BERKLEY TITLES BY JAMES ABEL

WHITE PLAGUE

PROTOCOL ZERO

continued . . .

PROTOCOL ZERO

JAMES ABEL

B

BERKLEY BOOKS, NEW YORK

BERKLEY

An imprint of Penguin Random House LLC
375 Hudson Street, New York, New York 10014

PROTOCOL ZERO

A Berkley Book / published by arrangement with the author

ISBN: 978-0-425-27635-8

PUBLISHING HISTORY
Berkley hardcover edition / August 2015
Berkley premium edition / May 2016

PRINTED IN THE UNITED STATES OF AMERICA

10   9   8   7   6   5   4   3   2   1

Cover art photos: Military transporter climbing © Dejan Milinkovic/Shutterstock.
Biohazard icon © Bakai/Shutterstock. Texture of ice © Serg Zastavkin/Shutterstock.
Design by Anthony Ramondo.
Interior map by Virginia Norey.
Interior text design by Kristin del Rosario.

Penguin
Random
House

ACKNOWLEDGMENTS

The author would like to thank the following people for giving generously of their time during the research and writing of *Protocol Zero*.

Thanks to James Grady, Phil Gerard, and Charles Salzberg, terrific writers and friends, for story advice, or for reading the manuscript.

To Dr. Charles Rupprecht, thanks hugely for talking to me about rabies. And to Dr. Fred Tilden, thanks for staying on the phone late at night, planning injuries to Joe Rush.

In Barrow, thanks to former Mayor Edward Itta, and to whaler, geologist, musician, and executive Richard Glenn. Thanks to the scientists of the North Slope Wildlife Department. Thanks to Harry Brower of the Alaskan Whaling Commission. And to Glenn Shehaan, who keeps science rolling in the High North.

Closer to home, thanks to my dad, Jerome Reiss, and my friends Lizzie Hansen and John Kukulka, for plot advice.

A thousand thanks to the U.S. Coast Guard, America's Arctic front line, for letting me fly and sail with you.

A thousand thanks to my agents, Esther Newberg and Josie Freedman. And to my terrific editors, Tom Colgan and Amanda Ng. And the whole fantastic team at Berkley.

Finally, to Wendy, with love, thanks.

No character in this book is based on any actual person, living or dead. Any mistakes are mine. PS, the ASRC is a real company, mentioned in the book. The author has only admiration for the way the ASRC has safeguarded the interests of North Slope people.

Anyone interested in learning more about Project Chariot—the plan to create a harbor in the Arctic by blowing up atom bombs—should read the splendid book about it, *The Firecracker Boys* by Dan O'Neill.

PROTOCOL ZERO

BARROW and the
NORTH SLOPE

Arctic

Barrow

Research
Camp

*Chukchi
Sea*

NPRA
National Petroleum
Reserve–Alaska

Alaska

0   100
Scale of miles

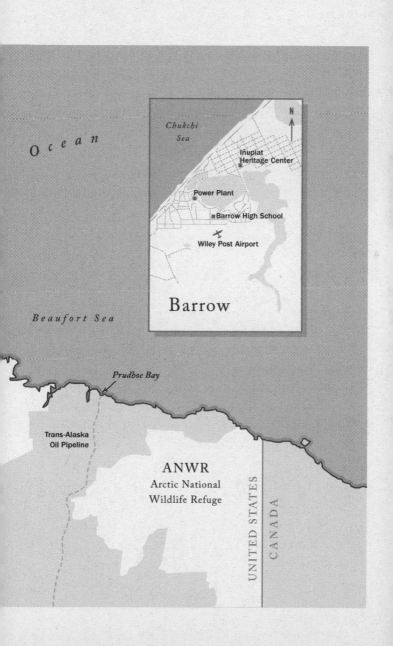

ONE

The police chief's emergency call had to bounce off three satellites to reach me. The first—over Russia—was snapping photos of their paratroops by the North Pole, on maneuvers. The second—over Arctic Canada—watched a U.S. attack submarine testing weapons, surfacing in ice. The last one was directly overhead above northern Alaska. North Slope Police Chief Merlin Toovik's voice came in loud and clear, from nine miles away.

"I need help, Colonel."

I stood, breath frosting, at the end of North America on a twenty-foot-high grass bluff overlooking the Arctic Ocean, a Mossberg shotgun over my back, in case polar bears showed up. Fire in the air, they usually turn away. My best friend and partner Marine Major Eddie Nakamura and I were trying to figure out what had killed the emaciated male bear at our feet. It looked like death by starvation. I wondered if it had been caused by a new germ.

"You know the victims, Colonel."

No other people were visible. No buildings or roads were here. The tundra stretched south for three hundred miles to the Brooks Range, in October, in a stark undulating beauty; an ocean of olive-brown high grass, filled with dips and hummocks, and spotted with the withered remains of summer flowers: once-yellow paintbrush, bright firewood, purple Siberian phlox, bell heather, and my true love Karen's favorite, the white-flowered anemones, which I gathered in bunches like a lovesick teenager. But it was worth her smile. Just about anything was.

The sea, thirty yards off, was black as anthracite and dotted with an early pancake glaze of ice. Locals had told me that the big pack would come in soon, to extend all the way to the pole, eight hundred miles north. The sky was a thick gray, the temperature hovered at thirty-six degrees. The Arctic sun looked as tiny and distant as Pluto. It rotated elliptically, staying low to the horizon, lava-colored but weak, more glow than heat, as if shy, as if frightened. Soon this remote landscape would fade to black beneath three months of night.

"Four people in trouble, Joe," Merlin said.

Ahead of us rose what looked like a mini Stonehenge; fantastic curving shapes rising up for fifteen feet; spaced as regularly as church organ pipes, and bleached gray by weather. They were bowhead whale ribs. Iñupiat hunters built the bone pile—bulldozing them there twice a year after the fall and spring hunts. The bones attracted hungry polar bears, who cracked the ribs and ate the marrow. The bone pile kept polar bears off of Barrow's streets, its supermarket parking lot, its backyards, and away from America's Arctic capital's kids.

"Joe, they were your neighbors," Merlin said.

No roads led in or out of Barrow. You arrived by snowmobile or four-wheelers, like we drove today, or you flew in or came by boat during the four months a year when sea ice was relatively clear. The nearest highway was three hundred miles away, at the oil fields of Prudhoe Bay.

The voice said, "Can you bring your medical gear?"

"Couple questions first, Merlin. How did you hear?"

I hit the intercom so that Eddie could listen. He was kneeling by the carcass, looking up, a small skull-saw in his gloved hands, and an unrolled scalpel kit in the grass. This bear had been sick, that much was evident from the fur patches stripped away. But what had killed it? Something usual and natural? Or the type of thing we secretly sought?

Merlin Toovik said, "The daughter called me, hysterical, screaming about sickness. She was crying too hard to make out words. But then I heard a shotgun. And the call went dead."

"You called back?"

"Yeah, tried both parents, her, too. No one answers."

"What sickness?" I felt a wave of fear hit my stomach.

"I don't know. I could barely hear. It was a bad connection. And there were funny noises in the background."

"Please describe them."

Eddie was frozen now, frowning.

"Grunting. An animal, maybe, but not one that I know. Too high for a wolf. Too low for a bear. Plus, she was inside their hut, she said, not outside. So whatever made the sounds was in there with her. Right beside her, sounded like. Weirdest, spookiest sounds, Joe."

Admiral Galli—who ran our small, secret unit—had been adamant when he'd ordered us not to get involved in local matters. Our mission had a public aspect, which Eddie and I had explained to Iñupiat leaders; but it also had a secret component, which we had reluctantly held back.

—*For their own good, Joe, the admiral had said.*

—*Sir, I disagree and think I ought to tell them.*

—*Not a chance.*

We were behind schedule with winter rapidly approaching. We needed to finish our study and go south.

Now, for a fraction of a second, the admiral's orders warred with Merlin's plea. I was seeing something in my head and it wasn't anything my boss said about an upcoming Arctic war game, due to start in the spring, about billions of dollars in weapons appropriations at stake, about national security. *Barrow will be flooded with VIPs, Joe: White House, State, Pentagon. We're behind the Russians in the race for control. And the Russians are getting belligerent again in Europe. If we don't get our act together, it will be too late. Something will happen up there, and we won't be able to handle it.*

What I saw in my head was a fifteen-year-old girl, and our neighbors for the last few weeks in the old World War Two–era air base where I'd been stationed with Eddie, where we'd lived in a Quonset hut among the university types who spent summers studying walruses, potential oil finds, ice melt, or, like our neighbors, nothing more threatening than seeds and moss. Our neighbors were a couple with whom we'd become friendly, two professors from a small New Jersey college, Ted and Cathy Harmon, and their daughter, Kelley. The parents were quiet academics who invited us over sometimes for poker games, cocktails, tirades on the warming Arctic, or rose hip tea.

The kid was smart and likable and wanted to be a scientist also. But she was also just a girl who liked normal teenage things. She'd sneak over to our Quonset hut at night—I had given her a key—to watch TV shows that her parents banned next door—*American Idol*, *The Vampire Diaries*—shows that Ted told me would "rot Kelley's mind." She also talked for hours with Karen Vleska, my fiancée, who'd flown in to visit a couple of weeks ago.

Cathy Harmon had taken me aside one day, squeezed my shoulder and said, "Thanks for giving Kelley a place to go. Every kid needs a friendly uncle. She doesn't have real uncles, so you and Eddie seem to be her choice."

"Colonel," Merlin said now, urgently. "I've got deputies ready and a copter gearing up. I've got Dr. Ranjay Sengupta along from the hospital. But I'd appreciate having you and Major Nakamura along, too."

I wanted to go. "Merlin, are you sure the noise you heard on the phone wasn't just static?"

A pause. From the silence, I knew I'd insulted him. "I know the difference between static and grunting. Also," Merlin said, "you and Major Nakamura have been visiting the villages all summer, asking about new diseases, rashes, hives, fevers, right?"

Eddie's brows rose. Despite the danger, I broke out smiling. It was impossible to hide anything from people here. They were scattered throughout an area the size of Wyoming, a county comprising America's northernmost outpost. America's Arctic Serengeti, filled with hundreds of thousands of caribou, wolves, grizzlies, foxes. There were about twenty million birds. But the human population was only 7,500, concentrated in eight small villages, with the capital, Barrow, home to 4,500 Iñupiats and a smattering of whites, blacks, Samoans, and Asians. Although hundreds of miles separated villages, somehow the Iñupiats seemed to know everything that outsiders did within days of their arrival. I'd told this to the admiral, advised him to let me speak plainly, warned him that lies backfire here.

Now I admitted, "We've asked a few questions about diseases, now and then."

In his pause I heard desperation. "If you won't do it for that reason, do it as a favor for me. Their bear guard is my cousin, Joe. Please."

That did it. People here did not ask favors lightly. Favors were more important than money. Favors were contracts. Favors were life. I told Merlin, "We're at the bone pile. Give me twenty minutes to get into town."

"Go to the rescue squad," Merlin Toovik said, and added, "I'm sure they told you not to do this."

"I was told to give you every assistance," I lied.

. . .

MY NAME IS JOE RUSH AND YOU WON'T FIND A DESCRIPTION OF my real job in my files at the Marine Corps. When I was seconded to the unit, my records were sheep-dipped— altered—to contain enough truth to fool a casual observer, the rest lies to protect the Corps, unit, and country from learning things that my bosses in Washington believe you ought not to know. Sometimes I agree with them. But often we fight.

Forty years old, the file says, and that part is correct, at least. Marriage status single; which was true that day, but happily due to change in three months. Six foot two. The photo shows blue-black hair, dark as the coal veins mined by my Welsh great-great-grandfather, eyes as light blue as those of great-great-grandma, daughter of a Norwegian cod fisherman, who met Gramper Bowen on the foredeck of the rusting steamer that brought them into New York Harbor as immigrants, 131 years ago.

They settled in Massachusetts, as the stumpy green Berkshire Hills reminded my ancestor of Wales. I grew up in the dying textiles mill town of Smith Falls, population 250, nestled between a thin, rocky river and a granite quarry, ten miles south of the Vermont line, on a two-lane cracked rural road.

There, generations of Rushes manned the assembly line of Brady Textiles, making button-down shirts in peacetime, Army uniforms during World War Two and Korea and Vietnam, but when the Brady company fled

Massachusetts for cheaper labor in Honduras, the Rushes became roofers and plumbers catering to summer-home owners from New York or Boston, who returned to their cities when the air turned chilly each autumn, and I climbed onto the creaky bus heading for my leaky country school.

I thrilled to TV commercials showing Marines—strong, confident men just a few years older than me—storming ashore on foreign beaches, rescuing hurricane victims, safeguarding the flag that we saluted every morning at Colonel David Harding High, named after the Massachusetts Civil War hero, killed during the Union's failed amphibious landing attempt to capture Fort Sumter, South Carolina, on September 8, 1863.

I never traveled farther than forty miles from home. I had friends, and girlfriends, but their smiles and invitations were, to me, traps to keep me in town.

So I left Smith Falls, and the higher-education part of my file correctly indicates that I attended UMass on an ROTC scholarship. The early Marines history is right, too: Parris Island, Quantico, antiterrorist guerrilla action in the Philippines. All of it real until Iraq and the secret germ lab I stumbled on there with Eddie Nakamura, when we were both lieutenants. The sick monkeys we found there—intentionally infected with disease . . . convulsing, terrified, dying—changed our lives, sent us to medical school, and made us experts on a kind of danger that most people fear, but put in the backs of their minds, not wanting to think about it, not wanting to remember it exists, not wanting to know.

Our enemy became smaller and traveled in vials and hypodermics or on air currents, in subway vents, or in bombs.

Awards? The Silver Star is there for Iraq, and a Navy and Marine Corps medal for actions taken in combat during the global war on terror—although the exact actions I took part in are secret. Our director once said that I'd saved "Thousands of lives, in Afghanistan and in the Arctic. Too bad we can't release either story, Joe. But we can promote you. You're young for a full colonel. Congratulations."

Under "skills" my file says that I can hit a running enemy at three hundred yards with an M4 carbine; and then, thanks to my M.D. degree, extract the bullet, clean the wound, administer antibiotics, and run any field hospital or bio lab in the world, to identify chemicals or germs.

I am also qualified to lead an assault on an enemy bioweapons facility, secure it, decontaminate it, and then interrogate its staffers, and kidnap them home to be tried and hung by military tribunal, under more obscure laws of the Republic. If my skill set seems contradictory to you, you're getting an idea of why I have fewer friends than I used to, other than Eddie, and my fiancée, Karen. It's also why my first marriage failed three years back, after I told my wife some things about my job. She'd been my college sweetheart and a loving, patient partner. But that disclosure—my attempt to save the marriage—came too late and put the last nail in a union that had been dissolving for some time.

That's the problem with secrets. Keep them and you drive away loved ones. Share them and you might do the same. Still, these days I kept no secrets from Karen. The admiral—former Coast Guard commandant—didn't like it. But I'd insisted when he asked me *as a favor* to stay in the unit, not retire, that I would only agree if Karen remained in the loop. The admiral had refused, argued, and then checked on Karen's high-security clearance. He'd tried to talk me out of it one last time, and then he'd given in.

"Because we need you, Joe. But if either of you talk, I won't be able to protect you."

I liked the admiral. Unlike the former director, who came from Wall Street and was destroyed by a financial scandal, the admiral was a true public servant: hero of Hurricane Laticia, hero of Deepwater Horizon, he deserved to keep the unit intact and strong. So I stayed.

"Joe," he'd said. "You're the best I got."

My memo to the secretary of defense six years ago—which brought me into the unit—suggested that the military should prepare for the possibility that the next big outbreak of human disease might come from a cold climate, not a hot one, not a jungle, as is usually assumed . . . but from a microorganism released by melting ice, after being encased in it for hundreds of thousands of years, or by an enemy who knew where to look for germs—new, terrible weapons—in cold latitudes.

On the day I received Merlin Toovik's phone call I had two months remaining in my one-year extension. Then I planned to move east with Karen, and start a biotech company with Eddie, looking for cures in the wild: good germs, not bad.

That was the plan, at least. But you know what they say about plans. Or at least what smart Marines know. Once battle starts, plans fall apart.

Eddie and I sealed the dead bear's brain and tissue samples into Ziplocs. The disease that had killed it was probably something normal, nothing new. We mounted our Honda four wheelers and turned south. We sped over the tundra, and ten minutes later I glimpsed the high cell-phone and radio towers and satellite farms ahead that constituted a first glimpse of town. Then would come the base, where Karen was waiting. She'd arrived two weeks back to train for her next polar trip, and she'd brought along a documentary filmmaker who looked at her in ways that annoyed me, trailed her around constantly, and gave Eddie and me the creeps.

I'd call her from the chopper. I'd say we'd be late. She'd be crazy with worry about the Harmons, but the film-maker would probably be happy to have a few more hours with her, alone. The jerk.

I was thinking, *Maybe they are okay. Maybe Merlin was wrong about hearing a shotgun. Maybe they're too sick to answer their phones. Maybe, even if he did hear a shotgun, someone is still alive.*

I needed to concentrate on driving or the Honda might turn over, but I kept seeing in my mind the fifteen-year-old high school girl, just a kid, who had adopted me as an uncle. I had no children of my own. You could say that I had adopted Kelley Harmon back.

The Honda skidded on slick tundra, began to go over, but the wheels caught and I righted it. I accelerated.

The biggest dangers start out small, one of my old instructors at Quantico used to say. Things sounded bad already. *Four possible victims.*

I had no idea how much worse things would get.

TWO

"Play Kelley's call again," I said.

The rescue squad's big, twenty-year-old Bell 412 copter rose off the tarmac, spun southwest, and headed for
the research camp. I was crammed with four others into
the cab, and through the window had a last glimpse of
Barrow. The triangular town hugging the last bit of coastline on the continent. The mass of one- and two-story
wooden homes sat on concrete pilings to prevent them
from heating up and melting the permafrost below. The
dirt and gravel roads, at 5 P.M., were alive with taxicabs,
kids on banana bikes, a truck hauling a big outboard boat
toward the beach and lagoon. Probably whalers going out
to scout for bowheads. The fall migration was due to start
any day.

Then the city was gone. We raced over a sea of tundra,
and through mist so thick that it felt like flying inside

lungs . . . the land rolling out in glimpses, in patches; thousands of elliptically shaped freshwater lakes, there because permafrost kept what little precipitation falls here from draining. Wiley Post Airport was gone. It was named for the American humorist who crashed there a century ago. Barrow's fame comes from death. The town was named for Sir John Barrow, English lord of the admiralty, who sent a thousand British explorer/sailors to their icy demise in a search for the Northwest Passage, Europe's quick route to Asia, over a century ago. Some of them sank. Some abandoned ships trapped in ice, walked off in search of rescue, and disappeared. Others died of sickness or starvation or they ate each other.

"Okay, here goes," Merlin said.

When I heard the terror in Kelley's voice, a fist seemed to cut off the air in my throat.

"Oh, God, God, no one's answering. I tried to reach Dr. Rush and Dr. Nakamura, and then your operator couldn't hear me. Everyone is screaming! I'm scared."

"Slow down, Kelley, okay? You've got all my attention. What's wrong? S-l-o-w."

We were dressed in zip-up float suits in case we ditched in water. We wore helmets equipped with mikes and earpieces and wore waterproof, calf-high Northern Outfitter boots. In the back we carried stretchers and medicines and sample bags and field surgical kits. Merlin was armed with a .45 Beretta, and he and his deputies wielded Mossberg shotguns. Eddie and I had our bear guns. Now there was a small clicking in my helmet, and over the rotor roar I heard the plaintive, terrified voice of the girl.

"We're all sick! Daddy said not to call. Said I was wrong. He said it was just flu. But he can't close his hand. He fell. He said a good scientist never jumps to conclusions, but I didn't! I didn't jump to conclusions! Oh, God! I wrote down the symptoms even before the sticking pains started. And Clay Qaqulik was babbling about little people. And Mom . . . I can't believe she and Clay . . . And the water tastes bad and . . ."

My throat closed up. This frantic voice was not the one I usually heard from her when she came over to watch TV, or to ask Karen endless hero-worship questions about being an Arctic explorer. *Aren't you scared when you're out in a blizzard? How did you get Coca-Cola to sponsor you?* I was used to her saying things like, "Why can't I spend summers like normal kids? The beach. Music. I'm, like, in prison. I mean, it's not like I don't like science, but my friends are at parties and I'm stuck here, looking at plants. I didn't ask to be an intern. They said it would help me get into college. They don't even pay me. I'm their little summertime SLAVE!"

My mouth was dry. My head was pounding with fear for the whole family, and I could feel my intestines clenching as the voices went on. It was Merlin now.

"Honey, slow, please, okay? Focus. What happened and when did it start?"

It was no use. Kelley was too scared.

"I saw that redheaded woman in the warehouse, bending over the water bottles! And then the water tasted funny and my throat hurt, but I thought it was just, you know, like when you wake up sometimes and it burns. And Daddy said

*the redheaded woman wouldn't harm us, and Clay . . .
(zzzzz) and Daddy screamed at Mommy because her underwear was (zzzzz) and I said, 'What little people?' And
Mommy said (zzzzzzzzzz)"*

Eddie said, cocking his head, trying to hear, "The
underwear was what?"

"Did she say bleeding?"

"I don't think it was bleeding. It was something else."

"Merlin, can you try that again?"

The voice had degenerated into a little girl's, the use
of the word *Mommy,* like she'd become five years old, like
she was cowering under covers, afraid that the bogeyman
in the closet was real. I felt trapped in the copter. My
mouth was dry. I was filled with a sense of being too late.
We still had a good fifty miles of tundra to go.

*"And then I was looking in the shaving mirror and the
glass bothered me, the sun was so bright on it, it hurt my eyes
so I just . . . just BROKE IT . . ."*

Dr. Sengupta, sitting opposite me, was a forty-two-
year-old from Mumbai who'd taken a three-year contract
at the hospital because he'd "Always dreamed of ice, since
I was a little boy. So when I saw the job description, I felt
I must come and see my dream."

He said, "Hmm, extreme light sensitivity."

Kelley babbling, jumping from one half thought to
another, the words becoming run-on, loss of control.

*". . . And Mommy coming out of Clay's tent and Daddy
yelling, 'How could you do that to me! You bitch!'"*

Eddie's eyes meeting mine across the four feet of cabin
that separated the two rows of passengers. Eddie's brown

eyes baffled. I knew he was seeing the same thing I was in his head; the Harmons, two quiet, middle-class researchers who don't use words like *bitch* in public, and don't brazenly sleep with their bear guards, certainly not in a small research camp in front of a husband and daughter. But perhaps we were misinterpreting what we were hearing. Or maybe, as Eddie said, "Maybe they had a dark side, Uno. Virginia Woolf times nine."

Merlin trying to slow her down. The girl talked over the police chief. Merlin trying to soothe her, trying to get information. The girl was out of reach, emotionally and physically.

"I'm in the hut. They're screaming outside. Clay says Daddy is trying to kill him! This is crazy! This isn't happening! Lalalalalalalala . . . I'm putting my hands over my ears. LALALALAAAAAA!"

I heard a clumping on the line, and thought she'd hurled away the phone, into a corner. The *lalala* sounded farther away. I wanted to shut off the sound. Something awful was building. Dr. Sengupta's eyes were huge inside his glasses, the deputies were still and silent, and the whole copter wobbled, as if the engine drew in the raw tension coming in with the call.

Then quiet, and another voice, a new one, Clay Qaqulik's, I guess, said, strangled, choking . . .

"I have to stop it."

A pause. Then Clay again.

"I have to. I'm sorry, Miss K."

And then I started in my seat because I heard a bark, or a grunt, close to the phone; a throaty animal sound . . .

The girl had stopped talking, Clay also. Something else was in there, in that research hut with them, sniffing at the unit. A series of more grunts followed. A flow of unintelligible sound: low and urgent, angry and primitive. Barking almost. Impossible.

Kelley screamed, "Stop it! Why are you doing that?"

Followed by the unmistakable *BOOM* of a shotgun.

And then nothing . . . zzzzzzz . . .

Eddie and I and the police chief and deputies bounced in the copter, transported into our imaginations. *What just happened?* The earbuds emitted static. The mist ahead thickened, to obscure not only air ahead, but earth below. The sky gone. The truth gone. The only sound the steady groan of engines.

"Play it once more, Merlin," I said.

The nightmare voices started up again. I thought back to Washington, to the admiral's small office on C Street, to the story he told us, to the secret part of our job.

"YOU ARE TO LOOK FOR WHAT YOU PREDICTED, JOE. FOR SOME-thing new and potentially dangerous popping up as the region warms."

Eddie, the admiral, and I had been sitting in a townhouse four blocks from the State Department in Foggy Bottom.

"Why send us now?" I'd said. "Did something happen?"

To answer, the admiral spread on his large desk a map of the North Slope of Alaska. Tinged brown for tundra, it formed the shape of a wild boar, the eastern side, or hindquarters, was the border with Canada.

"New fish species up there. New birds. Even a new kind of bear: half grizzly, half polar bear," Admiral Galli had said.

The western side, or skull and snout shape, jutted west toward nearby Russia across the Chukchi Sea, ending at the Eskimo village of Point Hope.

"Question is, are there new, dangerous germs as well?" the admiral asked.

He sat back. "We've been assigned a delicate task, and you two have been up there before, so you're going. All this land here, vast space, hardly any people . . . that made it a natural lab for the white-coat guys, in the past, you see."

Eddie said, "Weapons testing."

"And designing. This started during World War Two, and went through the end of the last century. The bad guys looking for new ways to kill us. Our brightest minds trying to anticipate what might come at us from across the Bering Strait: chemicals, gasses, germs."

"Meanwhile, we made some, too," I said.

"You want them to be the only ones who have it?"

"Nope."

"Of course not. It was a race. A germ and chemical race. And then, gentlemen, a few accidents started to happen. Montana: Army nerve gas experiment goes wrong, and next thing you know, fifty thousand sheep are dead. Nevada nuclear tests: Twenty years pass and the soldiers who witnessed explosions start to die of cancers. Atomic soldiers, we called 'em. Also a few locals, who drove through clouds of radiation emitted by the tests. You know these stories. If you're not familiar with all of them, surely you know some."

"And in Alaska, sir?"

"First, by the late 1980s, Congress was pissed off over these accidents, and the public outcry. Plenty of people opposed testing by then. This is before the chemical test ban treaties, big nuclear test treaties."

"So they passed a law," I guessed.

"Yep. HR-932. An obscure provision in a military appropriations bill mandated a kind of germ and toxics census in areas that had been used for testing. Every five years the secretary of defense is required to send out teams to, quote: *'Conduct a detailed examination of any general areas once used by the U.S. military for chemical or biological testing, in order to determine whether any lingering negative effects have harmed U.S. citizens, crops, or domestic livestock. If any such organism or public-health effect is found, the secretary of defense is directed to make full restitution for properties lost, both living and realty, and to assume responsibility for related medical costs.'"*

I'd asked the admiral whether, over the twenty-five years of the bill's life, so far, any of the secret surveys had located a new germ or toxic effect that had harmed U.S. citizens. Admiral Galli had sighed.

"Unsure, Joe. In 2005, surveyors found an accelerated strain of *hantavirus,* a potentially lethal disease transmitted by mice, in an area of New Mexico that had received large doses of radioactive fallout during a series of 1950s tests. Six, seven deaths among local Navaho."

"Washington took responsibility?"

The admiral looked strained. "The bill doesn't require anyone to do that. It only states that all costs are to be assumed. Remember, this sort of thing, once publicized, even a rumor, usually results in about twelve thousand people filing cases, lawsuits, studies, bills blocked in Congress, headlines all over the world. So the framers of the legislation wanted to alleviate any suffering caused by the initial testing, but also wanted to avoid opening a floodgate of lawsuits. Delicate situation."

Eddie quipped, "Yeah, you kill people, tricky problems pop up."

The admiral looked irritated. "These tests were conducted a long time ago. The people who carried them out were no more evil than you or I."

Eddie snorted.

"Colonel, this summer your job is to conduct the northern Alaskan survey. You'll go out with the annual Coast Guard medical team visiting North Slope villages. Coast Guard has been getting ready for the place to open up. They use the visits to get their pilots familiarized, see if equipment works. Your job is to treat anyone with medical needs. There will be a dentist and optometrist along. Look at flus, colds, broken wrists, everything. But I want you to ask questions, especially of the elders. Any new sicknesses? Anything they're seeing, even in animals? If you find something new, get samples. Those go straight to Fort Detrick. If the conclusion is that we've got a link,

Uncle Sam sends the case to the green hats in the Treasury Department, and then lawyers, and they'll start figuring out compensation."

"How do you compensate someone for dying?" Eddie said.

The admiral said stiffly, "What are you suggesting? That we do nothing at all?"

It was one of the few times I'd seen Eddie blush.

"Sorry, sir, my mouth gets ahead of me sometimes."

"Only sometimes?" the admiral said.

I said, "Sir, can you tell us exactly what happened in Alaska that may cause problems to pop up now?"

He sighed. "Oh, when it comes to the North Slope, that place was a biological dumping ground, and not just for us."

SOMETIMES I THINK THAT THE DIFFERENCE BETWEEN ALLEGED Western civilization and others is that somehow, we got the idea that *empty* means *useless*. Silence? Fill it up with earbuds and loudspeakers and TV monitors in airports. Time? Pack every available second with *multitasking*, another word for attention deficit disorder, with iPhones and BlackBerrys and games where Angry Birds fly around on a screen. Wilderness? Intolerable! Fill it up with condos or tour buses or, if you can't, drop in a golf course, at the very least flood the open space with experimental chemicals, bombs, drones, or man-made germs.

"Japan," the admiral said, sliding his finger on that map across the Bering Strait and onto Asia, northern

China to be exact, Manchuria. "In modern times, you've got the accident at their nuclear-power facility at Fukushima Daiichi, and winds capable of carrying fallout to northern Alaska. But previous to that, World War Two. Manchuria was where they had their germ facilities. Between 1932 until the end of that war, Japan had the most aggressive biological-warfare program ever applied at the field level. They set up their infamous Unit 731 in their puppet state of Manchukeo. They called it a water-purification department. It was horrible and brutal; and in that 150-building complex, they amputated limbs of the living, to study blood loss. They infected patients with syphilis: men, women, and children. They designed plague fleas that were dropped on enemy soldiers. Their laboratory experiments alone, inoculating prisoners of war with disease, killed an estimated ten thousand. Their use of toxics in the field probably killed another two hundred thousand. They tried typhus, cholera, plague, anthrax, shigella, a kind of dysentery, and salmonella."

"Christ," said Eddie.

"As you know, Japan actually invaded Alaska during World War Two, and temporarily occupied part of the Aleutian Islands. So far there has been no evidence that they used biological weapons in that campaign. Nevertheless, you are to be aware of this history as you undertake the survey."

"Next," I said.

"Next! The Soviet Union. The Soviets captured Unit 731 after World War Two, and used the documents—Japanese formulas—to augment their own program," the admiral said, as the big index finger pounded down again, this time in Siberia, western side of the Bering Strait.

"Sverdlovsk facility," he said. "Between the 1950s until the '90s, they weaponized and stockpiled over a dozen bio-agents including tularemia, plague, Venezuelan equine encephalitis, smallpox, and Marburg, a dirty little cousin of Ebola. Fifty-two sites. Fifty thousand workers scattered in an area where winds—on a fluky day—could take anything floating to Alaska. The Russians genetically altered some of these microbes to resist heat and antibiotics and, are you listening, resist *extreme cold*!"

"I think you should send us to Hawaii, not Alaska," Eddie said.

The admiral wasn't smiling. "We also know that there's new interest in Russia in these programs. Their president may have restarted them. Status, unclear."

"Yes, Hawaii," Eddie said. "Beaches. Surfing, you know, Admiral, Colonel Rush's fiancée is a surfer. Mai tais. Hawaii, sir. Definitely."

The admiral's brows rose. "Hawaii? Well, Major, our own Big Tom bioweapons tests were held in Hawaii."

"Where the hell *weren't* there tests, sir?"

"New York," the admiral said.

"Yeah, but the traffic sucks there, sir."

"Alaska," I said.

The admiral frowned. "Alaska! Starting in the sixties and seventies we tested live nerve gasses, sarin, near Fort Greeley, and later, in the 'Little Tom' tests, *bacillus globigii*. But the big bad wolf was Project Chariot."

"What was Project Chariot, sir?"

The admiral stood and walked to his top-floor window, which provided a pretty nice view of the Kennedy Center. "This is all public record now. It was the intentional contamination of groundwater near a village called Point Hope, with radioactivity."

"Why would you do that?"

"Because Edward Teller, revered father of the atom bomb, had an idea for peaceful use of atomics. Anyone can google this. Teller convinced D.C. that it was possible to create America's first Arctic deepwater harbor at Point Hope by blowing up a few atomic bombs at the location."

"Give me a break," said Eddie.

"Yep," said the admiral. "The Atomic Energy Commission approved it. It was one of those grandiose futuristic plans that looked good on paper. Re-engineer the planet! Project Plowshare, they called it . . . you know, like in the Bible . . . 'they'll beat their weapons into plowshares,' or something like that. The planet was 'slightly flawed,' Teller said. The use of nuclear bombs would dig canals, get rid of obstacles like mountains, *change the earth's surface to suit us,* he said."

"So what happened at Point Hope?" I asked, finding the little village on the map on the admiral's desk. It lay due southwest from Barrow, a few hundred miles off, the last tip of land before the Chukchi Sea on the west coast of the borough, the snout of the wild boar.

"What happened was that the plan was approved and engineers and Atomic Energy Commission people flew into Point Hope. They told the Iñupiats that the use of atomics in their area would be nothing more than a mild inconvenience. They said—while the locals secretly re-corded them—that the bombs dropped on Hiroshima and Nagasaki had not really had such a terrible impact on people. The villagers would temporarily leave. The blast—it would be 150 times more powerful than the bomb dropped at Hiroshima—would equal 40 percent of all firepower expended during World War Two—and instantly create a harbor where before had been a small creek. Then the locals would come home. The new deep-water harbor would show the might of America. Everyone would benefit."

"But it never happened, so what's the problem?" I asked.

"It never happened because the Iñupiats fought it, and stopped it. But before they did, Atomic Energy Commission staff started work.They wanted to know how ground-water flowed in the area, and so . . ."

I closed my eyes. "And so they put radioactive material in it, to track the flow."

"Yes."

"Cesium?"

"You got it."

"Didn't they clean it up, after?"

"They said they did. They got most of it. But as late as 2010, people were still finding traces in the soil."

"Cancer rates in Point Hope?"

"Slightly elevated."

"Proven connections?"

"No."

I thought about it. "Any other deposits of radioactivity in the North Slope, that maybe the locals *don't* know about?"

"Not to my knowledge," the admiral said, looking uncomfortable.

"But we don't know for sure," I said, envisioning those thousands of square miles of wilderness, tundra, mountains, beauty unparalleled, but also potentially a historic mix of poisons or chemicals deposited over the years by people regarding it as nothing more than a site for tests.

"Go north. Do the survey. We've done these surveys for twenty-five years now, without finding anything to worry about. It's pro forma. It's the law. It's just a study."

"Then why do you look worried?"

The admiral said, "Because when it comes to mutations, one never knows what is possible until it appears. And because your sworn enemy, Wayne Homza, is back It's backbiting time in D.C.!"

Eddie said, "Oh, shit."

MAJOR GENERAL WAYNE HOMZA HATED ME. HIS OFFICE LAY IN the war plans section of the Pentagon. He managed strategy scenarios relating to bioterror attacks on U.S. troops or towns. He was a formidable antagonist; an ex-street kid from Cicero, Illinois, who'd fought his way into West Point. He was blunt, powerful, and relentless—the kind of man who magnifies minor grudges. He was stuck planning for something that had not happened yet, so he was off the track for rapid promotion. He'd been trying to absorb into his command any Pentagon unit even remotely dealing with germs or toxics. The admiral believed that Homza wanted to become the biowarfare czar. Homza was politically adept, hungry for advancement, and constantly pushing for more responsibility.

"He's out to get you," the admiral told me.

The reason was, for the past two years, Homza had been converting research units into combat units. "We need fighters, not scientists," he said. "Guns. Not studies."

Homza had actually convinced the secretary of defense to switch our unit to his control a year ago, when I ruined it for him. Recalled to D.C. after my last Arctic mission, Eddie and I were summoned to the White House for a medal ceremony, the kind where the president thanks you personally, but where no one in the media knows, because what you did was secret. The kind where several VIPs are also in the room, since several people simultaneously receive awards.

The president had shaken my hand, showed me the medal—gold resting in blue velvet—explained that it would be kept in a safe, apologized for the secrecy, and said, "Colonel, this country owes you more than a secret ceremony. If there's ever anything I can do for you, I hope you will just ask."

I'd blurted out, "Sir, don't close us down."

And I'd seen the blocky-looking general across the room start, and stare, and then slowly smile at me. It was not a friendly expression. He smiled, I thought, like a shark.

"You're an interesting fellow," Homza told me that day, out in the hall. I knew then that he would keep watching.

...

NOW, IN THE COPTER, THE MEMORY DIED AWAY AND I GREW aware again of static in my earbuds. Perhaps the dead were trying to speak. Who could tell? Who can predict science? The pilot was pointing and we all craned to see through the thick white mist and light falling rain, an October drizzle mixing with a few flakes of confused snow.

Ahead I saw a small wooden shack with a long porch and a concave outhouse, both set inside a tramped down area of grass near a thin, long, elliptical lake, with ripples on the surface from the drizzle. I saw a parked ATV. I saw a pile of canvas-topped gear. I saw two bodies—lumps on the ground—growing clearer in the drizzle as we approached.

Eddie said, "This is bad."

I saw a lone red fox trotting off in the distance, moving in a sideways gait, absorbed into mist.

My dread for the Harmons was a cold clenching, a grinding in the pit of my belly.

The copter circled first, in smaller and smaller circles, to check if someone with a gun was hiding in one of the low areas between hummocks.

Merlin's voice was in my earbuds, quiet and serious.

"Those were the parents in the grass. Where are the other two, Kelley and Clay?"

"The cabin. Gotta be," Eddie said, staring at the buildings.

"Unless they left," said Merlin.

"Unless it's an ambush," I said, reaching for my gun.

THREE

"The shooter could still be here," I said.

Look anywhere except at the bodies, and the tundra presented a subtle, sweeping beauty; lovely, quiet, but as mute and indifferent as the huge snowy owl peering at us from fifty yards away. The rotors stopped moving. I had the door open and my shotgun out in case we took fire. The bodies out there, close up, lay in the loose-limbed tangled attitude with which the dead announce themselves.

Maybe the other two are still alive.

"Merlin, Eddie, and I should go in first. We have some experience in . . . uh . . . this."

Merlin nodded. "You Marines take the door. We'll spread out, hit the back and side. Stay low," he warned his deputies, two big, nervous men from Minnesota, cold-weather farm boys who'd found their birthplaces too boring, rule bound, or confining. One thickly dark haired, named Steve Rice; the other bald and bearded, Luther Oz.

All of us wore Kevlar vests. The deputies had their Mossbergs out. Dr. Sengupta hung back in the chopper, wanting to go but waiting for an all-clear. The pilot snapped off the safety on his sidearm, a Beretta .45, but I told him to stay put. We needed him to get home.

Eddie and I hit the ground fast, separated, and, communicating with hand signals, stayed low and quick-ran toward the cabin, just like we would have done in a potential enemy village back in Afghanistan, expecting fire. Anyone inside would have heard the chopper.

Did I feel someone watching from the cabin, or was it my imagination?

Fifty feet to go.

I'd not protested when Merlin made us sign some legal paper . . . "cooperation agreement between federal agency X and local law enforcement" . . . on the way here. The admiral would be angry, but I'd taken him at his word when he said, "*I value your judgment.*" Merlin needed us to have a legal, official role in case later on, he said, "The issue comes up in court, Joe."

I was aware of Merlin bending quickly over the two bodies—man and woman—sprawled amid the heather and sedges. He sought a pulse and my heart plunged into my belly when he rose and kept going.

Ten feet to the cabin. Is Kelley in there? Is Clay with her? Something just moved at the window.

I hit the ground, rolled sideways to avoid a direct shot,

and wriggled forward. The ground smelled of rain, voided bowels, and sweetish blood. Cold drops ran off my scalp, into my eyes and off my chin.

Up to the porch now, slowly . . .

Fucking creaky porch . . .

THE CABIN—FRONT DOOR TILTED SLIGHTLY OPEN—LOOKED AS accessible as every trap in the world, with that black slit inviting us in. I judged the place an eight-hundred-square-foot rectangle—*I hope it's only one room*—built from a conglomeration of weathered wood jutting up like a beached ship on posts hammered into the tundra, to set it a foot above the grass.

It sat thirty yards from the glassy lake—*natural water supply*—and another hundred from the shallow creek that probably swelled to monumental proportions in the spring, emptied into the Arctic Ocean, and served as a minor tributary to the Porcupine River, a major Iñupiat hunting grounds.

The Harmons weren't soldiers. They were gentle people who collected plants and oohed and aahed over seeds and algae. They fretted about genes, not germs.

We made it onto the porch. We stood on opposite sides of the slightly open door. I heard a low droning inside, and realized it was a mass of flies.

You go left, my eyes ordered Eddie. We've communicated in battle situations without talking since we were young lieutenants, in Iraq War One. And even before that, at ROTC, in Massachusetts, where we met.

Eddie's quick glance said, *If he's in there, he left that front door open. Step in, Marines, and BOOM!*

My hand signals told Eddie, *Ready? One . . . two . . .*

We burst in, me in the lead, Eddie taking the corners. Me processing the scene, thinking, *Nothing moving yet . . . two rooms: the bunk room and the kitchen area. Corners clear. Body one in the lower bunk. Body two on the floor. Flies. Lots of flies. Clouds of flies. That was what I saw move by the window.*

Eddie came out of the closet-sized, honey-bucket bathroom, and I smelled urine and shit from in there, unemptied buckets.

"All clear, Uno," he said, lowering his Mossberg, leaning against the wall in momentary relief.

But then the flies moved again as a mass, rising off the form on the bunk, to cross the window, a fast-moving shadow, a hungry buzz, and the relief was over.

Oh man . . .

Eddie knelt at the lower bunk. A poster above the upper one pictured a smiling female researcher in a Woods Hole Institute sweatshirt, holding up tweezers and a Ziploc bag: REMEMBER TO FREEZE YOUR SAMPLES!!! A second poster showed a big polar bear, teeth bared, and the caption: LOOK BEFORE YOU STEP OUTSIDE!

"Oh, Christ, One. It's Kelley."

She lay—what remained of her—in a torn heap of bedding, and I had to force myself to look at the mass of muscle, liquid, and ligature where her head had been. A bare foot protruded from the shredded North Face sleeping bag. The flies were a tropism drawn to the worst kind of luck. The stuffing poked out, soaked with black blood. She'd been thrown into the wall by the blast, smearing the planking with grayish brain matter, a raisin-sized bit of discolored bone wedged between planks, and then she'd bounced off and settled. The limbs showed all the animation of a straw doll's. A mass of strawberry-blond hair was pasted by blood to the wall. A single yellow strand glowed abruptly in a beam of sunlight coming through the window, flaring and dying as quickly as a soul departs a body.

That lone hair got to me more than the rest of the carnage. One hair. The strand you find in a teenage girl's brush, and it went along with the innocent items on the milk crate night table, sitting an arm's reach from the body; a Head & Shoulders shampoo bottle, a red-banded Mickey Mouse watch, a silvery palm-sized miniature digital recorder, a half-empty pack of Juicy Fruit gum.

"That mirror is busted over there," I said, jerking my head toward a part of the cabin otherwise untouched by violence. Something about it stood out . . . a mirror . . . shattered . . . a mirror . . .

"Shot up?" Eddie said.

"No. No pellet marks. Someone must have just smashed it."

"What are you thinking?"

"How the hell do I know?" I snapped.

I fought off a wave of sickness.

The upper bunk was untouched, a sleeping bag unrolled and zipped, just lying there. Mom's probably. The women slept on one side of this cabin, guys on the other.

Eddie knelt in the center of the room, by the second body. The shooter, from the look of things. Merlin's cousin Clay Qaqulik. Eddie going through the pockets. It's funny how, even in the wild, some people carry a wallet.

"It's Clay, all right."

He lay by his shotgun, but only half of his face looked back, one pale brown eye gaping, slick cheekbones visible on the left side, as in a medical school display. *The human male skull.* The rest of what had once constituted a face was splattered across the thick planking, with more gray matter glommed onto the legs of a small splintery wooden table, below a tin of canned milk, a box of Trader Joe's wheat bran flakes, a box of cracker-like Sailor Boy Pilot Bread, a half-played Monopoly game, with a plastic hotel sitting on Park Place, and a bagged half-loaf of Wonder bread—with a lone fly trapped inside, stuck to the condensation in the bag.

I also saw a pack of Zithromax, a five-day antibiotic, with three of the five pills missing. And an open bottle of Tylenol.

They were sick, sure, but with what?

The shooter's trigger finger—left hand—was still snagged in the guard of the Remington pump action and the left arm was twisted, dislocated. When he'd blown off half his face, the recoil had snagged the finger, torn wrist tendons as the blast pulled the shotgun one way, the man the other.

Eddie flicked his head toward the door, referring to the bodies outside. "Mom and Dad were on their backs, so—"

"So Kelley's still in her sleeping bag, which she would have tried to get out of if she heard shots. You think the first killing was here?"

"The shooting on the phone call was in here."

"So Clay comes in here first, and the parents hear it and run toward the house to help. He steps out and shoots them, too. He comes back in. He shoots himself."

In my head, I heard it: *BOOM . . . BOOM . . .*

Eddie said, "Or he shoots the parents first, Kelley's too scared to move. Then he does her. But why?" Eddie said, pulling on rubber gloves.

I tried to remember the phone message. "Kelley said something about Clay seeing things. Hallucinating."

Outside, Merlin and his deputies walked the perimeter of the camp, checking for people or evidence.

"I'm thinking Fort Hood," Eddie mused as we got out the Ziploc bags and tie-on masks, forcing ourselves to start the awful collecting: fingernail clippings, blood samples, hair bits for a toxics test.

Eddie said, "He wouldn't be the first vet who went around the bend. Kills three. Turns on himself. Alcohol . . . drugs . . . plenty of that up here . . . Or maybe being sick made everything worse."

I thought about it. I shook my head. "It doesn't explain the call. She said they were all sick. She was terrified *because they were all sick*. She didn't even mention a shotgun. Don't you think, if it was just about Clay, that the whole call would have been about him?"

Eddie sat back on his heels. He showed a lot of white in his eyes when he was concentrating. He shook his head.

"This won't have anything to do with us, or our mission. Don't look at me like that! I'm just saying."

"She called *us*, Eddie. She needed help. The mission? Who cares about the goddamn mission! *What the hell happened here?*"

"She's scared. Disoriented. Babbling. I can think of drugs or chemicals that would make you paranoid as hell."

"I want to test these bodies," I said.

Despite the cold, I felt sweat in my eyes. There was a quick, small movement to my left, and I instinctively moved sideways, grabbed for my Mossberg, only to see a miniature mammal, a rodent-like vole, scamper from under the bunk and out the open doorway.

I said, rapid breathing subsiding, "She said she kept a diary of symptoms. Book diary? Or computer?"

"Laptop's my guess. Or some new super mobile device that only kids and tech geniuses know about."

"Take the laptop. And," I said, eyeing two items on the night table, "that little voice recorder of hers."

We forced ourselves to start looking for a diary, whatever form it took.

I knew that shock and grief would come later, when we got home—and later still, would be added to the roll call of Marine bad dreams.

Eddie found another busted mirror in the honey-bucket room. Just a little six by six thing that had been hanging on the wall, and was now shattered, its glazed pieces lying on the floor.

I stared at it. Mirrors . . .

Something about mirrors?

...

I'VE SEEN DEATH ON BATTLEFIELDS, AND EXPERIENCED THE VIO-
lent deaths of friends, but even after many years of service
I'd never witnessed anything up close approaching this
level of violence on an American civilian family. The carnage mocked the normal setting: the set table, three places
for dinner, plastic fiesta-style plates, three plastic tumblers
with bowhead whale logos, the massive mammals etched
in black on the sides.

I saw a four-burner stove in the corner, attached by
hose to a propane canister on the floor. There was a larger
tank outside for heat even in summers, when temperatures
could drop into the twenties this far north. The cabin was
not insulated enough to be used by researchers in winter.
That was when most scientists, along with birds and
whales, migrated south.

*Gas leak? What are the symptoms of a gas leak? Light-
headedness, yeah. Blurred vision. Paranoia? I don't think
so. Mold? Is there mold here?*

"Four people. But only three settings," Eddie said.

"Meaning, Dr. Holmes?"

"An argument? A grudge? Three against one over
something that set Clay off."

"She called before that. She never said Clay was the
issue."

The camp emitted the stillness of a battlefield when
the death-dealing is done. Gradually normal sounds returned to the world. I heard the hiss of wind outside, and
the vague attentive scratch of a hail pellet at the window.

I heard the creak of Eddie, kneeling, Ziploc bag out, rubber gloves on, beside Clay Qaqulik. I heard a half dozen harsh, grating barks from that owl outside. One . . . two . . . three in a row . . . like it was counting bodies.

Four . . . Like the animal was mourning.

Six. Predicting more?

Deputy Luther Oz's voice reached us from outside.

"Chief. Over here! Four-wheeler tracks! Someone else was here!"

LUTHER OZ STARTED UP AN ATV AND HEADED OUT ONTO THE tundra to try to follow the tracks. Deputy Steve Rice strung yellow crime-scene tape, pounded steel stakes into the ground, and wrapped the camp perimeter. It struck me as ridiculous. What would the tape keep away? Wolves?

Merlin and his men picked up shell casings, dusted the cabin for fingerprints, and snapped photos of the bodies. Our collective attempts to control disaster are never ending. In South Sudan once, where Eddie and I searched for hidden labs and Ebola, we spent a week tending Dinka tribesmen wounded in the region's war with the Sudanese government. We were in a mud-and-wattle hospital near a swamp; no electricity, cots for beds, dank walls lined with silent patients—rebel fighters—awaiting donated prosthetics: artificial arms and legs made thousands of miles away.

Someone from the Red Cross had nailed a poster to the wall above the men waiting their turn to be fitted. RULES OF WAR, it announced to the amputees hobbling on rag-wrapped crutches around a packed-earth floor.

> You must treat prisoners humanely.
> You must identify yourself when taking a prisoner.

Eddie had laughed harshly. "'Rules'?"

There are no rules, of course, and now in this camp I knew that the tundra had mocked similar efforts over the centuries to apply "RULES" to disaster . . . British sailors walking off from an ice-trapped ship, heading south in a blizzard, in marching order, as if that would save their lives. Missionaries on their knees, sick with influenza, faces raised to heaven, as if prayers were contracts, bargains, rules. Here, Marine doctors Joe Rush and Eddie Nakamura sought order with tweezers—collecting hair, skin, and brain matter.

I noticed Merlin in the doorway, staring at the dead man on the floor. His voice sounded broken. "Clay and I grew up together. Except for his time in the Army, I saw him almost every day. He brings presents to my kids every Sunday."

"I'm sorry, Merlin."

"He was on my whaling crew. My dad hazed him good when we both were kids and went out with the hunters for the first time. The men gave us the jobs for the eight-year-olds. Clay took all their shit with a smile."

Merlin stepped closer, grief stricken. But he was also too good a policeman to be distracted from his job.

He said, looking directly into my eyes, "You've been asking elders about new diseases, Joe."

He stood only a foot from the body.

He said, "You were in Point Hope asking about flu and rashes. In Nuvvuak, you asked details of Jenny Aniruq's son's fever. You and Major Nakamura went to Point Lay to take samples of the dead walruses on the beaches, after that airplane spooked them and they crushed pups in the stampede. And the bears. *Why are you really here?*"

I lied, followed orders. "We're with the Coast Guard, helping out on their annual med-visits. Of course we ask questions. That's what doctors do, Merlin."

He was too smart to buy it. As borough police chief, Merlin's area of responsibility was a region the size of Michigan. He had more than a hundred officers answering to him; as well as detectives, drug experts, liaisons with federal agencies like the Bureau of Land Management and FBI. His eyes were almond-shaped dark brown with green-flecked irises. His complexion was olive. His shoulders were broad and powerful, as befitted a harpooner, able to throw a heavy missile far enough and accurately enough to penetrate the thick skin of a forty-ton bowhead whale. His hair was a short, thick brown, balding at both sides of his forehead, with gray streaks in back. His voice was soft but not unforgiving. I'd found during my brief time here that even the elders in Barrow, seventy and eighty years old, were often powerful men. During a health survey at the old folks' home, I'd shaken hands with one eighty-one-year-old ex–caribou hunter, holding back pressure so as not to damage his delicate bones. He'd looked offended. Suddenly the strength in him was enormous. He'd squeezed my hand like a Marine in a bar contest. He'd bellowed out, with great satisfaction, "Colonel, you are WEAK!"

Merlin Toovik demanded, "You have something to tell me, Colonel? Tell me, right now."

WELL! TWO ROADS STRETCHED AHEAD AND NEITHER OFFERED positive outcomes.

There had been no written language on the North Slope until a hundred years ago, and even in my brief time here I'd found that words were regarded as contracts. Tell someone you'll call them next week, and you better do it. Make an offer, you better keep it. The Iñupiats have stopped billion-dollar offshore oil projects in court when they believed that the oil companies lied to them. They shut down the Atomic Energy Commission when the commission lied at Point Hope. They pay top lobbyists in Washington to safeguard their interests in that cesspool of backstabbing arts.

You don't get two chances here if you lie.

Barrow, the little town eighty miles to our north—with its small houses and rural, tilting telephone poles and gravel roads and roller-skating rink—was run by leaders more sophisticated than half the VIPs I met at Washington cocktail parties. They spoke more quietly. They were more self-effacing. They wore Levi's and anoraks and sealskin boots. Yet, they were just as quick and brutal—when necessary—in getting things done.

I felt Eddie watching me sideways, wondering what I would say. And probably thinking that I'd already disobeyed orders twice in the last few hours, first when I'd come along on the trip, then when I'd allowed us to be officially deputized, which I'm sure had unpleasant legal consequences back in Washington.

I told Merlin Toovik our true mission.

His voice remained soft afterward, but there was no hiding the accusation. "You're here to check consequences from germ experiments and *dumped radioactivity*?"

"It happened seventy years ago and everyone on the North Slope knows about it and there's been no evidence since then of any damaging consequences, not here. Merlin, the likelihood is that your cousin went crazy and shot these people, and then he shot himself."

Merlin sighed, subsided. "Clay was not that kind of person."

I knew that the police chief was too experienced to believe this, that nobody was ever *not that kind of person*. I asked, "Did he take drugs, Merlin?"

"No."

"Drink?"

"As a teen. But his father shot himself while drunk. Clay never touched alcohol after that. He coaches . . . *coached* . . . girls basketball and made it a point: One drink and you are out."

Eddie suggested, "Maybe he hid it from you. I mean, you being the police chief and all."

Merlin said, "You can hide being a drinker in the city where you come from, but you can't hide here. Everyone finds out who you are."

"We had to ask, Merlin."

"No problem."

"We'll run the samples. I'll tell you everything. But right now we need to find Kelley's diary."

Merlin's eyes showed red, with moisture at the edges.

The sky was growing darker. It smelled wet and violent, like a sudden storm was brewing.

Merlin's voice cracked. "Oh, hell. What will I tell my aunt?"

TEN MINUTES LATER THE PILOT ANNOUNCED IN OUR EARBUDS that the weather report had turned worse, and that we had at most thirty minutes before we needed to get out of here.

After that, the gusting winds would rise to sixty miles an hour, and the chopper couldn't fly. Hail was falling in Barrow. We'd be stuck here for at least the night.

"Which would be no problem normally," I said. "But we don't know if the Harmons and Clay absorbed something toxic here."

"I wish we could find that diary," Eddie said.

We searched fast, under mattresses, in kitchen drawers, in the supply area stocked with canned tins of Dinty Moore stew and baked beans and Spam, Sailor crackers, PowerBars, and several dozen gallon-sized jugs of bottled water.

Someone put something in the water, Kelley had said.

So we took a few gallon jugs for analysis.

We found no diary. We found girl things: her summer reading assignment from high school, *For Whom the Bell*

Tolls; a backpack filled with pink sweaters and logo T-shirts; a suitcase under the bunk, which held mostly hip-hop music selections; a paperback dictionary; a small, stuffed bear with a red ribbon on its head; a selection of Nordic sweaters; cords and jeans and girlish undergarments.

"Maybe it's in her laptop, One."

"Power up the laptop. Does the battery work?"

"I see lots of files here, but no diary."

"Take it along. Hurry up."

There was no book-style diary in the cabinets or desktop. Or wedged beneath overstuffed chair cushions. And certainly not among her parents' gear, by the outhouse, the samples cooler, which seemed filled with seeds and other plant and lake life: algae, flowers, dried mud.

With ten minutes to go until we had to leave, Luther Oz returned on the ATV to say, baffled, that the tracks he'd followed had begun in camp, all right, and went out for half a mile, but then began making crazy circles, looping, carving *Z* shapes in the grass, leaving skid marks that turned back into tracks that eventually ended up where they started, back here.

"I don't get it," Oz said, scratching his head. "Nobody else was here. Someone went out, drove around in circles and came back. What gives?"

It was clear that within minutes the heavens would open up, and any evidence, whatever might exist in the open, tracks, hairs, chemicals, would be washed away.

Merlin suggested leaving the bodies here, the death scene undisturbed, a deputy guard overnight, but that was a bad idea, I responded, if there was something toxic here.

After all, we had not eliminated sickness as an element in this disaster. Or a chemical that could be anywhere in the camp. The cabin. The soil. The lake. The bodies.

"Better take them along, so animals don't get at them, and return later and do a better search," I said.

"*Imminnauraq*," muttered Merlin in the Iñupiat language.

"What's that?"

"Superstition. Little people. Jokers. Or, *Sinik Tagnailaq*. This lake," he said morosely. "A place where you don't want to stay the night. Stay and something bad happens. We never did love the idea of a camp set here."

Eddie said as we wrapped things up, "Why?"

"It goes back to the whaling years. Those New England whalers carried flus which decimated us. Back in 1870, a party of Iñupiat were coming back from the Barrow trading post, heading inland—infected but they didn't know it. It hit them when they overnighted here. Later their bodies were found, scattered along the trail. The lake got blamed for causing the fever. Then the Navy built this cabin for oil geologists. But there was no oil, so it was abandoned until the scientists came. More bad luck."

I shivered as the first drops fell, and envisioned a party of Eskimo men, women, and children camped by the lake, 150 years back, maybe a fire roaring. Then the first person started coughing, feeling feverish, and then the party tried to move out the next day, things getting worse, getting bad fast for people with no immunity to the whaler diseases . . . and the sick elders saying, *Leave me here. I'll slow you down. You'll live if you leave me behind.*

I said, "We wrap 'em up. We wear masks and gloves, even in the chopper. The bodies go to the hospital. We'll do autopsies tomorrow, when we're fresh."

"Disinfect the chopper," said Eddie.

"Rescue squad does it all the time," said Merlin.

"Anyone feels ill, after we get back, tell your people, call me right away," I said. "No matter how late."

As we loaded up, I asked Merlin, "Your cousin Clay. Any problems at home?"

"Not that I know of."

"Anger issues? Debts? Psychological history? He was a veteran, right? Grudges? Money problems?"

"Plenty of men in town are veterans. I'll have my detectives do the police work. Them. Not you, Joe. Thanks for coming. But you two stick to disease."

The bodies lay covered with plastic.

The rain began pummeling us.

"We need to get going," Merlin Toovik said.

WE LIFTED OFF. AS DUSK APPROACHED THE TUNDRA BELOW rolled out in multiple variations. Light browns grew darker. Glassy lakes produced whitecaps. Grass bent sideways as sheets of rain slashed at the crowns.

A lone caribou, almost a shadow silhouetted in moving mist, looked up at the passing chopper. The glass of the cockpit was smeared wet, streaming rain.

I saw a single ATV below pulling a small four-wheeled wagon. A hunter drove. A small boy sat on the cart, both people in jackets, hoodies and stocking hats against the wet, heading toward Barrow, hauling fresh meat: probably caribou, bound for the hunter's ice cellar, the fifteen-foot-deep pit in the permafrost dug behind many Barrow homes.

Like medieval monks looking up inside cowls, man and boy followed our progress, probably frowning. Everyone up here recognized the markings of the rescue chopper. If it was out, someone was injured, sick, or dead.

AS SOON AS WE LANDED—WHEN EDDIE AND I WERE ALONE IN OUR Ford truck—I called the admiral to tell him what had happened. He was angry that we'd disobeyed instructions.

"I *told* you not to get distracted."

"Sir, you told me to use my judgment. We may be looking at something new here, exactly why we came."

He wasn't fooled. "Spare me, Joe. You went because of that big damn heart of yours. Perhaps you can tell me what I should say to Major General Wayne Homza when he demands to know why two thousand lawsuits have suddenly been filed by Barrow residents blaming every cough, sniffle, and flu on radioactivity that was dumped three hundred miles away from them, over sixty years ago."

"Sir, in my opinion they would have found out in the end. It's better to be up front. That's been my experience up here, which is why you asked us to come."

"Hmph!" Admiral Galli grumbled, but he processed the logic and seemed to accept it, even though it meant he'd have to do a bit of dealing with the legal departments. Then he said, "I thought you said it was a shooting."

"After they all got sick."

"You think the illness caused the shooting?"

"Probably not. But if you're asking whether certain diseases or chemicals can heighten paranoia, the answer is yes. Sir, this location has been the site of many scientific inquiries over the years: digging, seismic, oil. I want to do more work before I sign off on Clay Qaqulik. I want to see the diary. And, sir, would it be all right if I used the research branch to run his social? I've got his ID card here."

A sigh. "At this point, why not?"

He clicked off but not before he connected me with his secretary, and gave her instructions to link me up with our research folks, a trio of Georgetown University graduates who spent their workdays in a Foggy Bottom basement, where the only light came from bulbs, lamps, and multiple computer screens. Conceptually as far away from the wilderness as you can get.

I'd never met our researchers—only spoken to them via phone—and thought of them as The Baritone, Chicago-Voice, and Valley Girl, since all of her statements came out sounding like questions. Valley Girl was the quickest and smartest, although her high-pitched, gum-cracking voice irritated me at times.

"I'll run his social? Hold on for ten minutes? This will be fast?" she said. "Or should I call you back?"

"I'll hold. Just give me an initial."

I sat there in the cab of the Ford with the heater running. The rain had stopped, and the sky was a uniform lead color. The ocean seemed more oily, maybe that was what happened to it before the big ice formed. It was calmer and looked darker, heavier. I saw a lone fin surface out there. Some sort of small whale. Minke or beluga, maybe. Then I saw a half dozen of them. A pod.

Over the phone came normal office sounds: a sucking noise—her gum, I figured—and keys tapping and a gurgling in the background that sounded like a coffeemaker. I heard music playing softly; something classical, Debussy, I thought. Impressionist. Swelling and ebbing. Maybe Ravel. Ten minutes became twelve, and twelve became fifteen. I might as well drive home while I waited, might as well risk losing the connection, which could happen, up here, at any time.

Suddenly Valley Girl was back. "Oh, wow! Cool! So Qaqulik is an Eskimo?" she said.

"Yes."

"In-teresting! Wow!"

"Interesting to you because he's an Eskimo? Or for some other reason?"

"He's got one hell of an impressive background, sir."

"He does?"

She told me highlights of Clay Qaqulik's background.

I gasped, and said, everything changed now, "He was *what*?"

FOUR

My mind was churning with the news about Clay Qaqu-lik as I walked into our Quonset hut. A CD of Ray Charles singing "Georgia" was playing, and the sight of my fiancée in her neon-blue and black spandex yoga suit made my heartbeat speed up. Then I saw the man who was in love with her across the room. I was in no mood for him and his camera tonight.

"Oh, Joe. I heard about the Harmons," she said.

Karen Vleska was uncoiling on the plush gold pile carpet, from one of those pretzel poses that seem impossible for a man to achieve. She did yoga when she was stressed. Just the sight of her small, lithe body—the toned arm muscles, the petite energy and vibrancy, and her most stunning feature, the head-turning silver hair, shiny and youthful, falling beyond her back and pooling on the carpet—set my heart pounding, even now.

"Joe, those people. Horrible," she said.

Mikael Grandy—award-winning HBO documentary filmmaker from Manhattan—was a lean, broad-shouldered man on the far side of the room. He infuriated me with his constant presence. He was filming her for an upcoming series, *Arctic Women Explorers*. Mikael was too smart to tell her of his feelings for her, but it was pretty obvious. It was in the way he watched her and held the camera, as if it were part of her, and it was in his voice. Always kind in a certain way, always attentive, and, as Eddie put it, *The slimeball is waiting*.

Mikael said, "I wish I could make my body do that."

Karen said, "Good things come with practice."

"Maybe you can show me, Karen."

You're asking for it, I thought.

A word about our temporary home, the Quonset hut, which was pictured, in an aerial photo last year, for *Smithsonian* magazine's cover story, "Barrow, America's Arctic Research Capital: The Frontier Town That Hosts More Scientists Per Square Foot Than Anywhere Else in the World."

The hut sat in an old Navy base, revamped into a research center: two square miles of seaside campus, fences gone, open to the tundra . . . freshwater lagoon to the south, a satellite farm—a collection of golf-ball–shaped geodesic domes—on the western property, where NASA guys from hut six launched weather balloons daily and monitored about five hundred factors affecting Earth's climate.

On the far side of the lagoon—accessible by a half-mile-long one-lane blacktop—sat a new twenty-five-million-dollar Arctic Research Center, where Eddie and I had our lab and freezers, filled with samples we'd collected all summer: a flu from the coastal village of Wainright; a rabies sample from an Arctic fox killed by hunters near Camden Bay; a batch of Arctic parasites—*sarcocystis pinnipedi*, shaped like crescent moons under the microscope—which were killing seal pups. A dissected brain of polar bear dead of toxoplasmosis, previously a warm-weather disease found in European cats, which had spread north as the Arctic warmed.

But at the heart of the base—the old cracked runway, the garages that housed snowmobiles and cold-weather gear, the rusted conveyer systems and hangars—were four rows of military-style Quonset huts that had become a summer campus . . . roughly thirty huts in all, looking from the outside like dilapidated World War Two–era housing, but inside had been fixed up nicely, and heated by natural gas.

Other than the curved roof, we might have been in a comfortable middle-class home in Minneapolis. Gold-colored pile spread from the entranceway, through a closed foyer and into the kitchenette, past the four-burner stove and refrigerator and across the spacious living room; in which sat a three-cushion couch and leather Barca-lounger, a flat-screen TV, landline phones, and four bedrooms grouped around the periphery, three with bunk beds, one with two singles, which Karen and I had pushed together.

Until two weeks ago, when Karen flew in, Eddie and

I had shared the hut, staying in separate bedrooms. But Eddie had insisted on moving to a hotel so I could have a "pre-honeymoon." I'd tried to pay for it. But Eddie had refused.

"Honeymoon gift, Uno," he'd said. "It's worth it to me not to have to deal with your grouchiness for two weeks."

Now I wanted to tell Karen details, try to figure things out, but not in front of Mikael. He saved me the trouble.

"Colonel," he said, turning the camera on me, "how did you feel when you found poor Kelley Harmon?"

"You *know* about that?"

"Do you think the bear guard suffered from post-traumatic stress? I understand he was an Army veteran."

"Where did you hear this stuff?" I asked.

"The checkout girl was talking in the Value Center."

"The checkout . . . how did *she* know?"

"The police dispatcher temp is her cousin," he said with pride, as if he'd just won a Pulitzer for investigative reporting. His series on women explorers would run nationally six months from now, and Karen hoped it would help her raise funds for a land trip next winter along the Northwest Passage. That meant the documentary was important to her, and so, by extension, was Mikael.

Mikael began coming closer, still filming, stuck to the eyepiece. Sometimes I wondered how he communicated with people in social situations with no machine around. He said, "I understand there was illness at that research station. Do you think it was connected to the murders?"

"No one has called what happened murder."

"Accident? Surely you can't think that."

"Too early to say anything," I replied.

"Do you think that possible sexual rivalry at the camp set the man off?"

"I think if you don't put that camera down," I snapped, "I'll do it for you."

He lowered it quickly, *Of course, sir, you are upset . . .* but irritation flashed in the intelligent eyes. Mikael emanated casual stylishness, a one-day growth of beard on the pale, blue-eyed face, the thick, black, wild hair combed with his hands, the brand-name, tight sweaters that emphasized the swimmer's shoulders and lean hips, the sense that he was always leaning forward, either fascinated, or hungry. He had the speed-talk of a Manhattanite, the smooth friendliness of a man who made his living by getting along with others. Allegedly he had a wife, but never mentioned her, and he wore no ring.

And the feeling he had for Karen showed in his lingering reluctance to stop filming. It wasn't professional. Not to me. He was the tourist gaping at the movie star, wanting to touch.

Karen had watched our exchange with no expression, which meant she was getting mad. The only disagreements we had recently regarded Mikael, his questions and appearances at inopportune moments. My dislike wasn't helped by his regular references to me—in their interviews—as "the Marine" or "your boyfriend."

I told Mikael, for Karen's sake, or more accurately, household peace, "Sorry I snapped at you. Tough afternoon."

"No problem. Karen, we can get more exercise shots tomorrow, on the tundra. You walking. Looking east, toward the Northwest Passage, contemplating the danger ahead."

I groaned inwardly. *Jesus Christ!*

Karen said, "Stay for coffee, Mike."

But the weasel was smart. He put down the camera and said he would come back later. After all, only fifty feet separated us from his neighboring Quonset hut. He said he'd give us time together, as if it was his to bestow. He said I should "recover from shock," maybe "lie down a bit."

Mikael waved at the door. "*Ciao*, guys."

"Mike, don't be shy. You're always welcome," she said.

When the door shut, she did not look happy.

"Joe, you embarrassed me. Are we going to have this discussion *again*?"

"He's in love with you."

"So? What's the problem?"

"*That's* the problem."

"I'm supposed to stay away from anyone who likes me?"

"No, it's . . ."

She poked me, angry. "I'm supposed to tell him, go away? I'm not interested in the documentary? I don't want to raise any more money for the trip? I've decided to retire and be a hermit and not talk to other men because my fiancée doesn't like it? Me Tarzan. Me Joe Rush. My woman stay in cave."

"Me in trouble," I said, smiling despite things.

"Goddamnit," she said, but after a moment—things

could go either way here—she smiled back. Our relationship was recent enough for anger to go away that fast. But you need to watch it. That happy phase doesn't last.

"Karen, I have to tell you something about Clay Qaqulik."

She gasped when I did. She said, "Graduated with honors from Vanderbilt? Army intelligence. Two years in the FBI? And then he quits and comes back here and hires out as the guy who cooks meals and fixes engines? I don't get it."

I nodded, frowning, envisioning him, a big, shambling, quiet man, mustached, usually in baggy old jeans and a ratty sweater, who looked like he'd never worn an FBI-style suit in his life . . . and played electric guitar with the Barrowtones at their Saturday night gigs at the roller rink . . . a sometime mechanic on base, fixing snowmobiles or truck suspensions, a handyman available to help out scientists, satellite repair folks, Arctic adventurers, visitor VIPs.

Now my computer folks had painted a picture of a crackerjack Phi Beta Kappa student, an award-winning FBI agent. A comer in Washington any way you looked at it, who up and left and returned to the North Slope and now used a socket wrench instead of a 9mm Glock.

Karen asked, "Is there a reason he quit?"

"They tried to talk him out of it."

"Personal problems?"

"Maybe he just didn't like it."

"Something happened. Cultural differences. Or, just because he was smart doesn't mean he didn't have problems adjusting. He just killed three people and himself. I'd say there were mental problems in there somewhere."

"I keep thinking about Kelley's phone call. They were all sick. *All of them*."

"The sickness could have exacerbated pre-existing stress."

"Yes."

"He's sick. With underlying problems. Add personal differences. Everything escalates. He picks up the shotgun. Wouldn't be the first time."

"No. It wouldn't," I said.

"Then what's bothering you?"

"I don't know. I don't know what the 'but' is. Maybe it's that I feel like I owe something to Kelley. Maybe it's that Merlin never mentioned the FBI. Merlin going on as if Clay Qaqulik spent his life here except for the Army. There's something else. Maybe the diary will help, if we ever find the damn thing."

Karen thought about it. "Did you get his tax records? If there's some other link there," she said, meaning, *like a mission, like his records are like yours, sheep-dipped*, "you might see who is paying him."

"We're not supposed to access tax records."

"I didn't ask what you're not supposed to do. I asked what you did do."

So much for protecting her from knowledge that would make her legally culpable. "I told Valley Girl to dig up tax records. That takes time. She has to sneak around to get them in order to leave no computer trail behind."

Karen and I met last year on an icebreaker that had

suffered sabotage. She was security cleared and no stranger to espionage, or even to spies, one of whom we'd uncovered on that ship.

She said now, considering, "You'll talk to Merlin about this."

"First thing."

"Or the admiral can find out more."

"I've pushed him enough for one day."

I remembered the dead man in that cabin, that lone remaining eye as stiff and lifeless as a marble. I also remembered the admiral's words back in Washington. *That town looks like the end of the planet, but it is less than five hundred miles from resurgent Russia, and along the longest unprotected coastline in the U.S. Military maneuvers coming. Shipping. Oil drilling offshore. You want to know the state of our Arctic satellite technology? Landing points in remote areas? You want to meet scientists whose work will impact national policy? It's presumed that the other powers want to know what we're doing up there.*

Karen made coffee, poured, stirred in sugar, gave me a mug, black. She was thinking along the same lines. "And *plants*, Joe. I'll be back here in a few weeks planning war games. You're on microbes. Take a walk around base, hell, look at the people in the other huts. Big oil. Diamonds. If Clay was working on something, why focus on the people studying seeds?"

"Unless the Harmons weren't really studying seeds." Then I laughed at myself. I let it roll out. I was tired. The most obvious explanation was still the first one. A man had cracked up. I told Karen, "Eddie said it's time to get out of this work when you start thinking that a fourth grader taking selfies on the Metro is really a midget snapping photos of you."

She drank coffee, cradled her mug as if it could spread warmth into her heart. "Oh, Joe. They took their child along! That girl! The poor mother. The last few moments, knowing that your child is . . . I can't believe they'd drag that girl into something bad, endanger her. Those parents are exactly who they said they were. *They had no idea what was going to happen out there!*"

"There are toxins that go right to the brain, Karen."

"And a high suicide rate locally. You know that. And alcohol abuse. Just look at those slogans on trash Dumpsters in town: *DON'T DRINK!!*"

"Merlin insisted that Clay didn't drink. And we didn't find drugs. Tomorrow we'll do a more thorough search."

Karen laid her hand on mine, leaned into me. I inhaled her smell of vanilla and fresh shampoo and detergent. More, I inhaled us, our mix, *togetherness*. Her eyes were the color of ice in a crevasse, a lone tear, a glass chip. I felt like I was home with her anywhere—in a Quonset hut, at sea, on ice—and it was this mixture of warmth and excitement that constituted to me the definition of love.

Her petite body was willowy and athletic, an inverted bow. Her voice was a soft Ozark lilt, but it could be candid to the point of bluntness. Her face was elfin, her movements liquid, her words usually punctuated by flying hands. But her most arresting feature was the silvery hair falling to the pit of her back; not gray, not old, it exuded youthful vibrancy. From the back she looked like a teen. She was thirty-two years old.

Karen worked as an engineer for Electric Boat, specializing in the operation of nuclear submarines. We planned a December wedding, and after that, when I left the unit, a move to Boston, where she would continue working on subs, and train for her upcoming all-women walk along Canada's northern border. I'd give lectures at the Navy War College in Newport and, with Eddie, start up a private company looking for new pharmaceuticals in the High North. Cures this time.

"Mikael was right about one thing, Joe. You ought to eat."

We'd planned a romantic evening; frozen sirloin from the AV Center, California burgundy, ten-dollar-a-bunch asparagus, microwaved Sara Lee apple pie, my fave.

We weren't hungry now.

We went into the bedroom and lay down, said nothing, held hands and, at length, undressed and made love, the slow kind, that goes with grieving, with wanting to feel human connection, to feel life in the face of something bad. Her flat, muscled belly rose and fell and moved in muscular circles. I saw tendons in her thighs bunch and release. I kissed the three-freckle constellation decorating her left hip. Later, with the light fading outside, her hair on my face, I smelled her perfume in the fresh linen. And in the little mirror on the wall—with the sled-dog logo on top, *Souvenir of the Arctic*—I saw two naked people lying there, lovers framed.

Mirrors. What is it about mirrors?

"Joe, you need to get used to Mikael. He'll be around in Boston, too, after we move."

"No problem," I lied.

"Did you know that he comes from White Russian nobility? His ancestor actually sailed under Vitus Bering and was given a land grant in Alaska by the czar. Not far from here! *Thousands* of acres."

"Fascinating man," I said.

"Mikael said his family would have still *owned* part of the North Slope if Russia hadn't sold Alaska to the U.S. That's so weird, isn't it? That this town, this place, would be part of Russia? During the Cold War? Russia!"

I asked, more interested, "So the weasel's family lost their fortune when the communists took over?"

"Don't call him a weasel. One minute they owned farms, and serfs, and even a small palace in St. Petersburg. The next minute, they're on the run, barely got out. They moved to Shanghai, and then fled to San Francisco when Mao took over. Mikael goes to Harvard. He doesn't brag, but he was nominated for an Oscar for his dolphin-killing film."

If he doesn't brag, how do you know? I thought.

We both heard the knocking at the door. It was now dark outside.

"Does Mikael still have family in Russia?" I felt her stiffen beside me, rise on one elbow and stare.

"Joe, that was a century ago, okay?" she said, getting up, beautiful, pulling on lace underwear—she wore it even in the Arctic—and black cords, pulling a white turtleneck over her hair.

The knocking came again. She said, "The *New York Times* called Mikael a 'visual poet.'"

"He touches you and he'll be a visual dead guy."

She giggled. "Short of that, Colonel, play nice. Now let's see who's here."

IT WASN'T MIKAEL BUT OTHER NEIGHBORS, SUMMER FRIENDS. What had been planned as a romantic evening turned into a wake, as people drifted in to talk, to remember, to grieve.

Still, I could not help but wonder, thinking of Clay Qaqulik as more than just cook and mechanic: *Is someone here not who they seem?*

"OhmyGawd! We heard about it in the post office!"

First to arrive were the brother-and-sister team—Dave and Deborah Lillienthal—employed by Longhorn North Oil Company, of Houston, which was expected to bid on undersea leases, up for auction soon by the U.S. Interior Department. Oil companies believed that a mini–Saudi Arabia existed fifty to a hundred miles away from Barrow, and it was expected that Shell, Longhorn, and Conoco would go head-to-head in bidding, trying to obtain rights.

In the interim, each company was conducting last-minute seismic surveys offshore to pinpoint areas in which they had particular interest, and to help them plan how much money to bid—billions would be offered for undersea land.

"The Harmons had such terrible luck all summer,"

Deborah said. "First their truck busted up, then their computers went down. Then they had that records snafu, remember, Dave?"

"Right, the closet that caught fire."

Dave and Deborah ran Longhorn's exploratory efforts: seismic ships, engineers, and archaeologists employed to select inland pipeline routes, bypassing Eskimo historic sites protected by federal law; water experts to avoid locations where groundwater might be polluted by construction.

In person, they were usually jovial corporate ambassadors; their hut, number six, was the party hut stocked with liquor and tonight they deposited two liter-sized bottles of Tito vodka on the table, along with tomato juice, a semi-fresh lemon, quinine water, and orange juice. Alcohol could not be sold in stores or restaurants in Barrow. It could, however, be flown in, if buyers paid for a liquor tax and air shipment, and bought a city license to drink. They could then pick up bottles at a hut by the airport.

As a result, a can of Bud might cost twenty dollars in Barrow. A bottle of vodka was worth hundreds. The Lillienthals carried a thousand dollars of alcohol in their arms.

"Figured we'd all need this," said Dave, pulling out logo mugs from above our sink; Sandia labs, Woods Hole cup, National Science Foundation glass, leavings of former visitors. No mug said, *SPY.*

He was a big, round ex-fraternity president at Texas A&M, two years older than his sister, and he was a ferocious eater and dedicated gym rat, with a Johnson City twang. The pudgy features gave him a cherubic air accentuated by the thick, curly hair cut close to his head. The red face said drinker, eventual heart attack, or both. The eyes were merry but the mouth was not. Dave was an engineer by training and his mission was to drill.

Deborah, mixing vodka and tonics, was small, skinny, and had the same facial features, except on her they were squeezed into a narrow face—big blue eyes, slightly bulgy midsection, small mouth but striking cheekbones—and she moved with a sexy walk that drew glances in town. She ran the daily morning phone tree conferences—from their hut—between company copter pilots, Eskimo elders in outlying villages, and headquarters. The elders would alert the company if fishermen or hunters were in an area, to keep copters away that day. The pilots were freelancers out of Anchorage. Longhorn had two seismic ships going back and forth offshore, looking for likely oil finds.

Dave took a long draw of Tito. "We've used Clay Qaqulik as a mechanic."

Deborah's voice was low, as if the dead could hear and take offense. "It could have been one of us." She smelled of Shalimar perfume and violets. She wore a moose logo sweater, background cobalt-blue, the animals white, over tight, faded blue jeans. Visitors took their shoes off usually when entering a Quonset hut, so as not to track in dirt or mud. Her socks also had a moose logo. She had small feet.

"Joe, I hear you're not just a colonel anymore," Dave said. "Now you're a gen-u-ine North Slope dep-u-tee, too."

"Merlin asked me not to talk about what happened."

Dave made a noise in his throat. "That would make you the only one in town *not* talking about it."

"Legal reasons," I said, accepting a beer, taking a draught. "You know, if there's a trial."

Deborah perked up. "Trial? Of who? Isn't Clay dead?"

"Good beer," I said.

"I heard they had rashes all over their bodies," said Deborah. She had a habit of idly raising and lowering one leg like a ballerina when in conversation. Eddie believed she'd taken dance training. She had the posture for it. Eddie also thought she slept with lots of guys, or at least was always seen in town hanging on to different ones. Visiting politicians. VIP visitors. Eskimo leaders. She liked putting herself on display.

Dave said, "Clay Qaqulik. What kind of past does this guy have? He was in the military, right? I mean, people get in trouble elsewhere, and no one asks questions here. Another beer, Joe?"

"No thanks."

"Purple rashes," Deborah said, opening the refrigerator. "You got any cheese? Rashes with little bumps all over. Is that true, Joe?"

They were grilling me. They wanted answers. Which made them normal. A knock interrupted their questions and our second visitor walked in—an enemy of the Lillienthals.

...

DR. BRUCE FRIDAY WAS A RETIRED PROFESSOR TURNED ENVI-ronmentalist from Rutgers University, in New Jersey. He was a sixty-two-year-old ex-researcher of ecosystems who Karen believed had the hots for Deborah. He grew nervous around her, fumbling during arguments with Dave, losing things: his glasses, a book. Karen always speculated, "*Something* happened between those two. Or he wants it to."

"Hell of an age difference."

"Maybe he came on to her, and she shut him down. It's like he loses control of his thinking when she's close."

Bruce was divorced, had lost his wife and two sons twelve years back to his passion for work. The wife had remarried. The boys were in business school, as if to reject his idealism, and never spoke with him anymore. He kept their photos in his hut; cracked, fading reminders of family.

I felt sorry for him, but he seemed at home on the base—a permanent expatriate. "Ecology is a science, not a social movement," he always said. At Rutgers he'd studied the way that all life-forms in an area—animal, vegetable, and microbial—interact. After retiring he'd signed up with the Arctic Warrior Fund and now studied the demise of polar bears. He gave speeches attacking oil companies, which he blamed for global warming. Usually, when in the same room, the talk grew heated between Bruce and Dave.

Bruce Friday was the oldest resident of the base. He'd been coming to Barrow for thirty-two years. These days he lived on a small grant from the Warriors and testified at government hearings about offshore drilling. *You can't clean spilled oil under ice, so don't allow any drilling!* Tonight he just held up his hands and said to Dave, "Truce?"

"Truce," Dave replied. "Beer?"

"Vodka."

"Tell me when to stop pouring."

"Don't," said Friday, looking wan and ill. "What a horrible day, Joe. Horrible, horrible day."

Visibly, he seemed poorly equipped for the rigors of Arctic research, with a hook-shaped body, skin that was the kind of white that erupted with cancers if exposed too long to sun, a mop of chestnut hair, more boyish than donnish, and round wire-framed out-of-date glasses that enlarged his gray eyes and gave him a permanently startled air.

But his appearance was misleading. Dr. Friday spent weeks on the ice alone, seeking bears and measuring snowmelt. He was an expert snowmobiler. He routinely went out solo to the bone pile, to gather polar bear hair, DNA. One time, I'd heard, he'd camped out on pack ice, and in the middle of the night it broke off and floated into the Chukchi. Rescued four days later by copter, the pilots found him dozing in a parka, the bones of an eaten fish beside him—and a bottle of Louisiana hot sauce.

Friday got me in a corner, pumped me with questions.

"Do you think Merlin capable of figuring this out?"

"He's a good policeman."

"I can't believe that replacement dispatcher spread the

story. If someone poisoned their water, the guilty person could just leave town, run away!"

"You heard about the water, too?"

"I heard it at the research center. I heard it at the Mexican restaurant. I heard it when I gave Luther Oz's sled dogs a run this afternoon."

Eddie should be here by now.

Bruce Friday went over to talk to Dave and Deborah. I noticed, as he got close to Deborah, that the liquid topping his glass began to shake. Deborah held Bruce's wrist, steadying it.

Where's Eddie? He should be here by now.

Without knocking, the diamond hunter walked in next.

CALVIN DEROCHERS CAME FROM ARKANSAS, THE ONLY PLACE in the U.S. where commercial diamonds are found. He was a home-educated geologist who insisted that, as in Arctic Canada, a huge cache lay somewhere beneath Alaska's North Slope.

"Canada's pulling out billions," Calvin always said. "I aim to find those kimberlite pipes."

His family had been slaves two hundred years ago; sharecroppers after that, then chicken-factory assembly-line workers. He was a short, powerful man, fullback more than cyclist, clothing bought secondhand, to save money for his project, and through sheer diligence he'd raised funding from a Chicago hedge fund—talked his way into their president's office—to pay for the rental hut, a copter pilot, geology supplies, and gear. But his time and money were rapidly running out as autumn began. He'd not yet found any evidence of what he sought.

"I'm sure some of those lakes were formed by meteors," he'd told me at one of our Monday night sausage grill outs. "Meteors did it in the Yukon, and the same shower could have easily hit here. Hell, man, you know what diamonds are? They're scabs on a sore. The meteor slams in. Then Mama Earth repairs herself and that kimberlite pipe is the bandage, and the scab shows up ten million years later as a Tiffany necklace. Uh-huh! They laughed at Chuck Fipke in ninety-one when he drove out to Lac de Gras, Northwest Territories. They laugh at DeRochers today."

He had a habit of referring to himself in the third person, had mortgaged himself to the hilt, for more funding, and I wondered how the wife and six kids handled this back in Arkansas. He was a tireless worker, and his hut was filled with books on diamonds, studies, reports from South Africa, treatises from Sierra Leone, maps from Arkansas. I thought him a homespun genius; a bit nutty, but interesting. Karen and I wished him well.

"I never understood suicide, Joe," he said, passing up the booze, boiling water for rose tea, his drink of choice.

"No?"

"How bad can things get for someone to kill himself? I mean, killing someone else, I get it, you get crazy. You have hate. But kill *yourself*? Never."

"Maybe he didn't kill himself," I said.

"Are you kidding? His finger was still in the trigger guard, right? And the dislocated arm, hell, pulled from the shoulder. Can't fake that! I took him along once as a guard. He was always quiet. I think that guy had secrets."

You don't know the half of it, I thought.

I said, "Is there anything that happened today that this whole town isn't aware of?"

Calvin DeRochers blew on his tea. I watched the ripples dance across the golden surface, and his greenish eyes came up slowly, met mine and stayed there, keen, smart, probing.

"You tell me," he said.

I TRIED TO CALL EDDIE. HE DIDN'T ANSWER.

Calvin's rent-a-pilot, Jens Erik Holte, arrived, a boisterous summer presence in Barrow and Norwegian American who spent his winters in Mexico. Then Mikael the weasel. Then the three-person visiting meteorology team from Boulder. And then three more crowded in: Alan McDougal, who ran logistics on the base; his wife, Candida, an anthropologist; and their fourteen-year-old daughter, Deirdre, a serious, attractive girl and casual friend of Kelley's. Deirdre sat mute in a corner, then broke into sobs.

I tried to cheer her up, which got her talking a little, wiping her nose with a bunched-up tissue. I asked, "Do you happen to know anything about Kelley keeping a diary?"

"Just that she had one. I never saw it."

"Was it on her computer? Was it a book?"

"I don't know." She blurted out, looking around, making sure all the other adults were in conversation, "Ask . . . *ask her boyfriend*!"

"Kelley had a boyfriend? She was only on base for a few days at a time. How did she manage to—"

"People always say they can talk to you, Colonel. Kelley said you and Karen, you can keep a secret. Help me. I feel awful. I don't know what to do."

I knelt on one knee to be at face level with her. It was something that Iñupiat adults did with children, and with the very old. They did not talk down to them. They always looked them right in the eye.

"Deirdre, this will stay between you and me."

The girl looked guilty, miserable. She *wanted* to talk. "She said she trusted you and Karen." The pressure in her face was palpable, awful. "She said . . . she . . . You *promise not to tell*?"

"Yes. I promise."

"She made me swear not to tell also. He works at the Heritage Center. Leon Kavik. He's older. Eighteen. She used to sneak away to see him. I wish her parents *had* known! They'd have sent her home!"

Her hands were twisting, and her eyes pleaded for understanding. I said, touching her shoulder, resting my hand there, "What happened wasn't your fault, Deirdre."

If we'd been alone she would have cried out, but her agony came out in a whisper. "It was! She'd lie and tell her parents she was at our hut, but she was with him! She lied! And I lied, too! Oh, God!"

Everyone stared at me when she ran out of the room

and into a bedroom, crying. I shrugged. I did not want to get her in trouble, but we were going to have to talk more. I wanted to see that boyfriend, and talk to Merlin again, first thing in the morning—and not just about the bodies.

You hid things about your cousin, Merlin.

Why shouldn't he have his secrets? Everyone else did around here.

Report from Barrow

Received by encrypted satellite transmission.

I attended a small wake at Dr. Rush's Quonset hut tonight, where many campus residents were present. So far, no one understands what has happened, what is at stake. But the police emergency operator who spread the initial story has been fired, so it will now be slightly more difficult to gain access to the department.

The bodies have been brought to the hospital, where they are in an isolated area in the morgue. There have been no other cases so far, not in town, but that could, of course, change and if it does, there will be widespread panic. I may need a way to get out, fast.

So far, the Eskimo Qaqulik is being blamed for the deaths. With luck, that will be the official finding.

Plus side: I planted microphones in the Quonset hut during the evening—one in the bedroom, one in the kitchen area off the living room—that should pick up conversation in either place. I'm receiving talk in the hut loud and clear.

Both Marine doctors and the submarine engineer Karen Vleska may need to be killed.

FIVE

Merlin Toovik was making whale bombs when I interrupted him at eight the next morning after I heard from Valley Girl. He was at a wooden worktable in his small, cramped, detached garage, wearing a lightweight Seattle Seahawks jacket and jeans in thirty-five-degree weather, concentrating and staring down at a foot-long copper-shaped missile lying on a coffee-stained blotter, tilted open at the tiny warhead area on top. I knew better than to interrupt while he poured black explosive powder from a spigoted plastic bottle into the finned missile.

When he was screwing the cap back, I said, "You didn't tell me everything, Merlin. Why not?"

"Found out about the FBI, huh?" He laid the missile aside and opened the cap of a second one.

"Merlin, not just that. He worked for you?"

The police chief looked up, visibly impressed, the muscles on his shoulders and arms straining against the fabric of the jacket. "How'd you find that out?" he asked, starting on a second missile.

I'd found out because "North Slope Police Department" was written on the dead man's federal income tax form, but I did not say that. I said, "Merlin, what was one of your detectives doing pretending to work for the Harmons? Yesterday you chewed me out for keeping things from you."

"Technically, no lie. He *did* work for them."

"I put my neck on the line for you."

"Look, I can't make a mistake on these bombs, Joe, or a few more relatives will be killed when we fire one and it doesn't work, or blows too soon. Give me a minute. Then we'll have coffee in the house and I'll explain."

I folded my arms and watched, fascinated by the process despite my irritation, as he loaded two more whale bombs. Whaling captains were the most respected men in the community. They ran crews of a dozen men, mostly relatives, and went out twice a year to harvest the big bowheads migrating past Barrow, using motorboats in fall, and paddling twenty-foot-long sealskin boats in spring, launched directly off the shore-bound ice.

At fifty, Merlin was considered young, not yet an elder. Shotguns hung in racks on the wall. There were two snowmobiles outside; fishing nets were drying in the yard. I saw three sets of rubber boots, two outboard motors against a wall, grease-smeared oilcans, clean fishing hooks.

"Do you know how these whale bombs work, Joe?"

Answer the question. Don't push him. He's testing you. You're on North Slope time here, not D.C. time.

"Tell me, Merlin."

He stood and stretched, getting the tension in his muscles out, and then he strode to the wall and easily hefted an evil-looking harpoon, about six feet long. The wooden shaft ended in a steel, wickedly barbed arrow-shaped protuberance.

"Most people think the harpoon is the whole thing, but it's just the steel part on top. Look down the shaft and we come to this little plunger, see? A trigger. See it?"

I want to know about your cousin, not the damn harpoon.

"Yes, I see it."

"Well, if the harpooner throws well and hits the bow-head—you only have a few seconds to do it before it dives—and you aim just behind the head . . . the harpoon goes in up to the plunger, then the whale's skin depresses the plunger, the plunger acts as a trigger, and the trigger fires the missile from the wooden shaft. A good throw blows up the heart. No suffering. Quick death."

"Then the whole wooden shaft there is a gun?"

"That's right. Hollow inside." He placed the harpoon back on the rack. "There! That ought to do it," Merlin said. "These things are humane. The harpoon stays in, and the shaft floats away, so we can recover it. The harpoon is attached to a floating buoy that marks the whale's location if it dives and tries to get away, still alive."

"Merlin, I'm not here to talk about hunting."

"Sure you are." Merlin signaled me to follow him into

the house, walking out the door. Over his big shoulder he said, "Just a different kind. Clay worked for the mayor, actually. He kept tabs on visitors. Too many of them are like you, Colonel. They don't tell us the whole truth about why they're here, just what they want us to know."

Well! He had a point there, I had to admit.

We passed outside and entered his one-story wooden house through a cold room—called a *cunnychuck*—where we left our shoes among hanging jackets, muddy boots, parkas, and anoraks. The living room was hot, from gas heat, and I smelled coffee brewing. A TV was on, tuned to MSNBC. The couch and sitting chair were Haitian cotton. The pile was colored gold. There was an exercise walker, from where Merlin's wife, Edith, waved to me. She wore spandex pants, a long floral-motif snow shirt, and sneakers and she was glued by earbud to Al Sharpton on MSNBC. The walls were decorated as in most homes I'd visited here, packed with family photos: graduation shots of nephews and nieces, high school football shot on a blue Astroturf field, Hawaii shots of Merlin and Edith on vacation—looking miserable in the heat—a shot of Merlin's crew on the ice, carving up a harvested bowhead with half the town helping. People atop the whale wielding carving knives affixed to long poles. People loading meat onto sleds. A smiling hunter holding out a piece of heart. I saw Clay Qaqulik in back.

Inside homes you always met extended families, in person, or in photos that filled up walls.

Merlin said, putting two thick ceramic mugs on the kitchen table, "Straight talk?"

"Straight talk."

"Clay was doing fine at the FBI until a North Slope case came up. Walrus ivory smuggling. Couple of low-rent jerks from Nome coming up with machine guns and a boat, leaving carcasses behind, harvesting the tusks and shipping pieces to Chicago, claiming they came from elephants. Know what the FBI did when the complaint came in?"

"What?"

"Laughed, Joe. That's what Clay told me his supervisor did: laughed. 'Fucking walruses,' the guy told Clay. 'We've got drugs coming in from Panama. We've got threats against the vice president when he visits Juneau next month. We've got bank robbers in Anchorage—and you want to go look for a couple of guys shooting walruses? Give it to ATF.' Clay quit the next day."

"What was he doing for you?"

"Not me, Joe. Us! The people who *need* walruses and whales to eat. Over half our food comes from subsistence hunting. And more than that, our culture. Walruses aren't just something to look at in a zoo, man. Not here. They're who we are for four thousand years."

He gestured tiredly at Al Sharpton on TV, who was haranguing a Republican senator about an upcoming vote on aid to the Central African Republic.

"That gets more play than us," he said.

"You didn't answer my question."

Merlin went to a different cupboard and opened it and instead of cups and saucers pulled out a three-foot-long rolled-up paper, like a blueprint, which he spread on the checkered tablecloth, after pushing away the remains of a pancake breakfast. He weighed the paper down with a sugar bowl on one end, a maple syrup bottle on the other. It was a map showing the North Slope borough, the same shape as the admiral's topographical depiction in Washington, only the admiral's map showed a cute caribou and a wolf on the bottom, and highlighted the wilderness, lakes and mountains—the vast, open possibility. Merlin's map showed the same area in plain, gridded white—as if the earth had been wiped away and what remained were perfect squares laid out as mathematically as in a Los Angeles real-estate guide. The squares were numbered. The tundra, lakes, and mountains had been reduced to mere geometry. I read out loud. "'Land allocation in the North Slope.'"

"Joe, our heroes here are Eben Hopson and Willie Hensley, who created the borough so we'd have some power over people who want to rip this place apart. They were fought by the state, the oil companies, by anyone who wanted access to land. *But we won.* And now we have our own borough. We can tax companies. That gives us money to pay lobbyists in Washington, lawyers, and scientists of our own to counter whoever wants to run over us. Greenpeace wants to stop our whaling. Interior wants us to stop eating birds. Oil companies want to drill offshore. Well, it's not so easy to come in and do whatever you want anymore. But it is always a fight. Hell, Joe, do you know how we became Americans in the first place? Russia *sold* us to you. No one asked us first."

"You don't want to be Americans?"

"*Of course* we want to be Americans. We've got the highest percentage of veterans in our population than anywhere else in the U.S. But like every other damn community, we want some power over our own fate."

"How did Detective Clay Qaqulik fit in to this?"

"Well, *helpful* Clay Qaqulik guided an Arkansas senator out to the Arctic National Wildlife Refuge, and listened to him on his cell phone, telling someone to try to get a gigantic open-pit mine in the place. *Cook* Clay Qaqulik made breakfast for the visiting president of the Northern Lights Drill Company, of Sweden, who, ignoring the Eskimo menial, bragged to advisers that even though he'd promised to build a pipeline if they found oil offshore, he'd move the oil by ship, save on taxes, cheat us. To them, Clay was a quaint piece of landscape, a dumb rube, and they said things around him that he reported. Well, I bet that Swede was surprised when Senator Maxwell demanded that they sign a paper promising a pipeline.

"Joe. I like you. Hell, you, Karen, and Eddie probably saved a few hundred lives here last summer. But you *still* didn't tell us why you're really here until yesterday."

"Clay was a spy for you, you're saying."

"He was my cousin and a trained investigator and he was undercover for me. He helped out."

"Spying on the Harmons."

"No," Merlin said, frowning, pouring coffee, stirring in sugar. "He was on another kind of case with them. Actually, he was trying to protect them."

"From what?"

Merlin sipped his coffee, made a face, dumped in more

sugar. "Clay believed that someone has been trying to stop their work all summer," Merlin said. "He hangs out at the base and he decided, too many accidents. Too many delays. But why? Why them? *Something is going on!*"

"Like what?"

A shrug. "Who knows? Something small and personal? Something bigger? Someone trying to keep them from going somewhere, doing something, seeing something related to *us*? Either way, if someone is breaking equipment, starting fires, that's a crime. And now, on top of that, the kid's on the phone. '*We're all sick.*'"

I thought about it. It made sense. I sat and sipped coffee, and let the acid spread warmth into my stomach.

Merlin said, "Anyway, right now you and I ought to get to the office. Major Nakamura has something to show us."

I started. *Why didn't you tell me that right away?*

Merlin added, "While you were parking your truck, my friend, he found the diary."

I'd shut my phone off so any ringing wouldn't disturb me grilling Merlin. The police chief was grinning now, enjoying this part. I sighed. "Okay, Merlin. You win."

Merlin changed out of a T-shirt and into a button-up. He added a bolo tie with a walrus-ivory clip, a carved hunter. He kissed Edith good-bye as she walked on the slow-moving treadmill. He took a paper bag lunch from the refrigerator and put on an anorak against the thirty-six-degree cold, whereas I needed a parka. I followed him outside. He stared at the ocean for a moment, across the street, beyond the beach. It was black, frothy with wavelets.

"Hmm, see that sky, Joe?"

"What about it?"

"Surely you smell *that*?"

I sniffed. "Pancakes?"

"Winter's coming," said Merlin, tapping his nose.

"Any day now," I answered.

"No, in about twelve hours," he said. "By tonight that ocean out there will be slush and ice."

I DROVE FAST, FOLLOWING MERLIN, MY RENTED TWELVE-YEAR- old Ford Explorer eating up the six miles of dirt-and-gravel road; past city garages and yellow bulldozers waiting for winter, past the blue Astroturf football field donated by a Florida woman for Barrow's high school, into the triangular mass of streets and past a restaurant that had once been a whaler trading station, abutting the beach, fronted by a bleaching bowhead skull—a popular spot for tourist photos.

I passed another tourist attraction: a signpost on a pole, nailed with wooden arrows pointing in all directions. They read: SEATTLE, 1,960 MILES. LOS ANGELES, 2,945 MILES. AYACUCHO, PERU, 7,691 MILES. PORT-AU-PRINCE, HAITI, 4,966. WASHINGTON, D.C., 3,600.

Many Barrow streets lacked street signs. Homes were designated by number for postal deliveries. We passed the Osaka restaurant where Karen loved the sushi. Backyards were little museums for people who loved the outdoors, filled with sleds, SUVs, hanging racks for drying fish or caribou hides. The tallest structures in town, grouped around one intersection, were Borough Hall, the Wells

Fargo Bank building; the Iñupiat-owned Arctic Slope Regional Corporation; and the two-story police station, in front of which we parked. Jail cells upstairs.

There was no need at this time of year to plug the engine into one of the electric heating sockets situated in rows outside any public building, like hitching posts in Old West towns.

Eddie sat in Merlin's small office, at Kelley's laptop. Its cover open, pasted with a mass of stickers depicting singing stars: Ed Sheeran, Meghan Trainor.

Eddie looked up. He seemed exhausted. On Merlin's leather couch I saw rumpled bedding. *He's probably been here all night.* "The diary is several files, some written, some recorded. All labeled something else. She would have made a pretty good researcher, One."

He'd given me downtime with Karen, while he and Merlin's computer guy went through file after file in the laptop last night. The remains of a delivered breakfast from Osaka—eggs on muffins, bacon, coffee, hash browns, and a big cup of OJ—sat on the blotter on Merlin's desk.

"This is as good as any research you'd see at Harvard, Uno."

"Tell me the symptoms?"

Eddie sat back, reached out, hit a button.

"Oh, man, listen to this."

Kelley said, in the recording, *"The little prickly feelings in my fingers are getting worse. I'm having trouble walking sometimes, losing feeling in my left leg, below the knee. I tap it. It's numb."*

"Nerve problems," whispered Eddie, making a list

while Merlin and I hung over his shoulder, riveted to the frail voice. Kelley quavering but staying focused. The kid sick and scared, but diligently making her "observations" file.

"Dad said we all have a flu or a cold and he broke out the five-day Zithromax. But that makes no sense. How come if we all have the same thing, we show different symptoms?"

"Name them," I urged the voice, the living speaking to the dead, to the past, to the void.

"I think it's the water. The bottled water tastes funny. Like there's metal in it or something. Scratchy. It hurts my throat. Mom said she saw the redheaded woman back in Barrow, in the airport, with our supplies. I bet that woman put something in the water. Water! I feel disgusting. I won't take a shower. My hair is so gross that I got angry at the mirror and broke it, when I saw myself. Ugh!!!!"

Eddie looked up. "Water tasted funny? Or her taste buds changed?"

"Write them both down. Also, irritability."

"But is that a symptom? Or is she just pissed off?"

"Just write it!"

Eddie said, "Maybe you caught it, Uno, speaking of irritability. What redheaded woman is she talking about?"

"It's got to be that Greenpeace girl," Merlin answered, frowning, hands on his hips. Outside the office, through glass, door closed, uniformed police officers were staring in at us. "From Anchorage. Tilda Swann. A Brit. She's also in PETA, an animal lover. Stop the whaling. Save the bears. Save the seals. The Iñupiats can go to hell."

"But why target scientists working on lakes?"

"I'm just telling you who Kelley's probably talking about. Firebrand is more like it. Odds are it's her."

Click. The girl's recorded voice said:

"I don't like the way Clay Qaqulik looks at Mom. He stares at her in the way that boys watch Jackie DiNardi in school. I saw him touching himself when she wasn't looking. I'm getting afraid of Clay. He's angry all the time, not like he used to be. He got on a four-wheeler yesterday and drove it in circles, faster and faster, crazy, laughing, on the tundra. He keeps cleaning his shotgun. Last night he kept staring into the lake for a long time. I asked him what's in there, and he didn't answer, just looked up fast, muttering about imminnauraq, *little people. I walked away. I was shaking. I couldn't even open the door latch, because my fingers wouldn't work right. I'm scared!"*

Merlin looked baffled. "Clay doesn't get angry. I don't believe I've ever seen my cousin angry."

"Mood changes," said Eddie, writing: *Headaches, hallucinations possibly, paranoia?*

"It started three days ago. We all have fevers. I told Dad we should go back to Barrow, but he's so crazy because we're behind schedule, after so many accidents all summer, and we still have three more sites to collect samples from before we can go home.

"And the fighting. Mom and Dad NEVER fight, unless it's over Dad's stupid labeling on his ice cream or Mom's terrible driving. Family peace is like end-of-the-world important with them. It's like they're one brain/two people, like Borg people saying the same thing. Like, Can I go over to Ellen's for dinner, Dad? 'ASK YOUR MOTHER,

HONEY.' Can we have pizza, Mom? 'WHATEVER YOUR FATHER SAYS, DEAR!' And now they're fighting over the samples, the weather, and especially about Clay and . . . Oh, my God! OH, MY GOD! I think maybe Mom had SEX with him. Nononono!!!!! DISGUSTING!!!!"

THE NARRATIVE ENDED BUT EDDIE SAID KELLEY HAD ALSO RE-corded other people. Returning to the menu, he found a file titled "BORG PEOPLE" and clicked on it. It was a log of people clearly recorded without their knowledge. I heard my neighbors' voices—recognizable from our evenings together—but an electric shock went through me. They were the Harmons, all right, but *different*, sounding harsh and cruel over the computer sound system. The mild-mannered restraint that I associated with them was nowhere in the recording. This was not subtle. This was Dr. Jekyll and Mr. Hyde.

CATHY HARMON: The water, Ted. The fucking water. The water burns, and I will not drink it. I told you to get different water, but you never fucking do anything I ask.

TED HARMON: I saw you coming out of the cabin with him. I go out with Kelley for an hour, and you two are in there!

CATHY HARMON: (laughs) Oh, you know what they say, if you don't use it, you lose it.

TED HARMON: I smell him on you.

CATHY HARMON: I do, too. I love it.

Eddie looked up at me. "Holy shit, One. Are these the same people we know?"

I looked over at Merlin, who was still and serious, staring down at the table.

"Merlin?"

"Nothing."

"Merlin!"

A sigh. "Clay had a crush on her, Joe. He told me at the family Fourth of July dinner. He laughed over it. He never would have done anything about it. He thought she was cute."

Eddie said, "Sounds like he did do something."

I shook my head, feeling the rage and confusion, the lust and pain that was palpable in this room, just as present as the appalling personality changes on Kelley's recording. "Having the urge isn't doing it. Everyone has goddamn urges. You need something extra to lose control."

CATHY: He can last hours, Ted. Hours. You want to go for a ride with me now? Come on, a ride. You and me. On the tundra. Like when we used to drive around. You know, blow jobs? In college?

TED: Get away from me. You disgust me.

I said, stunned for the teenager listening to this from her parents, "Write: *sexual aggressiveness.*"

Merlin sighed, thinking out loud. "You know what?"

"What?"

"Crystal meth. Ingested. We had a few kids on it last

year. Hyperactive. Meth mouth. Delusions . . . hmm . . . And screwing like rabbits. She said the water tasted funny."

Eddie shook his head. "You're thinking all four of them took *meth*?"

"Or were given it. I'm just saying . . . I mean, it's possible, right?"

I said, "Dr. Sengupta is running blood work this morning at the hospital. If any of them had drugs in their system, we'll know by this afternoon. The other chemscreens might take a little longer."

Merlin pulled a chair over, and sat down. "Well, they've had accidents all summer. Clay thought someone was trying to sabotage that project. So if someone was doing that, but it wasn't working . . . If someone got desperate to stop them . . . hell . . . Maybe someone showed up at the camp, landed on the lake. Float plane."

"She didn't say anything about a plane, Merlin. No tracks, either. No marks on the tundra if someone came down on those big balloon-tire planes. Kelley would have mentioned it, I'd think. And come to think of it, who was *their* pilot? Who took them out there?"

Whoever did that had access to their water.

"I think it was Jens. Yes . . . Jens."

"Merlin, if there's something wrong here, something they ingested, we're not hearing the Clay you know. None of them are normal. Believe me."

CATHY HARMON: You could take a few lessons from Clay, Ted. Mouth lessons. Tongue lessons.

Fingers. How to beat your three-minute-quickie record, hmm?

I stared at Eddie's list. I said, slowly, reasoning out loud, "You know: Funny tastes, bright light, numbness, fear of water, sexual aggressiveness. Pretty classic for rabies."

"Are you kidding? In *four* people? In a cluster? You have to be bitten by an animal to get it. *Four?*"

"I'm not saying it is that. I'm just linking symptoms. But you're right. One person could be bitten. Not four."

"It's not rabies."

"I know." I sighed. "Still, I'll ask Sengupta if he found bite marks."

"What's in their stomachs?" Merlin said.

The next two recordings had been made twenty-four hours after the first, same time each day, 3 P.M., with Kelley apparently sticking to her homemade scientific method, trying to reduce variables, I told Merlin, "Always taking samples at the exact same time." I envisioned her hiding her little palm recorder as she and her parents moved around the lake, collecting algae and plants; doomed researchers with glass sample bottles, nets, and tweezers, scooping up seeds, all the while their tempers rising, the barely suppressed rage building toward what would, in less than forty-eight hours, explode into shotgun blasts.

Apparently Clay Qaqulik was also testing water that day, as his voice started the next exchange.

CLAY QAQULIK: There is something out there moving around at night. It's not an animal.

TED HARMON: (snicker) Yeah, those little imaginary men?

CLAY QAQULIK: I don't make fun of your culture.

CATHY HARMON: Go eat your fucking ice cream, Ted. Stop it.

TED HARMON: Ah! Yes! Stop! The perfect request, wouldn't you say so, Clay? To halt? To cease? To hold off?

KELLEY: I can't stand this.

CATHY: Don't drink that water, Kelley! Stay away from those fucking bottles, I told you! Use the purification tablets on the lake water if . . . (cough) . . . if you're (coughing)

On the recording, someone was throwing up. Eddie jotted down, on the lengthening list on the yellow legal pad, "coughing."

KELLEY: I want to go back to Barrow. I want to go home.

TED: Home? What's the matter with you? Are you deaf? How many times have I told you that we have three more lakes to visit before (gargling noise, grunting)

KELLEY: Why are you making those noises?

TED: (grunting)

KELLEY: Daddy, you're scaring me.

TED: Fly . . . argh . . . in my . . . (cough) throat.

CLAY: Here's the last bottle. My eyes hurt. This light . . . so bright . . .

The recordings ended. Eddie sat back at the table. Merlin said, "That's it? No more?" Eddie replied, "Maybe that's the way they were all the time in private, Uno. Dr. Jekyll and Mrs. Hyde. Nice all the time to friends in public, at each other's throats at home."

"No, if that were the case, Kelley wouldn't have been surprised at their behavior. That kid is being exposed to this for the first time. Besides, if the parents were always like this, I can't see them spending all that time with us. They'd never control themselves, not with that much rage in the air."

"I guess," Eddie said. "But you never really know what goes on between a couple."

"What was that about light hurting?" Merlin said.

"Call the hospital. Ranjay must have started screening the blood, hair, and tissue by now."

COULD A MOLD HAVE CAUSED THE SYMPTOMS? WE HEADED BACK to the research camp to search for *stachybotrys*, a green/black compound that could, if breathed in or ingested, produce aches, pains, fevers, cough, mood sensitivity, and immune suppression.

Poisons? Sengupta ran chemistry panels, seeking evidence of heavy metals or lead exposure or unidentified poisons in the blood.

Eddie explained to Merlin, "We ought to have an idea of toxics in a day, two at most."

The redhead? Merlin said she was probably over at

Borough Hall, carrying a "STOP LONGHORN NORTH" placard at a public hearing today where Dave and Deborah Lillienthal were testifying. He sent two detectives to find her.

By the end of the day I'd found no evidence of mold or gas residue at the cabin, and the yellow crime-scene tape was broken in one place, beaten down, bear tracks at that spot, and lumbering off into the tundra. The ground was wet and we found no human footprints. Merlin made a thorough search. No people had been here since yesterday.

At the hospital, Dr. Sengupta's initial tests found, "No arsenic in the bloodstreams," he reported via phone. "No heavy metals so far, no raised lead levels, no illegal drugs. And no flu. Lungs clear. No infection in the blood. No hypo or bite marks anywhere I can see."

"Didn't hurt to check."

"However!" he said, excited. "All four of them had raised white blood cell counts, sixteen thousand in Clay Qaqulik, fourteen to fifteen thousand in the parents and the girl. So there's an invader in there, but I've not found any virus or bacteria so far. I'm going with something chemical. Gas, maybe. They breathe it. It dissipates in air. But wood can absorb it. Cabin scrapings may show it."

"We have the scrapings. Maybe you'll see something we missed."

I reported to the admiral as ordered and, when he heard the test results, he seemed less anxious. "No germs? Then that's it for you two," he said. "No connection! Get back to work, finish your survey. General Homza is breathing down my neck, just waiting for a chance to shut us down. I want to hear that you agree."

"Back to the mission, sir," I said.

"We're giving up?" said Eddie when I clicked off.

"If it weren't for Kelley's phone call, it would have been a suicide/shooting," I answered. "No question. If Kelley hadn't made the recording, it would have been chalked up to one more piece of bad luck. Tragic accident. Autopsy shows death by shotgun. End of story, man."

I punched in numbers in Washington, heard the phone ring on the other end, heard Valley Girl pick up in the computer section. She'd been instructed by the admiral's secretary earlier to "Give Colonel Rush what he needs," and so now remained under the impression that I could demand any accessible information, and she was to comply.

"I want to know about any studies or tests in Alaska, where any sort of radioactive material was deposited, especially on the North Slope. Seventy-year period. Note the ones we already know about and see if there's something we don't."

"Yes, Colonel."

"See what you can find on grants given scientists over that same period by the Defense Threat Reduction Agency. Anything related to toxics or germ tests."

Eddie's eyes were bigger now, and he nodded, meaning, Go get 'em, One.

Valley Girl asked, "How deep, sir?"

"Bottom of the sea. Run all service branches. Including Defense Security Service," I said, naming the Pentagon agency responsible for providing protection to private companies doing defense work. DSS helped out with electronic alarms, executive protection, armored cars, and even factory personnel screening. "*Alaska*. I want companies contracted to work on biowarfare. I want exact tests, years, and results. University research partners. Got it?"

"Colonel," said Valley Girl excitedly, chewing her signature gum. "Is something happening in Alaska?"

"You are not to discuss this with anyone, even at the unit, get it?"

She sounded intimidated. "Of course, sir."

"You're the best we have," I soothed. "So if you see something that doesn't make sense to you, too much money for a small project, too little explanation of a test, extra money for cleanup, *anything odd*, a gap, a closed file, a reference, use your judgment. I trust you."

Now her voice was happier. "Yes, sir!"

I clicked off. Eddie sighed. "Well, there goes our government grant work when we go private."

"Who needs it? We'll be capitalists, Eddie. No more government dole for us!"

"I got news for you, Uno. When we're in Leavenworth prison, that's government dole."

I smiled. "Why? I never told Valley Girl that anything I'm asking for relates to the Harmons. It's all mission. Background." I smiled. "Chickening out, Marine?"

"Galli will go apeshit."

I sighed. "I like the admiral, Dos, but right now he's more worried about Wayne Homza. Galli knew exactly what he was getting when he asked me to stay."

"The Light Brigade strikes again!"

"We find the redheaded woman, Eddie. And Kelley's boyfriend, Leon Kavik. This could all have nothing to do with Washington. Or testing. It's Friday night in Barrow, so I have a good idea of where those two may be."

SIX

I wanted to speak to Kelley's boyfriend. I ignored the voice in my head telling me that I should be with Karen. That it was 9 P.M. on a Friday night and I'd been working for over twenty-four hours. That I'd told her I'd take a break and meet her at the weekly roller rink dance. Instead, I called her to explain I'd be late.

"No problem," said Karen, with the barest hesitation. Perhaps I'd not heard it at all.

"Give me till ten," I said, as the Ford's headlights swung off road, illuminated the Iñupiat Heritage Center.

The little voice in my head said, *Hey, isn't this how it started with your ex-wife? With excuses? Wasn't this what you said you wouldn't do if you fell in love again?*

Getting out of the truck, I told that voice that Karen was a different person, not like my ex-wife. I told that voice, eyeing the two-story-high museum where Leon

Kavik worked: *Karen has security clearance. She understands the importance of this. Sengupta's toxic screens haven't come up with any hits. Maybe the boy can help.*

The Heritage Center sat on North Street, near Arctic Family Medicine, the home for the elderly, and across the road from what looked like a small wooden shack but was an entrance to Barrow's oddest feature, a three-hundred-million-dollar, 3.2-mile-long underground tunnel carved into permafrost, snaking through the city, to bring potable water from the lagoon, fiber optics and phone lines. Inside the tunnel, temperatures remained at forty-eight degrees.

"Oil taxes built the Utilador," garrulous Dave Lillienthal always argued, over vodka, at our dinners on the base. "Oil paid for the old folks' home."

Bruce Friday usually snapped back: "One day you'll blow a pipe offshore and kill or scare off every whale within a hundred miles."

"Oh, posh! More Tito, Bruce?"

I wasn't interested in their arguments now. I saw a lone figure inside the glass door, behind the admission area, wiping the counter, stooped, weighted, depressed.

Karen understands about completing a mission. What's one more hour to wait?

Something about the scene in there reminded me of an Edward Hopper painting, *Nighthawks*. It was the sense of weary figures killing time, a diner in the painting, a museum here; but in both cases, night pressed in against human life. The figure beyond the glass door looked startled when I entered. He was tall and thin, wide nosed and thin lipped. He wore a spotted sealskin vest, thick workman's painter pants, and a red-checkered flannel shirt. His stomach bulged over his silver buckled belt.

"We're closed," he said in a neutral tone.

"Leon? I'm Joe Rush. I'm helping out Chief Toovik. Can we talk about Kelley Harmon?"

He knew from my tone that this was an official visit. The look in his chocolate-colored eyes grew wide. He assumed I was a detective, at first. He glanced back into the museum, as if seeking help, but the only help back there was history; glass cases filled with Iñupiat harpoons, old skinning knives, wolverine-ruffed polar bear fur parkas, mouth-chewed, softened sealskin boots.

I saw a big blowup shot of Merlin on a wall, standing on ice, bent toward the sea, eyeing the back of a bowhead whale with a harpoon sticking out. I saw black-and-white photos of elders; when they were young, carving up a caribou.

A stark, fishy odor filled the modern atrium, its rankness at odds with the curated, well-lit exhibits. The smell—I knew from visits here—meant that someone had been in back, in the community workshop, with a bucket of bloodied seal, building a new *umiaq* for the spring hunt.

"You're a Marine?" the boy said, looking puzzled, handing back my ID. He seemed hemmed in by the counter. I felt that he wanted to leave. But it was unclear what he wanted to get away from. The investigation? Or the deaths?

"I'm a doctor," I said. "We're trying to figure out

exactly what happened out there. I'm sorry, Leon, I heard you knew Kelley pretty well."

Most museums are filled with artifacts from elsewhere. This one existed to explain the Iñupiat way of life to visitors, and to help educate young kids in town.

The boy said, softly, "Yes. I was a friend."

"I know it's late, Leon. Just a few questions."

"What's the point? I told the police what I knew."

He wasn't sullen, or defensive. It was more like I heard futility and grief. I said, softly, "Sometimes, when you're trying to figure problems out, little things help."

"She needed help *before*. And she didn't get it."

He walked out from behind the counter. He locked the front door, shut off the overhead lights, so a soft glow from streetlamps outside made the parka in a glass case seem alive. He beckoned me to follow and I trailed his slumped form down a shadowy corridor, into the glass-walled workshop in back, illuminated by a red nightlight. I saw a half dozen long, sturdy wooden worktables, tools on sideboards. This was where local artists carved walrus ivory into statuettes. I saw knives on the wall, neatly arranged hammers, saws, screwdrivers, and small jeweler-like hand tools. He took a stool. I sat down, too, making sure I stayed at eye level, to show respect.

"Leon, what do you mean, she needed help *before*? What was wrong before today, before the shooting?"

He rolled his eyes. "Isn't it obvious?"

"Not to me."

"She's dead," the boy blurted out. "Of course something was wrong."

"Do you have any idea what?"

He looked bewildered. "What are you asking me for? How would I know?"

"Did Kelley say anything about tension in the group?"

Leon Kavik had large hands, and I saw a long, healed scar on the right palm as he held both hands up. There were high school textbooks on the worktable . . . *Chemistry Two* . . . and I realized that he did homework here.

He said, "'Tension'? No, unless her mother was driving a car or someone ate her dad's ice cream . . . or that HBO guy, the one with the camera, was around. Pushy, Kelley said."

"When's the last time you saw Kelley?"

"A week ago, when they were in town. We rode to the quarry on my motorcycle. She looked for dinosaur bones. She found part of a mammoth bone, to use as a paper weight."

"Did she seem sick to you last week?"

"The police asked that. No."

"Think about it. Coughing? Headache? Sniffles?"

"I told the police! She wasn't sick."

"Did she say anything about her parents fighting, or *them* being sick?"

"She said they were like Moonies, always smiling. Never disagreeing. Borg people, she said. But sick? No."

Which means, if he's right, that the symptoms hadn't started a week ago. They came on fast.

"Leon, this is helpful because it helps us pinpoint when any sickness started. Because they all had fever. Did she say anything to you about Clay Qaqulik?"

"Just that she liked him, I mean, as a person."

"Did she mention anything about their water supplies?"

"Like what?"

"I don't know. The taste? A shipment being late. Problems with food or water."

"Well, they had accidents all summer, but that was equipment breaking."

I watched him for signs of guilt; stiff posture, twitchy hands, change in tone. Kelley's friend had said, "He has a temper." I didn't see it yet.

I asked when he'd met Kelley and he said, "Here, when she came in to look around the center."

I asked what they did together.

"Ride around. It was tough to see her because she was hardly ever in town."

I asked whether he'd been bothered by that.

"What does that have to do with what happened?"

"I'm just curious."

"Well, it was a pain, that was for sure."

"Made you angry?"

"Yeah. Sure. Her parents worked her to death."

"By the way," I lied, "I heard that you helped them with supplies, loading up food and water."

He looked surprised. "No. I never did that."

"I just asked because someone said they remembered you helping in the warehouse. You were a big help, they said."

"Ha! I was never even there. Kelley warned me to stay away when her parents were around. They didn't want her to see boys. They were tough on her back home, too. No boys."

He seemed more hurt than angry, but who could tell? I was fishing. I switched direction. "Leon, what did she tell you about their project?"

"Not a lot. They collected stuff in lakes. Algae. Fish. Plants."

"Did she say why?"

"She said species are dying out as the North Slope warms. And new ones are popping up. She said her parents concentrated on basic collecting, what's the word, *cataloging*. She said they shipped their stuff back to New Jersey—and to a school in Norway."

I'd not heard of this. "Norway?"

"Joint study. To write up everything they found. She wanted to go there. She showed me pictures. She said in Norway there are lots of big Arctic oil and gas projects."

"But the Harmons didn't do anything related to oil?"

He shrugged miserably, as if an inability to answer was an insult to Kelley. "I don't think so."

"You're doing fine. Tell me more. She said plants are dying out."

"Yeah, my cousin lives down in Teller? He says a lot of their wild berries are dying off as it gets warmer there. I guess that's the kind of thing that the Harmons were looking at, I mean, in the lakes."

I watched him carefully for guilt or anger. A sharp intake of breath. A *tell*. I saw only pain, but plenty of liars look as innocent as babes.

I don't know why we discount young love as *puppy love*, as if the number of years you've spent on Earth qualifies you to experience more sincere emotion, as if age is a requirement for love, as if we cynical adults have cornered the market on wisdom about the one thing that too many of us don't appreciate until too late.

"Kelley told me maybe I could get a scholarship to Prezant College. You know, for my work."

Leon swept his arm toward the table, and I realized that the artwork was his: the exquisite six-inch-tall walrus-ivory Eskimo woman, sparkly flecks of baleen as eyes; the baleen mask—made of a whale's mouth filter—a black smooth surface etched with figures of seals; and a small painting that caught my attention most: a lone hunter in a parka, his back to the viewer as he stood on a floating bit of ice, lost at sea, rifle over his shoulder. Sky a claustrophobic gray.

"He looks lonely," I said.

"He's in trouble because he did not pay attention. He will float off and die because he made one mistake."

I FOUND KAREN DANCING WITH THE FILMMAKER, AND THE SIGHT, Mikael trying to get closer to her as she kept her distance, his arms outstretched as if to embrace her, the quiet pleasure on his face, filled me with rage.

It's your own fault, Joe.

The roller rink was one of Barrow's big social centers on Friday nights. There were no movie theaters in the city, no bowling alleys, malls, or bars. None of the nexuses of idle leisure marking other towns. There were church meetings and socials. There were potluck dinners at churches. There were high school sports contests or traditional Eskimo dance groups, where Karen had dragged me onto the floor last week for the "everyone invited to join" dance.

When she saw me, she waved me onto the floor, smiling. Mikael Grandy turned and his grin faltered but he gamely retreated toward the folding chairs and four-person tables grouped in a semi-circle facing the raised stage. Grandy did not have his camera. The fucker hadn't even brought it.

Karen put her index finger over my mouth, which meant, *Not one word about Mikael.* She put her head on my chest. Her arms went around me. The tension began to drain away.

The skating rink was over a half-century old, a vacuum to be filled with weekly performances of the Barrowtones, a half dozen middle-aged amateur rockers: the electric-piano-playing Eskimo Ph.D. geologist from the Iñupiat-owned Arctic Slope Regional Corporation; the guitar-playing Serbian who owned one of the town's three pizza joints; the long-haired San Francisco–born radio jock; the Arkansas guitarist who played like Stevie Ray Vaughn; and, I saw with surprise, Deputy Luther Oz doing pretty good on the drums.

We danced—so did five other couples—to oldies, "Devil with a Blue Dress" and "The House of the Rising Sun" and we slow moved to "Georgia on My Mind." I wiped the deaths away. I felt her small, strong body move with mine, her arms warm against the back of my neck. I'm not a good dancer, I'm too stiff, but she made me melt and manage synchronization. When the third dance was over, she took my hand and led me to a table. The asshole was sitting there, nursing a can of Pepsi from a machine out in the hall.

"Where's the camera, Mikael?" I asked, feeling Karen stiffen beside me. My voice had been too rough.

"All work makes a filmmaker lose his edge, Joe."

"You're a good dancer."

"I go to clubs sometimes in Brooklyn," he said. "Maybe if you and Karen come east, I'll show you around."

"I heard your family once owned a big piece of Alaska."

A shrug. "The czar giveth. Then he selleth to America."

Karen looked terrific in light brown cords and a cobalt-colored fitted sweater, a gold necklace showing a miniature walrus-ivory snowy owl between her bud breasts. Her hair smelled of coconut shampoo. When she took my hand, Mikael studiously avoided looking in that direction. Eddie Nakamura strode up, glanced down at the filmmaker with displeasure, smiled broadly at Karen, shook his head at me as he sat down, meaning: *I can't find the redhead.*

"Long Cool Woman in a Black Dress" began playing. About four dozen people had wandered in off the street, a few were sipping from beer cans, more women present than men. The single women often danced together, the single men were usually at tables, watching the women. The dancers' ages ranged from the twenties to the sixties.

Overheard from the adjacent table, during a pause, Alan McDougal, who ran the base, and diamond hunter Calvin DeRochers, talking about the Harmons.

Alan said, "Ted was so determined to finish up this year, despite the accidents. The guy never gave up."

Calvin said, "We used to sit around for hours poring over the maps of the lakes. Man, ten thousand lakes! Me thinking, Which ones have the diamonds? Him going on about plants and algae . . . Who cares about that goddamn stuff? Huh?"

The music was free. Someone had fixed up one of those rotating mirror spheres so it threw sparks of bright, multicolored light across the audience and stage. The mood was slow and easy, even when the music was vibrant. The Barrowtones usually played until 2 or 3 A.M.

"Are you looking for me, Colonel?"

The sharp, British-accented voice startled me, coming from close behind me. I turned and looked into a stunningly gorgeous woman's face, framed by a lioness mane of red hair so close that it almost brushed my head. The eyes were deep aqua, the nose classic, and the teeth as white as in a TV commercial. She seemed to throw off heat. The freckles—a light copper color—were so numerous they seemed more like a tan. The lips glistened. Karen's shampoo smell mixed suddenly with something stronger: musk and alcohol and tobacco.

"*I'm* the one looking for you," corrected Eddie.

"You're a major. He's a colonel. He's the boss," she said, staring boldly into my eyes. "Want to dance?"

"Have a seat. Join us. Let's talk."

"I don't want to talk. I want to dance."

It was not a social invitation. I recognized a calculated preemptive strike. Merlin had told me she was a professional agitator. Mikael stared up at the model-quality face with fascination. Eddie looked wary and Karen surprised. If I stood up, if I danced with her, I knew instinctively this would cripple every future argument with Karen limiting time she spent with Mikael Grandy. *I'm not the one who walked off with that woman!*

I needed to ask questions. I stood up. Tilda Swann reached for my hand. No way, I thought, but followed her out onto the floor anyway; an act that, I knew, constituted a strategic loss on the field of domestic tranquility. No sex for you tonight, Joe!

I tried to ask questions but she was having none of it, not at first. She was the kind of dancer who probably got sex-crazed cavemen to kill each other with clubs. She closed her eyes, pretending not to be aware of me, yet her rotating hips managed to stay close, and her arms wove circles in the air . . . the effect one of abandon, and of consciousness of the eyes upon her. She was trying to irritate and she was succeeding. She was so beautiful that most men in the rink stared. A guitar player hit a bad note. Deputy Luther Oz, on the drums, glared with disapproval. He'd heard Merlin warn me in the chopper to keep to the medical end, leave interviews to the cops.

When the song was almost over, when she knew I'd be walking off in a moment, she leaned close, breath warm in my ear. "Blame it on Greenpeace," she said.

"You don't strike me as a victim, Ms. Swann."

"Because I'm good-looking? Your oil rig has an accident? Your whaling ship spills oil? Blame Greenpeace!"

"Are we going to talk or just rant?"

"Fire away, *mi* colonel! Batteries three and six aimed at the *Rainbow Warrior*!"

It was like starting a conversation in the middle; no preliminaries. Well, two could do this. She did not seem like someone who would respond to any subtle strategy except to mock it, and she was clearly clever enough to recognize any roundabout approach.

I said, "Okay, straight out. You were seen tampering with the Harmons' water."

She stopped dancing. Hands on slim hips. Then she smiled. "Good for you! Who exactly saw me?"

"We have a record of it."

Lips curling. "Uh-huh. A camera, you're saying?"

"Audio recording," I said. Her perfume was getting to me.

"Oh, audio! Someone *heard* me tamper with water. I wonder! What do you hear when that happens, gurgling? And who is this 'we' anyway? The Marines?"

"The police, Tilda."

"I'm a little confused. Which one are you?"

"I'm helping them out," I said.

"Are you sure?" She resumed dancing, rotated her hips like a Brazilian at Ipanema. The top and bottom parts moved in entirely different rhythms. She said, "What are you really doing here anyway? In Barrow?"

"Dancing."

"Touché. Oh, too bad, the music stopped. So tell me, Colonel. *Just what did you guys do to them?*"

"Excuse me?"

From our table where Karen watched, and I could feel her eyes on us, we probably looked like a couple caught up in intimate conversation. Tilda Swann's eyes sparked with passion, and her fragrance overcame the mélange of sawdust, sweat, and bad electronics that seemed a permanent background in the old rink. The finger that poked me in the chest was slender. The wrist was encircled by a single silvery bracelet. Her rage, unfeigned, blotched her angular cheeks with color.

"What was it, Colonel? What did you guys do on the tundra when nobody was looking? What was *tested*? A gas?"

"What are you talking about?"

"Anthrax? Radiation?? Give me a break, jarhead. Two detectives show up at my hotel this afternoon and want to know if I was anywhere near the warehouse that held water for the Harmons? It's not just me, you know, that you're accusing. My organization is used to being attacked."

"No one accused you. You've got the wrong idea."

"Really!" The finger poked me again. The floor had cleared but we remained in front of the stage, face-to-face. I grabbed her wrist to stop the poking. She didn't even look down at her hand. People stared at us. She was fury incarnate, that blown-up passion represented one of the finest acting jobs I've ever encountered, or the best ambush.

She said, softly, "I want you to know that I called Washington. We have people there and in London and every fucking capital in the world. And, Colonel, those people are making inquiries. Why are two Marine officers here, asking about bad water? Why are local detectives in Alaska co-opted into the goddamn U.S. military machine?"

"How do you know what I've been doing?"

"*How do I know?* Because when someone starts asking about me, I ask about them, too. That's how I know!"

"And how well did you know the Harmons?"

"Little accident? Little gas leak? Planning on blaming Greenpeace? It won't work. I'll find out what you did."

WE WENT BACK TO THE TABLE, WHERE KAREN PAID MORE ATTEN-tion to Mikael than before, like I wasn't there. *Screw you, Joe, for ignoring me.* Tilda pulled up a chair between me and Eddie. Karen smiled dazzlingly and asked Mikael to dance. She flashed me a look when she stood up. Not rage. Just a kind of raw intensity. Karen looking from Tilda to me, sensing more than just antagonism. The whole scene one of crazy feminine misinterpretation. Planet of the women. Planet of miscommunication. Planet of trouble for Joe Rush.

"I didn't touch their water, Colonel. I didn't even *know* them. But if you're thinking that somebody tampered with supplies, why not talk to those two perverts from

Texas, brother and sister, my ass. Why not grill the pilots and mechanics. No. Gotta be Greenpeace. You know why people always think it's Greenpeace?"

"Why?"

"We're convenient targets."

Eddie said, "I thought it's because you always claim the credit!"

Karen was back and she'd had enough. "Joe, let's go home."

IF I THOUGHT IT WAS COLD INSIDE, THAT WAS NOTHING COM-pared to what happened when we stepped outside, and into the small, streetlamp-lit parking lot. We were on another planet. Merlin had been right. In the time between my entrance here and my departure, winter had arrived. The temperature had plunged. The season had crashed down with all the swiftness of an avalanche in the Rockies.

Everything was the same, but different. The night air was brittle. Our breath had steamed out before but now it shot away in small, white puffs. Even Karen, mad as she was, stopped dead and looked outward . . .

I had the sense of the horizon contracting, the planet shrinking, the sky losing its third dimension: depth. Altitude sucked down, gravity grown monstrous. Distance seemed eradicated and the scale of the place shrank. There was a *drawing-in* feeling, a sense of reduced possibility. There was, in the air, a palpable promise of isolation.

Take care of yourself. Winter is back.

I shivered as the air knifed through my parka. The stars blinked, as if startled, then cloud cover smothered them up. The moon went from a low orb to a suggestion. Breathing seemed like something we needed to plan. The smell had altered, too, the briny ocean tinge was gone, as was the peaty wet mud and decayed floral essence of autumn tundra. Now an almost sterile frigidity had replaced it.

And the rhythmic background *shoosh* of that vast sea across the road—as we rode silently home—went from liquid to something filled with friction. As if shore was trying to extend, reach out, become tectonic.

"I had to talk to her," I said.

"Of course."

I did not need this shit. "There's nothing to apologize for."

"Oh? Maybe it's me that needs to do it, you mean?"

We slept in the same bed that night, but as separate planets. We woke the next morning and said we were sorry and the argument had been stupid. We made love. We made up.

Outside, there was frost on the window. Outside, the sky had a sucked-out, ominous cast. Inside, we made coffee and cooked our breakfast, but the residue of something distasteful remained in the hut. I was glad when Eddie arrived to pick me up, for us to head over to the lab, to check the samples. I was glad to get away from Karen, I had to admit. The truck passed the Harmon hut, where the lights were off. It passed the oil hut and Bruce Friday's hut and the hut where Kelley's friend lived, where lights glowed.

Goddamn Tilda Swann!

We took the curving half-mile road that linked the huts to the new twenty-five-million-dollar Arctic Research Center where we had our lab, and planned to redo Sengupta's toxic tests just to be sure. Eddie said, "Uno, can I just say one thing?"

"No."

"It's that when you two were dancing last night, I mean, speaking as your friend, it looked pretty close."

"What did I just tell you?"

"I'm only trying to explain—"

"Your superior officer, Major, gave a direct instruction, and it is for you to shut up."

"But our unit doesn't follow instructions."

I sighed. "Then do it as a favor, Eddie."

He quieted but the phone began buzzing. I was surprised to see that the call was coming from the cellular phone of Valley Girl, except if it was 8 A.M. in Barrow, then it was 4 A.M. in Washington, when Valley Girl would never, ever be at work. She'd not even be awake. Valley Girl came in at ten, left at nine at night.

"Joe Rush!"

It was her, all right, but she was home, she said, not at the office. She sounded scared, her voice an octave higher than usual. This was the first time in three years of speaking to her that I'd heard her words come out as exclamations, not questions.

"I'm being arrested," she said. "Men are here from Defense Security. I'm in my bathroom. They're in the hallway. I need help. It's because of what you asked me to do."

SEVEN

They were going to put Valley Girl in handcuffs when she walked out of her bathroom, she said, crying. They'd banged on the door of her townhouse fifty minutes ago, four of them, at 3:10 A.M., shown Pentagon ID, seized her laptop and desktop computers, searched her two-bedroom apartment and warned her that another agent was under the bathroom window, outside, so don't try to climb out. They'd taken all drugs from her medicine cabinet before letting her shut the door. They'd terrified her cat, Ephraim, who was meowing under a couch.

There's no way they'd let her go into her bathroom alone normally, no way they wouldn't have confiscated the cell. So someone is listening to us.

"They think I'm a traitor, like Edward Snowden," she said, voice quaking.

I asked her, playing to the larger audience that moni-

tored us, "Did you do what I told you to?" I envisioned
listeners in a cubicle, or van, vultures who ate sound.

"Yes, Colonel."

"Do anything extra?"

"No, sir."

"Explain exactly what you *did* do?"

"I went to appropriations to see if monies had been
allocated for toxics or germ testing in Alaska, going back
seventy years. I cross-referenced grants. I checked AEC
and Threats Reduction, and PC's and PU's (private companies and universities) contracted for this sort of work.
I ran all social security numbers of the victims, like you
said, for links."

"Try to break in anywhere?"

"I backed off if I saw 'Classified.'"

"Which you did, I gather."

"In 2008. Something called 'Enhancing Warfighters.'"

"How did you learn that Enhancing Warfighters existed, so you could make that request?"

"I found a reference in a grant to U Alaska, and another in an Army cognition study downgraded to normal
classified two years ago."

I considered. "You're saying that you sent in a proper
request asking for details of Warfighters?"

She sniffled. "Like we always do."

"Did you get an answer?"

"It's that these people showed up."

I nodded, but of course she could not see me. She was
terrified and I was growing angry. I cautioned, "Listen
to me. If there's anything else I need to know, *now* is the

time to say it. If you did something else, forced a back door, tried your way in somewhere, hacking, *anything*, tell me now. I won't be able to help after this."

She was crying openly. I envisioned a shaking female hand cupping a tiny phone. "Are you kidding? I saw the scare movie that the security guys showed us when I joined up. It's just . . . just that . . ."

I felt my breath catch. "Just that what?"

"Well, you said to concentrate on toxics or germs, and Enhancing Warfighters was experiments, all right, on volunteers, but with magnets. Do magnets count?"

"'Magnets'?" I asked, surprised.

She'd always had a good memory, one reason I used her. "It's called 'transcranial magnetic stimulation.' The Biosciences and Protection Divisions carried it out. Trying to get soldiers to do tasks better, using electrical current, magnetic coils . . . something about revving up cortical brain tissue. I didn't exactly understand it, sir."

"On human subjects, you said?"

"Volunteers, sir. And in military prisons."

"So you asked for more details?"

"Yes, Colonel. You said to look at any experiments involving people or livestock, so I did."

If this description was honest, she'd not exceeded instructions. In my three years of dealing with her, I had found her never to exaggerate. I said, "You did right. You used judgment and initiative."

Which means, if she's telling the truth, her normal request triggered this raid, not any breach.

I asked, "Was Clay Qaqulik part of this brain study?"

"I never got that far! The security people showed up."

"Okay. Don't worry. Sarah, keep the line open and tell the people outside—in a loud voice—that you'll walk out holding a phone."

"But why should I say . . . Oh, my God! OH, MY GOD!"

"Just leave the phone on so I can hear. Calm down. Tell the person in charge that I want to speak to him."

A minute later I was speaking with a woman identifying herself as Air Force Major T. J. Cobb of the Pentagon's Office of Defense Security. She had a soft, feminine voice, a hint of southwest twang; Arizona maybe, or New Mexico. But there was no softness in the accusation coming over the line.

"You admit, Colonel, that you ordered Sarah Kemp to try to break in to classified files relating to certain activities that occurred in 2008?"

"Are you a lawyer, Major Cobb?"

A pause. "How do you know that?"

"Because you talk like one. And because only lawyers use the word 'certain' that way. They do it when they don't want to tell you what they mean."

"Sir, I'm asking the questions," she responded smoothly. "Yes or no?"

I said, harshly, for emphasis, "I did not order her to break in anywhere, nor did she try to, so don't suggest she did. She made a legal request through channels. You will not handcuff her. You will give her time to dress properly and then politely escort her to wherever you've been told she is to go. You will leave food and water for her cat. You will not mistreat her, am I clear?"

"Colonel, I report directly to General Wayne Homza."

I sighed. *Why am I not surprised?*

I snapped, "And he works for someone else, and *she* works for someone else. Get it? A chain? *Am I clear?*"

"Yes."

"Yes, *what?*"

"Yes, sir!"

Standoff. She wouldn't tell me more.

In the background, I heard Valley Girl crying, and then the sound grew distant, so I envisioned big men escorting a tiny girl—I always imagined Valley Girl dressed out of a sorority house . . . she probably looked nothing like that—down carpeted townhouse stairs, into predawn suburban Virginia, toward a couple of big black Chevrolets—the Pentagon seems to be the only loyal customer left for GM's rattletrap vehicles—with tall antennas on top.

I called the admiral via encrypted sat-Skype to relay what had happened and up swam his secretary, Pauline, a large, pear-shaped fifty-nine-year-old chain-smoking grandmother, who sounded hoarse and showed none of her usual cheeriness. Her mascara had run down her rouged cheeks. Uh-oh, I thought. Pauline was not normally emotional.

"The admiral is gone, Colonel."

"Find him, please, Pauline. Is he at lunch?"

"No, that's not what I mean," she gasped. "He's been

replaced. General Homza took over and he's in Admiral Galli's office now, going through the drawers." Her voice became a whisper. "They were shouting, him and the admiral. General Homza said to patch you through if you called. I'll be reassigned, sir. They're shutting down the unit."

"You'll be fine, Pauline," I soothed, hoping I was right. "Let me talk to General Homza."

Click . . .

The screen went fuzzy for a millisecond. It did that sometimes from solar flares. Suddenly leaping forward on-screen was Homza, a blunt, fit-looking, middle-aged man wearing the two stars of a U.S. Army major general, and sitting behind the admiral's Civil War–era walnut desk. Posture, ramrod. Behind him was the left side of the admiral's World War One oil of the Coast Guard cutter *Tampa,* being torpedoed by a U-boat; flames high, crew members leaping into the sea.

The eyes of the man looking back at me were steely-gray, inside wire-rimmed spectacles; the jaw was smallish for the round face, the cropped hair thinning, the few remaining bristles those of a tough, aging boar. I judged him a hard fifty. The mouth was set, the voice tight; the overall effect one of vigorous disapproval.

"Colonel Rush," he said, neutrally.

"May I ask, sir, what has happened?"

"Well, where to start," he said with disgust. "The admiral has been running this unit haphazardly." His disapproval hinted at satisfaction, *I told you so,* and suggested that any alleged lapses had provided Homza opportunity. He went on. "Special privileges. Avoidance of rules. Your girlfriend for instance, Colonel. Granted security clearance!"

"She had that already, sir, at Electric Boat."

"Not from us. Starting now, share classified material and your pillow talk," he said, as if those two words constituted a perversion, "will have dire consequences." He looked disgusted. "Are we clear?"

"Sir, my original deal with the admiral—when I extended my tour—was contingent on Karen being in the loop."

He looked astounded. "Your deal with the United States of America is not. Your personal life is not my concern. You've also shared information with local police. Admiral Galli failed to discipline you. *Strike two.* I've long argued that we need to rein in loose cannons around here, your unit in particular."

I thought, *Put everyone under your control, you mean.*

I said, "You're closing us down?"

"You had your people in D.C. exceed your mandate, poke around in places that don't concern you. Strike three. When this mission is done, you'll be moved out of research, into field units."

I did not back down. "Sir, if by *exceeding mandate* you're talking about Project Enhancing Warfighters, Sarah made a legal, logical inquiry. I was sent here to check on special projects. I'd say that human experimentation counts."

I saw a sneer. "Colonel. That sounds like Auschwitz. I'm authorized by the secretary of defense himself to tell you that, in Warfighters, no work was done near Barrow. Furthermore, all volunteers in that failed experiment are fine today, living wholesome lives, in different places, and none suffered side effects. So let's put this to rest."

"That was always my intent, sir," meaning: *Then why not send me what I asked for?*

He seemed surprised that I was still pushing. Generals don't explain things to colonels. But his eyes shifted. His jaw muscles clenched. He didn't just order me to shut up. Something else was going on here.

He said, "We don't think it's in the public interest to advertise every detail of every experiment. There isn't a government anywhere that isn't, at any given moment, looking at new germs, electrics, gasses. We both know what happens when you tell the public that. Shit blows up, shit that you'll agree we do not need."

"Sir, my people aren't the public. Sarah's vetted for classified material."

"You are *not* to involve yourself further in an investigation that has no bearing on your mission. Just finish up, fast."

Surprise! I'd been expecting to be pulled out, if Homza was closing the unit. "You're keeping us here, sir?"

A sigh. "Your patron Admiral Galli made one last argument. He said the locals like you, and can make trouble in Washington if they feel jerked around. And that although *we* do not think a quarter-century-old law relevant here, it *is* law, so someone has to carry it out. Five years from now, there will be no need for this. This is the last time."

Now I understood.

"You're ordering me to find nothing?"

A pause. "You've been up there for months and found nothing so there is nothing to find. You and Major Nakamura take four more days, file your negative report, and come to D.C. At that point we'll discuss your future, and also the future of Sarah Kemp, who for now remains in custody."

"Like a hostage?"

He drew in a sharp breath and I took a deep one. "Sir, I'd like to see the files on Clay Qaqulik. That's my right as investigator. I want to see Warfighters to determine if it *is* part of my mission. Or, General, I respectfully request that we include a note in my findings stating that I was instructed to avoid asking certain questions."

He didn't move for a moment.

"Thin ice," he said.

"Sarah only did her job," I said.

"Remember what I said about pillow talk, Colonel."

He clicked off.

THE SCREEN SHOWED GRAYISH SNOW. I TURNED ON THE LIGHTS. Eddie Nakamura was seated at the opposite table in a lab coat, his mask on, preparing to run a back-up screen on the samples—blood, skin, and hair—that we'd taken from the victims and cabin. Ranjay had done one already.

Eddie said, "Way to go, One. How to make friends and influence people."

"Hey, he's sending the files. It worked."

"Sheep-dipped? Or real?"

"Who knows?"

"Sometimes I think on the day that Lord Jesus comes back to Earth, even then, the assholes will still play politics."

Clay Qaqulik's files were forwarded to us twenty minutes later, and I consumed them, looking for any connections, links, hints. He'd been stationed in Germany and California, not Alaska. His psych reports were clean and his FBI files complimentary. Unless his records had been sheep-dipped, there was nothing indicating involvement in any Army experiments.

Eddie looked puzzled. "Then why the big deal when Valley Girl asked for this? All they had to do was send."

"She gave Homza the opportunity he's been waiting for. He couldn't care less about the files. Politics is right."

"What do you make of Major General RoboCop?"

"He's telling us he is big and we are small. He's offering us an opportunity to fall in line, Eddie. That stuff about discussing our future? For Homza, training the rogue dog is a special challenge."

"We're rogue dogs? Woof!"

"Finish the screen, Eddie. We leave in four days."

The clock was ticking now. Four days was nothing. In Eddie's gloved hand sat a small rectangular plastic dish the size of a tape cassette, lined with three dozen small, half-inch-deep wells. Eddie deposited different blood samples into each well, then poured in reagents. He refrigerated the dish. If, during the next twenty-four hours, a sample turned bright green, it meant we had a poison.

If the sample remained unaffected, it was harmless when it came to the specific toxics that we tested for.

"Hey, One! What are you going to do about Karen? You told off RoboCop, but truth is, he can yank you, or arrest you, he can stick you in ward seven," he said, referring to a fourth-floor hallway at an Air Force mental hospital in Nevada. "Or he can do it the bureaucratic way, bust you down, post retirement, wipe away your pension."

"You're a bundle of laughs today," I said. "Anyway, it's not like Homza can hear what we say in our hut, right?"

Two days later all the results were in on our tests.

"Nothing."

THERE ARE NO FUNERAL HOMES IN BARROW. THE IÑUPIAT BURY their own dead. A *cakewalk* held before the burial—the sale of homemade cakes and pies—raises expense money.

The cemetery was a half mile from the airport, a small patch of tundra dotted with disorderly rows of crosses and markers, dwarfed by sky and horizon, rich with wildflowers in summer, but summer was over, and a big yellow borough-auger drilled loudly through thin topsoil, slashing into permafrost, to carve out a resting place for Clay. Four-wheel-drive vehicles circled the cemetery like wagons.

Tomorrow we'd go home.

On our last day in Barrow, Karen stood beside me at the graveside, as Clay's wife, neighbors, and friends remembered him, and a northeast wind whipped away every second word. The chill in the air seemed small beside the frost that had marked our Quonset hut since the dance. Nothing overt. No arguments. But something about my dance with Tilda Swann had set off a red flag inside my fiancée. I didn't push. She would talk about it when she was ready. The truth was, I'd dreamed of Tilda for two nights running: graphic dreams, sex dreams, pumping bodies. It made me wonder if Karen's intuition had picked up on even my dreams.

I'd told Karen about our orders shutting her out of things, and she'd shrugged. "No problem, Joe. You retire in a few months anyway." She'd been more concerned about the deaths we'd come to commemorate.

"Clay was a servant of the borough," Mayor Rupert Brower was saying. "He was my friend."

Karen had plunged herself into her prep for her film over the past few days. I'd hit the investigation hard, testing soil samples from the camp, food samples, wood scrapings, victims' medical records, from here, and home.

We've found nothing. And Merlin's detectives found nothing useful in their interviews, either. No sign of aberrant behavior. No drinking or drugs. No big problems or depression, mood changes, or resentment of the Harmons. Nothing useful on the tip lines. Nothing found at the site.

No speaker uttered the words *suicide* or *murder*, but even among a people who lived with sudden death—small plane crashes, snowmobiles falling through ice, fishing boats capsizing—what had happened stood out as special tragedy. Merlin Toovik remembered Clay as a skilled hunter. I met Clay's sobbing wife, a bewildered nephew, an Army buddy from Germany who flew in from Juneau. I looked over the grouped residents of our little Quonset hut community.

The Harmons will be shipped south, but somehow this service is for all the dead, although the earth only receives one on this day.

Calvin DeRochers, the diamond hunter, stood to the side, near fourteen-year-old Deirdre McDougal, who was weeping. I spotted morose Leon Kavik, staring at the ground. Alan McDougal made a speech about how he'd only known Clay for six years, but that Clay had been a kind, smart, generous man.

My eyes roved over the crowd. Dr. Sengupta stood beside Bruce Friday, and wore enough clothing for three people, and still stamped his feet to keep warm.

Mikael Grandy stood alone, camera sweeping right to left, discreetly aimed at Karen, then on me.

But funerals have a way of putting smaller problems in perspective. Karen and I moved closer, until my arm was around her shoulder. By the time we got to the Presbyterian church for the post-funeral singspiration, the warmth I felt was not only from gas heat. It was us. Our argument was over. Whatever had been wrong, I knew, would be okay, at least for a while.

Truth was, our year together had been exciting, but part of that was that we'd lived in different cities. Our periods of togetherness—thus far—had been enhanced by the knowledge that they'd be short and sweet. Oh, we'd talked by phone every day, texted, e-mailed—all the modern substitutes for actual presence—and we'd look forward to the next romantic rendezvous in the Costa Rican mountains, or the white, deserted beaches of North Carolina, or the Broadway play weekend in Manhattan. All great.

But after our meetings, I'd go back to Anchorage. She'd fly back to California.

I told myself now that the mundane parts of our life together had not yet been given a chance to settle in, and turn from boring routine to intimate rhythm, which is what they do when relationships work. Our issues had been big tricky ones; not small, insidious ones. We'd settled on where to live, how to stay in contact when one of us was in the field, how long to hold off on having children. Karen did not want to be an explorer and mother at the same time.

"Once I have a child, I'll be there one hundred percent," she'd said.

"I can wait a few years."

"It will be a challenge, you and me, Joe."

"You mean, having children?"

"No. I mean, just living. Because one of us will usually be traveling. Because there will always be aspects of our work we can't discuss. Because we'll need to get used to the other person . . . the one you love . . . being in danger. You with diseases. Me and my long Arctic walks."

I shook it off. When we gathered up our parkas, I saw her turn and make a hand gesture to Mikael Grandy, who was in a rear pew, and it meant, *Not now, not today, go away.*

"Let's take a drive," she said. "And talk."

The wind had risen, and snow had fallen last night, so two inches of fresh fall coated the town. It looked more like sand, hard and granular, the way it collected on rooftops and stop signs. Barrow is technically a desert. Little precipitation falls but what does stays there all winter. Plows move it around at night, pushing drifts into piles that, during the day, spread out again.

We wore extra layers, stocking hats, fur-lined gloves, calf-high boots, and wool socks with liners. The ocean had a glaze, stretching to the horizon. Night had fallen with particular sharpness. The stars were bright, a rarity in a place where 90 percent of the time the land sat beneath thick cover of clouds.

When she walked past my truck I said, confused, "I thought you wanted to take a drive."

A smile. "You'll see, Marine."

So! A peace mission. We strolled down empty streets, stopping finally before a two-story home with detached garage, and a warren of chain-link cages cramming the side yard. I heard deep excited barking from many throats.

"Oh, *that* kind of drive," I said.

"I took the dogs out earlier this week, when you were at the lab. Luther Oz let Mikael and me borrow them, once he saw me mush. Twelve-dog power. Got my sat phone and trusty GPS. Help me start the engine, Joe."

The huskies were enormous, shaggy, and more wild than domesticated, each one chained to a small wooden box that served as home. They knew Karen, eyed me but gave up suspicion when they realized we were going running. They leaped and howled with excitement when they saw her pull the wooden sled from beside the garage and lay the harnesses on the snow, in each animal's place. This was the last dog team in Barrow. The Iñupiats used snowmobiles on the tundra. They were cheaper than dogs and didn't have to be fed every day. This team was a last vestige of the old Arctic. Hell, Deputy Luther Oz—who raced in the Iditarod each year—spent hours catching more than two hundred fish a week with spread nets just to feed the animals.

We unchained the dogs. The harnesses went on smoothly. The last animal to be fitted was the lead, a five-year-old female named Justina.

"Climb on. I'll start it out," Karen said.

I sat legs out on the sled's pile of woolen blankets. I smelled dog and mildew and the sharp tang of ammonia. She stood behind me on the runners, the woman I'd fallen for, my personal explorer, my one in a million. She shouted, fiercely and happily, "Hut-hut-hut!"

The sled rammed forward at twelve miles an hour, out of the backyard, up over the packed-down snow on the road. We skittered hard across someone's backyard, past hanging caribou skins, and across a frozen lagoon and out onto the tundra. We passed the airport runway lights, with the streetlights of town receding. The dogs headed at a happy gallop toward the raised-up natural gas pipeline in the distance, source of Barrow homes' heat.

"Beats the horse carriage in Central Park," she called.

I forgot any investigation. I saw furred dog tails wagging. The sense of space pressing in; the lab, the base, the hut, disappeared. Karen's voice floated in from behind.

"I apologize, Joe."

"Why?"

"Because you were just doing your job at that dance. You know why I've been spending so much time with Mikael? To show you I'm independent. Truth is, I used him to make myself feel like I wasn't getting tied up. I mean, he needs to be here, but I went a little overboard."

"Thanks."

"And then I saw you with Tilda Swann and I was furious. Like you were flaunting someone else in my face. But you weren't doing that. I was."

I thought, recalling last night's torrid sex dream about Tilda, *Accept this gift and shut up.*

"I want us to work, Joe. I want it so badly that I get scared."

"Me, too."

"I thought Marines never get scared."

"We hide it better."

"Want to drive?" she said.

"*Now* I'm scared. Explain how to steer this thing."

"Pick a direction."

"Right."

She shouted out a sharp command, "Dee! Dee!"

Justina suddenly veered off to the right, looping the whole team, the sled, and me that way. Amazing.

Now we were running away from the pipeline, and straight away from Barrow, and toward the oil fields of Prudhoe Bay, two hundred miles ahead.

Karen shouted, "Haw!" and Justina smoothly and instantly veered back the way we'd come.

"Stop! Okay, Marine, let's see you try."

We reversed position, Karen sitting on the sled, me standing in the back.

"See that flat iron bar above by the back runner, Joe?"

"Yes."

"It's a brake. If you stand on it, it slows the sled. But you still need the command for them to pull up."

"What's *that* command, Karen. Moo?"

"Just yell 'stop,' silly. Like I did."

I yelled, "Hut, hut!" and off we went again. *Joe Rush, Arctic dog team commander.* I gathered up my Marine colonel's voice and shouted a resounding "DEE"—turn right—except the dogs ignored me. I tried, "Haw! Haw!" and a dozen heads whipped around, regarded me with doggy disdain, and kept going straight.

Karen was laughing. Then she said, "Oh! Look up, Joe. Look at the stars!"

They seemed closer and brighter. Then there was a sudden disturbance up there, like a razor blade drawn across darkness. A slit opened and I watched in awe as molten color—green lava—began spilling out, dripping down in luminous sheets.

"Aurora borealis," I breathed.

The lava faded to a luminous gas, swirling in the southwest quadrant. It sharpened back to the lava-like mass that colored even stars and flared brightly and disappeared so suddenly that they left an ache in space.

We stopped the sled, the dogs lay down, she got on beside me and pulled up a free blanket. "Now this *really* beats Central Park," I said.

She giggled. "Ready to hear a super-classified submarine crew war game secret? Death penalty if you talk?"

"They'll never get it out of me." From the teasing tone,
all I knew was that something amusing would come.

"I was on the *Virginia* a couple years back, war game,
north of the Bering Strait. Scary scenario, actually. The
deal was, Russia's in the Ukraine again. We're threatening
reprisals. They up the ante in the Arctic, face-off, and we
suddenly lose all sat coverage, we're stuck on the surface,
fire's destroyed guidance. We have to get to Nome."

"You navigated by stars," I said.

"Right, except the game was, *The Russians can hear
everything we say* . . . so one of our chiefs, a guy from
Louisiana, shrimper family, told us about this game his
people played in the Gulf. *They made up constellations.*"

"What do you mean?"

"Think about it, Joe. Look up. See Polaris? The North
Star? See how it's part of Ursa Minor, the bear?"

"Yes, I know it."

"The Greeks named it. They knew that if they drew
lines connecting those particular stars, you'd see the outline of a small bear, and they named the whole image,
see?"

"So what was the game? Rename the image?"

"No! Better! Because the images are arbitrary. Take
those same stars, connect them to *other* stars, thirty degrees south, and turn your pen northwest and hit that
red-looking star, see it? Good! Connect *those* dots instead
of the Greek ones, you get a squatting monkey."

I started laughing.

"It was the simplest damn code," she said admiringly, and lowered her voice, became a ship commander directing a helmsman to change course. "Head for the monkey's chin."

I loved that laugh. Karen taught me new constellations. The fat zebra. Flipper. She was right. It was easy, and had us howling. "Head southwest from the giant toad."

Funny, yes, but as we stood under the stars, holding hands, the sad truth about the deaths of new friends came back to me.

"Occam's razor. The simplest explanation is the truth, Merlin will announce a suicide/murder."

We started back. At length I saw, in the distance, hemmed in by vast night, the small glow of human-made light in Barrow. I knew that probably a thousand new diseases come into existence every year. You never hear about them. A goatherd in Turkey develops rashes from a new skin virus. His fever spikes. He recovers. The rash disappears.

A Boston two-year-old comes down with a cough that lingers, and the child does not respond to antibiotics. Three days later the girl is cooing at her mother, cured not by medicine, but by natural body defense.

In less than twenty-four hours we'd board the evening Alaska Airlines 737 and head south, me to D.C. for a talk with my new boss, she to Nome for upcoming war games.

In ninety days I would retire. In ten months so would Eddie, and then Karen and I and my partner and his family would take up residence on the East Coast. We'd never have to deal with General Wayne Homza again.

It struck me, as we glided along, that for the past twenty thousand years—from the time before the Romans to Wayne Homza—the land around us had simply sucked up lives with mystery. That Kelley and her parents, and Clay Qaqulik, were going to go down as the latest additions to a list stretching back to the days when mammoths and saber-toothed tigers walked these rolling plains.

If Clay Qaqulik hadn't fired his shotgun, all four of them might have recovered and told the story one day of the scary time out on the tundra, when they'd become ill with something no one ever ID'd.

At first I thought the chirping sound was coming from Karen's parka. Then I realized it was my phone and, seeing it was Eddie's number, calling, clicked it on.

"Colonel Rush?"

It wasn't Eddie but I recognized the musical intonations of Dr. Ranjay Sengupta, who had released the bodies for a flight home tomorrow morning. They'd be leaving at 9 A.M.

"What is it?" I asked, assuming it was one more piece of nonstop North Slope or State of Alaska paperwork.

"I think you had better come to the hospital. I am afraid that we have another case," Dr. Ranjay Sengupta replied.

EIGHT

It was hard to think about business when all he could imagine was sex.

George Carling—38, respected whaling captain, board member of the Arctic Slope Regional Corporation, coach of the Alaska state championship high school wrestling team, and descendant of a Danish-born whaler—and his Iñupiat wife sat at the long conference table on the third floor of the ASRC headquarters, trying to concentrate on the oil people's words, but his heart was roaring with anticipation, his throat was dry with lust.

Longhorn Oil's Dave Lillienthal, smiling at the dozen assembled board of directors, including George, said, "Believe me, our drilling will be done under the safest specifications. We will stop work when you are whaling, to avoid driving bowheads away."

Unlike Native Americans in the lower forty-eight, Alaska's Eskimos had not been given reservations by the federal government, in exchange for signing away rights to land. They got money, and established corporations under the Alaska Native Claims Settlement Act. Each tribe's corporation had authority over their land. Any Iñupiat was an automatic shareholder, and received tax-free dividend checks annually. The ASRC, George's corporation, owned twenty million acres on Alaska's North Slope.

Dave Lillienthal said, "Longhorn North would be grateful if the ASRC supported our pipeline route, in Washington."

So far this morning the board had approved a bid by a Los Angeles–based Arctic Tours Company to acquire a fifty-year lease for an eco lodge on sixteen thousand acres of land south of Barrow, to bring in tourists. They'd gone thumbs-down on an application by a Minnesota-based copper mining company to dig a mine to the west, even though the company promised that half their employees would be Iñupiats.

The proposed pipeline route/offshore drilling plan was the main thrust of today's meeting.

"What can we do to get you to agree?" Dave asked.

Board members were almost all whaling captains, the most respected leaders in their villages. They were responsible for the lives of their crews, usually relatives and friends. They brought food to their people, and so, in meetings like this, they wore two hats. As board members, they wanted to expand business. As whaling captains, they wanted protection for the hunt. In fact, their captains organization, the

Alaska State Whaling Commission, paid lawyers in Washington, D.C., who filed lawsuits against oil companies when plans conflicted with hunting times.

Merlin Toovik, sitting beside George, said, "Put your promises on paper, Dave. That would help."

Dave sighed, nodded as if that was a good idea, but then said, "That's complicated. That sets a precedent. But we promise. You know our promise is always good."

It was little Deborah on whom George concentrated, his mouth dry, and heartbeat strong, as he anticipated the pleasure in store for him across the street, up in the Wells Fargo Bank building when this meeting was over. George imagining that small dancer's body naked, lying on the Naugahyde couch by the window; George remembering the feel of those slim arms around his neck, and those soft fingers gliding down, the dirty things that she whispered; George in wonder at the excessive physical zeal of which he'd been capable during the last three days, even with his wife at the hotel. Like he'd become twenty years old again. George shook his head in wonder. He and Agatha must have done it four times last night . . . and STILL this ceaseless urge made him hard right now, made it difficult to hear the mélange of babble from the brother, as he delivered the same promises that captains had heard from so many corporations over the years.

"There will be many jobs for local people."

George read the lips of one of the Point Hope captains, a young man, and angry. Lies.

But Point Hope people were always angry. They never trusted outsiders and George could not blame them. First they'd been decimated by diseases that the whalers carried in the 1800s. Then the U.S. government had tried to blow up the village with atomics, during Project Chariot, and government scientists had dumped cesium in nearby water.

"I'm sure none of you want," Dave Lillienthal said, looking around, palms out, "to go back to pre-oil days, when you chopped ice for drinking water."

The sister actually thought she could influence his vote by sleeping with him. George found this amusing. But he was not going to turn down excellent sex.

George tried to take notes but his fingers began going numb again, damnit, he was losing feeling at the endings. The tingling and deadness had come in waves over the past two days, starting a day after he'd arrived in Barrow. In fact, when he'd walked into this room an hour ago, he'd almost fallen into the chair, because his right leg didn't work right. Fortunately no one had noticed.

I must be getting a flu, he thought.

George caught sight of his reflection in the window and it disgusted him; the clean-shaven squarish face, bullet head, and fleshy cheeks on a trunk of a neck, a worker's face, strong, the same as always and yet it seemed wrong to him, ugly, something he did not want to look at.

Like this morning, at the hotel, after the post-sex shower . . . First the water had felt slimy, like there were chemicals in it, and then his reflection in the bathroom mirror was so disturbing that'd he'd draped a towel over it to shut the sight of himself off.

Weird. Well, he'd gotten flus before. Whatever this stupid thing was, it would go away.

Dave Lillienthal got his attention again, holding up the TV clicker, gesturing at the teleconference screen in front of the room, by the coffee and ham and turkey sandwiches. He said, "Our engineers in Houston want to show you our new drill machinery, safer and more efficient than before."

George distracted, catching Deborah's wink. George thinking, *I can't believe I'm so hard!*

Last night he had been incredible, insatiable, better than when he was courting Agatha, better than his honeymoon or even anything he'd imagined when he was a teenager watching James Bond. He'd done it with Agatha again and again and left her gasping, both of them gloriously sore, and STILL he'd seen her with the towel this morning, gotten aroused and gone at it again.

And now he could not stop glancing at Deborah, the way her hair fell around her face . . . the way her slender fingers caressed a pen. He smelled her Shalimar fragrance over the scents of coffee, Paco Rabanne from Dave, leather chair cleaner, and muktuk. Someone had it in a pocket, or breathed it.

And now, in his head, pain, growing . . . Boom . . . Boom . . . Boom!

"As you know," Dave said, through George's headache, as if he needed to remind them of what they all never forgot, "in the days of your grandparents, the Iñupiats had no plumbing. In the Indian Affairs schools children cried themselves to sleep at night. The Iñupiat language was banned in class."

A captain from Wainright, and one from St. Lawrence

Island, both more than seventy years old, nodded, remembering.

Dave said, "It wasn't until you taxed oil that you took control of your own destiny. But if you shut us down, if offshore fails, you go back to the past."

The board thanked the Lillienthals and asked to discuss this in private, and the brother and sister left. They'd paid for the coffee and sandwiches; turkey on wheat, ham on rye, bacon cheeseburgers from Northern Lights Café.

George's headache was worse now, so bad that he forgot the sex, as the board argued about offshore drilling. Some favored it because without oil tax money, the borough would go broke and without oil the ASRC would lose business. Others feared that a spill or explosion would drive away whales. Everyone felt the pull of logic on both ends, but half of the board came down on one side, half on the other.

"George? You're not saying anything," Merlin said.

"What?"

"We're going around the table."

His hand wouldn't move. He told them he needed to think more, needed to pray on it. He sat there trying to look normal, caught sight of his face again in the window, and turned his eyes away.

But then the numbness passed as suddenly as it had come, as it had several times already. It would probably go away by itself in the end. The meeting ended without resolution. George waited until he was the last to leave—so no one saw where he went next. He made his way outside and across the street to the Wells Fargo Bank building, and up in the el-

evator to the fourth floor, where she waited in the tiny, unoccupied Teens Against Drugs suite. Longhorn funded the organization, so she had a key.

"Georgy."

He could not control himself. He had her gasping. She lay eagerly below him on the couch. His knees pressed into thick carpet and he knelt behind her, ramming. His big hands encircling her tiny dancer's back, squeezed her small breasts. A coffee table was knocked over. The smell became rank and musky. All of it drove him to new heights.

He looked down, and son of a bitch, HE WAS STILL HARD.

"George, how old did you say you were? Seventeen?"

He made a grunting sound, like an animal.

"A little bird told me that you didn't vote in there, Georgy. Is there something bothering you about our plan?"

George knew that the "little bird" was thirty-six-year-old Patrick Ahmogak from Nuigsut, who had once worked as a marine mammal spotter on the BP seismic boats out of Prudhoe Bay.

Deborah jerked up on the couch when he answered, looked alarmed and asked, "What did you say?"

"I said I want to think about it."

"Why are you making those noises?"

"What noises?"

"George, stop that! This isn't funny! Speak English!"

He stood up. He could see the reflection of a startled, ape-like man, naked in the window, and a small woman, head turned to him, her white body stiff on the sofa. He sat beside her. He tried to explain about the headache. Except she backed off and then stood, quickly gathering up her clothes, looking frightened. He tried to reach out to soothe her, but his hand remained at his side. She was dressing, telling him that no one was supposed to know that they spent time together and she'd see him later and just STOP MAKING THOSE NOISES!

And that was when George realized that he'd only thought he'd been speaking English. Because the sound of barking in the room, the sound that he believed to be coming from outside, from a dog, was actually coming from deep inside his own throat.

George dressing now also, baffled and afraid. He needed to see a doctor. He'd go to the hospital. But he waited for her to leave first, as she always did, to keep their secret, before he took a step toward the door to leave.

He fell down.

His foot would not work. It simply refused to function. He told himself to stand but the command did not reach his limbs, so they did nothing. Instead little shooting pains started up in his ankle, worming their way toward his hip, so that his knee began stinging, too.

He lay on the carpet. He fought away fear. He was a captain and he had faced many dangers worse than this, he thought. There was the time that the engine stopped forty miles out, during a fall hunt, in a storm, and they'd been towing a dead thirty tonner and he'd kept the crew safe until help arrived. And the time on the tundra when he'd been alone, hunting caribou, and the snowmobile engine jammed and he'd walked twenty-nine miles home in a blizzard. So now he lay there and waited for opportunity. He waited for the numbness to pass and he told himself that he would then get up and go to the hospital emergency room.

He could see a clock on the shelf and at length thirty minutes had passed, then forty. His throat seemed to be closing. He was thirsty, REALLY thirsty but at the same time the thought of water in his mouth was repulsive, and he watched the clock and waited for the bad to pass.

George told himself that when he got to the hospital, he would need to tell doctors about the symptoms. He tried to think back and pinpoint when they had begun. He'd been fine four days ago when he and Agatha had boarded the flight from Wainright, his village, to Barrow. He'd felt fine on the plane, and on the first night here, at the potluck at the high school. That was the evening he had gotten into that argument with the woman from Greenpeace, the fiery Brit who was always trying to stop any kind of development on the North Slope.

"Longhorn is lying to you," she'd said. "Nobody can clean up spilled oil under ice. Why not make this land into a beautiful park for tourists, and make money that way."

"That's all we need, thirty thousand tourists a year," he said. He'd been to several public parks and remembered crowds, trash, blaring radios, buses. George had told the woman, "You want to put us in a snow globe, and shake it, so snow falls on the quaint Iñupiat people. You want us to be the endangered species, not the animals."

That same evening he'd had a pleasant talk with Alan McDougal, who ran the research base, and told him that caribou herds were growing instead of shrinking even with pipelines crossing part of the borough. Then he and Agatha *had stayed up until two, catching up with his cousin, Ned, and his wife and son, Leon Kavik, in Browerville. He'd felt a bit of headache the next morning, and attributed it to the hotel bed, and the odd angle with which his head had lain on the overly soft pillow. And then later that day he'd felt a little fatigue, and Agatha had taken his temperature and told him it was low grade, little cold probably, 99.2, a nuisance, a go-away-fast fever, not worth thinking about.*

George tried to move his hand. It worked! He filled with gratefulness. He tried his feet. They slid forward a few inches. He felt as if he had won an Olympic race. He stood. He felt dizzy. His fever had spiked.

Get to the hospital, he thought.

Outside, it was night, and he swayed as he left the building, needed to grasp the handrail by the steel steps, barely aware of the frigid metal against his hand. Cars were passing, their headlights brighter than usual, painful, in his face, causing him to turn away. His throat hurt badly. He bent over and threw up in the snow. When the episode was over he realized that his saliva still ran freely from his mouth over his chin, dripping, Christ.

Finally, he was scared. This was no small cold. This was no flu. Cancer?

George walked into the middle of the street to hail a ride. A cab passed but did not stop. The driver already had a passenger. In Barrow, you didn't flag cabs. They were on radio call or you found them outside the AV Value Center, where they picked up shoppers. But gasoline cost so much—as much as seven dollars a gallon—that no taxi driver would simply drive around, hoping for fares.

Another pair of headlights approached. Fearing that if he waited longer, he'd lose mobility again, George stumbled into the road and held up his arms. The Subaru began skidding. It loomed and swayed but stopped. The driver was a scientist he recognized; Bruce Friday, who regularly came to Wainright to research polar bears.

"What's wrong, George?"

"I need to get to the hospital."

Dr. Friday helped him in and he coughed on the man, sprayed his whole face, mumbled, "Sorry." Dr. Friday said not to worry and wiped the spit off with his parka sleeve. Back at the wheel, he eased down on the accelerator to keep from skidding. The hospital, like any building in Barrow, was minutes away.

When they pulled up at the ER George's hand refused to grasp the door handle. Dr. Friday came around to his side and helped him out. George, staring at Friday's gloved hand, had an urge to bite it. He started laughing. Friday asked him if he was able to walk, and slipped an arm under his shoulders. Someone must have changed the lighting in the ER, because it was like floodlights in a theater, like one time when he'd walked on stage at the University of Alaska auditorium in Anchorage, to receive an award for mentoring the wrestling team. The light hurt.

At first they made him wait, but when he started throwing up they ushered him into a curtained-off cubicle. The nurses took his blood pressure and blood and a young doctor—she looked fifteen years old—asked about symptoms.

He tried to get it out. The curtain seemed to be billowing and voices in the big exam room, from other cubicles, seemed to echo and then the beating sound in his head was like the end of a kivgiq, *the winter messenger feast,* when all the dance groups in the borough crowd into the high school gym, when, at 2 A.M., after the five-day-long celebration, all the drummers from all the villages marched in, in groups, and stand in a solid line, in their traditional dance clothes, and hit those whale liver–lining and hide handheld drums at the same time. The dancers stamping. The stands filled and everyone—young and old—visitors from D.C., moms with infants on their backs, whalers, and hunters . . . all clapping . . . magnificent!

BOOMBOOMBOOMBOOM!

Like a thousand years of drums mixing together under the basketball banners. He blinked. He was hallucinating. He thought he was in that gym, the stands filled, the dancers stamping. *BOOMBOOMBOOMBOOM!*

Then his vision changed and there was a new doctor there, that Indian fellow, from Mumbai, positioning a mirror to look into George's throat but the light spiked so harshly that George reached and swept the mirror into the corner, where it shattered.

"Turn down the lights!" he screamed.

Faces went out of focus. There were more faces there, the two Marine doctors who had flown into Wainright earlier in the season, with the Coast Guard. All three doctors bending over him, looking down at him, looking worried, asking questions that he struggled to answer.

Suddenly he was convulsing, thrashing, trying to hit the doctors, flailing, and when a nurse tried to put the plastic cuffs on him, restrain him against the bed rests, he lunged *with his teeth, tried to bite her, felt the crazy heat spread through his synapses, like poison, like a sizzling electricity cauterizing thought, the sun was in his chest, a furnace, consuming tissue as fuel.*

Nurses wheeling in medicines.

"George, look at me. George!"

"What's happening to him, Ranjay?"

"Oh, my God! Look at the monitor!"

BOOMBOOMBOOMBOOOOOOOM! . . .

I STOOD WITH EDDIE AND RANJAY, BESIDE THE DEAD MAN. HIS agitation had exploded in the final moments, and he'd been trying to speak, but no words had come out.

"It's the same thing the Harmons had," said Eddie.

"It's in town," said Ranjay.

"Did we bring it back with us, in the chopper?"

"If we brought it back, why did *he* get it? Why not us?"

"You think it started here?"

We heard voices from other ER cubicles, as doctors had normal conversations with patients. Where does it hurt? We're going to do an X-ray. Take these pills when you get home. Illness, but something familiar. Disease, but something we understand.

"What the hell is this thing?" said Eddie.

All three of us doctors, in our imaginations, now filled in sights to go with the voice recordings that Kelley Harmon had made, out in a deserted research camp. And what I imagined was terrifying. Clay Qaqulik holding a shotgun . . . yes, we'd known that . . . but all four people convulsing, babbling, and feverish.

Dr. Ranjay Sengupta said, in a whisper, "Contagious?"

I left the cubicle and walked to the ER window. Outside it was night and I looked over the rooftops. I saw headlights moving. I saw lights in windows. In those homes people were watching television and making love and sleeping. I wondered if, in those houses, there was also something else, lurking, small enough to seem invisible. Or was it in the caskets awaiting flight out? I looked at the ER doors, portals for the sick and injured. At the moment they were still, as was the hallway. I did not want to think about what I saw in my mind's eye, which was more people coming in, convulsing, screaming, like George.

Eddie said, "We go home tomorrow, One."

"Oh, not now, Two."

I went back into the cubicle. The man on the table looked yellow in the artificial light, and the pain he'd suffered at the end remained etched in agony lines of his mouth. My eyes swept the cubicle, the medicine vials, the tools of my job, all of which had failed us this evening.

I saw the mirror shards on the bright linoleum, in the corner, I recalled George sweeping the instrument from Ranjay's hand, barking something about too-bright light.

Mirrors . . .

And then it hit me.

"Shit."

The other two doctors stared at me, understanding

that I'd made a connection. But it was a bad one, a very, very hideous connection, a connection that I wished would turn out to be wrong.

"We knew it. But we ignored it," I said.

They both drew in closer.

"We ignored it because we said it was impossible," I said. "Tell me, why did we come here this summer, Eddie?"

"To check if there have been changes, new things . . ."

"*Changes*, Eddie. Because the place is warming. Because the Slope's been a dumping ground. Because new species are arriving. We *saw* it, but didn't believe it."

He knew what I meant, his eyes growing wider. I uttered a single word then. The word has terrified humans for two thousand years.

"It's a one-hour test," I said. "We can do it right now. At our lab. After we leave, disinfect this room."

Ranjay backed from the bed slightly, not because he feared the corpse. He feared the idea.

"But you never get four people with it, *never, that has never happened*," he said. "I've seen this, yes, in India. Many cases. *But you never get a group!*"

"You're right," I repeated. "Quite right. *So far.*"

NINE

"It cannot be possible," Ranjay said.

The twenty-five-million-dollar U.S. Arctic Research Center was a concrete tower sitting on the tundra, a half mile from the base and satellite farms, jutting up like those old forts forming the French Marginot Line before World War Two. Inside were labs assigned to scientists. The amenities were first class but security stank. When it came to the Arctic, Congress didn't take the Arctic seriously.

I remember meeting a Senate aide on a fact-finding mission up here once. He'd asked me if the Eskimos spoke English and shops accepted U.S. dollars.

"This *is* the U.S.," I'd responded, and watched the man's cheeks color. "That was a joke," he replied.

Now, in our lab, I said, "Here goes. We test for rabies."

George Carling lay naked, under a sheet, in a bright light that would have driven him crazy before he died. I smelled formaldehyde and a more corrupt whiff from the man on the table, who had been alive hours ago.

Eddie, Ranjay, and I wore aprons, gloves, plastic visors. Sengupta shook his head, but looked distraught. "We considered this possibility, and discarded it."

"But we didn't *test* for it, Ranjay."

"Because you never get cases together, never a cluster. Never!"

The Harmon bodies waited in a walk-in freezer, down a long, lab-lined hall.

"Rabies, one hundred percent fatal," said Eddie morosely, watching me unwrap an enormous hypodermic, World War One size, more wicked-looking sword than needle. "Ebola deaths, ninety percent. Plague can be treated. Rabies? *Hydrophobia?* Once the symptoms hit, good-bye."

I bent over the body. I probed with my gloved index finger at the base of George's powerful neck. His feet hung upside down over the end of the table. The flesh was yellowish in death, even paler under the light.

Rabies, I knew, was a Lassa virus, a zoonotic brain infection named after Lyssa, Greek goddess of mad dogs. The Greeks understood rage enough to give it a god. By the twenty-first century, rabies had been shut down as a major killer in developed countries, but still killed fifty thousand around the world each year, usually in poor nations, jungle countries, where bite victims could not reach or afford the painful series of shots that could—only if administered before symptoms appear—halt the disease.

"Rabies kills *one by one*," Ranjay argued. "If it spread the other way, my God"—he shuddered—"you'd have millions of fatalities."

I found the spot where spine flowed into brain, a nerve highway or, if I was right, the road by which the virus had migrated to George's skull, taken root, and spread back to set fire to his thinking, burn along his nerve endings, shut down speech, and, in the end, with a swiftness defying the usual timetable, stop his heart.

"The symptoms were there," I said. "Come on, Ranjay, a laundry list of what we heard on Kelley's recordings."

Rabies is one of the most hideous diseases in the human imagination; the basis of vampire and werewolf legends. The virus infects through an animal bite, although, on rare occasions, it has sickened lab workers who got it in their eyes or mouth. Rabies transforms a pet into a salivating killer. It lives in superstition. I think we were all fairly terrified now.

"I grant this. Yes, Joe, water becomes disgusting. I had a case, a farmer, peaceful man, screaming as they brought him in because it was raining, that water hurt. But for five people to have it . . . no, impossible."

Eddie said, "Plus, he died too *fast*."

I shook my head. "It wasn't mosquito-borne encephalitis. Or West Nile. Negative on herpes variations. The guttural noises. He thought he was speaking English."

I inserted the needle into the mass of muscle and flesh, the brain stem. I drew back on the plunger, watching the hypo fill with a dark gray mix of blood and brain tissue.

"Of course, none of our dipsticks were positive. Rabies doesn't hide in blood. We *came* here to look for mutations. Then maybe we found one but refused to see it."

"Too bad Clay Qaqulik blew his brains out," said Eddie. "Can't test it."

"Even if George tests negative, we'll do the others."

Just weeks ago the research center had been packed with scientists from around the world; its hallways a mélange of languages: Swiss German from the glacier people, Norwegian or English from the ocean currents people, German-German from the Max Planck Institute's climate people.

The locks on the doors were old-fashioned number punchers, there were no eye scans or fingerprint panels. The walk-in labs had key locks, and inside freezers, areas were assigned by rack and shelf space. Preserved samples ranged from algae to whale livers, the only security a few yellow-and-black BIOHAZARD stickers on crates, vials, shelves.

"Good thing the bodies were refrigerated," Dr. Sengupta mused. "Because we are at the tail end of the period when the virus can be detected after death."

Eddie shook his head. "You're imagining things, One. That cabin's been the site of research for decades. Who knows what the hell someone dumped there. Occam's razor. The most likely explanation is probable."

I slid out the needle and injected most of the extracted fluid into a five-ounce sample bottle, which Eddie sealed. This would remain our primary sample, which Eddie walked into the freezer down the hall. The place was so deserted that I heard his footsteps receding. George's tissue would be stored beside our collection taken over the summer; toxoplasma from a four-year-old we treated for anemia in Point Hope—victim of a parasite normally found in cats farther south, but recently beluga whales have tested positive for it. So have people eating their dried meat. Stored rabies from Arctic foxes. And the prize, a disgusting foot-long tapeworm, *diphyllobothriasis,* normally found in Pacific Ocean salmon, but they've been moving north as oceans warm.

"This is all we need, another 1348," Eddie said. He'd returned.

I moved to the microscope table and dripped a single drop of George's fluid onto a glass slide.

Thirteen forty-eight, I knew—using a tongue depressor to thin the sample, so light could pass through it—was the red-letter date for plague researchers. It was a year when the smartest physicians on Earth did not even dream that microbes existed, and when infected fleas somewhere in central Europe boarded a sailing ship in the fur of a few black rats. By the time they scurried ashore in Marseille, the crew was dying of a new disease. And the fleas kept biting: a baby in a market, a husband and wife as they made love in a hut, a swineherd, a nobleman. Rank and money made no difference. They all began to die.

"Now we air-dry the slide. Ten more minutes," I said.

Bubonic Plague was what those terrified Europeans called the dark buboes that erupted in those medieval groins and armpits, that had victims coughing black blood and dying by the thousands. And then the disease got worse. *Something changed in its DNA*. It went from being transmittable through flea bites, into a killer that floated in air, lived in human breath, murdered if you kissed a girl, if a stranger coughed on you, if you took a steam with a friend, if you shook a hand and picked a food particle off your teeth. Bubonic Plague exploded into the catastrophic Pneumonic Plague, the Black Death, which rampaged across a continent and slaughtered one out of four people. Graveyards were overwhelmed. Societies collapsed. Armies of flagellants marched across Europe, through villages of the dead and dying; parades of half-naked, half-starved supplicants, praying, whipping themselves, crying for God, blaming the suffering on human sins.

"Now we stain our slide," I said.

"I am very fearful. I am thinking . . . about Constantine's experiments," Dr. Sengupta said.

Constantine was a Texas researcher who worked on rabies in the 1960s and his conclusions scared the shit out of me. That's because Constantine worked in a huge cave, Frio Cave. And on the massive vaulted ceiling of that damp place lived a colony of three million silver-haired bats. Bats that fled their home each dusk in clouds of winged movement, spread through a thousand square miles of landscape, and were susceptible to rabies. The strain they transmitted was particularly virulent.

Thirty seconds and the slide will be dry.

Constantine was curious, I knew, why there had been a few isolated incidents where hikers in remote areas—

people who insisted they'd never been bitten by animals—came down with rabies.

They'd been in bat caves, he found.

Constantine's theory was that under the right circumstances, rabies could travel in air.

To test this, he placed caged coyotes in that cave, beneath the squirming bats on the ceiling, so the coyotes ate and slept in that air saturated with bat guano and effluence. Half of the cages were built with iron bars, enabling bats to enter the gaps. For the rest, steel mesh covered the bars, stopping bats, but the mesh would admit airborne virus.

Constantine's question was: Would the mesh stop rabies?

"All the animals died," Sengupta said.

Eddie shook his head. He did not want to believe. "That was closed space, Ranjay, the air thick with bat shit. There's no connection between transmission in the Arctic and coyotes trapped with three million bats. Yeah, Constantine proved aerosolization possible, but not here."

I gingerly moved our slide to the microscope, careful not to cut myself. Rabies virus is big enough to show up on a high school lab student's microscope. No extra-special equipment required.

"Maybe I should have my sons and wife leave town, go back to her mother's, in Mumbai," mused Sengupta.

I heard my heart beating. I envisioned the Harmons in their camp. I inserted the slide beneath the eyepiece. At that moment we all sensed ourselves standing at a border between a world we knew and a different, frightening one that might exist a moment from now.

"Bird flu," I said, adjusting focus.

Same story. Mutation. Bird flu originated in winged vertebrates. They passed the disease on to pigs—dropped a seed into their food maybe, who knows—and the pigs sickened and transmitted the flu to humans.

But then, again, something *changed*, we knew. The middle stage disappeared. I envisioned it. Somewhere on a Chinese farm, in a fetid sty a thousand miles from Beijing, air filled with alterations, maybe a local factory dumped chemicals in the water, maybe the temperature rose just a little bit, or nature stepped in, but for whatever reason suddenly DNA mutated and that flu bypassed pigs as hosts and went directly from birds into humans.

You no longer needed a pig to get it. You could catch it from a heron on a rooftop in Paris. You could catch it from pigeons you feed bread crumbs to in Central Park.

"Host shift," said Eddie.

"Mutation," said Sengupta. "Evolution at its finest."

I considered Barrow, the homes, and church singalongs, the value center, the high school—any town, every town, with a thousand places for a virus to move between hosts.

I took a seat on the stool. I watched bright light shine up through the slide. I peered down.

"Oh, shit," I said, uttering the most eloquent exclamation of inadequacy on the planet.

My head was an anvil. What I saw in the eyepiece

matched the photo on my screen. The bullet shapes were unmistakable. I was staring at a quivering mass of microbes, thick as bees in a hive, bumping and shifting as if trying to get out; the spiked coatings like defensive antenna on a mine in the ocean, or an armored dinosaur; and beneath that, I saw the shadow of the virus's protective envelope or shield; and inside *that*, like explosive powder that Merlin had poured into his whale bomb, the killer: looping spiral DNA.

"Rabies," I said.

Eddie gasped. "How the hell did George get it? He was nowhere near the Harmons."

I turned away, heading down the hall for the freezers and the three Harmon bodies. Eddie and Ranjay trailed along. "George doesn't even live in Barrow. He flew in a few days ago. The Harmons were in the field then."

Sengupta said, "Then the starting place is *in town*?"

"Let's wait and see what we find with the Harmons. Maybe they'll be negative."

An hour later we stood amid the three bodies, now all laid out on tables, a little party of the dead.

Stunned, despite the fact that I'd anticipated this, I said, "And not a single bite mark. Anywhere."

I heard a droning sound over the quiet whoosh of our air-circulation system. Looking out the window, I saw the contrail of the afternoon Alaska Air Flight to Anchorage, and, from there, many passengers would board other planes, to New York, L.A., Paris, Hamburg, Moscow . . .

The contrail disappeared into the gray.

Sengupta said, "We must call the CDC in Atlanta. I have only two doses of rabies vaccine at the hospital. We will need more."

I tried to think. I shut my eyes. I flashed to flu season in New York. People crowding subways and buses, coughing. Workers and kids coming home at night and going straight to bed. Patients flooding ER rooms, lining up in local pharmacies. Whole offices of workers short of help.

I looked out the window, southward, toward the lights of Barrow. Almost five thousand people there.

What we've got here—if it's contagious—is much worse than a flu. It makes you angry. It makes you crazy. It kills you ranting and screaming, stark raving mad.

Sengupta laughed softly. "Just think. I *wanted* to come to the Arctic."

"So the possibilities are . . ." said Eddie.

"One. Worst case. It's evolved. It's traveling in a new way. Mutation. Evolution. Aerosolization."

"Two?"

"The starting point is in town, in a single location they all visited. Point source, not contagious."

"Is there a three?"

"*Intentional.* Someone gave it to them. Kelley said Tilda Swann was tampering with their water supply. It was out in the open, in the airport supply area."

Ranjay said, "Where would someone *get* a sample?"

"Like we did. Sick dog. Dead fox. Hell, anyone could walk into the freezer where *our* samples are kept," I said.

Sengupta recoiled. He was not a soldier, trained to look for enemies. "That is crazy," he said. "Why would someone do that? If you wanted to hurt someone, there are other ways, easier ways to do it. You are talking about a very, very insane individual."

Eddie said, "You don't think it's a weapon, One!"

I knew from our unit files that in those old Soviet labs, across the Bering Sea, as recently as thirty years ago, scientists had tried to weaponize rabies.

"We treat it like it's contagious," I said, reaching for the phone. "Your wife isn't going anywhere, Ranjay. No one in town is. We need to quarantine this place, now."

TEN

"Oh, pshaw! It won't be rabies," the distinguished-looking doctor on my computer screen said.

It was ninety minutes after we'd made our discovery, the amount of time it had taken General Wayne Homza to gather up the five faces looking back from the split screen. I'd alerted D.C. from the Quonset hut, not the lab, because of the crappy security. Just over the past few days Eddie and I had overheard detectives interviewing people in other labs through the vent system, a veritable highway for talk.

Bruce Friday telling Merlin, *"Where was I on August second, when the Harmons had the lab fire? Hmm! Oh! Anchorage. At the Cook Hotel conference on polar bears. Here's the photo."*

Anthropologist Candida McDougal, Alan's wife, saying, *"Leon Kavik was yelling at Ted about Kelley, just furious that he couldn't see her more."*

I'd been quite rational in my step-by-step presentation. I'd told the men and women on-screen that something terrible and inexplicable had infected five so far, but we must anticipate more. I'd listed possibilities, that the rabies might be man-made or a natural mutation. I'd suggested the investigation split into two paths: tracking the infection backward, and considering that the Harmons had been targets from the first. That's when Homza, incredulous, had sneered, "Targets? The *algae* people?"

The CDC, in the U.S., has the authority to call a national medical emergency. And its chief, Dr. Rudolph Gaines, looked like one of those M.D.s on old 1970s medical TV programs, when doctors were godlike, a status to which he seemed to feel he belonged. Silver hair. Pale blue eyes. Smooth movements. White coat. He radiated *soothing*.

"Rabies simply does not present this way," he lectured. "We'll send up a couple of epidemiologists. They'll repeat the test. False positives! It happens all the time. You're a warrior, Colonel. You believe intent exists where there's merely understandable error. You're simply not a rabies expert, sir. No shame in that, my friend."

"How long will this confirmation take?"

"Hmm. Our plane is in Haiti, on the cholera now, so our people will use commercial flights . . . back and forth to Barrow . . . we'll want the bodies back here. Retest, all total, electron microscopy, antibody tests, antigen, amplicon tests, oh, I'd say six or seven days at the most."

"Six days? The whole town could be sick by then."

"I very much doubt that."

He gave me—and the four other faces on screen—a sincere, sympathetic doctor look.

"Colonel, please understand. Two years ago we had a similar panic in Braxton, Missouri. False positive! One hundred people vaccinated and then we find out that the preliminary was wrong!"

"We tested four people, sir. *Four* tests!"

"But the same equipment, same lab, same testers. I admire your zeal and dedication. Let's begin from scratch. Tell me, what would you have us do right now?"

I answered immediately. "Protocol four."

The faces seemed shocked. Protocol four was one of those secret plans, hopefully never to be used, to attempt to impose *rules* on danger. It called for an executive order to seal off a small town, in the event of a contagious outbreak. Protocols one to three involved similar measures in a major city, military base, harbor, or airport.

I said, "To be safe. Nothing leaves or enters until we track down the source. Hold any planes out of Barrow on the runway, and get more serum up here . . ."

In disaster films, it looks relatively easy to seal off a populated area. The president makes the call. The troops move in. The fences go up. Voilà!

But in the lawsuit-crazy U.S., protocol four took a lot more into consideration, involved coordination of multiple moving parts. Governors secretly notified, health officials secretly on board, judges secretly signing papers, a whole set of contingencies designed to cover the asses of the decision makers later, after the emergency was over, when the lawsuits and finger-pointing began. Protocol four was as much an act of political preservation as it was an attempt to control a deadly outbreak or attack.

Now the man in Atlanta listened, as if he was considering it, but he wasn't.

"Premature."

"Would you say that if the disease had broken out in, say, Greenwich, Connecticut? Or Beverly Hills?"

"If you're implying that I regard life differently for a native population, or a poorer one, that's offensive."

"Really? Beverly Hills stops funding candidates if garbage collection gets held up for more than forty-eight hours."

"Colonel, you can't test for rabies until symptoms appear, and you know it. You want passengers to sit in planes for days? And have the news get out? Panic! And *shots*? There's no stockpile of vaccine for this disease. It is not a mass threat. At summer's end, what few supplies exist have been diminished. How many people in that town? Five thousand? We don't have enough vaccine in the entire country to treat a quarter of that amount."

"Then perhaps we need a crash program."

I heard a groan from the speaker on my laptop. It came from General Wayne Homza, whose bristling visage stared out from the top left box. The general looked like he'd swallowed a lemon. He was undoubtedly envisioning the cost of mass manufacturing a drug instead of spending the money on weapons or troops.

Dr. Rudolph Gaines sighed. "Phhhhpt! Because of five

presumptive positives? Only two companies make the stuff and they're in Europe. And even if they started a batch, it would be a year before they had any supply for the FDA to check. So let's come back to Earth, Doctor."

"In the meantime, what if more people die?"

"No need for theatrics," he said unpleasantly. "I'm not saying ignore your problem. I'm saying this will turn out to be something else. We want to get it right, sir. Of course, I'll be grateful if General Homza allows you to stay on, you know, to liaise with the locals. Calm them."

Homza smiled with his lips only. His eyes wanted me out of there. He radiated force. "Yes, he will assist," he said. It was like watching a piece of wood talk.

One by one the faces before me signed off, and other ones grew larger as their space expanded on screen. Gone was the Alaska state epidemiologist, state department of health, a timid political appointee Merlin had called, now grateful to be relieved of responsibility. Gone was the Federal Aviation Administration deputy administrator, who'd listened in about the part concerning quarantining an airplane. Gone was the White House rep, who had been silent the entire time, taking copious notes.

Homza's face filled the screen. I flashed to a story I'd heard about him once at a hotel bar, at a conference on biowarfare. The source had been a colonel who'd attended West Point with Homza. The story was that Homza's father had been a violent drunk who routinely beat his mother, and killed her with a garden rake when Homza was eleven, at school. Previously, the father had been released early from prison after agreeing to participate in a University of Chicago study on domestic-violence causes. The story was that eleven-year-old Homza had been restrained in court, trying to attack a testifying psychologist. "You studied him? You should have shot him," the boy screamed over and over as guards dragged him from the room.

Now Homza's brows drew in. From thousands of miles away, he watched me.

"You are a troublesome man," he said.

"I'm just trying to complete my mission, sir."

"If we find proof that you've shared security secrets with enviro-agitators, I will prosecute you."

"There's no proof because I didn't do it."

Close up, Homza's lips were thick, his jaw powerful, a nut cracker, his eyes blunt and deep blue, and I could see the swell of muscle beneath his taut shirt and crisp tie. He'd trained to be a weight lifter, I'd read somewhere. He was legendary at the Pentagon gym.

"Perhaps, Colonel, you believe that because you will be retiring in a few months that you have more latitude than others to do whatever you want."

This was true, actually, but I said, "No, sir."

"If you do think that, I suggest you reconsider. You are in until we say you are out. I can and will bury you, Colonel."

"Yes, sir."

"I've checked you out. In the past you've had the protection of powerful people. "Then, *in front of the president,* you asked that a key policy, a necessary policy, be changed. Well, one word about contagious rabies and you go down. We sell a story up there until we know more. You will be our mouthpiece."

"Sir, what exactly do you want me to do when the CDC gets here?"

"I admire loyalty. I reward loyalty."

He was gone.

I FELT THE AIR GO OUT OF ME. I LOOKED OUT THE WINDOW AND saw Mikael Grandy trudging away from our hut, glancing back. I had not heard the door close. Shocked, I turned. Karen was in the doorway, snow still dusting the shoulders of her parka, stocking hat over her hair. Her beautiful mouth moved, but no sound came out. How much had she heard?

She said, "Don't worry. I sent him away before we got inside."

And then, in a very quiet voice, "Rabies?"

I slumped. "Yes. But they won't believe it yet."

She took a step into the room, which seemed smaller suddenly. "Infectious? Is that possible?"

"We don't know."

She nodded. "You said you wanted them to seal the town, quarantine everyone."

"Yes, until we know for sure, because . . ." My mouth snapped shut and we stared at each other in bald understanding. I'd forgotten about her, forgotten, in the urgent moment, that I was talking not only about shutting in myself and strangers with death, but her, too. I felt sick. I'd seen my friends dead, heard the agony in the way they died—the pain, the terror. Then I'd asked . . . no, *demanded* that my superiors order the woman I loved shut in with a possible killer, intentional or accidental, either way.

I felt my face go hot, my mouth dry up.

"Got to take precautions," she said. She was a scientist. She understood. She meant it. But it wasn't the point just now. The point was, I'd forgotten her.

"I know."

"Can't have the thing spread, if you're right."

I could have said, *You weren't here, Karen.* I could have said, *I planned to tell you,* or, *There was no time to call.* But there had been time. I'd had over an hour to call. She'd been within phone reach all day.

I just said, "No."

"Want some tea? Mikael got a package from his boys at HBO, from Zabar's," she said. "Russian tea. New York sesame bagels, chorizo sausages, and cheese, air-dropped supply."

Tea! I suppose that every couple have their trigger words, which, when said, raise the alert level to DEFCON two. My first wife used to say, *take a nap* when something bothered her. My mother preferred, *bake pies.* My father opted for, *couple of cold ones.* I glanced at the thermostat, set at sixty-seven. But the room had gone chillier.

"Sure," I said, hoping that what had just happened would have limited consequences. Joe Rush, great at professional problems. There's nothing like ignoring personal ones, hoping they'll go away.

Why do I screw up every relationship?

The tea tasted odd, metallic, *wrong*, but I attributed that to the acid surging out of my stomach. The bitter taste went down and came back as harsh bile. She cut up the chorizo. We sat snacking silently on Mikael's gift. The TV went on—I wanted sound—and an announcer out of Anchorage said something about a dispute in the Bering Strait between Russia and America, the Russians wanting to move the border—which has never been nailed down—to give them more space. *"Sources inside the State Department confirmed that the Russians offered a trade, they will back off on the Ukraine if Washington agrees to a small shift in the Arctic."*

"Everybody wants a bigger piece," Karen said at length, chewing. So we were both going to ignore it.

Ignore threats and they come back.

But it was easy to ignore this particular threat that night because an hour later my phone rang and Merlin told me that a sixth case had shown up at the hospital. It was a child this time, a six-year-old, the son of one of the Cambodian taxi drivers. The boy had been complaining of a headache for two days. Now he was vomiting, running a high fever, and he was losing feeling in his right hand.

Seven hours later, he died.

EDDIE, RANJAY, AND I SAT IN THE MAYOR'S OFFICE WITH MERLIN, in Borough Hall, a new comfortable building built with oil tax money. Exhibits—artifacts and photos of Eskimo dances, or bowheads—were displayed on walls or in glass cases inside the bright atrium. I'd been ordered to downplay rabies. I'd been threatened with arrest if I disobeyed. My intestines burned as Ranjay filled his bosses in on the medical situation.

Ranjay seemed relieved that the CDC believed that our tests had been flawed. He wanted to believe that the rabies was a false alarm. When the mayor asked me if I agreed with the CDC opinion, my words came out in my normal voice, but I was surprised that my throat didn't cut them off.

"CDC has a pretty good record," I said.

Sengupta nodded, admirably devoid of ego. "If the CDC believes we made an error, that is good enough for me."

At least the mayor followed our recommendations to cut down on panic or illness. Schools closed due to *flu*. Pets that have not been vaccinated to be inoculated at the vets for standard diseases: distemper, animal flu, rabies. *Wash your hands more. Cover your mouths when coughing. There is illness in Barrow,* the mayor told the North Slope's eight villages, over the radio that night.

And we waited.

Sixteen hours later, two CDC experts got off the morning 737 from Anchorage, looking young and concerned, advising Eddie and I to steer clear of the labs as they worked. They seemed certain before they started that their tests for rabies would turn out negative.

Another day passed before they knew they were wrong.

"You seem to have been correct, Colonel," Dr. Rudolph Gaines told us, stiffly, on the next conference call. "I am now suggesting, one and all, that we recommend to the president that he proclaim Barrow the nation's first protocol four."

ELEVEN

Thirty-six hundred miles from Barrow, Alaska, the angry man sat in the second-floor study of his luxurious, log-sided country home, on a forested three-thousand-acre mountain property, watching Quonset hut one in Alaska via satellite. It was a crystal-clear view right down to magnified fresh polar bear tracks crossing the base; stars out, new snow reflecting prisms of light between huts. He saw the curving roof beneath which his two operatives sat, their voices encrypted and distorted so that any listener—if they'd managed to break in—would not know if men or women spoke.

The first voice, even modified, came across as tentative, fearful, tailing into a soft *wooooo*. "If it wasn't for Rush, they would have called the first deaths a shooting. They wouldn't have found rabies. It's not fair!"

A fire roared in the big room, smelling of hot, popping

resin. The angry man was fortyish, with a cherub's pudgy cheeks and body, sloped shoulders, and thick chestnut hair. Black eyes. Soft mouth. Soft hands. Red silk robe. The plainest face in the world. Natural camouflage. Because of this mild appearance he'd been underestimated his whole life. Because of his intelligence, he'd used that to his advantage.

The second voice in his ear was lower, a rumble rising to an opera soprano's note, earsplitting over the screwed-up sound system. "If you would have let me infect him at the beginning, this wouldn't have happened-d-d-d-d."

"It's not my fault . . . ault . . ." the first voice whined.

"Nothing ever is." The second voice remained calm. It was the voice of a professional chewing over a problem. "The quarantine starts in an hour. Whatever we decide, it has to happen now."

The angry man curbed his rage. He demanded of his listeners, "You understand what's at stake?"

No answer! Had the satellite spun beyond range? The man was almost apoplectic. Had his communication system failed? No . . . no . . . just a delay, a traffic interruption above Earth, where messages whizzed through space; a phone scammer in Mumbai, tricking a retiree in Florida; a Chinese destroyer receiving orders as the ship maneuvered off the Philippines; a diplomat in Tokyo whispering endearments to a lover in Havana.

The first voice was back. "At stake? Many millions."

"Millions? *Billions!* We're on a deadline! You made a promise! You assured me!"

The roaring fire illuminated original oil paintings;

American West motif, Remington buffalos, Bierstadt Yosemite, flatboat river men. The desk was Zairian mahogany, the carpet Italian, the rugs from Iran. A wall of leather-bound books featured works on strategy, military, and finance. Beyond open silk curtains, floodlights illuminated a crushed stone driveway, an armored Mercedes, and a private forest of pine and birch, the leaves brittle in October. Down the hall slept the angry man's twenty-seven-year-old *trophy wife* . . . He'd heard older, jealous wives of colleagues whisper that term at last night's cocktail party in the capital, a ninety-minute drive from here.

Stupid women go dry, lose the urge to have sex at forty and then blame men for getting it elsewhere. Now I understand why Moslem men have five wives.

The second voice—the professional—said, "He's with his fiancée now, asleep. We hear their breathing. I know the combination of the lock on their door and—"

The first voice cut off the second. "Are you crazy? That would focus everything on *what he's saying*. And you'd leave tracks in the snow!"

The angry man tried to ignore electronic interference, earsplitting over the German-made speakers, fucking things were supposed to be the best in the world. Krauts, he thought. They killed my great-grandfather.

He spat out rapid questions.

"You said he shares ideas with the fiancée?"

"Last night he told her what he wants to do next. They both know the idea. He's figuring it out!"

"That major, Nakamura, does he know, too?"

"He's been out at the campsite for the last day. He's

not aware of what Rush wants to try. And, sir, once the quarantine starts, it will be much harder to get to him. They'll be bunking soldiers in all the huts."

The angry man tried to ignore the hot sensation coursing through him; throat dry, fists clenched, temples throbbing—and he had an idea. "If you can't reach him, what about *her*? Is Rush the kind who would lose focus? Fall apart? Or come at things harder?"

"He's crazy about her. That's for sure."

"That's not an answer."

"I'm not a mind reader, sir."

"You will stop him or distract him! Do you hear!"

The angry man had grown up on the streets and learned early; when you have an enemy you hit hard, right away, with all you have. You don't strategize or negotiate. You don't whine. You don't allow a modicum of thought in the foe as to the possibility of equality between you. But he'd permitted himself to start slowly in Barrow—and it had come back to haunt him. So he explained what he wanted now and the professional went quiet. The angry man heard: *Weeeee.* Then the pro said with some delicacy, negotiating, taking advantage, "Sir, once the quarantine begins, I'm stuck here."

"Double."

"Stuck with soldiers. No way out."

"Triple."

"If I get caught?"

"You're supposed to be good."

"Even the best get caught if you wait too long."

The angry man swallowed the insult. His voice softened considerably. This was a tell. Anyone who knew him understood that you did not want his voice to go mild. It meant he'd left the red zone, where he generally resided, and entered a worse one, purple alert, DEFCON one.

"If you're caught, I can probably get you out at some point," he said.

"Even from military prison?"

"I said, *at some point*. But if you feel like you need to refuse, I understand."

"I'll do it," the professional said quickly, understanding that he had pushed things too far.

The angry man slammed the phone down, stomped down the hall to his dozing wife. *Fucking bitch would sleep through a bomb.* Action usually made him feel better. He dragged her awake by her long blond hair. She'd not seen this rough side of him yet and she started screaming, which excited him, so he hit her a couple of times, but not in the face. Hell, she wanted money to shop every day? The art galleries? The vacations? Fine. He'd bought her, so to speak, and he'd get what he wanted now.

THE NIGHTMARE STARTED THE USUAL WAY BUT THEN THE FACES changed. I was in a tunnel carved into a cave, its high ceiling shielded by steel netting strung up top to contain— rock. I stepped forward, hyperaware, carbine in hands. I had trouble drawing in air because of the protective mask over my face and the heat in my ears, in my throat. My Marine squad advanced behind me, down, down, in hell's direction. Blue smoke curled from air vents in rock.

Alarms screeched. The cave exited into a hallway. The hallway had a lab. Inside were medical cabinets. Surgical instruments. Steel manacles fixed to operating tables. No people at first . . . but then . . .

Then the child-sized figure charged out of the smoke.

Iraq. In memory. Eddie and I were first lieutenants, dispatched from the main thrust of invasion, patrolling outlying villages, making sure they were clear of ambushers. We found nothing until our Humvees and armored carrier stumbled onto a brand-new highway in the middle of nowhere. It led to a ratty abandoned village, except, when we entered the huts, we found they were mock-ups, a false town, a trick to fool reconnaisance. In one hut we found an iron door set into the rocky side of a mountain. We blew open the iron door. It led down into the cave.

That brought us to Saddam's hidden lab.

As the child form rushed at me, through dream smoke, I knew what was coming next and I filled with dread. The dream came sporadically. That day changed my life and sent Eddie and me to med school on the Marine dime, made us hunters of different kinds of deadly weapons, the kind you can't see, that float in air, seep into lungs, take a healthy person and twist them into a shrieking, burned-up furnace. That rewires evolution and turns ten million years of anatomical progress into a contagious degenerating mush.

The figures that usually burst through the smoke in my dream were monkeys, with pink faces and pink hands, as they'd had on that day in real life. Infected monkeys. But tonight they had human faces. I saw Kelley and Ted, Cathy and Clay, furried bodies, friends' eyes, and the alarms ringing, as they shrieked like animals, rushing to attack.

My hands rose by themselves. I squeezed the trigger. I screamed as bullets made my friends dance and fall back, their furry chests blossoming red.

"Joe! Get up!" Karen was shaking me.

I opened my eyes.

The red digits on the nightstand read 3:50 A.M.

"Christ." My body was soaked with sweat, and I smelled ammonia. Sweat. Nightmare. Me.

"The dream, right, honey? The monkeys?"

She'd been with me once before when it happened, on a vacation. Now I lay inside a cone of night-table light. I still saw Kelley's face, blowing apart. I went into the bathroom and washed my face, looked at myself in the mirror. Did the light bother me? Did it hurt? I saw blanched skin, saw a man who had just shot his friends. A man who had not answered his phone when Kelley tried to reach him.

"Why them?" I asked when I came out. Rhetorical question. Either Karen or I uttered these words ten times a day.

"It's not your fault, Joe. If you'd answered that phone, nothing would be different."

"People have dreams for reasons."

"Joe. You take things on. That's the reason."

"Maybe. Okay. I do. But maybe there's more. Maybe we've all been trying to figure this out the wrong way."

Wide awake now, we weren't going back to sleep. She looked for the coffee in the kitchenette. "Meaning what?"

I sat at our little table and saw the white wall as a blank canvas and filled it with the dream to help me think. Dreams are clues. They're always clues of *something*. The problem is figuring out what they mean. You think a dream means you should quit your job. But it means you should divorce your wife. You think a dream means you need to see the dentist. But deep inside, where you don't want to look, you fear you have cancer.

"Karen, I said it last night. What if Clay Qaqulik was right from the beginning? What if this all goes back to someone trying to stop the Harmons' work?"

She had a lovely frown, the way it deepened the gray in her eyes, softened it, added amber. Intensity became her. When you're in love, even musculature becomes mystery, even at moments like these. "Joe, you're thinking that someone infected them on purpose?"

"I'm just saying, maybe the way to crack this isn't to track the outbreak, or analyze the bug. We go back to Clay. Restart *his* investigation. See? And we finish what Ted and Cathy started, do their work, complete their project. Maybe there's a consequence of their work that no one is seeing. If you understand the consequence, you understand what is going on."

Her silver hair swooshed back and forth. "Algae? How would algae relate? Anyway, if it was intentional, murder, why kill people in town, too, who had nothing to do with the Harmons? Who didn't even know the Harmons? Joe, you're overthinking."

"If it's contagious, it got out after."

"Murder, Joe? Listen to what you're saying!"

"People have been trying to weaponize rabies for three hundred years."

"You're still halfway in your dream, Joe."

"Good. Helps me think."

"But why murder someone by using rabies?"

"*Because no one would think it was intentional.* Look, maybe it's not contagious. Contagious is logical, but it's also possible that someone wants it to look that way! See what I mean? So many explanations are still possible."

"You're doing mind tricks on yourself."

"All the time."

"Give yourself time to wake up."

"I'm up. That's the point."

She cocked her head. She smiled, but not with humor. "Well, Colonel, this would be one hell of a time to decide it's *not* contagious. Listen!"

I heard the droning—the big engines and propellers overhead—and went still. I moved the curtain aside, looked out. Was someone there, walking toward our hut in the snow?

No. My vision must have played a trick on me. No one was there. Lights flicked on in the Longhorn hut.

I looked up. The C-130 troop carriers, blotting out constellations, looked fearsome. Karen switched on the TV. I saw snow on screen and heard static. The satellite embargo must have begun. Barrow was closed off.

"You don't look surprised. So you knew, too," Karen said, and sighed. "I figured you knew. They might need me on the sub. They called last night."

We stared at each other. I'd been warned not to tell

her by Wayne Homza. She'd been warned not to tell me by Electric Boat. So at precisely the moment when man and woman need each other, probably reached for each other across the city, we'd been told to shut out our partners, to link ourselves to duty over love.

We dressed swiftly, warmly. The thermometer outside read twenty-seven degrees. A dusting of snow covered the base, and parachutes bloomed above. We took go-cups filled with hot, sugar-sweetened Folgers.

I started up the Ford, the heater roaring, Karen snug beside me. Our pathetic rebellion against the government. No using seat belts today. Mikael Grandy and Dr. Alan McDougal were exiting their huts, too. They looked up at the sky.

"Someone should have told Merlin. Or the mayor," Karen said.

At four A.M., a few people were up normally, restaurant owners heading out to prepare breakfasts, hunters getting an early start on the day. More lights flickered in homes as we bounced toward the airport. People emerging from houses, staring at the sky, not yet understanding. Lights glowed inside the police station, where detectives on tonight's rotation probably stared at corkboards, at results of investigation that had left us helpless; lines of infection stretching from homes to garages to airport; as we interviewed family, friends, and neighbors, filling in schedules, looking for intersection points, checking refrigerators for similar products, testing blood.

"No roads out of Barrow, but anyone could leave by snowmobile or SUV, use their GPS, and hit the tundra,"

Karen said. Which was why the Rangers would cordon the town.

The world closing in. We rounded a corner and saw, in an efficient show of force, at sea, the U.S.'s sole working icebreaker, the Coast Guard's *Wilmington*. And the nuclear sub, the *Virginia*, a dark moray eel shape, risen through light slush. Barrow had no harbor. Neither ship would land.

Karen said, "The *Wilmington*'s got a chopper, and Coast Guard snipers. The *Virginia*, drones. I'm on call if they have problems. They're to block offshore."

"Thirty-six wasted hours," I said, remembering General Homza telling me on the phone. *I'll head the task force, personally. When we land, I'll call you. Stay put.*

Great. Can't wait.

An hour later, Karen and I—in the crowd at the airport—watched white parka–clad troops hemming us in, as efficient as hindsight. I thought, *A day and a half of passengers scattering from Barrow across Earth, while the CDC people ran tests, gasped over the results. Refused at first to believe that rabies killed five . . . And now, nine.*

Eddie—back from the field—pushed through the crowd, stood beside us, and put it more graphically. "Idiots."

The Rangers moved efficiently as the crowd grew more agitated. On the tundra, the last few feet of open view was sealed off by concertina wire—a razor wall. Oh, the city had known that rabies was loose. They'd been alerted by the mayor and Ranjay. But they'd been given an impression that the danger was smaller. They'd been told to watch for sick animals, to make sure their pets were inoculated. They'd not been told that rabies may have assumed a new form.

Now the mayor looked like a fool before his own people. He was angry and—like anyone with family here—afraid.

Rangers moved onlookers back, maintaining a thirty-foot buffer area inside the wire. In the airport they'd be double-checking hangars and offices. Our old Navy base to the north would return to its original function, housing military personnel. The huts were being gas-bombed right now, to kill germs. No one was allowed back in for the next few hours.

In quarantine drills I'd practiced, soldiers set up tent cities outside the infected area. Impossible here. Too cold. In drills, supplies arrived on roads. Here there were none. In drills, medicine worked. And these troops had been vaccinated, but if we faced a new strain, we all risked infection. There were no good choices, I thought. Only degrees of danger.

Standing atop the bank building, as Karen, Eddie, and I did with Merlin and the mayor ten minutes later, we got a complete view as Hercules aircraft disgorged more Humvees, .50-caliber machine guns on top, beginning patrols along the perimeter. Rangers toting M4 carbines stood on higher rooftops, setting up terrestrial jammers.

"Full cooperation from communication companies," Eddie said. "As pre-agreed for in a protocol four event."

No cell-phone calls or YouTube presentations would be leaving Barrow to go viral. No chance of millions of people in Moscow, Tehran, Beijing, and Mexico City watching minute-by-minute panic: *American town quarantined!*

The crowd continued to swell.

Guards opened a gap in the wire and a lone Humvee drove inside. A single officer got out and climbed onto the vehicle's hood to face the crowd, now easily more than a thousand people.

"Major General Wayne Homza," Karen said.

From a distance, he looked shorter, bullish, but size meant nothing. His voice was deep and resonant, containing the right mix of authority and respect for the audience. His posture was as straight in person as on screen. I liked that he exposed himself. My respect rose a notch. I hoped he was more than just a self-serving featherweight attack dog. I saw formidability. He'd need flexibility as well.

He announced, voice clear in the silence, "We're handing out free surgical masks and rubber gloves for anyone who wants them. Go home. Stay calm. Food will be distributed. Doctors will be at the hospital. Anyone experiencing headaches or fever, please go to the emergency room, at no charge.

"In one hour I will meet with you at the high school. It's too cold for all of us to stand around out here. I will answer all questions. We'll talk, calmly and rationally. One hour."

A man's voice cried out from the crowd, clear to us on the roof. "We need to hunt the bowheads now! They are here."

"Sorry, sir. No boats going out."

I recognized the man as a whaling captain. "We promise to come back. We need to hunt before they pass!"

Homza nodded sympathetically, but answered, firmly, "We will supply all the food you need."

"I don't want *your* food."

"Sir, I'm not partial to Army food, either, half the time." He smiled. "But we'll make do for the time being. For safety."

"Ours? Or yours? Once the whales pass they are gone until spring."

The mayor turned to me speculatively. I'd dreaded this moment. Protocol four calls for local authorities to be notified before quarantine, but Washington had decided that an unannounced arrival would be best in this case. I'd argued over it. I'd said, "General, if the town was New York, would you keep people in the dark?"

"I won't honor that insult with an answer."

Merlin asked me now, "Joe, did you know about this?"

"Yes."

"And you didn't tell us."

"No."

Eddie looked from my face to Merlin's. "He was ordered not to. He was threatened."

The mayor made a disgusted sound, spun on his insulated boots, and headed for the rooftop doorway. Merlin looked sad. "Who's side are you on, Joe?"

Eddie said. "You know the answer. Uno, tell him. Say something, man!"

Karen said, "How can you ask that, Merlin?"

The point was, I hadn't told them.

Merlin turned to leave.

PANIC RIPPED THROUGH THE HIGH SCHOOL AUDITORIUM.

Classes were suspended: No gatherings of more than five to form in public for the time being, General Homza said, but since there had been no advance warning of the quarantine, the auditorium was filled with one last community meeting, people who wanted answers; angry, yelling, fearful parents, whole families, old and young, everyone shouting at the same time:

—Why are troops here?

—This is the United States of America! You can't do this to us!

—You're treating us like criminals!

—We are French tourists. You must let us go!

The big room seemed smaller, and I could sense that razor wire outside, a half mile off, as if it had drawn town boundaries in, constricted even the air supply. A half dozen Rangers stood in front of the stage like security guards at a rock concert, hands at belts, sidearms conspicuous, but no M4s in sight. Gutsy call, General.

Karen whispered, "In this town there are probably as many firearms as people."

On stage, Homza, floodlit, looked out at the standing-room crowd, people shoulder to shoulder, packing exit doors, sitting on steps, in aisles, spilling out into hallways, glued to intercom boxes overhead. More like firewood waiting to ignite than people. A cross-section of America: Eskimos and whites, blacks, Samoans, Cambodians, Pakistanis. I saw elders with walkers, guaranteed front row seats. I saw community college students. The handful of neighbors from the base were grouped together.

I saw, in all eyes, fear.

"I am Major General Wayne Homza, heading the task force charged with protecting you, and keeping any disease here from spreading. You're afraid, I know. Angry that we've shut you in. I'd feel the same way. It's no fun to make sacrifices. God chooses us for different challenges and gave this one to you. But by keeping whatever has happened here local, we may save lives. Yours. And others."

The president, I knew, would probably be on TV, telling the nation that a U.S. town had been quarantined, *"An unprecedented act for the safety of its citizens and all villages on the North Slope."* That hopefully the situation would be temporary. The rabies would disappear. That the disease might not be contagious. That nations that had received travelers from Barrow had been notified. That his difficult decision had been based on a CDC recommendation to protect four hundred million Americans. That his heart was heavy.

The general acted more diplomatically with civilians than I'd thought him capable. He said, "I hope that we will, together, defeat a danger. I've brought along top epidemiologists to pinpoint the illness's origin. And special agents from the Army's investigative units to coordinate the investigation with your officials, determine whether a crime or terrorist attack has occurred."

Eddie whispered, "Coordinate? Or take over?"

Homza was no fool. Safety aside, he had to realize that the outcome of this quarantine would determine his professional future. The last thing he needed was a riot. He said, "I want our stay to be brief. We will do everything possible to make you comfortable. I will take questions now. Please line up at the microphone and identify yourself before speaking. Remember, our precautions are for your own good."

"No, they are for *your* good. Martha Nukinek died yesterday and my neighbor, Mr. Kunisakera, is in the hospital," said the first questioner, a slim woman with a moon face, long black hair, and wearing a thigh-length snow shirt. She carried her infant in a sling.

The general nodded sympathetically. "No one wants this thing to spread. You must see that."

"Don't tell me what I must do! You people have wanted to kill us ever since you tried to blow up Point Hope."

The place erupted with shouting.

"Why can't I use my cell phone!"

"You're working for the oil companies!"

Homza, by the fifth question, was drowned out. What would he do? He was used to people following his orders. I saw him pause, unrattled. His eyes calmly found me, third row up, right side. He'd known I was there all along, I realized. His head flicked. It was a summons.

"I'm going to have someone who many of you know up here," he said. "Many of you remember Colonel Rush, who was here once before, when he stopped another outbreak."

He waited for me like a master calls a dog. A dog told to "shut up" one minute and to "speak" the next. A dog threatened with a cell if he disobeyed. He shook my hand when I reached the stage, so the crowd would see friendship; I felt the hard grip, saw the challenge in his eye. He said, "You know what to do. You know these people."

He meant, *Are you one of us? Prove I can trust you.*

I looked down from the stage, beyond the guards, at a handful of supportive faces; Merlin, shrewd, Karen, nodding as if to say, *You'll do the right thing,* then turning to scan the crowd with a fierce, protective attitude that sent a bolt of love into my heart. *That's my man up there! I'll kill anyone who harms him!* I saw a flash of red hair and a beautiful face: Tilda Swann taking phone videos. She couldn't broadcast them yet but she was making a record.

Mostly I saw lots of strangers, ready to erupt.

"Some of you know me. I'm Colonel Joseph Rush. I'll answer your questions. But, please, one at a time."

"What kind of doctor are you anyway?" demanded a professor from the community college.

"I work in a toxics and disease unit. Public safety."

"What experiments have you done on rabies?" asked a part-time worker at the oil field at Prudhoe Bay.

"None, ma'am. My partner and I have been up here all summer, studying microbes. Standard study."

Tilda Swann pushed her way to the front row, and held up her phone. Mikael Grandy in back, filmed also, looked excited. Happy. *What a great story!* He panned the crowd. He pushed his way down the aisle, lens on Karen, as the night manager at the elders home screamed at me, "You gave people this disease!"

"Sir, that isn't true."

At the mike stood a huge Samoan, the high school football coach, shirt hanging loose, rolls on his chin; I knew him vaguely from Saturday morning basketball . . . skins against shirts . . . scientists teamed with locals. His family of five boys stood beside him as he barked: "I heard that you soldiers got vaccinated but there's no serum for our kids?"

I was ordered to take it. Essential personnel need it, they said. If you get sick, no one can do the work.

I explained, calmly, "Anyone who came in contact with victims will receive preventative inoculations. That includes nurses and families of detectives working the case." *Locals, not just outsiders.* I saw sporadic nodding in the audience. I said, "Also Dr. Bruce Friday, who was sprayed with saliva while rushing a man to the hospital."

The coach insisted, "Why can't we all get it?"

Because there's not enough to go around.

"We'll be flying up additional serum," I said, hating being the one to explain the too-late policy. "If you have been in contact with a sick person, if you have exchanged fluids with them, saliva, liquids, you are top priority for the next round."

But if more symptoms appear, or if the disease is fast spreading, it will be too late for you.

The next questioner was one of the younger whaling captains, maybe thirty-nine years old. He said, "I heard that Longhorn North flew medicine in for *their* people. They get special treatment! They're not essential personnel!"

"That just is not true, sir."

What is true, though, is that they're going to fly in vaccine. A private supply, that the company bought. How the hell did people here find that out already? The Longhorn people will receive standard inoculations for people who may have already been infected; one rabies shot on the first day, plus a dose of immune-globulin, then three more shots scheduled on the third, seventh and fourteenth days, a painful process guaranteed to stop rabies . . . unless this is a resistant strain.

A middle-aged woman—lawyer, for the borough— took the mike. "I heard there are three thousand doses stored at the airport, and you refuse to release them!"

"Ma'am, that rumor is just not true."

I saw Karen straighten up, turn, and begin pushing her way up the aisle, toward the exit.

Is she leaving? Why would she—

Karen suddenly stopped and doubled over, coughing.

Oh no. Nonononononono!!!

I'd missed a question. The speaker was the clerk at the liquor shack by the airport, a spare, serious young man with dark-framed glasses and a wisp of scraggly beard. "Why can't you use all the vaccine you have on kids and elders!"

Karen straightened, caught her breath, went out.

People nodded at the question. But the answer—if I voiced it—would trigger an explosion. *It's worse than you think. There aren't enough doses for all of you in the whole country. The best we could do was to fly in a lousy one hundred and twelve doses. We're scrounging for more.*

God help us if an inoculated person comes down with it.

Merlin suddenly stood beside me. He put his meaty arm over my shoulder, claiming friendship, which was no small thing. He reminded the town that Eddie and I helped save everyone here a year ago, when we stopped an outbreak on a ship offshore. He said that "his friend" Colonel Rush had cooperated with the police from the beginning, that I was the one who had identified the disease in the first place. He told them that without my input, the disease might not have been identified at all.

The screaming subsided to a low, angry rumble. Merlin and I moved offstage, surrendering the limelight back to Wayne Homza. The general squeezed my shoulder and nodded at me as we passed, playing to the crowd. His crisp uniform smelled of pipe tobacco, and close up, his eyes were neutral, light gray, and intelligent. "Stay here till the meeting is over. Research center. One hour."

The audience had calmed a trifle, but that trifle made a difference. Homza began answering questions again.

"I saved your ass there, Joe," Merlin said.

"I know." *Where's Karen?*

"Tell me now, Joe. Push comes to shove, can I depend on you? If I can't, I don't want you near me. I don't want you fucking my investigation. You're in the middle. I get it. But don't lie to me again."

In the pause before I replied, I flashed to the prison at Leavenworth, Kansas, where Eddie and I had once interviewed a U.S. Army private—Horace L. Scruggs—disgruntled kid from Tampa—a pimply beanpole with a low IQ, sentenced to forty years for sending anthrax through the mail to the vice president. I saw the kid's cramped cell, his moist, concrete world. I heard the echoing bootfalls outside, a drum that never stopped. I smelled steamed beef and Lysol and a rank, perpetual chill, alive as memory. In Leavenworth, time is geology. The institution is a steel casket for people who remain alive.

Screw around with me, I'll put you in Leavenworth, Wayne Homza had said.

"I promise," I said.

I thought, *Why did I say that?*

THE LAST QUESTION CAME FROM A HALF-BENT ELDER SUPporting himself with palsied hands on the shoulders of a teenage girl, granddaughter, probably. A sickle-shaped, white-haired man in a white anorak. His voice wavered but he not was not weak, mentally. He'd seen trucks passing the old folks' home, slatted ones filled with children, he said, because their small pink hands had been visible, fingers on wood, little pink fingers in the cold.

"What are you doing with these children?"

The stunned audience fell silent. Perhaps elsewhere they would have discounted the question. But this man had been a respected community leader. He was not senile. I saw that many people here were prepared to believe that the Rangers would have actually been transporting innocent children into a disease area. It did not bode well.

Homza answered smoothly. "Yes, sir. Trucks. But those were not children inside, but monkeys we've brought for lab purposes. Our doctors will be working round the clock to defeat the sickness. These creatures will help."

He was interrupted by the strident, British-accented voice of Tilda Swann. "Torturing innocent animals!"

It was so irrelevant that it killed some tension, even made one person laugh out loud. The meeting ended. The crowd headed for the exits, talking loudly, a mix of rage, fear, hope, argument. At least, for the moment, dispersing.

Outside, a parking lot, as in any high school. Cars and SUVs lined up at exits, orderly, taking families home, as if they were leaving a basketball game, a PTA meeting.

I kept remembering Karen, coughing. I needed to know where she was. My heart pounded with fear for her. I pulled out my cell phone but the jammers stopped it from working. There was a landline inside the school, in the office. Long distance calls were out but maybe local lines functioned. I could try the base. Or the hospital, where I hoped she had not gone.

But will there even be anyone at the base, or are they gas bombing the place, disinfecting?

The hallways were deserted. I heard my boots echo as I hurried toward the office. I was so worried about Karen that my defensive instincts weren't working. I only heard the other footfalls, the running ones, at the last minute.

I whirled. It was one of Homza's Rangers, a guard who'd stood beneath the stage while he spoke. Hispanic guy. I relaxed, but tensed up when I saw his eyes. He was wary of me.

"The general said to get you, sir. Now."

"After I make a quick call, Sergeant. One minute."

"The general said you are to come immediately. The general said if you resist, to restrain you, sir."

"What . . . *restrain me?*"

"Please come along. Now."

The phone inside that glass office was only ten feet away. I wanted to make sure she was all right. But a second Ranger appeared. It was clear that only one course of action would be permitted. The first guy had his hand on his sidearm. No phone call for me, not now. I went with them, praying inwardly, *Let her not be sick.*

TWELVE

Karen Vleska was getting puzzled, sitting in the passenger seat of the late-model Subaru Outback, bumping out of the main part of town, off the grid of gravel streets, onto side roads crossing onto tundra. The Subaru headed south, toward the gas pipeline and pump building and the lines raised above the permafrost. Everything she saw was inside the wire perimeter that the Rangers were setting up.

I hope that Alice Aghokeak isn't sick with rabies, like Bruce said!

A few sporadic homes here, maybe one every half mile, in Barrow's outlying area. One-story shacks with lots of space between them. The Subaru had good snow tires and she heard the crunch of gravel and crushed snow.

"Bruce, why is she here?"

"She lives out here, has a little house."

At the wheel, Dr. Bruce Friday hunched forward, in the posture of a perpetually bad driver, but as usual, although he looked incompetent, he fared well. Both gloved hands gripped the weathered wheel. His battered vehicle had served him for years, and smelled of blooded meat and preservative chemicals and ketchup and cheap cold cuts.

The radio—which normally worked—was out, a victim of Ranger jammers.

With basically the entire town at the high school, they passed no other vehicles. The sky was overcast, typical for autumn, with a seasonal blanket of gray fog. Bruce seemed nervous, but considering what he'd said while convincing her to come here with him, that made sense.

"Alice said she was sick. She hates hospitals. She said you've been nice to her. She'll only talk to you."

"Symptoms, Bruce?"

"She can't feel her hands. I couldn't get her to go to the doctor!"

"You should have made her go."

"How? Ha! She's 180 pounds, and she's mad."

"My God. Does she have fever?"

"Yes. High fever."

"How does she sound?"

"Sound?" He seemed to think about it. "She made— at first I thought she was coughing—grunting noises."

"Joe has a theory that it may not even be contagious."

"That's crazy! Then how could it be spreading?" Friday said. He sounded almost offended by Joe's idea.

"That's what I said."

Back at the school, Karen had suddenly felt nauseous

during Joe's speech. It was probably her period coming on, dizziness, bad cramps as always, so she'd headed out toward the bathroom, run into Bruce in the deserted hall. He'd hurried her out of there after the dizziness passed. She'd seen no one else in the parking lot. "Alice Aghokeak's running a 102 fever," he'd said.

"Why ask for me, Bruce?"

"People trust you."

"Let's find Ranjay, take him, too."

"Ranjay's busy at the hospital."

"You're a good person, Bruce," Karen said now.

She picked up her cell phone to call Joe, let him know where she was, and then remembered that the jammers would block communication. She'd tell Joe later. She'd seen Joe freeze onstage when she started coughing. He'd be worried. He'd think she was ill. But he'd understand why she had to leave. Bruce's urgency was infectious. Something off with the whole scene but with all the craziness, there was no time to analyze that. Some fraction of her mind thinking, *Why had Bruce been with Alice to start with, and not at the high school with everyone else?*

Karen remembered Alice from the Barrow dance group: a lightbulb-shaped, forty-year-old, overweight woman who never stopped shoving Sailor Boy Pilot Bread into her mouth during breaks. And yet, on the floor, with twenty hand drums beating, with her thick, fur dance mitts on, she looked so feminine, a flower stalk in wind, a young girl, a virginal presence in the "Newlywed Dance."

The road dipped slightly, passed into a shallow tundra bowl. She could no longer see the town or the specks of soldiers a half mile off. Ever since Calvin DeRochers had told her about diamond finds and meteor strikes, she saw tundra lakes and depressions in a different way; wondered if embedded in the permafrost down there was, as Calvin insisted, a fortune find rivaling South Africa's or Arctic Canada's in wealth.

Calvin was always going on about meteors, slamming into Earth eons ago. The impacts like an infusion of microbes. Vaccination from space. Microbes that could alter rock. It would be funny if he was right, she thought. It would be *fair* for the driven Arkansas man to emerge from the Arctic as a gem millionaire. For a moment she flashed to Calvin. His charts. His talks. His theories. Calvin going on about the vast tundra here *seeming* as unimportant to the rest of the U.S. as, say, Saudi Arabia was in 1900. A wasteland. An icebox. But Karen knew from briefings and after her short time in the High North that the world was pivoting here. All the upcoming war games, the oil, the planning, all of Joe's frustration went to that fact.

She went back to what Joe had said this morning, after his nightmare. *What if all this sickness somehow goes back to someone trying to stop the Harmon project?*

Bruce Friday slid the Outback to a halt beside the north side of a dilapidated one-story wooden house, completely cutting off her view of the soldiers. No smoke rose from the pipe chimney. The roof canted sideways. The walls seemed sucked in and the *cunnychuck* door, the outer entrance to the house, was secured by a clothesline strung between the knob hole and the shadows inside.

"Bruce, there's no truck or snowmobile here. Maybe Alice left."

"Her son dropped her off here. She's inside, all right."

There were no footprints in the snow, either, she thought walking toward the frigid-looking building, but then again, the sandlike snow was so granular that the slightest breeze shifted it and covered up footsteps in a minute. Still, no dog tracks. No caribou hides strung in the backyard. No hunting equipment. Nothing usable in view.

"Looks deserted, Bruce."

"She'll freeze in there. Hurry."

She followed Bruce through the *cunnychuck* and into the living room. She stopped dead, her logical side needing a moment to catch up with her expectations of what she was supposed to see. The place was deserted. It *smelled* long deserted. It smelled like it had not been heated in months. Like even ghosts had left. There was no furniture. Karen called out, "Alice?" as if some voice might answer and dispel reality. Karen turned and saw fresh red paint dripping down a living room wall.

MURDERER MARINES!

YOU KILL OUR LOVED ONES! NOW WE KILL YOURS!

She was so taken aback that she froze, said, "Bruce? What?" and only vaguely registered the quick movement behind her as the floor creaked and an arm circled her neck with shocking force, and she was lifted off the ground.

Bruce looking sad and sick, from five feet away. *Who*

is behind me? Karen fighting, trying to kick, claw, scream now, but the arm cut off her air. Karen thinking, *Kick a shin or instep. Stomp on that black boot!* Karen feeling something cold pinch the side of her throat, just a touch, and then the itchy cold sensation moved left to right and a hotness flooded her mouth and spread into her throat and the air was filled with reddish spray that fountained onto the scuffed white wall and beaded it and ran down the side like water.

She buckled.

Karen flopping like a fish. Karen clawing at her throat, unable to draw in air. Karen's elbows hammering on the floor, her boots pistons, working on their own, as the pool around her grew slicker and soaked into cracks in the floor, the old ship timbers transformed into a home, and then losing purpose yet again. Wreckage. Ghosts.

"You," she said. "Not . . ."

Only seconds had passed. Karen's life was running out. Bruce bent over her, looking disgusted but also fascinated, as if studying her. And then another face was there, too. Two faces.

Karen Vleska, scientist, explorer, scheduled focus of an upcoming HBO documentary on the opening Arctic, which would now be canceled. Karen dying, but not on an Arctic trek, the way the documentary would have suggested she might.

Her final emotions came wordlessly, as she looked up at the two faces.

Terror.

Surprise.

THIRTEEN

I'd expected a conference but got an inquisition.

The Rangers drove me to the lab building on the tundra, within view of troops positioned a few hundred yards off, beyond concertina wire. We removed our boots beneath the NO DIRTY FOOTWEAR! WARNING! AVOID LAB CONTAMINATION! sign. In a foyer, rows of metal racks held pairs of combat boots. Mud dried on the floor.

Despite the somber mood there was something silly about Rangers, M4s on backs, walking around in stocking feet.

The building had no elevator. The guards followed me up concrete stairs, and past a glassed-in conference room where, grouped around a long conference table, standing and arguing, were about ten soldiers and civilians. A diorama of confusion: Merlin and the mayor at the far end of the table, standing, arms crossed, as if to say, *We do not like what we're hearing.* A couple of Ranger officers poking something on the table, a map probably, and gesturing as if trying to convey orders. *This is what we want you locals to do.* The two CDC doctors watching, in an attitude of semi-helplessness. *We haven't found out anything yet that can help you.* I saw a naval officer. A couple of state public health officials. And a man and woman sitting together, in uniform, glancing up sharply to meet my gaze as I passed, giving me a look of interest and recognition. Army investigators maybe. *We've heard about you!*

But Homza wasn't there. The Rangers escorted me down the hall to the lab I shared with Eddie, where the general waited with a cute, gamine Asian woman, in her midthirties, in an Army sweater. Homza cradled a mug of steaming coffee. The woman sipped a Diet Pepsi from a can.

"This is Lieutenant Colonel Amanda Ng, who's running our special investigation unit," Homza said, his gray eyes probing. "She'll report directly to me twice a day. I report to the White House every six hours."

Both of them regarded me with a flat, appraising intensity bordering on suspicion. Their careers would be elevated or destroyed by what happened over the next few days. I was the bug under a microscope. They needed to know if I could hurt them or help.

Homza nodded at Ng. It meant, Go ahead.

Ng said, "I want straight answers, please. Did you have anything to do with the eruption of this outbreak?"

"What?" I was stunned.

"You were assigned to Alaska to seek out organisms

that might be harmful. You're dead center in this. Yes or no? Did this thing come from your work, your lab?"

"No, Colonel." I felt myself growing warm.

"Did you, at any time this summer, find what you were sent here to look for, illness resulting from a U.S. government program?"

"No." The warmth was turning to heat.

"Did you or Major Nakamura discover the existence of any prior testing program—directed by any branch of the armed forces—that may have caused this disease to erupt?"

Homza just watched and weighed. I said, "How can you ask that? We're the ones who reported the rabies."

"Which could mean you had prior knowledge," came the high, musical voice of Amanda Ng. "It could mean you're playing catch-up, minimizing damage."

"You're accusing us?" I asked, disgusted.

She shrugged. "Asking. I want to get to the bottom of this, as quickly as possible, and for this quarantine to end. I assume you do, too."

"No," I snapped. "I like it this way."

She turned to the general. She had a mildly exotic look. Her face was heart shaped, her nose and mouth small. She was well proportioned, her honey-colored skin glowed, and her hair, almost blue-black, was cut in a shag that brushed the nape of slender neck. Her eyes were burnished light, and seemed to catch the fluorescent laboratory glow. The Army sweater she wore had built-in patches on the shoulders, and was thickly knit. A gold cross hung from her neck.

"General," she said, shrugging, "Colonel Rush may well be telling the truth, but I still think he should be removed from any further investigation. That way, if he's culpable, he cannot impede work. We've got independent experts here from the CDC for disease tracking. My suggestion is to put him on the medical side. Use him as a doctor. Sideline him and Major Nakamura from our part; available, but out."

I smiled bitterly. "So far, your independent experts have missed half the clues, Colonel Ng."

The edge of the general's mouth twitched. He nodded at her, but to show that he heard, not necessarily that he agreed yet.

The general turned his gaze on me. "You've been part of cover-ups before," he said. "I've got your records now, all of them. Colonel Ng is familiar with them, too."

I knew what was coming next and felt sick. I was under orders not to discuss this with anyone. My orders had been clear when I was awarded the presidential medal by the last occupant of the White House, not the one who sat there now.

Never bring up what happened in Afghanistan.

I felt a tickling in my throat. In my head I saw a caravan of tarp-covered Army trucks driving toward a joint Army/Marine base in Asia. I saw the dust they threw up. I saw all the trucks but one pull to the side of the road when I ordered them to over the radio. I saw one truck race toward the concertina wire and sandbag gate, where I stood.

"You killed eight Marines, Colonel," Ng said.

My throat had gone dry. "Yes."

"You fired a .50-caliber gun at the truck, knowing full well that it was filled with fellow Marines."

"Yes. I blew that truck up."

"And the incident was covered up. Anything you want to explain?"

In my mind I smelled alkaline dust and oil fumes and the faint latrine/diesel odor of a tent camp filled with thousands of military personnel. I heard the driver of the approaching truck, a Moslem-American, a kid from the Midwest, a tortured and disappointed man who had sneaked chemical-packed oil drums into that truck, singing prayers over the radio. The Marines in back—who could not hear him—were returning from a humanitarian mission, a food drop at a refugee camp. They did not know that the driver was trying to ram the wire. The servicemen and women in the base didn't know they were being attacked. The guards were too stunned to fire. I leaped into their post and gripped the twin handles of the .50-caliber. The guards stared in horror. I watched the tracers arc into the hood of that truck, watched the canvas top engulf in flame. We felt the shock wave roll across the dun-colored desert, and watched the mustard-like gas cloud drift from the wreckage, reach a small flock of sheep, and their shepherd. They began to convulse, puke, go into mass seizures.

You saved a thousand lives, the president told me when he awarded me the medal. *I'm sorry no one will ever find out.*

"It was the worst day of my life," I said now. "I would do it again."

Homza sipped coffee. I couldn't read him. He was probably one hell of a poker player. Lieutenant Colonel Ng seemed to take my admission as confirmation of twisted proclivities. She told Homza, "Cover-ups become SOP." She meant *standard operating procedure*. "I don't know this officer. I don't know if he is covering up something now."

Homza sighed. "Colonel Rush, this is why I've never liked the idea of all these little independent units."

My God! He's playing politics right now!

We all sat on lab stools, bar-stool height, except the smell in here was Lysol, not beer, formaldehyde, not peanuts. I comprised the third point of a triangle where the other two edges were hard stares.

Otherwise the lab seemed normal. There were tables on which sat books and a microscope, a computer, printouts. Rabies studies. Rabies treatises. Rabies histories.

I wish I'd had time to call Karen.

Lieutenant Colonel Amanda Ng said, "Tell you what, Colonel Rush. If there's something you need to tell us, do it now and there will be no consequences."

"My word on it," said Homza.

"I've told the truth, sir."

General Homza stood and brushed off his uniform pants. He said, noncommittal, "The others are waiting for us. Why don't we go down the hall and all have a chat."

...

I KEPT REMEMBERING KAREN IN THE BACK OF THE AUDITORIUM.
Karen doubling over, coughing. Karen rushing out.

I hope she is okay.

Homza sat at the head of the table, Lieutenant Colonel
Amanda Ng on his right. The power seats. On Homza's
left were a couple of majors: Kevin Jackson and Kendall
LeMoyne, who commanded the day and night shifts out
on the wire. Jackson was towheaded and crew cut, with
a flinty New England accent, slate-gray eyes and the remains of a bad case of acne scars on his sallow face. Le-
Moyne was a bulked-up, dark-haired and neatly mustached
man who occasionally touched his gold wedding band,
or glanced at the map of Barrow on the corkboard. Little
black pins in the board denoted troops, white ones were
food distribution points, green ones showed important
civilian locations: Borough Hall, the hospital, the prison,
and there was a jagged curl shape drawn around the town,
like a strand of rotini. That was the wire.

On the left side of the table, moving down, were the
CDC epidemiologists who'd been testing and retesting
victims for rabies over the last two days, and who, in my
opinion, had caused the delay in quarantine while they
questioned their own findings.

They were a sharp-faced, balding black man named Dr.
Harlan Morgan, from San Antonio. And a wide-hipped,
sloppy-looking woman from New York, Dr. Janette Cruz,
who wore wire-rimmed glasses around her neck on a
string, and showed small food stains on her white coat.
They'd both looked mildly hopeful when Amanda Ng

suggested that Eddie and I might have had something to do with the outbreak. I guess that would make their failure to identify the virus less embarrassing.

Eddie called the two CDC docs the Tweedledums. They always agreed with each other, even finished each others' sentences. Karen had told me she thought they were lovers. She's good at spotting this stuff.

The number two with the Army's investigative unit was Captain Raymond Hess, out of D.C. The two Iñupiats, Merlin and the mayor, still seemed resentful that I'd not warned them of the quarantine. They sat at the far end of the table, clearly relegated to the status of locals privileged to get any information at all, and there to take orders.

Homza said crisply, "Captain Hess? Where are we? Theories? Foreign attack? Probe? Terrorism?"

Hess wore a West Point ring. He spoke confidently and made good eye contact with Homza. "Sir! At this point, foreign attack seems unlikely. The victims are civilians. There's no military target of note here. The spread seems random. Domestic terrorism is a consideration. A bigger outbreak could impact domestic oil supply, although if it was an attack, why not hit Prudhoe Bay. Why here? We'll be looking into victim background, spread pattern, lab samples, and anyone," he said, glancing at me, "who worked with rabies this summer. It's quite possible the outbreak is natural in origin."

Homza's eyes slid right. "CDC?"

Dr. Harlan Morgan said, "Spread. We'll do a house-to-house survey, seeking connections. We'll watch the monkeys. Is the illness contagious or spreading in another way? We're monitoring anyone coming into the hospital. Blood tests on family members. Daily blood from anyone who's come in contact with a victim. I suggest that we set up four or five satellite medical posts, to avoid crowding."

Dr. Cruz added that she and Morgan awaited results of the DNA tests on the strain taken from George Carling, to see if it was a known one, if it came from nature, or if it was man-made and had come to life in a lab.

Amanda Ng asked, "You can tell the difference?"

"Absolutely. There are hundreds of strains around the world but we've analyzed them. A couple of days, we'll know if we're dealing with a known strain, lab strain, or mix."

The naval officer—from the sub—explained that the *Virginia* and the icebreaker would remain offshore as long as ice stayed away and allowed it. Major Kevin Jackson went to quarantine logistics, patrol schedules, areas where electronic jamming was in effect, two monitored rooftop areas where authorized sat calls could go out, rules on public gatherings, and efforts to keep the troops separate from civilians, in case the rabies spread and vaccinations did not work. It was a quagmire of problems.

"At night we'll have searchlights mounted on the Humvees," Jackson said, eyeing Merlin and the mayor, who'd been pretty much ignored up to then. "It would be a good idea if police came with our patrols, house to house. We'll be doing spot checks, mobile teams, looking for home laboratories or sick people hiding away and—"

Merlin spoke up. "You want my people going with you through all the homes?"

"Yes, sir."

Merlin and the mayor exchanged glances. They didn't like it. Merlin nodded. He'd do it.

"Good! Also, we want an announcement from you, Mr. Mayor, that people should stay away from the wire. No gatherings of more than five. No one out after eight P.M. You will—"

Mayor Brower cleared his throat, interrupted the major. The mayor shook his head vigorously, agitated. "Actually," he said. "You will *not* tell my people what to do."

On the table sat mugs of steaming Maxwell House coffee, a sugar bowl, a half gallon of milk, and a glass bowl piled with chocolate- and coconut-flavored PowerBars.

The major blanched, glanced at the general for assistance. Homza handled the interruption smoothly, showing none of the harshness of which he was capable in private. "With all respect, Mr. Mayor . . ."

The mayor cut him off. "'Respect'? You didn't respect us enough to tell us you were coming. Or to let us know that a protocol four event—yes, General, I know what it is—had occurred. You're not putting my police under your command, or this major's command, or anyone's. Plain and simple."

Homza sat back and sighed, refusing to be baited. My sense of him as a thinking commander had been rising all morning. He said, low key, "I understand that you are upset, Mayor. But martial law is in effect. Cooperation would be best for all. I have trained experts here, highly qualified to end the quarantine as safely as possible."

"The same experts who failed to recognize rabies, even after Joe told them it was here?"

The general's eyes flicked to me. He was playing it soft before he made threats. That's the way drills suggest we do it. "Mayor, believe me. In this kind of situation, it is best to work together."

"You've run a quarantine before?" the mayor said.

Homza pursed his thick lips. "We've planned them, gamed them out in great detail, sir."

"Gamed. You've *gamed* them." The mayor drew himself up; he was small and gray haired and wore a button-up blue-and-white-striped cotton shirt and a spotted sealskin vest with a walrus-ivory bolo tie. I'd been in a hundred meetings on "ways to handle locals." The mayor was the guy D.C. paid no attention to. And now he addressed the meeting with dignity and force. "Martial law ends at some point, General. And when it does, you'll want cooperation with building permits, pipelines, bases, training. Cooperation as any federal Arctic projects go forward."

"I don't see how that is relevant just now."

"Yes you do. We're not rubes here. You fly in and see a few houses. Ice. You figure you can do what you want. We've got lobbyists in D.C., good Georgetown lawyers. I can pick up this phone and call our Senators. We've stopped the oil and can do it again, and if we do, *when we do*, I'll make sure everyone knows you are the cause.

You personally. General Wayne Homza. Who fucked up the North Slope."

"Mayor, there's no need to make threats."

The mayor's finger went up. "There's more. The weather's going bad. You have no housing if you bring in more people. You can't kick us from our homes. That'll look bad. You're unprepared for Arctic ops. You don't have the men to manage a growing crisis. Will you bunk your people in the infected zone? You really think you can do your job without us, and get out of here before the big freeze hits? Because once it hits, your guys will freeze out there in those stupid tents. How will you explain that failure in Washington? They'll want a scapegoat. They always do."

In the beat of silence, Homza pulled out a pipe and packed it. I would have guessed him a cigar man. I was unsure whether he was thinking about his career, the best way to run the quarantine, or both. He asked the mayor, "You're suggesting an alternative?"

"Joint," said the mayor, as if he'd never made a threat. "You and us. Together. My people do NOT work under yours. We split up jobs. However we agree to do it."

I sensed muscles working beneath the general's bland expression. "Done," he said, ignoring the anger flashing on Lieutenant Colonel Ng's face.

She tried to fight it. She invoked the two magic words, or at least magic to her: *national security*. She reminded us that the law specified that where a national threat exists, the task force has the lead. "General, Mayor, may I respectfully point out that we have jurisdiction?"

"Meaning, I have that," said Homza.

I flashed to Karen in the auditorium, coughing. I was worried about Karen's health. I was only peripherally aware of a soldier entering the room, whispering to the general, until the halt in conversation snapped me back to the present. But this time the expression in Homza's face was not accusatory, and what I saw filled me with dread.

"Joe, let's go outside for a moment," said the general. That use of my first name, not my title, ratcheted up the fear. Homza looked softer. Ng looked confused. Hess was staring. *What just happened?*

But somehow I knew. I was a Marine officer who had visited the homes of men killed in the line of duty. I knew that expression on Homza's face. I'd seen mothers faint under it, and strong fathers weep. I'd worn that expression myself in the past, a look that officers shared with priests. A look that said afterward . . . too late.

Eddie?

Karen?

You think it won't happen to you. You think if it does happen, it will never be today. There is no way to prepare for it. It is the sum total of human fear, love, and mortality.

The general repeated himself, but not with anger, not with the expectation of instant obedience this time. I heard the future in that voice. I heard years ahead.

"Colonel, let's go out into the hall for a moment, okay?"

FOURTEEN

Steel yourself, General Wayne Homza had said.

I was awake but my body moved too slowly, as if in a nightmare. My legs propelled me toward the cabin and police cars, the floodlights shining out from windows that seemed misshapen to me, manufactured rhomboids, not rectangles. Deputy Luther Oz's face loomed, broken into pieces, as in a splintered mirror. Deputy Steve Rice's jaw looked elongated, Pinocchio's nose. Gusts whipped up snow, made the scene grainy and colorless, interference on an old TV.

Had someone put the hat on my head? Had someone slid on gloves? I tottered through the black gap of open doorway, and into a bright frozen diorama of hell.

A crime-scene tech was taking photos. A medical examiner—from the gray hair and slight form I thought it was Sengupta—was bent over the head. Beyond his back

I glimpsed a single denim-clad leg, woman's or teen's, from the size of it. I saw the boots—weathered brown insulated Merrells—identical to Karen's.

It is not Karen, I don't care what Homza said.

I heard more vehicles, outside, grumbling, rattling, converging on the cabin. And now, looking up, I saw graffiti on the wall. No, not just graffiti but a message. Red paint oozed, dried slowly, ran from a chest-high starting point to the dusty plywood floor.

MURDERER MARINES!
YOU KILL OUR LOVED ONES! NOW WE KILL YOURS!

The police photographer moved left for another shot, revealing her entire body. The thing on the floor, the thing with a face turned away had Karen's silver hair, Karen's puffed-up Outfitter parka. I told myself it wasn't her. That someone had sheared off hair that looked like hers, attached it to an adult-sized doll. A doll that spilled a sludgy pool of blood onto the floor. Camera flashes exploded on the pudding-like surface. I'd seen blood in Afghanistan. I'd tended to Marines on the field of battle. This was different. This was her.

Sight became blurred as sound grew magnified. I heard whispering detectives in a corner, snatches of talk over the scuff of boots on wood, snap of a forensic glove on someone's wrist, electric buzz of the tripod floodlight.

From the body temperature, it happened within the past two hours.

I disagree. Rigor is delayed in the cold.

The jaw. The eyelids. Rigor's definitely beginning.

I said to no one in particular, to myself, to hope, to fantasy, to too late, "That's not her."

SOLDIERS GRIPPED ME BY THE CHEST, DRAGGING ME OUTSIDE.

Someone was screaming. I heard a man's screaming, agony and grief. I had to tell her something. It was important to get back there and tell her I was here, with her. My flailing boots connected with someone's leg, and there was a howl. A Ranger fell back, writhing on the ground. There were too many of them. The doorway and cabin receded. My boot heels formed drag marks in the hard, granular snow.

A calm voice, a soothing voice, in my ear said, "Can we let you go, Colonel? Can we let go of you now?"

"Yes. I'm . . . I'm good."

"The general wants to see you."

"Tell the general to go fuck himself."

"Yes, sir. This way please, sir."

When had the crowd behind the tape arrived, and the growing collection of small trucks, ATVs, SUVs, even, in the snow, a bicycle? Civilians made death entertainment. They snapped cell-phone shots as police in departmental parkas and flap-eared hats kept them back, at the tape. Someone in front held a better-quality camera. That someone wore Mikael Grandy's festive red-and-white striped pullover hat. I broke away from the man guiding me. I saw Mikael's camera lower when I was almost on him. I ripped through the tape like a runner at the finish line. He doubled over as my fist slammed into his solar plexus. Mikael on the ground, gasping like an animal. He tried to kick back. He tried to cover himself. I didn't care which part of him I made contact with as long as I hit something.

"You were here! You followed her everywhere!"

"I'll sue you," he shouted.

"That fucking camera! Even now!"

They pulled me off as Lieutenant Colonel Amanda Ng helped him up, and Raymond Hess picked up his camera, stared at it . . . *evidence* . . . as I was spun around and marched toward the idling Humvee. The rear door was open and Major General Wayne Homza sat inside, a smoking pipe in his mouth.

"Get in, please, Colonel."

I brought Karen up here early so we could be together. Then I ignored her. I kept going when everyone told me to stop.

"Colonel, I gave you an order. Get in!"

HE SAID NOTHING AT FIRST.

We sat there. It seemed like a long time, but probably wasn't. He watched me, maybe giving me time to collect myself; maybe wondering whether I had anything to do with the death. *Lover's quarrel? Plotters turning on themselves?* Homza worrying this murder into his larger problem. Homza deciding things. The windows fogged and blue smoke swirled and a thick, sweet borkum odor filled my lungs. The heater made a growling noise. I heard the rumble of more vehicles arriving from the main part of town.

You left her alone, Joe. But you couldn't leave the Harmon deaths alone.

"Colonel Rush?"

I thought, *If you go down now, you lose the opportunity to find whoever did this.*

I saw the abyss in front of me. It was waiting and it was an abiding blackness, an eternity more real than any Leavenworth cell. Grief was becoming rage and the only question was how it would consume me. I could plunge in now or hold myself back a little longer. I could make a deal with it. I could use it for clarity in exchange for self-destruction up the road.

All you had to do was go along with everyone else and call the deaths suicide/murder. We all would have gone home.

"Colonel!" Homza packed and relit the pipe, drew in smoke and said, watching, "Under other circumstances I'd release you now, give you time off."

"I don't want time off."

Everyone you love, you destroy.

His brows went up. He puffed smoke. "You're a singular person. I'm not unaware that you're the only one so far who seems to have any idea of what is happening. Everything you've predicted has occurred. Now Dr. Vleska is killed."

"I don't believe in coincidences, General."

"Me neither." The general's eyes swept the cops, soldiers, crowd, bored back into me. He said, "Locals getting back at big bad government? You heard that shouting in the school. Accusations. That would explain the message. That?"

"Looks like it," I heard myself say, using every ounce of discipline to achieve a semblance of normal voice, to speak from a place of focused, rational thought. "One of George Carling's relatives maybe. Someone close to someone who died. They know she was my fiancée. They couldn't get to me. So, yeah, looks like. *Looks*."

"You know, the mayor made some points in there. I need five times more people than I have. He was right about the freeze coming. He was right when he said our scenarios were never designed for the Arctic. Now, a murder," Homza said.

"Murder takes up manpower. Murder diverts."

"Give it to the police? Local problem? What do you suggest I do with this?" Homza said.

"I don't know what *you* should do." My head hurt. I said, "But I know what I want to do. Permission to speak plainly?"

He made a wry face and blew out smoke. "Considering what you say when you don't have permission, this ought to be enlightening. Go ahead."

"You don't much like me and everyone knows it."

"Correct."

"Let's use it." I told him what I wanted to do. I explained it in some detail. It was important to sound rational. In control.

He said, considering, "You're serious?"

"Why not? If I screw up, I'm blamed. If it works, you

get credit. If I'm guilty, Colonel Ng still finds out. You can't afford to miss an opportunity. You're on a clock. You don't want to have to explain in Washington later if I could have helped out now. And the best part for you . . . I'm gone in six months, either way. Expendable."

"I do like that part."

"This is exactly what I told Karen that I wanted to do this morning. Exactly what I said when we were sitting in our kitchen and . . ."

My mouth slammed shut. I thought back to the early morning, before the quarantine began. I went over our talk, starting in the bedroom, moving into the kitchenette, rambling over my theories. Laying it out, just as, in the privacy of that hut, I'd been laying out thoughts for days.

No, no, no, no, no.

There's no way someone could have heard, I thought.

Then I thought, *A four-digit combination lock to the front door. Hell, half the time the neighbors would just walk in when we were there. How long does it take to install one of those stick-on mikes? Thirty seconds?*

Homza said, "If I give you what you want, you'll need some backup, some way to talk to me."

"Major Nakamura. But that's it. You, me, and Eddie."

Homza said, "If I do this, Colonel Ng will still be all over you. This isn't a pass. You're a cover-up suspect until you're cleared. All three of you, actually. Her, too."

"I lost it back there, but I'm over it."

"No you're not."

"For now, I mean."

He stared at me, making up his mind. He hummed softly for several seconds. Not a tune, just a single flat note. He was a humming thinker.

I pushed. "Sir, Atlanta will analyze the samples. Police on forensics. So give Amanda Ng what she wants. You were probably going to take me off investigations anyway. We both know that whole chat back there with her was an act."

Homza turned red.

"My condolences," he said. "Okay, do it. Now get out."

IF YOU'RE IN CHARGE OF QUARANTINING AN AMERICAN CITY, AND if you've ordered electronic jamming across town, you're going to give yourself the ability to call the White House. A spot free of jamming. Encrypted override equipment. A way to phone home if no one else can.

My two Ranger babysitters stood twenty feet off as I punched in numbers. I had no doubt that Homza would have Lieutenant Colonel Ng double-check whoever I called. I was on the weather tower three hundred yards beyond the lab building, on a steel platform twenty feet above the tundra. At my back was an unmanned trailer-cabin filled with passive electronics enabling NASA and NOAA to monitor Arctic weather at four altitudes, as well as tundra methane release, incoming ultraviolet light, outgoing albedo effect (heat radiation back to space), and probably about nine hundred other streams of information normally forwarded to Washington, New Mexico, the Pentagon, the Energy Department, or Woods Hole.

"Prezant College Science Department! Melissa speaking."

I turned my back to the wind to make reception clearer. I told the secretary—she sounded about fifty—that I was a Marine colonel phoning from Alaska, that this call constituted an emergency, that I needed to talk to the head of the department right away.

"I'm sorry, but Dr. Willoughby is in a thesis defense. It should be over around noon and then she has lunch with the provost after that."

"Did you hear me say emergency? Get her on the line!"

The voice that replaced hers five minutes later—she'd had to physically go find Dr. Willoughby down the hall—was sixtyish, female, and southwestern. This voice was heavy with shock and sorrow. I felt sympathy from her, cooperation.

"I'm Eliza Willoughby, Colonel. You're in Barrow right now? You knew the Harmons then?"

"Yes, ma'am."

"Awful, awful, awful. I've known Ted and Cathy for more than thirteen years. I've had them to my home. Kelley plays—*played*—lacrosse with my nieces. I don't know what I can tell you that might help you figure out what happened, but please ask anything you want."

I asked for a rundown of the Harmon project. She hesitated a moment, then gave the same basic explanation that Kelley had in her diary, and that her boyfriend, Leon, had told me at the Heritage Center. The Arctic was warming. Species were dying out. Scientists were behind the curve in understanding *what was there in the first place*.

"Not enough studies have been done," she said. "So the Harmons basically collected everything at their nine sites. Then they shipped samples back and spent the year analyzing."

"Any practical or commercial applications to this?"

"Like I said. Basic work. To find out what's there."

"And the Norway part?"

I heard a soft intake of breath. I was not sure if that constituted surprise on her part, or more thinking.

"Oh, you know about that," she said.

"Tell me what you know about it, please."

"Well, I guess you could say there *is* possible commercial application on that end. We've partnered up with the Arctic University in Tromso. Tromso is Norway's Arctic capital, you know. Ever been there, Colonel?"

I curbed my impatience. I didn't need a travel log. I said, politely, "No, ma'am."

"Call me Liz. Well, Tromso lies at the same latitude as Barrow," she said. "But what a difference! Glass cathedral. Excellent hotels. Fine restaurants and a splendid university. Lovely as a Currier and Ives postcard. Just top-notch."

"What's the connection with the Harmon project?"

"The Norwegians are way ahead of us in the Arctic, as is every other northern country. When *they* collect biological samples—they're not interested in the DNA yet—they check commercial applications first."

"Please explain."

"Drugs. You probably know that many useful drugs—natural substances—have come from tropical rainforests. The rosy periwinkle, for instance, a flowering bush. Those alkaloids upped the cure rate on childhood leukemia to eighty percent. A miracle, really, from the jungle."

"And in the Arctic?" I said, looking out at the expanse of white stretching south for hundreds of miles.

"That's the point. Nobody knows what's there yet," she said. "So the Norwegians have bioprospecting companies. They go out on the ocean, in big ships. They suck up everything on the bottom and grind it up and test the compounds against all kinds of ailments. Systematic."

I tried to envision an enormous ship plunging through white-capped Arctic waves off of Europe, 3 A.M., floodlights shining down from A-frame winches, nets hauled from the turgid sea, filled with life.

"They test everything?" I said. "Plants? Fish?"

"Mostly bottom life, but some fish, test it to see if it's *worth* analyzing. They grind tissue into compounds they mix in with diseases, bacteria, virus. If they find an application, a possible drug, *if the target microbe dies,* they decipher DNA. You see in the tropics, researchers have it easier. You've got more people there. Folktales or shamans identify cures. When tropical researchers go into a jungle, they find locals, ask questions, track stories, and send samples back to labs."

"But in the Arctic?"

"Impossible, especially a mile down in the sea. The Norwegians just grid the sea and suck it all up and test."

"Sounds like a long process."

I envisioned her nodding, getting into the academics of it. "Laborious, yes. It takes months just to analyze what you pull up on one trip. But they've had successes! A herpes drug came out of Tromso last year. They've got another compound that shows promise against nerve damage, and a product out now that does a pretty good job against acne. All new! So when they approached us, about sharing our Arctic work, we signed an agreement with them."

"With the university there? Or a company?"

"It's connected there. It's socialist. Better, if you ask me. Look at their health-care system! The best in—"

"Please, Liz, can we stay on point?"

"Sorry. The university and the company work together. Anyway, once the Harmons are finished analyzing samples, we ship 'em to Tromso. That's what we did last year."

"Any finds yet?"

"Unfortunately not."

"Ted Harmon was in a rush to finish up this year, get each site in. Was that because of this deal?"

"No. He's just diligent. Always has been. Systematic. He hates falling behind."

I thought about ramifications. "Would the Harmons have gotten a cut of profits if they found something?"

She chuckled. "Well, I would have said yes a few years ago, but if you've ever read an academic contract you'd know that his percentage, even then, wouldn't pay for Kelley to go through one year of college."

"Low, huh?"

"Microscopic. The trade-off is that a professor gets

tenure, security, but you give ninety-nine percent of any discovery to the school."

"But you just said he wouldn't even get that now."

A sigh. "Thank the U.S. Supreme Court, Colonel. Two years ago they ruled that a natural substance can't be patented. They took the incentive away for medicinal research. Even if Ted and Cathy found something, no, they'd get nothing, *we'd* get nothing. Many schools have stopped their programs now."

"But not in Norway."

"Well, over there, it's a different law," she said. "If they patented a discovery, it stands."

"Which is why your school made a deal with a Norwegian school, instead of doing the work yourself. They make the discovery. You share profits."

I heard Dr. Liz Willoughby sigh. "Legally it's a gray area. Even if you give the Norwegians the stuff, the problem is the natural substance *still* lies in the U.S., banned from patent. The Norwegians have their program going anyway. It costs them nothing to do a few tests. If they find something, maybe *they'll* pay for a legal challenge.

"Colonel, we do it because we're scientists. Basic research. If you ask me, if you want to make money up there, stick to oil, minerals, natural gas. Is anyone looking for *those* things where you are?"

VALLEY GIRL ANSWERED ON THE SECOND RING. I KNEW SHE WAS relaxed and back to normal because each sentence came out as a question again. She was back to being irritating.

"They let me go?" she said. "Thanks to you?"

I told Valley Girl to double-check everything that Dr. Liz Willoughby had just told me. I asked her to try to dig up any business arrangements between Prezant College and the University of the Arctic, in Norway. I asked her to check both Dr. Harmons' buying habits, credit rating, debt situation, savings, and to see if they'd stocked away any money to pay for Kelley's college education.

I asked her also to get hold of Ted Harmon's grant application and cross-check which exact Arctic lakes— there were ten thousand of them on the North Slope—he was supposed to visit with any other applications for mines, pipelines, or business endeavors planned for the same spots. Who exactly owned the land the Harmons were visiting? The feds? The state? The Iñupiats? The borough?

"I can do this fast? I don't have any plans tonight? Thanks again for taking care of me," said Valley Girl.

Yeah, I take care of strangers. I couldn't protect the person I love, I thought.

NO CARS WERE ON THE ROADS EXCEPT A POLICE DEPARTMENT Explorer. No people walking. Shops were closed. Why visit a relative, when there might be sickness waiting? Why go out when you could lock your door and watch my Ford rattle by on the way to the base? Barrow was a ghost town filled with people. Barrow was Edgar Allan Poe's *The Masque of the Red Death*. The only thing moving were the sled dogs, restlessly, as I passed the yard where Karen and I had hooked them up just a few days ago.

I made a left turn off the coast road and passed the Ilisagvik College sign and entered the Quonset hut area. Dusk was falling and the world looked gray: gray clouds, gray light, gray earth. Lights glowed in huts and off-duty troops were returning from the dining hall. I punched in the four-digit combination to the door of my hut.

The officers who'd moved in while I was out had made themselves comfortable. Two exhausted-looking lieutenants in stocking feet lounged in the living room, staring at the TV, which got no reception, since the sat jamming killed that. I heard snoring from a bedroom. A captain came out of the bathroom, saluted, and said, "Sir!"

"Get out," I barked. "All of you."

"Excuse me? The security staff and docs finished up here. They said we could move in, sir."

His gaze followed mine into the bedroom I'd shared with Karen. Our single beds, pushed together last night, had been moved to opposite walls. A stranger's knapsack lay on her bed, and thonged slippers sat on the floor beside it. There was a paperback copy of *The Things They Carried* on the crisply made bed. It had been rumpled when I left. The smell was sweat and canvas, leather and testosterone. I saw a man's wallet on the dresser, and packs of spearmint gum.

"Didn't you hear me, Captain?"

"But where should we go, sir?"

They'd wiped away all trace of her. They'd eliminated her essence. They'd smoothed out marks that her body would have made on cushions, blankets, a pillow, on a towel she folded in the bathroom.

"I don't care where you go. Wake the others. Get out!"

"Sir, you're shaking."

"I am not shaking."

"Your hands are shaking."

They trudged off grudgingly, glancing back, exhausted from their flight here, from the cold, from wondering whether the vaccinations they had been given would protect them. I was authority, but not one of their officers. Maybe I didn't have the power to kick them out. But they were reluctant to challenge me. Sullen, they left. The wind gasped, receiving them.

I stood in the Quonset hut, wondering if someone, someone outside, or in another hut, had just overheard everything I'd said, or would the jamming kill transmissions? I'd told the general: *Karen and I talked about my theory this morning*. I made sure any exposed computer screen in the hut was covered to mask any remote camera. To create the sound of a tantrum I kicked a chair over. I lifted the small table, and threw it into the couch. Anyone listening would be hearing me screaming, kicking things around. Joe lost it.

They probably can't be listening anyway, because the jamming is blocking any mikes, if there are any.

Quietly as possible, I started taking the place apart, looking for bugs.

DID YOU EVER SEE THOSE OLD MICROPHONES IN BLACK-AND-white movies? The ones as big as ice cream cones? That radio singers crooned into? Mikes so big they required a stand? Eddie and I once watched that kind in an old Marine film about listening devices. The audience broke out laughing, trying to envision a spy taping those big fat mothers under a chair. Anyone assigned to units like ours trained in eavesdropping techniques. Strategies. Equipment. Finesse.

So now I unscrewed the backs of kitchenette chairs and peered at the screws. Were they equally shiny? Were they the same size? Was one gone, something else in it's hole?

Nope.

I stood on a chair and unscrewed lightbulbs, and fixture parts. I figured that in a Quonset hut, if you wanted to place a mike, you'd go for the most-used spaces, living room or kitchen, or the most intimate area, bedroom.

If someone got in when we were out, it could be anywhere. But if someone did it during a party, then the living or bedroom is logical. It will be freestanding or adhesive. No time for screws.

I knew that there were pencil mikes and pen mikes and mikes that looked like fixtures. There were mikes the size of contact lenses. Mikes you stuck under coffee tables, under phones, in curtain rods, under any piece of houseware with a raised bottom. God only knew the latest mikes. The Chinese had them in kitchen equipment. The Koreans wired up cars. The Russians had a false-tooth mike and the Cubans had a false fingernail. That one, when I'd seen it in Washington, had blown me away.

I found a furniture tack that looked shinier than the rest in a row of brass pieces running across the top of the faux leather sitting chair. I took it off and used a hammer on it. It was just a tack. I tore off felt pads beneath a laptop, and tried a scissor on them.

They were just felt.

"One? What are you doing?"

I whirled and held up both hands in a *stop* gesture. I shook my head violently, meaning, *Shut up!* Eddie stood in the doorway, dressed for the field. His expression was a mix of horror, at the news about Karen, and bafflement. But I saw quick understanding appear on his face.

I snapped out, "What do you think I'm doing? Having a drink, that's what."

He began to move toward me, in sympathy. I stepped back and shook my head and let him see my rage. I shoved my hands into the air, *Keep away. Don't touch me.* He halted, getting it, but not liking it. His shoulders slumped. His eyes said, *She was my friend, too.* I let him see what I needed. It was not sympathy just now. I shifted my head to the right, then left, scanning. We communicated by glances.

—*You're looking for bugs, One?*

—*I think someone's been listening to us.*

—*Okay, let's get to it then.*

I understood the effort required on his part not to speak of Karen. As he bent beneath the sink cabinet, where the hut toolbox was stored, I started talking again, just in case someone listened in. "Want a drink, Eddie?"

"I got back as fast as possible."

"They cut her throat. They cut . . ." My voice really did fail me at that point. "Her throat."

We took the place apart together, babbling. Me trying to sound broken. It wasn't hard. Eddie trying to pep me up. Eddie in the bathroom, with a Phillips-head screwdriver, removing, one by one, screws on vanity doors, the knob on the toilet, screws on the overhead light fixture.

"You were right, One. It was rabies."

"Being right is shit."

Eddie peering at a screw that looked duller than the rest.

I need to sound useless.

"Eddie, I can't stop seeing her, lying on the floor."

Eddie laid the screw down, inside a towel and folded the towel over it and raised a hammer and coughed loudly when he smashed down. He unfolded the towel.

We saw a normal, half-bent screw, with a chipped top.

Together, talking memories, we tipped the couch on its back. We went around front and looked past a sea of dust balls at tacks affixing the fabric in place.

"I wanted to go to Costa Rica for the honeymoon. She wanted Sweden," I said.

Hmm. I reached out and unpeeled a small brown dot off the false leather. It looked like faux leather, but it was a lighter shade, and had adhesive underneath. It seemed to have no purpose. I said, "So I told her, okay. Sweden." I saw no other similar stick-on dots under the chair. I took the dot to the kitchen table. I tried to cut through it with a scissor. The blade would not penetrate. It did not seem to be encountering fabric. My head was pounding. Eddie pulled out his Leatherman. The serrated blade sawed halfway through.

It was fabric. Thick. But no mike.

I said, sick of chatter, "I want music." I switched on a disc already in the CD player. Cajun. Her favorite. Loud. I turned it louder.

We continued looking, kept it up, changed places, in case one of us missed something. I tilted over a kitchenette chair that I'd already looked at. A screw fell out. So did fresh wood shavings. I stared at the shavings, retrieved the screw and bounced it up and down in my hand. It looked brand-new. The thread felt prickly. It seemed to emanate purpose. It had been shoved into the hole because the wood there was worn away, stripped of grooves.

Eddie came over and examined the screw with me like a jeweler staring through a loupe. We put our heads together. We whispered over the raging music.

"It's just a screw, One."

"Someone got in here and replaced the old one with this."

"No, it's just a hole. How could anyone get in?"

"How? It's a stupid four-digit code on the door. Anyone could have seen one of us punch it in. Or at a dinner. The quarantine started. No one was here. They knew we might look for bugs and they got in fast and took it out."

Eddie sighed, and said with exaggerated softness, "It's a screw. A goddamn screw. That's what screws do. They fall out after a while."

I hated the sympathy in his face. *Poor Joe, grasping at straws.* I felt a red film in my head replace the glow from the fluorescent light. My legs were trembling. The urge to hit something surged into my shoulders. A cold sensation spread up from my belly, and became a hard beat in my head, as if the Arctic was inside, not just out.

"Yeah," I hissed. "And there's no rabies. And it can't be contagious. And there are no fucking microphones because that's just crazy and—"

I stopped. "Shit, Eddie. You're the best friend I have."

He was white. "Just tell me what you want to do."

"Let's go over to Longhorn, have a drink," I said.

"They told me at the airport, security is looking for you. Someone named Hess."

Outside, we crunched over toward the oil company hut.

"I'm going to be part of it," he said. "Whatever it is."

"Don't worry about it."

His face floated inches from mine. "Don't *worry*? We're Uno and Dos. We're the team. If you don't tell me, I'll be there anyway and probably screw it up. You'll tell me eventually. So tell me now."

Eddie's face close. Eddie's force and rage and love an unqualified lifetime offer. *You won't stop? Then why would I ever stop, whether or not I think you're right?*

I told him what Homza had okayed for us. He didn't like it. But he did not protest.

"Do you have a better idea, Eddie?"

"I don't have any idea," he said.

We knocked and did not wait for an answer and just walked into the hut, as we'd been doing all summer. They were all there. My neighbors. My friends. Karen's new buddies, turning to me, consoling me, pouring drinks for me. The fly lights on the shiny web, moves his wings, thinks he's free, unaware that the trap already has him.

Which one of you did it? Listened to us? Killed her? Went after the Harmons? Introduced the disease?

Come on in, any old time, Dave Lillienthal always said.

Said the spider to the fly.

FIFTEEN

"More Tito, Dave! Man's best friend."

I gazed up drunkenly at the Longhorn North Oil exec, who stood over me as I sprawled in his massive corner chair. I held out my glass. He shook his head. He said, "You'll make yourself sick, Joe, if you don't slow down, man. Have some coffee."

"Dave, why keep all this goddamned liquor here if you won't give people any? All you do is offer drinks, and when I ask for one, you say no."

Dave Lillienthal grew hazy through the bottom of the olive-green plastic tumbler. He walked off and Deborah replaced him, looking down at me; wan, small, and horrified. Stiff as a petrified stick. She kept her voice down, as if she did not want others nearby to hear.

"I'm so sorry about Karen. She was a terrific person."

Was it you, Deborah? Was it your brother? Who was it?

"You don't look so good yourself," I slurred.

"Oh, Joe! I bonded with her right away. What she was, she was *kind,* Joe. A rare quality to find in someone so accomplished. This all must be awful for you. I can't imagine what you're going through. Anything Dave and I can do, just say it. Um, do you mind if I ask a question?"

"Deb, whenever someone asks if you mind a question, it means you won't like it. Just ask."

"Theoretically, I'm curious, I mean, if someone slept with a person who has rabies, and got vaccinated after, how much time has to pass before that person knows the vaccine works? You know, that they're safe?"

"Who did you sleep with, Deborah?"

She spoke in a low, embarrassed voice, hard to hear over people crowded into the hut, party central usually, wake central tonight. The chair was new, overstuffed, Haitian cotton. The window looked out on my hut, where lights glowed, as the soldiers had come back.

"Joe, I told you, theoretical question."

"Are you afraid you gave it to someone? Or afraid someone gave it to you?"

"I shouldn't have brought it up. Forget it. I know you loved her a lot. She was so happy with you."

I shrugged. I drank. I slumped down further and said, "Now I'll ask you one. Karen and I wondered, how much would Longhorn lose if your pipeline doesn't go through next year, if drilling gets blocked?"

"Don't even think that."

"How much? And what would happen to you and Dave?"

"We'd have to close the Anchorage office." She moved off. Dave was back to refill my glass. He seemed, despite his protests, to keep me supplied. I gagged, rose, and lurched to the bathroom, making sure to lock the door. There I groaned loudly, patted vodka onto my face, like aftershave, washed out my mouth with it, and spilled some on a sleeve. The rest went down the sink. I urinated into the toilet but made sure to drip a bit, stain the crotch of my pants.

I refilled the tumbler with cold water, made sure to keep the ice and the fresh lime. I swayed slightly on the way back to the chair, my grieving man's throne. *Don't overdo it.*

"Joe, you okay?"

Calvin DeRochers, the diamond hunter, stood there now. He'd discarded his usual jeans and U Arkansas sweatshirt for something more formal, for the impromptu wake. White button-up shirt, collar crisply jutting from his homemade knit sweater. Creased beige cords and newer Columbia boots. For here, he was dressed up.

I mimicked him. "Am I *okay*? I'm great. I'm the greatest I've ever been. You guys," I said, morosely, switching mood, sweeping my free hand to encompass all: the three McDougals, Eddie, Merlin and his wife, and Deputy Oz, Bruce, a few members of the Barrow Iñupiat Dancers, "are the greatest pals a guy could want. I love you all. Karen loved you, too."

"Joe, maybe you shouldn't go back to your hut tonight . . . where you . . . well, you know, memories. Why not sleep in my hut? I've got an extra bed in my room. Soldiers in the rest, but it's comfortable. Eddie can come, too. Both of you. Better to be with friends instead of strangers."

"Yeah, thanks, Calvin. Friends!"

"And maybe a little cutting down on the booze."

"Hey! What booze? This isn't booze." I grinned. "It's water." I broke up laughing.

"I'm serious. Vodka won't help. *Talking* helps. You want to talk about anything, I'm here. Calvin," he said, speaking of himself in the third person, as usual, "is here for you."

"Thank him if you see him. Hey, Calvin! I'm the one who's sorry for *you*. Another summer over. No diamonds."

I watched his face. I saw no guile or regret, no guilt or anger or even disappointment. I saw patience. But that meant nothing if he was a pro. He shrugged. "Calvin will be back next year. The diamonds are here. Waiting. They're *here*!"

JENS ERIK HOLTE, CHOPPER PILOT, WANDERED OVER NEXT. IT was like they all waited and took turns with me. When there was an open spot, somebody filled it.

"Karen promised to take me dogsledding, Joe."

"Yeah! Sledding! Those dogs are big!"

"How do you get them to turn?"

"Make the right noises, man, and they do it! But they wouldn't listen to me. Hey, Jens, you flew the Harmons from site to site, right?"

"They hired me after their first pilot got his leg busted

in that car accident. They were good customers. They always paid in advance. Not everyone does that, you know."

"You ever think the accidents weren't *accidents*?"

His eyes widened. "You mean, someone tried to stop them?"

I scratched my head. I squeezed my temples, as if I had a headache. I let him wait. I said, "That diary. Thing is, I'm reading back in Kelley's diary, the print files. *There's something in it* that I read, I can't figure out what it is, but *there's something she said that's the answer. I know it!* And, wait! You're Norwegian, right? Ever hear of a city called Tromso?"

"It's our Arctic capital," he said with some pride.

"Ever been there?"

"Me? I'm from Oslo. I served in the Air Force in Bodo, but never went to Tromso, no."

"Now you're a citizen here, right?"

"Yes."

"You had to take the test? Who's the first president? What's the capital of Minnesota? How many states in the U.S.?"

Jens Erik was down on one knee, the way we'd been told Iñupiats speak with children, the elderly, or, in my case, a grieving drunk. He held a sweating can of Foster's. His silver hair was brushed back, and his eyes were the blue of ice shining up in a glacier, or rather, if color could look sad, it would look like Jens's eyes.

"Jens, what's the capital of Minnesota, anyway?"

"Who the hell remembers?"

"That proves you're American," I said. "You can't answer basic questions about our country."

Jens Erik laughed and took a drink. I said, "You must have a brand-new social security number. I bet those numbers are so high now, you immigrants must need a card the size of a movie poster to get all the digits on it, that or the digits are so small you can't see them anymore. Got your card, Jens? Lemme see it. I wanna see your card!"

He smiled. "Who are you, an immigration agent?"

I fumbled for my wallet. "My card, see? Nine digits."

"I don't carry mine around," said the pilot. "The guy at the agency told us, don't keep it in your wallet. You might get mugged. Keep your card in a safe place."

I said, "Where's your safe place, Jens?"

He laughed. "You a thief?" he said.

ALAN MCDOUGAL OFFERED ME THE SPARE BEDROOM IN HIS HUT but I said I'd already accepted Calvin's invitation. Deirdre McDougal came over and said nothing but held my hand. I felt badly for pretending with her that I was drunk. Eddie tried to take my glass away, but I loudly told him to buzz off. I finished the water, lumbered to the liquor table, poured in more Tito, and did the bathroom spill-it-out routine again.

I heard people talking outside the bathroom.

—*He asked my social security number!*

—*He was asking about the pipeline!*

—*He said there's clues in Kelley's diary.*

Eddie went person to person, making excuses for my drunk condition, glancing back at me and shaking his head occasionally, *Poor Joe*, telling them that I'd been babbling "crazy theories." I held the blackness at bay but at all times Karen stood offstage. People moved around me like marionettes, or two-dimensional images. I felt crushing grief ready to flood in. I saw a black void stretching into the future.

You brought her here. You could have stayed out of things. You were even ordered to stay out.

"Joe? I saw Karen at the high school. She was coughing. I thought she might be getting sick. I'm so sorry."

Bruce Friday had brought over a kitchen chair and reversed it and straddled it so his arms lay on top. He was drinking a Coke. He emitted a slightly moldy odor, a guy who lives alone, for years, who uses mothballs instead of a washing machine. His arms looked thin beneath his shirt, skinny impressions, but close up the muscles in his wrists and hands were powerful. Scarred. Corded. I saw white patches on his cheek, discolorations where frostbite had healed over the years.

The Longhorn hut was decorated more expensively than the government one in which I resided. The furniture was plusher, the paint fresh. The kitchenware was top of the line—restaurant quality, not Army surplus, like ours. The photos on walls, unlike personal momentos in other huts, were corporate: a shot of their gigantic floating Arctic drill rig, the *Bowhead,* exploring off Greenland; a shot of Dave and Deborah shaking hands with Alaska's former Democratic senator, on this base; a shot of one of their seismic ships off Arctic Russia, escorted by a Russian icebreaker—Longhorn had drilled there; a shot of Merlin, Deborah, and the secretary of Homeland Security, on the bridge of a U.S. icebreaker, poring over a nautical chart.

"You talk to Karen?" I asked Bruce.

Head shake. "I told that Army captain, Hess, that I saw her at the high school. Seems I confirmed what someone else already told him. By the way, Hess is looking for you."

"It's not like I'm hiding, you know."

"Karen was with a child at the school. A little kid. I saw the kid take her hand, lead her out to the parking lot."

"Boy kid or girl?"

"Sorry. I saw them from the back."

"Parka color? Pink would be a clue."

"Dark green, I think. Or maybe it was blue."

"Did you see where they went in the parking lot?"

"I wish I did. I stayed in the building."

"Hey, Bruce, I wanted to ask about your polar bears . . ."

He looked surprised that I'd switched the subject to this, but he gave his usual answer. "They're not *my* bears. They're Earth's, Joe. The living bounty of all."

"I wondered all summer. You want to block off their territory, block development where they live, right?"

"They're dying out, Joe. They need protection. They need a federal designation, an off-limits habitat. Where they hunt. Where they breed. Where they raise cubs."

"And if their habitat was protected, how much exactly—how many miles of coast—would that include?"

"All the way across, Joe!"

"Wouldn't that stop any new pipeline construction, sea to shore?"

"I hope so," Bruce Friday said, rising to leave.

"By the way, Bruce, you ever find any bears out on the tundra this year, dead from rabies when you autopsy them?"

Bruce Friday stopped, turned, stared at me.

"Rabies? No. Foxes get it mostly. In bears it's possible, but almost unknown."

"JOIN ME FOR A DRINK, MERLIN. YOU LOOK LIKE YOU NEED IT."

"I don't drink, Joe. You know that."

"Scared of a little vodka, Chief? Come on. One sip."

"I haven't had a drink since I was nineteen. I hate the taste."

"Merlin, we may have missed something at that cabin."

He grew very still. "What?"

"Well, five of us get out of the chopper, see? Eddie and I go into the cabin right away, see? And your deputies *split up and go out by themselves* and then come back and tell us they found nothing. But we never checked what they said." I smiled. I hoped it was a shrewd, suspicious smile.

Merlin stood up. Color blotched his powerful face.

"You're saying a cop was involved? Covered things up?"

"You told me that Clay Qaqulik didn't share his theories with you. You said he worked alone. Why would one of your own people do that? Maybe he didn't trust *you*, Merlin. You personally."

Merlin's eyes narrowed, then he sighed. "You're upset, Joe. I understand."

I shrugged. I took a long drink. I drank all my water. I said, more aggressively, "Eddie and I were in the cabin. We couldn't see outside. Luther took the ATV out on the tundra. What did he do there? You went through Clay's pockets. I'm *upset*? You think I give a damn about your sensibilities? It never stops! Poor us! Always victims! Don't give me that poor-us shit."

Merlin's face loomed very close, so I could see the pores, the gap between two lower teeth, black hairs in his nose, the half-healed scar of a shaving cut on his chin.

"You are drunk." *I'll pretend you didn't say that.* "Clay and I grew up together," he said gently.

"Yeah, yeah, family, all of us brothers. Merlin, who's the guy you arrest half the time in killings? The husband. The brother. Why not a cousin? With a bank account in Oahu? Pipeline money. You have one of those accounts, Merlin? Dave here pays you on the side? Is that it?"

"Stay away from the office," he said. "I don't think it is such a good idea for us to work together anymore."

Merlin picked up his hat and left.

MIKAEL GRANDY HAD HIS ARM IN A SLING, AND HIS SHIRT BIL-lowed out due to bulky bandages beneath the fabric, wrapping his rib cage. He approached gingerly. I was surprised he would come near me, surprised to see more grief and guilt than pain on his stupidly handsome face.

"I fell in love with her. I never met anyone like her before. She was strong, and she was loyal. She loved you. She told me that. She told me because I, uh . . . I confessed how I felt. All she could talk about half the time was you. How you'd buy a little house. How you'd live back east. How she wanted kids one day, but not yet. I'm not going to press charges against you."

"Why are you telling me this, Mikael?"

"I need to tell somebody."

"Right. Plus, your film of her death will make your show a big hit, huh? You'll tell the story of the Marine savage who broke your ribs at conferences. You'll tell the story when you win your gold statuette next year. You'll say, *I felt sorry for Rush. I couldn't take that poor Marine to court.*"

He did not reply. I saw truth in his face, a flush, but also something deeper resembling genuine sympathy.

I asked, "Did your family really own part of the North Slope way back when, Mikael?"

"We would have been millionaires today." He winced when he shrugged. "But my grandfather used to tell me, in Brooklyn, millionaires have money, but this does not make them happy people."

"What would you be today, if Russia had kept Alaska? Duke Mikael? Count Mikael?"

He cradled the hurt arm. "Duke."

"Where was the land your family would have owned?"

"I'm not exactly sure. But the communists would have

wiped away our claims anyway, even if Russia had kept Alaska."

"You never even went looking for the land? I mean, you're here! You didn't even want to see it?"

"What would be the point? I concentrate on today," he said. "The grand days of my family are over."

ARMY CAPTAIN RAYMOND HESS, AMANDA NG'S INVESTIGATOR, found me in the chair a half hour later, said he'd looked all over for me, checked the labs and my Quonset hut. Said, in a tight, irritated voice, as if I'd purposely avoided him, which I had, that he "needed to clear up a few questions."

Hess was a trim, balding man with almost invisible eyebrows, an oddly high voice, watery light blue eyes, and a West Point ring on one finger, a thin wedding band on another. His collar was starched above the Arctic-weight Army sweater. He'd draped his parka over the back of his chair. He looked an old thirty, and had a lean bullet shape, tapering at the head. By now he'd know that he was supposed to pay extra attention to me. He'd have been told in no uncertain terms that if Colonel Joe Rush and Major Edward Nakamura *were* involved in a cover-up and he missed it, he could kiss his career good-bye.

A toilet flushed. And flushed. And flushed. I'd "finished" my third glass of vodka. Hess's nose wrinkled. He smelled urine on me, or maybe the liquor I'd rubbed on my clothes. I was sprawled, legs stretched, head lolling, a sneer on my lips.

"Army security," I said. "You guys are even worse than the Federal Bureau of Incompetency."

"Let's go back to the research center, Colonel. We have a room set up for quiet talk."

"For interrogations."

"Discussions."

"Discuss away," I said, leaning back, watching the man's irritation grow as blotches on his too-white face.

"It really would be better at the center, sir."

"For who? Whom? Is it *who* or *whom*? I never know. How are you with grammar, Hess? How'd you do in high school English?"

"Colonel, please don't make this difficult."

"Her death is easy so far, Hess?"

I had to give him credit. He remained polite, if stiff and disingenuous. "Sir, we're on the same team."

I stood up. I breathed into his face. Up close, his skin seemed to lack pores. There was nothing wrong with his approach. I had to be eliminated as a suspect. Also, like all the troops here, he had to know he was in danger, if the vaccinations didn't work, and the rabies turned out to be contagious. He'd been parachuted into a strange town and denied full support. In quarantine *drills,* the security contingent included dozens of personnel. But Barrow lacked logistics for a larger team. The admiral— the old head of my unit—had warned Washington for months that the country was unprepared for an Arctic emergency. The emergency was here. The country was still unprepared.

I snapped, "Hess, you can't order me." As if the effort had been too great, I fell back on the chair.

"Colonel Rush, you—"

"Hey, Hess! Did you volunteer for this? I bet you did! How'd they trick you into volunteering? You might get infected, bring the germ home to your wife and kids. That's why that bitchy colonel only took along three of you, you know. Until they know the vaccine works. You're expendable. How's it feel to be the guy they could lose and not care?"

He was red now. I allowed him to escort me into a rear bedroom, the one with the air vent above the right-hand bed. The shaft ran directly to the living room, where I hoped conversation was quieting, as people positioned themselves beneath the vent, straining to hear. Or maybe they'd be behind the bedroom door, government-contract quality, even thinner than the old piece-of-garbage security doors that the FAA approved on pre-9/11 commercial aircraft.

Someone out there, I prayed, was desperate to listen.

Hess was smart. He didn't start off with rabies. He started with Karen. He told me how sorry he was about her death. He asked about the status of our relationship. He made it seem he cared about her.

Our status is that I'm responsible for her murder.

I said, "We were engaged to be married in two months."

Had things been "good" between us recently?

We fought and made up and fought some more.

"They were very good," I said.

Did Karen have enemies in town? Had she said anything about work problems? Had I shared sensitive information with her?

Ah, here we go on rabies. Yes. I shared information.

"No," I said. "Tell me something, Hess." *We're all on the same team?* "What kind of weapon killed her?"

"I'm sorry, Colonel. I can't tell you that, sir."

"Can't? Or won't?" I knew he couldn't.

"Same thing, sir."

"Leftie or rightie? Man or woman? Give me something."

"Did you and Dr. Vleska ever discuss your work here, or the investigation into the Harmon deaths?"

"We were threatened if we talked about work. We discussed honeymoon plans. Want to hear them?"

"Yes."

I'd asked Eddie to watch for anyone hanging around beneath that air vent. I envisioned people jostling and quieting and looking up. I told Hess loudly what I'd *really* told Karen, and wanted people in the other room to hear. "Everything's connected. General Homza is wrong when he thinks she was killed by a local. They couldn't get to me, so they went after her! It's not about the quarantine! It's the same people who killed the Harmons!"

I raised my voice until I was shouting.

"GIVE ME ANOTHER DAY WITH THAT DIARY! THERE'S SOMETHING IN THAT DIARY! I KNOW IT! I'M CLOSE, I'M VERY CLOSE!"

Hess's voice sharpened. "You have the diary?"

"An F-drive copy. Not the original, asshole."

"Sir, I'll need you to hand it over. It's evidence."

I argued, shouted that I needed the files. He threatened to have me arrested if I did not surrender them. Under martial law, he could do it.

I begged him to let me keep the diary. I said that it was my right to have a copy. When he didn't back down I grew more belligerent, told him to go fuck himself, shouted, refused, and finally gave in, making sure my voice carried.

"Just how small is your brain, Hess? Is it even there?"

"We'll go and get it now, Colonel."

I'd alienated everyone I could think of. If someone here was guilty, I hoped I'd hit on the thing they feared. Hess escorted me from the bedroom, a drunk, shamed, broken presence, except as we passed the group outside I glanced over and winked, as if I'd just pulled a fast one on Hess. I saw my look register. I saw Mikael Grandy frown and look sharply at McDougal. Deborah Lillienthal stared. Dave had been pouring himself a vodka. He looked thoughtful. Eddie watched them all, trying to see a tell.

Outside, the night was dark, and the wind came off the sea and sliced at my face with the sharpness of an *ulu*, an Eskimo knife used for skinning. I glanced back at the hut and saw a white face, Deborah, in the window. Deborah who'd feared she was infected with rabies. *Because you slept with someone. Who?*

Soldiers moved between huts. Smoke whirled from stovepipe vents. Someone approached Hess and told him that sleeping arrangements were changing. All the civilians would sleep in two huts, or in town, if they had friends there. Soldiers needed the other huts.

My fists were clenched. My jaw throbbed. I felt blood coursing in my arteries, trying to burst out; a fury that was pure and directed and craved outlet. I was filled with the rage of a man who had, through his pride and maneuverings, killed his future.

In our hut I retrieved one of two F-drive copies I'd made of Kelley's diary files, and gave it to Hess. He didn't see me shove the extra one in my pocket. He probably saw the spittle that I made sure hung from a corner of my mouth. Joe Rush, half drunk, in a rage.

A rabbit's foot. A talisman. *An answer,* I hoped.

If Homza came through on his promise, I'd be transferred off base—suspended from the investigation.

You'll be alone, General Homza had warned me.

Well, I was already alone. I was more alone than I'd known possible.

Watching Hess drive off, I spoke softly, out loud, to thin air, to whoever had killed her. Who, I now believed, had wiped out Clay Qaqulik and the Harmon family, and then eight others in town.

"Come and get me," I said.

SIXTEEN

The first quarantine death occurred three days later. It was not from rabies.

Whynot Francis, hunter, father of three, whaling captain, stood twelve feet beneath the earth in his ice cellar, behind his one-story Barrow home, that morning, enraged at the soldiers who had sealed off the town; at the growing fear, at the lines of panic-stricken people flooding the hospital, coming in with any symptom at all; normal coughs, normal aches, normal fevers, imaginary pains. Everyone waiting, holding their breath, waiting for something terrible to occur.

They will not keep me here, *he thought.*

Whynot was a stocky, balding, pigeon-toed man, plain faced, with a bowlegged walk. He had a master's degree in geology from the University of California, and worked for the Iñupiat-owned Arctic Slope Regional Corporation, ad-

*vising the board on which tribal land could be leased to
outsiders, which should be retained.*

*Whynot took an annual spring trip each year to Phila-
delphia, where his college-age daughter was an English major at Penn. His wife was an anthropologist, who studied
the psychology of nonnative scientists who came to the Arctic.*

*That morning Whynot considered the hacked-off chunks
of raw seal, musk ox, and caribou around him—and a
diminishing supply of bowhead. It not only fed his family
and in-laws, much of it went to the old folks' home, the
Presbyterian church, and to Uncle Glenn and Aunt Flo,
after Glenn broke his leg in July.*

There was not enough food. Whynot's anger crested.

*"We're going out. To hell with the soldiers," he called up
to the four faces peering down at him through the wooden
trapdoor opening. Above that was thick fog.*

*The cellar was fifteen by ten feet. Its permafrost walls
gleamed with ice. Permafrost went down eight hundred feet
in Barrow. Many homes had these cellars. Whynot's meat
lay in piles, not neatly cut as in a butcher shop, but in
hacked-off chunks, ribs rimed with frozen blood, white bones
protruding, ice crystals coating it, nature's freezer burn.*

*Whynot climbed up the aluminum ladder. Up top waited
his two favorite cousins, Lewis and Aqpayuk, his brother-in-
law, Edward, and his best boyhood pal, Walter Aiken, who
had played tight end for the Barrow Whalers state champ
high school football team when Whynot was quarterback.*

*Whynot told the others, "I served my country in Iraq. I
fought for the United States. These soldiers have no right to
keep us here."*

Three of them nodded agreement but Edward looked nervous. He was a shy, heavyset, kind man whose bad eyesight required the use of thick-lensed glasses. He tended to sweat when nervous, and he was sweating now. He was a reliable and highly efficient crew member.

Edward said, doubtfully, "That general said the Coast Guard will stop boats from going out."

"We'll go the long way around. The ships won't see us in the fog."

Whynot kissed his wife, Violet, good-bye and made sure his eighteen-foot-long powerboat was secured in its hauler to his Durango. He loaded the whaling dart gun, harpoon, and whale bombs. The crew piled in and they bumped through semi-deserted streets toward the beach. Normally small boats were launched from a protected point, a small cove north of the old Navy base. But the road was blocked, so Whynot figured he'd just back the rig up in town, onto the black beach.

Almost all the soldiers were out at the barricades. So no soldiers spotted the truck hauling the boat.

Bowheads were enormous compared to the small aluminum outboard boats. Normally this time of year, scouting crews would go out, range around as far as thirty miles away, and report back to Barrow by radio. When the migration began, all the other crews would go out, too.

But all radio reception was jammed just now. Whynot knew that if he got lucky today, if he spotted whales, his crew would be alone.

The whales were much, much bigger than the little boats. Normally several boats would haul a floating carcass home.

Whynot's elders had told him to go for the young ones, as they are plumper. Bowheads could live for over two hundred years. Some had been harvested with harpoons in their hides dating from President Andrew Jackson's day.

"Cold," Whynot told Edward and Aqpayuk, in the cab with him, as he backed onto the beach. "I haven't felt cold like this, this time of year, ever."

"The sea will freeze soon," said Aqpayuk, a backhoe driver.

"The whales must be coming," said Edward.

"If this cold settles in for a few more days, soon we can ride our snowmobiles away, around the soldiers."

Edward said, as they backed the boat into the water, "The general said the quarantine might end soon." Meaning, Let's wait and not go out today.

"No! The ocean will be solid by then. No hunt!"

Whynot's friend Walter guffawed from the cramped backseat of the extended cab. He was a good spotter, an alcoholic who sometimes disappeared for weeks on Nome's Front Street, its row of bars. He'd fly off. Later, someone would get a phone call. Someone else would go fetch Walter, and bring the sick man home.

"Once the whales pass, they are gone," he said.

Edward kept at it, as they bounced off in a thick fog. "The general said the Coast Guard has a chopper, snipers."

But any reference to threats hardened resolve. Lewis, a teacher at the high school, growled, "The Whaling Commission. The duck in."

These were references to other times that outsiders had imposed their will on Barrow. The International Whaling

Commission, which regulated global whale hunting, had ordered it all to stop in the 1970s, when scientists said the species was on the edge of extinction.

"Only six hundred left, they said," Lewis said. "We said there were more. The commission said we were wrong. Turned out there were thousands of bowheads. The ban was lifted. If we would have gone along, hunting would have stopped."

Walter agreed. "And the duck in. Those federals said we couldn't hunt ducks. Too many ducks shot down south, by sport hunters. We didn't listen. We eat those ducks. We killed what we needed and, together, took the ducks to their offices and dared them to arrest us. We were too many. Civil disobedience worked. It will work now."

"What's that?" interrupted Aqpayuk, quietest man in the crew, shielding his eyes, gazing west. They'd left the fog area. They were in the clear. He gazed in the direction of the Coast Guard ship, which was not in view.

"Where?"

"That speck."

"It's a drone!" announced Edward.

Their parkas were powder blue. The boat was white. Whynot *manned the steering console.* To hell with the drone, *he thought.*

Despite the speck growing closer in the sky, Whynot *felt a surge of excitement. Hunting!*

The drone—it looked like a big model plane—came closer and began circling as they reached an area of slush, and began powering through, rocking as the hull made contact with more solid area. The drone flew about a hundred feet up. Whynot pushed the throttle forward. The boat surged ahead. The drone fell back but sped up. The boat—now more than a mile out—hit a completely ice-free area and reached more turbulent waters where the Chukchi Sea met the Beaufort. The drone stayed with them, like a prison searchlight tracking an escape.

Whynot moved the steering wheel left to right, left and right, zigzagging to see what the little drone did.

It adjusted.

"I don't like that thing," Edward said.

"Do you think it is armed?" asked Aqpayuk.

The seas grew calmer as they left the junction of currents. Glass. Perfect for hunting. The whales, if they were out, could come up at any time. They could be five miles from shore or thirty. The men started to see solid ice bits. Suddenly a message came over channel six, the international channel. They'd passed beyond the area being jammed.

"This is the U.S. Coast Guard cutter Wilmington to the boat which has just left Barrow. Please turn around."

"Well, it was a good try. Let's go home," said Edward.

Walter snorted. Lewis asked, from the prow, "How long can that thing stay in the air anyway?"

"I'll shoot it," said Walter, hefting his rifle.

Whynot told him to put the rifle down. Destroying property was not something he wished to do. "It will go away," he said, although he was starting to doubt this.

The radio started up again. "This is the U.S. Coast Guard cutter Wilmington to the boat that has just left Barrow. You are violating quarantine. You are ordered to turn back. Please acknowledge."

Whynot mimicked the tone. "'Please acknowledge.'"

They rode along like this for a while, the drone sometimes dipping, sometimes making a wrong move but adjusting, sometimes disappearing into low mist but reemerging. The ice bits became more numerous. The whole sea was starting to freeze. Edward ducked his head, as if that would make him invisible. Whynot eyed the thing. Walter gave it the finger. Aqpayuk said that back in Barrow, probably lots of people knew they had gone out. They'd be on landline phones. "Hey! Did you hear! Whynot's crew went out!!!!"

This gave Whynot more resolution. Iñupiat means "the real people" and the people were with him, urging him on.

Edward groaned. "Look! Here comes the helicopter."

This time the thing in the sky was bigger, red, coming fast, a swiftly moving bubble.

Edward said, "You think there's a sniper on board?"

Walter scoffed, "What are they going to do, shoot us?"

"I heard those snipers are trained to shoot out engines on boats. I read it in Parade *magazine. They clip on a harness, hang out the door. They shoot up drug boats."*

"Drug boats?"

"Yeah, those fast-moving ones—faster than us—that come up from Colombia, heading for Mexico, with cocaine."

Whynot was outraged. "You're comparing us to a cocaine boat?"

"I'm just saying the snipers are good."

Whynot barked, "You're saying that whaling—our families have been whaling for a thousand years—is like selling cocaine!?"

"You know that's not what I'm saying," said Edward as

the little drone veered off, made a wide U-turn, summoned back toward its launch point. It passed the incoming chopper. One craft grew smaller, the other larger.

So Whynot increased the zigzagging. His anger was cresting. That these people would barricade his town! That they'd treat citizens like prisoners! That they'd send a sniper to try to stop him from whaling! That they did not even send vaccine to cure people of a disease they claimed was fatal!

"We should give up," counseled Edward.

Walter and Aqpayuk didn't say it, but Whynot could see from their bland expressions that they now agreed. And his own more logical side said that perhaps it was time to give up. But his fury grew. He did not want to back down. Perhaps if he pushed this confrontation a bit longer that red helicopter would turn around.

Except it wasn't turning. It was getting lower, and now, looking up, Whynot saw the door was open and someone was harnessed to the side, one boot on the runner, and the person was positioning a rifle of some sort, aiming at the boat.

"It's a girl," Aqpayuk said in wonder.

"A girl!"

Those who would survive today would learn later that the sniper had been trained at the Guard's facility in Jacksonville, Florida. Her name was Gail Mullen. She was twenty-five years old. She'd proved her marksmanship several times over during Coast Guard drug interdiction patrols off Panama. There, during 2 A.M. chases in the Pacific, against boats moving twice as fast as Whynot's, she'd brought her .50-caliber rifle to bear on an engine, and, after drug runners ignored warnings, put a round into that engine, made the boats stop, the crews give up. She'd trained to shoot out engines, not to hurt people.

She was a little nervous this time, though, because she knew that the people below were not drug smugglers, but just whalers. These men had not been confined to town because they were evil, but because they might be ill. Gail Mullen hated her job at that moment. The boat below cut right, and left. The figures in baby-blue parkas looking up at her. No drug bales aboard. Just five guys.

Gail heard her pilot over the loud-hailer, urging the whaling crew to change course, using information he'd been supplied with from town. "Captain Whynot Francis, please turn around."

Below, Whynot grew furious at the mention of his name! The government knew everything about everybody! The use of his name was supposed to make him feel small against their hugeness, make him back down because just by saying his name they were telling him that they knew who his family was, where he lived, they knew his history. He'd learned in college that in some parts of the world, primitive people never reveal their real names to outsiders. They believe that if you know someone's name, you have power over them.

Whynot saw that this was true. He was an unimportant asterisk to those in that chopper. Those who wanted to stop a four-thousand-year-old hunt.

He told himself to stop, turn around, Edward was right.

He pushed the throttle ahead.

At that moment two things happened. The first was that the copter hit an air pocket and dipped as Gail Mullen pulled the trigger. The second was that Whynot swung the wheel left. In a fraction of a millisecond, the object in the rifle sight stopped being an outboard engine, and became a man.

The bullet slammed into Whynot's chest with force enough to knock over a man ten times his size. He went over the side, into the freezing water. The crew thought the shooter was going to fire again. Aqpayuk ducked. Walter ran for the steering console. Edward grabbed the gaff, already looking over the side to where Whynot floated facedown in the sea, a spreading mass of red around him.

The boat, released from human control, began swinging in a wild arc, bounced off a piece of ice just as Walter got it under control, and powered down, gliding toward his captain.

Aqpayuk stood up, holding up his hands, like a bank robber caught by police.

Walter, calling Whynot's name, brought the boat beside Whynot's body.

Edward roared at the chopper, "You shot him!"

The chopper hovering. The body starting to sink until Edward gaffed it, like a dead whale.

The sniper in shock up there.

The word—a shooting death—to spread in town when the boat returned.

They killed Whynot Francis! They shot him down like a dog! They're going to kill all of us! They said vaccine would come and they lied!

SEVENTEEN

It got worse in town after that, fast. Deep winter arrived early that night. A November-type freeze slammed the coast in mid-October, as news of the accidental shooting death spread. A cloak of ice descended upon the tundra, wire, soldiers stamping to keep warm out there.

Before Whynot's death, some residents had brought food out to the wire for soldiers. That stopped. Some citizens, a few, veterans mostly, had acknowledged passing patrols with waves of the hand. That stopped, too. A sullen rage gripped the city, a sense of building fury.

General Homza considered sending Rangers house to house, to seize firearms. Merlin and the mayor talked him out of it. *Shooting will start if you do.*

Previously I'd thought of Arctic seasons in terms of color, white winters, floral summers. Winter was *feel*. At twelve below zero skin became paper. At thirty below, outerwear did, too. Oxygen was fragile. Breath solidified inside your nose. Teeth hurt. Light had substance. Earth was Pluto, so far from sun that heat was misnomer, legend, memory, grail.

"Hold still, Chase. This will hurt."

The nine-year-old boy looked scared, watching the hypodermic. His mother carried a sleeping infant on a sling, on her back. The boy made no sound as the rabies vaccination went in, from a supply—two hundred fresh doses—that arrived that morning. I'd been assigned to the airport, where twenty children stood fretfully in line, in the terminal. The room was unnaturally quiet. Most adults present glared at me. I felt them blaming me, the Army, the general, Washington, D.C., for the outbreak.

Making everything even harder was the fact that a preventative rabies regimen, for those who may have been exposed, was four vaccinations over a two-week period.

Eddie was at the hospital, examining anyone coming in with fevers, aches, possible early signs of rabies. We took blood. We were off the criminal investigation, separated so that Amanda Ng and Raymond Hess could question us one at a time, which they did at least once a day. Back in D.C., Ng had told me, our old boss, Admiral Galli, was being grilled to see if he was hiding anything about the origin of the disease.

"The White House needs to be on top of this," Ng said.

"Brave boy. Bring him back in three days, for the next shot," I advised the boy's mother, who looked about twenty-five.

She regarded me disdainfully, zipping up her son's parka. "You are not going to vaccinate all of us, are you?"

"Ma'am, that just isn't true. The supply comes in slowly. Ma'am, you were Clay Qaqulik's next-door neighbor, I see. Did he ever talk to you about the Harmons?"

"You," she said, and I understood the word to include the soldiers, Homza, Eddie, "*you* killed Whynot."

She led the boy out the heavy swinging door. Outside the terminal, vehicles idled; cars, snowmobiles, a four-wheel ATV. Some families arrived with the kids in sleds pulled by snowmobile, breath frosting in the cold.

I asked the next family in line about Clay. I asked everyone. It was useless. Whynot's death had thrown up a wall. The father growled at me, over his shoulder, as he left, "You people always ask, you never answer," and opened the door, to let in a blast of Arctic air. I felt the eyes of the others in line. The silence grew deeper than the resentments. Rangers stood in the corners, in case force might be needed to control civilians. But this morning, at least, it was not.

On my way home in the Ford I spotted two Iñupiat men with ice probes, long, thin iron poles, standing beyond the beach, on newly formed sea ice. They were probing thickness. Only later would the reason become clear.

I checked in with the general via encrypted cell, and urged once again that we explain the truth about the vaccine shortage to the community.

"Open your mouth, and the cell door in Leavenworth will close it," Homza said.

...

THE NORTH SLOPE BOROUGH RESCUE SQUAD HANGAR HAD been designated one of three food distribution points. The squad's Lear jet and copters had been moved to a different hangar, to provide more space. Each morning two big Hercules arrived from Fairbanks, carrying supplies, which were then forklifted into the hangar. Portable heaters hissed as soldiers took old ration coupons from people in line, and handed out new ones, freshly printed, good for three days.

I filled my knapsack with Ronzoni spaghetti, Folgers coffee, white rice, and cans of Green Giant peas. I took a package of frozen hamburger stamped UNITED STATES ARMY. There were canned pears and Devil Dogs and Coca-Cola and cartons of Marlboros on another table. There was Heinz ketchup. There was Bumble Bee tuna. There was A&P brand white bread. People in line brought their own bags, cardboard boxes, or knapsacks to load.

Someone behind me bumped me roughly. I turned and looked into the florid face of a man I recognized as one of the baggage handlers at the airport, that is, when the airport worked. He was a big white guy with long greasy hair jutting from his soiled stocking cap, bad teeth, bad breath, and bad posture. Stuffing spilled from a rip in his oil-stained parka, poked out from peeling duct tape he'd applied to cover the rip.

He stared back at me, wanting to fight. He sneered. He said, smiling in challenge, "Must have tripped. Sorry."

I turned back and heard him snicker.

You're a lucky guy, I thought, considering what I could have done to him, what I wanted to do, but I recognized my own misplaced anger. I needed my anger for someone else.

Don't waste it on him.

THE REPORTER/PHOTOGRAPHER POOL ARRIVED BY HERCULES transport. Pressure was growing in the rest of the country for the White House to prove that the city was getting humanitarian aid. The reporters stayed outside the wire. They milled about on the tundra in a group, like a herd of musk ox, staying close to one another. Fish do that to hide from predators. Reporters did it as if that might shield them from germs.

They snapped photos from a distance. They interviewed soldiers two hundred yards off, where the disease was allegedly held at bay by thin wire. I took a break from vaccinating and watched them through a window, and saw the way their breath seemed to be absorbed into one mass of rising fog, mist the color of gauze-protective masks.

What's it like to be working the wire, soldier?

Aren't you scared that you might get sick?

Do you have plans to handle a riot?

What if you are ordered to fire on civilians?

Someone in line said that the mayor had agreed to talk to reporters, along with General Homza. *As you can see everything is under control.* Meanwhile, a film crew in the chopper circled the town, hovered over the high school, and the icebreaker at sea, hovered above the hospital, so the camera operators could get steady shots.

The reporters filed back into the Hercules and it took off, headed back for Anchorage, or Fairbanks.

The rest of the world would see the film that evening.

No civilians in Barrow would see it, as satellite reception was jammed. General Homza, who had access, didn't care.

I went back to vaccinating. Our supply of rabies serum ran out. We had over three thousand unvaccinated people in Barrow. I checked in with the general. I told him, *nothing new.*

"YOU'VE GOT FROSTBITE IN YOUR LUNGS."

The Ranger in front of me had to be all of twenty-three years old, a tall, fit-looking warrior whom I'd insisted on examining when I heard him wheezing, saw him wince with each breath. His voice had gone scratchy. His lungs sounded like cracking ice. He said he'd patrolled the wire for four hours last night, and the pain had started then.

"In my *lungs*, sir?" He didn't believe it.

"I'll write you a note. Take it to the hospital. Where are you from, soldier?"

"Florida. People get frostbite in their *lungs*?"

...

THE CITY LAY SHEATHED IN COLD, ITS ANGLES SHARPER, ITS AIR clearer, any delineation between land and sea beginning to blur into white void. The ice out there starting to thicken. Light seemed dimmer, and lasted a few minutes less each day. The planet seemed to shrink.

Up here, in the old days, this time of year, people would disappear into their sod houses or subterranean homes, bundle up, bunch up, live off body heat and stored animal meat and, like bears, begin the long hibernation. If winter lasted too long, they'd starve, eat pebbles to try to keep hunger at bay. If the sea ice moved the wrong way, it would suddenly sweep onto land, as fast-moving mountains that the Eskimos called *ivus*. A family could go to sleep at night and never wake up. The *ivu* would crush them, Merlin had told me only a few days back, when we were friends.

Now we did not speak.

Streetlights glowed beneath the thin, cold moon.

Henry David Thoreau once said you can gauge the health of a society by the trust that its members have for each other, even if strangers. By that measure we were all sick. The country was sick. And it wasn't a sickness that came from a germ.

The "polar spa" was a joke of a slummy two-story building that stood a few blocks from Arctic Pizza, across the street from the beach. The white paint job was the only thing new about it. On its side were depicted three polar bears wearing Ray-Bans, sunning themselves on lounge chairs, on an ice floe, while orcas leaped at sea.

Inside, the place was falling apart. In summers it functioned as bottom-of-the-barrel bunking for spillover researchers during weeks that scientists packed town; slept
in cots at the community center, like hurricane victims,
and tripled up in hotel rooms. Unlucky grad students
ended up here.

I lowered my binoculars, standing on the rickety roof.
Out on the tundra, the weather had caught the Rangers
by surprise. They were the Wehrmacht in Russia, 1942.
Machinery stopped. Humvees needed to be plugged in
when parked, but there were no electrical outlets there.
No one had anticipated early winter. No one had provided
proper equipment for sustained land-based winter Arctic
ops.

I watched Rangers tottering around. In the round
binocular *O*, halos of freezing breath trailed men walking
or stamping in the snow to keep warm.

Come and get me.

I went inside where it was only slightly warmer, made
my way down stairs that seemed ready to collapse. The
bunk room was designed to sleep fifteen in tiers of racks
that ringed the walls. The saggy mattresses were assaulted
by cross currents, drafts slipping through wall gaps and
plastic sheeting stapled to sills. An ancient gas heater
chugged away in a corner, coughing fitful bursts of lukewarm air against the steady assault of cold.

I slept in a bunk farthest from the heater. It was warmer
by the heater, but its chugging would mask the sound of
an attack. I wore long underwear, a Marines sweatshirt
and a stocking hat, even indoors. I removed my Beretta

92A1 pistol from the back holster and broke it down for cleaning. I pushed the right side button and rotated the breakdown lever and moved the slide forward and cleaned the gun. I made sure to rack it back when it was on the frame. It was a heavy pistol, with a Teflon-based black finish. It had a thick grip. The trigger needed extra pressure. It fired fifteen rounds.

Eddie was on duty at the hospital at the moment. I was alone.

There were four big bunk rooms, each equipped with the antique gas burners. The floors were concave plywood. Locker-room style showers ran rusty and cold. The kitchen looked as if it had been installed in 1920, and featured a vintage Maytag, four-burner stove, and metal cabinets filled with plastic glasses featuring logos from the 1964 world's fair.

I spent hours with Kelley's diary files over the next two days. I ventured out for walks, advertising that I was alone. Once, outside, I noticed a North Slope police department SUV pull up across the road. The windows were up. Deputy Luther Oz sat inside. I nodded at him. I felt a glare through his sunglasses. Slowly, he pulled off.

On the fourth morning—no vaccine supply that day— I ate Army-supplied oatmeal with cold water and raisins and powered up the computer for the hundredth time and inserted the memory stick and called up Kelley's diary, the written parts. The bunk room smelled of mold. The words of a dead fifteen-year-old teen popped up. I scrolled back and forth, trolling, reading inanities written months before the Harmon deaths. I went over the same stuff for the twentieth time. Sometimes I concentrated on specific passages. Sometimes I skimmed. I chose random pages and started at the bottom, moving up, hoping that something I missed before would pop out.

> I had an argument with Mom about candy. She said I can't bring Snickers bars along. So how come Dad can have his own ice cream and I can't have a few bars of candy?

I randomly chose another day.

> Mom got another parking ticket. She's always leaving the car where she can get a ticket! Dad gets mad about the tickets, but she always thinks she'll be out of the store before the cops see the car.

I jumped forward. She was in Barrow now.

> I met the new guide today. His name is Clay and he seems pretty nice. He offered me pickled *muktuk*. It's good!

> Dad's birthday is coming. I want to play a joke on him.

The diary told me about her crush on Leon Kavik. It told me that she feared acne was breaking out on her face. A girl named Jessica back home was making fun of Kelley on the Internet. It was useless. Maybe there was no answer here. Maybe the diary was just the ramblings of a teen.

Someone was banging on the outer door. *BAMBAM-BAMBAM!*

I shoved the pistol in the rear holster. My breath frosted in the hall. The *cunnychuck* door was closed and the front door had no knob, just one of those four-digit punch-in codes, even to exit. It lacked a spy hole. I held the gun low, at my side.

"It is Ranjay!"

The little Indian stood stamping and freezing. He was growing a beard, probably because facial hair might raise warmth by a fraction of a degree. His Honda SUV was plugged into the electrical outlet outside; the only modern amenity the place offered. He was alone, a bundled up ball with legs, Humpty Dumpty style, wearing two hats, one pulled over the other, the whole effect pushing his nose down and his mouth up. Ranjay as Picasso painting. Arctic cubism. The white period.

"Joe, for God's sake, let me in. This is awful!"

His hands were in his pockets. I smiled at his war-orphan look and backed up and he entered. He stood in the hallway, shivering. He had no tolerance for cold. Maybe there was something else in a pocket, not just hands. Maybe he'd pull it out.

"Want some coffee?"

"Anything hot will do!"

I walked at his side to the large, cold kitchen. This room had been old when Khrushchev and Nixon held their kitchen debate in a mock-up U.S. home, at the American National Exhibition in Moscow, in 1959. I opened a metal cabinet and extracted a tin of Folgers. I measured out three heaping tablespoons for the Braun and poured in cold water. We sat at the chipped Formica table and smelled coffee brewing. The mug into which I poured Ranjay's portion read, "Cleveland Indians" and showed a grinning comic-book Native American, with a red-faced leer. Mine read, "Yakutia! Come to Russia's Arctic Diamond Week!"

"No new cases for three days," Ranjay said, cradling the mug. "People are getting angrier. Something will blow."

"It's spreading slower than we feared."

"Maybe not spreading at all, Joe. Like Ebola. It broke out. It killed many. It went underground, disappeared."

"What about the monkeys that Dr. Morgan injected with rabies?"

"Dead in three days."

I gasped, stunned. "That's a huge increase in speed."

"Huge," he said morosely.

"But this also means," I said, brightening a little, "that if there are no new cases in town, maybe it's not airborne. Wait! Morgan and Cruz would have checked that, put sick monkeys with healthy ones, just like Constantine did with the coyotes in Texas. Any spread?"

"Not yet."

"Good. They also inoculated sick monkeys, to see if the vaccine works. Any of those animals fall ill?"

"So far, no. So far, the vaccine seems to work. So maybe

the spread is point source. But, Joe, it's only a few days since we started. The vaccine may just slow it down, not stop it. Too early. We need more time. But I don't know how much time is left before the whole town blows up."

I sat back. It was too early to relax. He was right. There were no good options.

If it just disappears, if the quarantine lifts, we may never find out what happened. If we stay, we'll have a riot soon. If we leave, Karen's killer may get away.

Ranjay looked upset. His hands squeezed the mug. He changed subjects. "Joe, they made you a scapegoat. You are the reason we discovered the rabies. I myself pooh-poohed the notion, yet you were diligent. I do not like what they have done to you. It is not fair at all."

"Thanks, Ranjay." I was moved. But I also did not trust him. It was nothing personal. I did not trust anyone except Eddie, and Eddie was elsewhere most of the time.

Ranjay said, "I think that often in life, the man who sees things first is the one that others do not want to know, my friend."

"I wish I saw things better."

He drank. I drank. He added more sugar. We watched each other over china rims. He had not unzipped his parka yet. At least both of his hands were visible. I could move a lot faster than Ranjay. If Ranjay made a move for his pocket, I'd beat him, I knew.

"Also," he said at length, more quietly, "I've been round the clock at the hospital and did not have an adequate chance to say how sorry I am about Karen."

"Thank you."

"Joe. It is funny, in my country, we arrange marriages. I arranged my own marriage, you know. I was in London. I dated English girls. It did not work. You people believe that if you have a feeling, the logical parts will follow, after you marry. We believe that if the logical parts are there to start with, feeling will follow. But in your case, I would say that everything was there all along."

"Very eloquent, Ranjay."

"What have you found out?"

"Excuse me?"

Ranjay's eyes dipped toward his mug, and he lifted it, so I could not see his face. He said, lowering it, "You are a clever person. You would not have made only one copy of her files. You are asking everyone many questions. You are looking at other copies, aren't you? You've not given up."

I considered, my heartbeat rising. "Yes."

"Find anything?" His brows were up.

"Like what?"

"Some clue. Some reason why they had the accidents."

"I think I found a thread," I lied.

We were interrupted by more knocking. Ranjay rose as I did, casually drifted beside me down the long hall. A bulb was out. The remaining glowing sixty watt, hanging from a loop-wire, seemed ready to expire. There were no windows in the hall. The knocking grew louder. I reached out, punched the code, opened the door.

"Hi, Bruce."

Now I had two visitors. As we all went back into the kitchen, it struck me that although I'd seen Ranjay's

Honda outside, Bruce's late-model Subaru Outback was not in sight. It was probably around the side of the house.

"This place is a shithole," Bruce said, looking around. "An igloo would be better than this."

"I don't mind. Want coffee?"

Bruce removed his gloves, rubbing his powerful hands. "Arthritis," he said. "Coffee, yeah."

Bruce sat on my left, hat off, jacket on, but inside the polar spa, wearing extra layers made sense. Ranjay regained his seat, on the right. I couldn't see them both at the same time but I relaxed a little bit. With two people here, one wouldn't try something, I figured.

Bruce told Ranjay, "I heard there's no more vaccine coming."

"We've used all the supply in the U.S. We're trying to get more from Mexico."

"I heard you've got frostbite cases."

"Three Rangers didn't cover up their faces enough. We warned them. I gave a lecture to them when they got here. They didn't listen."

Bruce told a story about his first winter in Barrow, about going out into a garage and picking up an ice ax without gloves on. The next day, his fingers turned blue. The blue crept up his forearms, in his veins. It was poisoning. Frostbite. It had come because he touched metal. Just touching metal had almost killed him. "But antibiotics did the trick," he said.

Then he asked Ranjay, "How long before Homza—if there are no more cases—before he bags the quarantine?"

"I do not know," Ranjay said.

Bruce and Ranjay made eye contact. A silent message seemed to pass between them. Ranjay rose abruptly and said he had to go to the bathroom. Bruce said, jokingly, "Don't let it hang out too long in there, or it'll freeze, man."

After Ranjay left, Bruce pulled his chair closer and said, sympathetically, "You're a quarantine in a quarantine, Joe. I can't believe Homza kicked you off the base. That they even think you might be responsible."

"Thanks."

"What are you going to do when they lift the quarantine, *if* they lift it? I mean, no new cases in three days. It can't go on forever?"

I answered truthfully. "I haven't thought about it." I had no vision of a future, just Karen, these walls, the pistol snug against my back, the laptop.

"You could work with us," Bruce suggested. "We have bear people in Canada, at Resolute Bay, and in Norway in Svalbard. Helping the planet, Joe. Sounds corny, but it's not bad work. It gives a feeling of accomplishment. When my divorce went through, I felt a void, and those animals helped fill it. You could do worse than that."

I heard a shuffling noise behind me and turned, but no one was there.

Bruce leaned closer, drawing my attention back, "It's not a lot of money. But Karen said you were quitting the military. Maybe it's too early to bring this up?"

"No. Thanks. I appreciate it."

"Lots of people get the bug. That Tilda Swann, the Greenpeace woman. I heard she's staying on to work here."

I remembered her fired-up expression, her rage, her face in mine. "You mean, she's quitting Greenpeace?"

"Keeping a hand in, another way. She might give lectures at the eco lodge. You know, Joe, I had a feeling that time in the roller rink that she had a thing for you. You've had a loss. A terrible loss. It's never premature to think about building a new life."

"What?" I grew hot. "Premature? Karen's not even dead a week."

I heard a whispery noise and turned. Ranjay had come into the room, and stood just two feet behind me. I hadn't heard him enter, hadn't heard until he was close.

Bruce gazed up at Ranjay. "You make out in there, Doc, without losing man's best friend to the cold?"

Ranjay approached the table. I heard Bruce's chair scrape closer.

"You know, Joe, we, Ranjay and I, that is, feel . . ."

Then there came more knocking at the door.

BRUCE AND RANJAY EXCUSED THEMSELVES, MUMBLING HELLO as Lieutenant Colonel Amanda Ng and Captain Raymond Hess entered. The polar spa was a regular Club Arctic today. I didn't offer coffee. I didn't offer anything. I said, "Back to check what I say against what Eddie said?"

Hess said, "Sir, Drs. Morgan and Cruz completed their DNA run on the rabies."

Ng watched and waited. She wanted to see whether I looked frightened or curious, guilty or alert. Hess watched Ng watch me. It was a watch-athon. I was tired of their relentless insinuations.

"I can wait if you can," I said.

Amanda Ng sighed. "Colonel, looks like we're dealing with something that came from a lab."

HERE'S THE THING ABOUT RABIES. IMAGINE THREE PEOPLE catching it, one from a bat bite, one from a dog, one from a raccoon, each case thousands of miles from the others. The first victim is a seamstress in Jakarta, the second a kid in Des Moines. The third is a farmer in Yakuta, Siberia. All three fall ill after a short period of incubation. All show the same general symptoms. All, untreated, die.

So you'd think they all had the same exact thing, but that is not true. Sample their brain tissue, strain out the virus, get it under a good microscope, an electron one, one that really shows the spirals and tracks of DNA, and you discover tiny differences. Extra spikes on Indonesia. Fewer coils in Des Moines. Slight discoloration in Siberia.

Those CDC docs from Atlanta, I knew, had brought along with them a thumb drive library of rabies DNA variations . . . a thousand across the planet, each as identifiable as a fingerprint is to the FBI. Ng was saying that the strain here was different, *new*, probably man-made.

Hess pulled up a chair now. They'd given up the good cop/bad cop routine two days ago. They looked as tired as I felt. I admired their persistence and resented it. I wished they spent more time on other things, but I supposed that, in their shoes, I'd check out Joe Rush, too.

Hess reasoned, "You're sent up here specifically to look for new strains. And now, *that's happened!*"

"If it's lab born, it doesn't mean it came from us."

Amanda Ng leaned back. "Who then?"

"I have no idea."

"Colonel, Major Nakamura has told us a very different story."

"Cut it out. If you even talked to him at all, he said the same thing I'm saying."

"*You've* been briefed on old military programs. *You* were warned against disclosure. I can guarantee you immunity if you tell us anything relevant, right now."

"Immunity? From what?"

"From retribution of any sort should you disclose to us a secret program. This comes from the SecDef himself, get it? A personal guarantee. Did you discover a connection, some old program? Were you ordered to bury information?"

"How many times are we going to go over this?"

Ng stared at me. "So you insist that it's coincidence? You looking for new strains and one occurring?"

"I don't believe in coincidence."

"Someone trying to get you blamed, then?"

"I am being blamed. And you," I said, "don't know for sure it came from a lab. It could have evolved."

They rose. They pulled on their parkas. I had a sense of the cold deepening outside, of the heater inside coughing fitfully, ready to expire.

Ng said, "Chew our offer over. Full amnesty. Hess, let's go."

I SHOT AWAKE. IT WAS 3 A.M. EDDIE WAS STILL GONE AND I'D heard footsteps. I turned on the lights, breath frosting once I left the bunk area and went room to room.

No one was there. Jesus!

THE NEXT DAY THE SUBMARINE WAS GONE. APPARENTLY THE ice was freezing up, putting the sub in danger of being crushed. Soon the icebreaker would depart.

I returned to the beach on a walk and saw a sight that amazed me, a large polar bear on his belly, wriggling forward on ice one hundred yards offshore, spread out, hauling himself by claw. An enormous bear can move on ice so thin that a human would plunge through it. It has to do with weight distribution.

Sometimes a thing that seems impossible at first glance stands there right in front of your face, I thought. *Go back and look at the old stuff on the F drive again.*

I went back inside the polar spa and back to the F drive—the written part of the diary—to the first reversal the Harmons had suffered, a car accident.

> Dad says no matter how long it takes, we're not going home until we finish up at all nine sites. Dad says . . .

I went back to May again, reread her entries about her crush on a high school English teacher named Mark Wong, her musings on whether her parents were as boring when they were kids as they were now, read about her pet beagle who was too fat, and how cool Mini Cooper cars looked, how Mom and Dad pulled out maps of the North Slope, and pointed out the lakes they'd be taking her to this summer.

B-o-r-i-n-g.

Mom going on about lake number one, and the oil pipeline proposed to cross it. Lake number four, where, in 1839, Russian fur trappers had planted an Imperial flag. Lake number eight lay inside the National Petroleum Reserve, designated a strategic area during World War One, when the nation feared a cut off of Mideastern oil. Bigger lake number nine, Dad had said, and the surrounding tundra, final site they would visit, might one day house a new eco lodge, where tourists would sleep, eat, and view the Arctic tundra on big, heated, rolling glass-sided carriers.

I started to scroll away and stopped.

Eco lodge? Lake number nine?

They never got to lake number nine.

I read:

Dad says that Merlin Toovik and the ASRC board will vote next month on whether to allow the pipe-

line near lake number one (that he hates) and the
eco lodge by lake nine (that he loves).

I envisioned a new eco lodge rising out on the tundra.
Wealthy tourists coming from New York, Berlin, Moscow,
Singapore. Heated bedrooms. Hot showers. Tundra tours
in big-wheeled or tracked vehicles, where Mom, Dad, and
the kids could snap photos of bears and caribou, while
sipping Coca-Cola or premium champagne.

*Hmm, I've thought about diamonds. I've wondered
about oil and pipelines. I've thought strategic. I considered
medicines, personal grudges, land acquisition, bioweapons,
cover-ups, even Mikael Grandy's inheritance.*

I'd not really thought about the eco lodge.

Nah. How?

Eco lodge?

EIGHTEEN

It seemed impossible that the temperature could drop further, but the big red needle on the thermometer outside the front door of the polar spa read minus five, a record for the end of October. My breath hovered. A Humvee patrol crunched past. I heard, from across the street, from ice pack that had only a week before been ocean, a hard, steady cracking, as if the last atoms of water there were solidifying into granite, making fluid a memory, a petrified artifact from long ago.

Eco lodge?

The borough police headquarters was in a rectangular two-story building with blue metal siding, across from Borough Hall and the Wells Fargo Bank building and ASRC headquarters. It was Barrow's power intersection. Blue-and-white Ford Expeditions—four-wheel-drive Arctic patrol vehicles—were tethered by electrical wires to outlets outside, like horses a century ago, connected by reins to hitching posts. The stairway was steel, mud-catching in summer, and the steel was slippery with an ice sheath that made me slide around despite the rubber soles on my insulated boots. The railing was also coated with ice. Overheated air enveloped me when the front door swung shut. Light seemed yellowish, and cops stopped what they were doing to stare as I made my way to the duty sergeant at a front desk. They knew who I was. I was the guy who gave their kids vaccinations, but I was also the one who might have unleashed illness in their town.

"I asked you not to come here," Merlin said.

His office was glass-enclosed. There were framed eight-by-ten photos on the desk of Merlin and his kids on vacation in New Mexico, hiking; Merlin and his wife throwing a feast when his crew had brought in the first bowhead of a season. Happy shots. His living room packed with neighbors eating fresh meat, pouring on hot sauce, sipping the peach juice infusion that Merlin had made.

The family scenes were at odds with the opposite cork-board wall plastered over with tacked-up eight-by-tens of the Harmon research camp; the bodies, the angles, the huts. There was a Barrow map, with *X* marks showing homes in which rabies victims had resided.

My eyes stopped at the shots of Karen, a whole series: her body from a frontal angle, a side shot, a blown-up facial showing pale skin and bruises, a shot of the neck where a blade had ripped through.

Merlin said, somewhat more softly, "It's better if you

stay away from my guys. Everyone's on edge. We had a near riot in the church last night. Luther talked them down."

"I need to ask you about the eco lodge."

His head inclined. His eyes narrowed. He sat up straighter and put down the photos.

"Why?"

"The last lake the Harmons were supposed to visit. The one they never got to. Number nine. It's slated for the lodge, right?"

If I learned something important, my agreement with General Homza was that I'd call him on the encrypted phone. Homza had told me, *Even my adjutant won't know about our deal. That stays between you and me.*

Merlin regarded me neutrally for some moments. His eyes flickered to the corkboard. He must have decided that his resentments were secondary to any possibility that I might have stumbled on a meaningful theory or bit of information.

"What about the eco lodge, Colonel?"

Now he calls me Colonel instead of Joe.

"Is the lease sale final, Merlin?"

"It will be signed in a few days in Anchorage. Our signatory was down there when the quarantine began. The quarantine won't stop the closing. They're hacking out final details now."

"Outsiders will own the lodge?"

"The land remains ASRC land. It will be leased out for fifty years to the eco outfit."

"What outfit is that?"

"Great Arctic Circles, from L.A. They came up here and made an impressive presentation. They showed maps and statistics. Over a million tourists visited the Arctic last year, mostly in Europe. Ships. Treks. Polar bear safaris in Canada. Ice hotel in Sweden. Hunting in Siberia. It's a booming industry, they said. The annual lease fee is substantial. Low-impact use. Other proposals we get involve mining or drilling. This seemed . . . friendlier."

"Who owns Great Arctic Circles, Merlin?"

He sat back and regarded me flatly. One advantage of working in a small place, I thought, was that in Barrow, things were not as compartmentalized as they are down south. Merlin was not only a police chief, but a whaler, a board member of the ASRC. He was a pillar of the community, a member of the local elite.

"A consortium," he said. "Hotels."

"They've built other eco lodges?"

"They own two in Siberia. They sent up a fellow by the name of Klimchuk, a lawyer. They'll put ten million dollars in escrow. If they can't finish the job, they forfeit it. They're guaranteeing twenty percent of the jobs to locals. The North Slope will be an Arctic Serengeti, Klimchuk said. He showed profit charts on eco tours in Tanzania. He said Arctic tourism is the future. If they make ten percent of that African haul, they're ahead."

I asked him if I could see the plans and he shrugged, *Why not,* and opened a file cabinet. Minutes later I was bent over a photo of the lake and a ratty-looking cabin that was there now, alongside of an artist's sketch of the proposed eco lodge. It was a long one-story ranch-style structure, its twin wings enveloping the curved end of the two-mile-long tundra lake. There were viewing platforms on the roof. There were, in the sketch, tourists sipping drinks and watching a herd of caribou pass. Those people, in the artist's mind, probably came from homes in New York and London, Munich and Rio. They were people who paid to climb Kilimanjaro, to dive for sharks in the Marianas, to go on motorized big game photo safaris in South Africa. People who had killed off even the raccoons in the guarded communities in which they lived. But who paid tens of thousands of dollars to watch lions kill gazelles while they sipped beverages.

In the sketch, I saw big-tired tundra vehicles, glass-enclosed rolling living rooms, parked near the lodge. There was an airstrip. Small boats hugged a dock. Visitors walked from a private plane toward the lodge, with staff carrying luggage. Everyone seemed happy. Huge flocks of migrating birds blanketed the sky.

I said, thinking out loud, "Do the new owners get mineral rights, too, if they happen to change their mind, decide to dig or drill?"

"No. When you lease land in Alaska, you only get surface rights. Not below."

"Oil? Diamonds?"

Merlin shook his head. "That would violate the lease. They'd forfeit the bond. They do the lodge, or nothing."

"What about a rerouted pipeline aboveground."

"Nope. That would violate terms."

Maybe this is just one more bad idea. Drop it.

I said, "Number nine is the only lake that the Harmons were supposed to visit that they never reached."

Merlin's eyes left mine, slipped outside the office. Lots of police had gathered by one of the desks.

I said, "Is there anything special about this lake, Merlin? At all?"

Now more officers were at the desk. Merlin's eyes came back. "Not that I can think of. I mean, they're all different, but nothing particular about nine stands out. It's on the edge of the Porcupine herd caribou migration. But so are other lakes."

"I want to go there," I said.

His eyes widened. Then he frowned. "And do what?"

I looked out the window. The world was white. *The lake will be frozen. And not just frozen like ice freezes lakes back in Massachusetts, where people drive cars on them. Frozen like you could drive a personnel carrier on it, full of Marines.*

I made up an answer as I went along. "I want to finish what the Harmons started. Fly out with an ice augur, drill a hole. Hell, take samples and send 'em back to Ted's college, just like he would have done."

Merlin's chair creaked as he sat back, put his big hands behind his head, and moved his head slightly, right, then left, as if to encompass the barriers enclosing the town, the Rangers barring exit. Whatever the hell was going on outside his office, it had the cops agitated, I saw.

"Just exactly how would you get there?" Merlin said.

I can't ask Homza for a copter. I'm supposed to be out of the investigation, out of favor with him.

"You'll help. You'll ask the general for permission to take a borough copter. You two are cooperating, right? You'll say it's part of your investigation into the Harmons and Clay. Rangers can come. You'll say there are no villages near lake number nine, so we can't infect anyone. We'll come right home. That chopper is big enough to carry a small augur."

"It will be fifteen below tonight. Temperatures are still dropping. The Harmons would have quit by now."

"Maybe that was the whole point, to stop them."

"And what do I tell Homza is the reason I want to go?"

"You're investigating four possible murders. All four victims were slated to go to that site. You want to eyeball it. You want to check the cabin for prints or evidence, in case someone else was there."

This time when his gaze moved I followed it. Outside the glass wall, Deputy Luther Oz was standing there, eyeing us. Oz saw me notice him, and joined the officers clustered around the desk.

I had another thought. "Merlin, you said lodge buyers can't go after minerals. Does that mean the ASRC can sell mineral rights to someone else, if the lodge is there?"

Merlin stood, back to me, looking out at the road, where three Army Humvees suddenly shot past, fast, heading for the airport. Something was happening. Merlin said, "No. That's part of the deal. We leave everything alone. But before we agreed we had *our* geologist take samples, see if there might be minerals there. Negative report. Everybody wins."

"You mean the Harmons won? Karen won? Clay?"

"I'm surprised you'd trust my guys to come with you," Merlin said coolly, turning back to me. "After what you said about me being involved. Remember? Me taking oil money?"

"I was drunk. I didn't know what I was saying."

"The thing about being drunk," said Merlin evenly, "is that you may not know *what* you're saying, but you mean it. And there's nothing out there but ice. There's never going to be enough vaccine for everyone in Barrow, is there?"

"No."

"You knew it all along. You lied by omission. Again."

"Yes."

"Good-bye, Joe. I have to get back to work."

Suddenly alarms went off in the building. I saw cops putting on body armor and throwing on parkas, rushing for the exit. Luther Oz burst into the office, snapping on a Kevlar vest. "The airport," he gasped. "Shooting at the airport."

I followed Merlin and Oz as they ran from the office, both carrying heavy shotguns. Outside it was snowing lightly. The cold hit us like a fist. I heard shots now, from a distance, the steady *snap-snap-snap* of M4 carbines. Merlin rolled down the passenger window. Oz was driving.

"Stay out of it, Colonel. Stay away. I don't owe you anything anymore. I see you there, I arrest you," Merlin said. Their Ford disappeared into the falling snow. The shooting in the distance picked up. I heard lots more weapons now.

NINETEEN

The Rangers manning the roadblock trained their M4 carbines on me as I slowed the Ford. I did not know them, and to them I was in civilian clothing, driving a civilian vehicle. They looked tense and angry, eyeing my Marine ID, as if they refused to believe that I was really the person on the card. Ogrook Street was a gauntlet of small homes, with frightened faces pressed to many windows. The airport, my destination, was a quarter mile away.

"Can't let you through, sir. Please turn around."

The quarantine plan called for defensive zoning if violence broke out, to try to contain it. These twenty-two- and twenty-three-year-old Rangers had quickly and efficiently blocked key roads, but from their tense attitude I had a feeling that the source of the shooting had not yet been identified.

The lieutenant at my window—a tall, chisel-faced Creole from Louisiana—would brook no argument. The privates at his side, their carbines trained on me and on an approaching snowmobile, were ready to fire. They seemed more angry than scared. Someone had shot a Ranger.

I said, pushing it, "Lieutenant, let me through."

"Sir, you are not my commander. My orders are to arrest anyone who will not turn around."

He'd do it, I saw. Argument was useless. "At least give me an idea what's happened."

He considered for a moment as wind whipped up a gust of diamond-like specks, hard, granular snow in his face.

"Sniper, sir. Shot two guys at the wire."

I turned the Ford around and headed for the military base, encountering no other roadblocks. But on the way I saw a sight that struck me as wrong; a few people, men, women, and children, in their yards, loading up snow-mobiles and pull-sleds, as if the day was normal, and they could leave town. They were dumping in knapsacks, food, snowshoes, cross-country skis. Rifles or shotguns went in last, so as to be easily accessible. They couldn't leave town, so this made no sense. Yet they kept loading, in fact, seemed to be hurrying their families to finish up.

Then it hit me. *That's why those men were out on the ice, probing the thickness. They're going to break out, just drive off over frozen sea.*

Some quarantine. I heard my own bitter laugh over the Ford's engine, not the kind that comes from some-thing funny.

The coast road was deserted, and at sea, farther off than where it had been yesterday, the *Wilmington* had turned, a red speck, limping west toward the Bering Strait. The ice must have thickened so much it threatened to trap the ship. It had to leave. Usually ice didn't solidify so much for another month. But the cold snap had deepened. The *Wilmington*'s departure meant escape had just become an option for anyone in town who was scared, or blamed the Army for the outbreak, or was guilty, or just wanted to get out. Now they could mount up and disappear into the white while the troops were occupied on land.

Or does the sniper know that? Was the shooting intentional? Is it a diversion to occupy Rangers while people— while Karen's killer—gets away?

It was all falling apart, I thought, pushing down on the accelerator. All the careful strategy drawn up in warm classrooms at the Navy War College. The fine plans were about to be busted open by plain old ice. I'd been to some of those meetings with Eddie. We'd sat in classrooms with other alleged "experts." We'd made lists of questions to be dealt with in the event of a quarantine of a U.S. town. But no questions and no strategies had regarded the Arctic.

Because no one in Washington, including me, had thought that a quarantine could occur in such a cold, remote place.

Now Homza would be scrambling to adjust, calling for more troops, more wire to block sea escape, air patrols, more housing, but extra help was hours away at best!

Eddie's favorite expression came into my head, in his sarcastic voice. "SNAFU: Situation normal. All fucked up."

At least I was still cleared to enter the base. I drove in as a half dozen troop-packed Humvees drove out, filled with somber-looking Rangers. I passed the Quonset huts and the community college building at top speed. I took the curving road to the lab building, Homza's headquarters. The car slid sideways on an ice patch, almost plowed into a snowbank. The wheels caught at the last second, and the Ford veered right but straightened and made it to the labs.

That was when my encrypted phone started buzzing. But when I glanced at the screen, I saw that it wasn't Eddie, or the general, but Valley Girl back in Washington.

Not now, I thought.

I burst into the building. To hell with orders to avoid tracking in mud. I stormed up the stairs to the general's office. There, amid a scene of controlled anarchy, officers manned phones, snapped out orders, drew arrows on a chalkboard, peered out windows toward the airport, but the windows did not provide a close enough view.

I smelled bad coffee and chocolate cake. The snow against the windows sounded hard, abrasive, constant.

Homza stood alone inside his office, on a landline phone. But before I could get to him, his adjutant—a major named Garreau—blocked my way. He was a bulked-up Georgian with long sideburns, thinning reddish hair, and the tense, ready-to-leap attitude of a good guard dog.

"Doctor, not now. He said no one gets in."

"I need to see him. This relates."

"Perhaps I can help, Doctor."

You? You don't even know I'm supposed to report to him.

You're not even addressing me as "Colonel." You're talking to me as if I'm a civilian, an outsider, which was what Homza and I agreed to pretend that I am.

Garreau regarded me with a cold politeness. He repeated, "Can you tell me what this is about?"

I stopped dead. What *was* it about? A theory? One more unsubstantiated speculation? Guesswork? Hope? I was here for Homza's permission to visit lake number nine. A body of water so anonymous it lacked a name. It just had a number.

"I'll wait," I said.

He frowned, preferring that I leave, and not complicate an emergency. He said, "It might be a while."

"Yes, I understand. I'll sit here. I give you my word. It's important. You'll tell me when I can go in."

He nodded and turned to attend to more pressing business. My phone started up again, tinny and insistent. I ignored it, trying to get an idea of what was going on in town by listening to conversation. Sniper shots—from a single shooter, it was believed—had hit two Rangers thirty minutes ago. But no one had heard the shots. It was believed they were silenced, which made sense, as some hunters in town used suppressors, and any good sniper would have known that—especially in such a small place—the sound of firing would have pinpointed his location.

"One critical. One dead," I heard someone say.

"No one on rooftops, sir."

"No shell casings found so far, Major."

"Shooting's stopped, sir. It's possible whoever did it

got away into that utility tunnel, that fucking Utilador, sir. He may be moving to another spot."

I heard a lieutenant call the *Wilmington*, now twelve miles away, asking the icebreaker to dispatch drones to scan the city rooftops. Or a chopper and Coast Guard sniper.

My phone began ringing again.

I might as well answer. Valley Girl sounded back to normal, each sentence—even the mundane ones—ending in a question. She sounded proud today, and the accent was extra irritating. She cracked gum, chewing, between words.

"I did what you asked me to do, Colonel?"

"Get to the point, Sarah."

But she did things her own way. She repeated what I knew already, confirmed the business arrangement between Prezant College and the university in Norway, confirmed that Professor Ted Harmon's original grant application said that his research was precisely what he'd claimed it to be. Go to nine lakes. Take samples. Gather up everything indiscriminately. Freeze it and ship it back.

Nothing new about this. Why did you call?

Valley Girl said, "Colonel, I also went back? I took another look at people you asked about? On the base? And I found a funny thing?"

I sat up straighter.

"What funny thing?"

"Well, that Norwegian guy? Jens Erik Holte? The helicopter pilot who works for different people?"

"Don't make me keep asking!"

"I checked his social security info? It was fine. Birthplace? Jobs? Voting? Credit? Then I went to get a pizza? With mushrooms and peppers? I was in the car and I was thinking? I have this friend I went out with? At Interpol? Like he has my job there? I was waiting for the pie? They always take long if you want extra peppers, like, I don't get it, it takes the same amount of time to put on regular peppers or extra ones. You put peppers in your hand and sprinkle them on the pie, right?"

"Get to it, damnit!"

"You've been so nice to me so I asked my friend to check that pilot. But in Europe, see? Like, I figured, *all* his records won't just be here since he came from somewhere else."

"And?" My heart was slamming in my chest. "What about Jens Erik Holte?"

"Well! That's the thing, Colonel. Everything is fine with him here, in America? Just perfect."

"But in Europe?"

"He's like this retarded guy in an institution? Same age, but like, IQ down the drain! Like, he's been in hospitals since he was *five years old!* Same ID. Same name. Same little village birthplace. See? But it's another person! So who's on your base, claiming to be him?"

I HUNG UP AND TRIED TO GET TO HOMZA, WHO WAS ONLY TWENTY feet away, yelling into the phone. Major Garreau blocked me and had his Rangers push me out. I tried to explain. But Homza had played his part perfectly with his men.

Garreau "knew" that I was out of the investigation, a suspect. The adjutant was not inclined to listen to anything I had to say.

I ran out of the building and got into my Ford. I took the road back to the Quonset hut area. I left the Expedition running in front of hut thirty, the last one on base, the one in which all my summer friends now resided, and in which Jens—who bunked in town with a girlfriend—often hung out—drinking coffee, making small talk, *hearing information*, during the day.

The campus looked deserted. *He doesn't know you know.*

I made sure that my Beretta was ready, but kept it in my holster, the snap loose. I walked directly into the living room. My throat was raw and I felt my heart beating. Normally the place slept eight but now it held more than twenty. The smell of too many people hit me.

Sleeping bags lined the periphery of the living room, some occupied, some rolled up during the day. Think London, World War Two, the underground tube, the blitz. I smelled eggs frying. I smelled feet. I saw, at the kitchen table, Alan McDougal playing chess with Deirdre. A poker game was in progress between three base roustabouts. I saw CDC Dr. Janette Cruz fiddling with the TV, don't ask me why, because it got no reception. Bruce Friday came out of a back bedroom in stocking feet, saw me, and froze, fixing on the urgent expression on my face.

Bruce was in jeans and a heavy knit pullover, a time-faded white sweater. He held a stack of eight-by-ten color photos of polar bears in his hand.

I tried to sound casual but I doubt it worked. "Hey, Jens here?"

"Why?"

"I just got permission to take a chopper out to lake number nine. I want him to fly it."

His eyes grew huge. "How'd you get permission to leave?"

"Persistence. *Is he here or not?*"

Bruce glanced around. "I was taking a nap. I don't know. Did you hear? About the sniper? My God! I knew if Homza kept the lid on, this place would blow. I told Homza! You can't lie to people. You have to tell them the truth, especially if they don't trust you to start with."

"I know."

Bruce said, "People have had enough."

I raised my voice to make an announcement. I told everyone in the hut, "I've got permission to take a chopper. Anyone see Jens?"

No one had seen him.

"Tell him I'm looking for him if he comes back."

Nods. Grunts. *Who cares?* The poker players went back to their game. McDougal seemed thoughtful. Deirdre looked miserable. Dave Lillienthal came out of a bedroom with a glass in his hand, and a half-filled bottle of scotch.

I left.

Heading back into town, I left a message for Eddie to call me. I thought, *Maybe I'm overreacting. Maybe he's got a secret that has nothing to do with rabies. Maybe I'm frustrated so I want the answer to be Jens.*

Where to look? If he was the sniper he'd be moving,

and finding one man in Barrow—if he did not want to be found—was like finding one flake of snow in a field of drifts. There were hundreds of homes here; the community center, the Heritage Center, and restaurants, all closed, but accessible with a pick of locks. There was the roller rink. The environmental observatory. The long utilities tunnel. Add in city garages, schools. About two hundred permafrost cellars, a public library—even the old, abandoned, half-buried sod houses near the sea, mounds jutting up from tundra, cramped dark spaces where, centuries ago, humans spent winters huddling to keep alive.

Look for his car.

I passed his girlfriend's house. No cars there. I knocked. No one home. I started off again. He could be anywhere. He could be crouching in someone's home or backyard or an abandoned house, amid busted stoves and discarded refrigerators. He could be inside a parked car. On a roof.

Try Eddie again.

Jens had been the pilot who worked with the Harmons after the original flier was hurt. Jens would have heard their plans. He had time and opportunity to tamper with supplies. Jens was the invisible fifth member of their party. Jens, in fact, was the invisible member of at least a half dozen projects here; oil surveys, water surveys, pipeline surveys, even Eddie and me going out.

As I passed the big AV Value Center I caught a fast blur of movement to my left. I slammed on the brakes and skidded sideways and almost hit a snowmobile pulling a sled as it bounced out of a yard, crossed the road three inches in front of me, and zipped toward the beach. A second Polaris followed. Escapees. My heart clung to my throat. The sleds pulled away. Looking back were women and children, huddled beneath blankets. Everyone scared. It was just a question of what you were more scared of. Illness? The Army? Secrets? The North?

Those families believed that the icy tundra was safer for them than here, and the drivers were probably taking their chances heading for the nearest village, a hundred miles away, a three- or four-hour journey if they were lucky.

I sighed. I pulled out my phone. If any of those escapees were infected, if they were vectors, they could turn a bad situation to start with into a disaster, if they reached another town.

I punched in the general's number. He needed to know that people were running from the quarantine. There were no good choices here, just gradients of bad. No one answered. I sat for a moment deciding which danger to address. Go back to the base or the roadblock? Alert the Rangers? Assume they knew that people were escaping by now?

They'll see it. They'll spot snowmobiles leaving, fanning out on the ice. Someone will see it. Meanwhile, Jens might be getting away.

I headed for Eddie, at the hospital. I thought, *We lied to them from the first. If there'd been serum, if we would have leveled with them, they'd have given us a few more days of cooperation before trying to get out.*

I saw blue smoke puff up in another yard, another

family mounting up on snowmobiles. A Chevy Blazer roared past, crunched onto icy beach and reached the sea ice and turned right, toward Prudhoe Bay, driving right over the Arctic Ocean, as if navigating a clear, straight highway, instead of a boundary-less plain.

If Jens is responsible, he'll know what this microbe is. He'll know whether it is contagious.

If he killed Karen, I'll do the same to him.

Three minutes later I pulled up to the hospital. As I leaped out the cold hit me like a glass wall. I found Eddie eating a PowerBar in the corridor outside the emergency room, inside of which Ranjay and an Army surgeon operated on the wounded Ranger.

Eddie looked exhausted, standing there in medical whites. Eddie saw my face and threw the PowerBar in a freestanding ashtray.

"It's Jens, Eddie. Valley Girl called. Bogus name. The real Jens is institutionalized in Norway."

"Who is he, then?"

"No idea."

Eddie frowned, thinking fast, thinking what I'd told myself at first. "Phony name doesn't mean he's guilty. People hide out here. End of the world. Leave your family, job, divorce, nineteen thousand traffic tickets."

"Let's find him."

"You told Homza?"

"I'm blocked."

"Merlin?"

"He won't have anything to do with us."

"Pain in the ass Ng and Hess?"

"They're at the front line and can't be reached."

"You're just Mr. Popularity, aren't you, Uno?"

"Get your goddamn parka on," I said. "He can't get around without his truck, not in twenty below zero. His damn truck will be parked *somewhere*. We find him, we worry about the other stuff after. Meanwhile, people are mounting up, heading out on the ice."

"Oh, shit," Eddie said, eyes wide.

A SATELLITE, IF ONE HAPPENED TO BE LOOKING DOWN FROM space, would see the triangular town, and then a speck, a snowmobile, heading from the populated area into the voidish white . . . and then a second speck, and a third, and then a fan-shaped parade, some Ski-Doos or Hondas turning right, toward the oil fields. Some left, toward the next village along the coast. Some making a wide U-turn to bring them back to land, behind the Rangers.

Most people will stay, but I bet over a hundred make a break.

Eddie checked Itta Street and Ahkovak Street and Takpuk Street, looking for Jens Erik Holte or his metallic green Isuzu truck. I took Egasak and Pisokak. Eddie at the library. Me at the quarry. Eddie at UIC Car Rentals. Me at Utilities and Electric and KBRW radio and the Piuraagvik public athletic center.

Nothing.

If Jens is the sniper, his car could be inside the blocked-off area, I thought, scanning the elementary school parking lot, going around back, peering into the garage, bumping back onto the street.

Twice I was flagged down by nervous troops in Humvees, checking IDs of anyone out, telling them to go home. I said I would. I didn't. I passed a Humvee chasing a snowmobile, which eluded it by slipping into a yards-wide passageway separating two homes. The Humvee was too wide to get through.

Minutes later I passed a different Humvee whose crew had cornered a snowmobile in a front yard. The snowmobile driver had his hands up. Soldiers advanced on him, carbines out. The driver looked middle-aged, heavy, miserable.

I reached my own street, Stevenson, which ran along the Chukchi Sea. The shoreline was eroding here, and at several places homes had been abandoned and soon would crumble during winter storms. I headed over to Kongek Street, for a second try at the house where Jens lived with his girlfriend, Michelle Aikik. I pulled up before a one-story shack with a neat front yard, a freshly painted door, a corrugated iron fence, a freestanding garage, open, that had Michelle's rusty blue Subaru Impreza inside, an electric wire extending from the engine block to an outlet.

I did not see Jens's truck there. But I knocked.

Nothing.

I banged on the door. I knew she was in there if her car was here.

Nothing.

I grew worried about Michelle. She was a slender,

observant, cheery presence at the post office, always helpful when inevitable delays kept packages from reaching
Barrow from the lower forty-eight. I'd seen her at the
Saturday night dances. I usually nodded hello at restaurants. Her brother, Philip, was a roustabout on the research base, working with scientists who tagged bowheads.

She still did not answer the door.

Heart in my chest, I tried the knob. It opened. I
walked into the *cunnychuck*, stood amid the hanging
parkas, saw no wet marks on the floor, heard a dog snort
inside the house. What was her dog's name? Waggy?
Wilmer? It started with a *W*, I recalled, envisioning a big
animal, St. Bernard or Malamute. Northern dog.

"Waggy?"

It stood there when I opened the inner door, three feet
off, its big gray-and-white tail swishing back and forth.
Beyond the enormous head I saw artist renditions of Jesus
on the wall: Jesus on a cross, bleeding; another on a cross,
not bleeding; Jesus with his palms up, eyes to heaven.
There were porcelain Jesuses. There were lots of photos
of Michelle's extended family. I smelled wet dog, pancakes, old electronics, dog food, fresh laundry.

"Good boy, Waggy. Michelle? Jens?"

Nothing.

I stepped into the house. I looked around, leaving
mud.

No one here.

"Shit!"

I walked out of the house and heard Michelle's musical
voice from the side of the house. "Doctor?" I turned and

saw her emerging from the ground, from the open wooden trapdoor of their ice cellar. She was bringing up meat from below, frozen ribs, moose, from the big size. The ribs looked like a bloody harp.

"Doc, how are you?"

It was funny, but her smiling face and normal-sounding voice got to me. She radiated kindness, just as she always did behind the counter at the post office. I felt sympathy coming off her. *Karen*.

"I'm looking for Jens, Michelle. He here?"

"He went out, Doctor."

"Do you know where I can find him? It's important."

She walked toward me. Ice bits twinkled on the meat. Her face was a study in sympathy.

"I'm sorry for your loss."

It hit me hard. It got past my defenses. I looked away for a moment and blinked and did not trust my voice to come out the usual way.

"Thanks, Michelle."

"I just wanted to say that. Why do you want Jens?"

"Oh, a job came up."

"Good! He'll like that. He's getting cranky sitting around, doing nothing. Hey, do you need any meat, Doc?"

"Excuse me?"

She nodded at the wooden trapdoor leading down to her ice cellar. "Jens is as good a hunter as any in town. He had a great summer. We've got more than we can use. Caribou. Musk ox. Don't be shy. That Army food stinks."

"By the way, does Jens have a silencer on his rifle?"

"Sure. Doesn't spook the caribou that way."

I started to say no to her offer but then I turned and stared at the ice cellar. What is an ice cellar but not a huge freezer, I thought. *And what else can you keep in freezers?*

I said, slowly, "Maybe I will take something, if it's really okay. Can I go down, take a look?"

My heart was going crazy. I borrowed a flashlight and declined her offer of help, trudged to the gray, weathered wooden door and reached down and pulled the heavy thing back on its rusted hinges. There was a jury-rigged system of electrical wires down there, a freestanding light switch. I flicked it. Dull yellow illumination gleamed on earthen walls coated with slick, permanent ice.

The ladder was wooden. I felt the rungs bend beneath my weight, heavier from the extra clothes and ballistics vest. I stood at the bottom, looking around. I was in a large, squarish room, eleven feet high, my breath frosting as it would in a Manhattan meat locker. The cold down here was a thousand years old. The meat lay stacked irregularly in piles. I saw a pile of frozen fish. I saw hacked-off chunks of sinew and bone, ribs and fat. The smell was cold.

Michelle's voice drifted down from the small opening. "You good down there, Doc? I need to go into the house."

"I'm good!"

I stood and slowly pivoted. I thought hard. *This is a natural version of what Eddie and I use in the lab building to store samples in, disease samples, to preserve them, so that they can be unfrozen and brought back to life.*

Was it possible?

I saw that my breathing had quickened from the puffs dissipating as they left my mouth. I felt mucous freezing in my nostrils, felt my moist lips cementing together. I opened them.

Gotta watch that.

It won't be in the meat. There are lots of places to hide things in meat, cavities, rib cages, or the piles . . . but Michelle lets people come down here and take what they want. Jens would be crazy to hide anything in the meat.

But the walls . . .

The walls weren't solid. They *looked* solid as steel, but anyone could easily chisel out a small opening in the permafrost, and then, within twenty minutes, use a spray bottle, and ice glaze would cover it up again.

My boots crunched. Even the *air* down here seemed to be ice. The meat smell was hot and wet. I let the flashlight beam enhance the weak bare bulb light. The beam played over the walls, glaze, and came back at me in an ice reflection.

Check the ice thickness.

All you'd need to conceal a small vial would be a few inches of space, tiny opening, four-inch-deep hole.

It won't be here. You're imagining things.

I went slowly, inches at a time, letting the beam move like a mini searchlight up a wall, right, left, down.

Take two steps over and start again at another spot.

This is crazy. There's too much wall here. I won't find anything. I'm wasting time.

I kept going.

I saw a thin spot where the light looked sharper, an area

where the ice seemed thinner. I pulled out my Leatherman and dug at it. The tip broke through, I hit earth. Solid, packed, two-hundred-thousand-year-old earth.

Sighing, I moved left.

I saw another interesting patch about seven feet off the ground. I moved the ladder. The cold here was more severe than outside. It was a cold that had been nurtured and preserved, enhanced, cold that formed the base of cold. I needed a new word to describe it, not just the English, *cold*.

I felt the air creep through my mittens and my fingers. I felt it start to turn my trachea white. I felt it inside my elbows. I used the Leatherman on the spot seven feet up. I broke through. I poked the Leatherman into earth.

Solid again.

Leave. This is stupid.

I moved the ladder left three feet, climbed up, letting the flashlight beam play over the upper level of ice. I moved around the basement, using the ladder as if I occupied a private library and climbed up and down, getting new volumes in reach. Somewhere at this depth, not here, but at the quarry, researchers had found frozen mammoths, petrified cartilage of sharks the size of Bradley Fighting Vehicles, creatures that fell to the bottom of a Jurassic Ocean long before Jesus walked the earth.

I saw another inch-wide spot where the ice seemed thinner. I poked it with the Leatherman. The blade punched through the last bit of glaze.

And plunged all the way in, into a hole.

I stood there, breathing fast. I shone the flashlight

beam into the hole. The cold in my chest grew warmer. It dropped into my belly. My breathing came sharper. I saw something in that hole.

I reached in and withdrew a small plastic box, maybe four inches long. Metal was a bad idea down here. Touch metal with skin, the skin would adhere, rip off, and frostbite would set in. So he'd used plastic.

I opened the case with bare fingers and saw, nestled in velvet inside, plastic vials. Sample vials!

The light changed from above, went shadowy, probably from clouds, the Arctic gray veil.

I closed the box and put it into my parka pocket. I climbed down and moved the ladder so that its upper tip now protruded, once again, out the open trapdoor.

You did it, Jens. You infected people intentionally. The Harmons. The people in town. You faked an outbreak.

I'd take the vial to the general. I was extra aware, going up the ladder, that what I carried in my pocket was deadly. I took each rung slowly, feeling the rungs dip from my weight. I concentrated on the vial, and the rickety ladder. If it broke, if I fell, so could the vial.

I was so aware of the vial that, poking my head out, I was only vaguely conscious that a figure stood nine or ten feet away, and when I looked up, I saw the muzzle of the rifle.

He didn't say anything. He just fired. I was already pushing off, into the air, but I was too late.

Two shots hit me.

I was falling. The trapdoor was a far-off geometry. Miles away, whole universes away, was gray Arctic light.

TWENTY

The ballistics vest took the two impacts, both over my sternum, bull's-eyes, normally guaranteed death shots. I'd pushed backward as he fired. I was flying away from that opening, falling in a kind of slow motion, splinters flying off the door above as he fired, *automatic weapon*, and when I smashed into hard earth below it was unclear which pain was worse, the concrete feel on my back, or the sensation of having been hit with sledgehammers in front.

My shoulders had taken most of the blow.

I couldn't breathe for a moment. My vision returned. I'd struck the earth with the top of my spine, and shoulders, and then my skull had rocketed back and slammed into the ground. The parka had provided a minimal cushion. It was like an airbag had gone off inside my brain. The earth burst up in splinters around me. He was firing diagonally through the trapdoor, as he moved toward it. He didn't see me yet. He was spraying. I'd thrown myself out of his line of sight; now he needed to look down to see me.

Did the vial in my pocket break? Are the germs out?

The pain was a freight train in my ears; a jackhammer. I felt a cracking sensation in my chest when I breathed. The three-fingered mitten was inside the Beretta's trigger guard. I saw my arm go up, swiveling toward that square of light. The pistol bucked, *crackcrackcrack,* as if firing by itself, firing from twenty years of Marine survival instinct.

I pushed backward. My back was an anvil and a hammer slammed down on it. I was dizzy. My fifteen rounds were exhausted. As I groped for a second clip I saw that my only advantage was that while *his* rifle was silenced, my Beretta was not, my firing would be magnified down here. My shots might be audible in the neighborhood. If so, they'd bring onlookers. They'd attract attention. They'd lure soldiers if any were near, or if someone phoned them. *Someone is shooting a gun down the block!*

Jens would know that he could not stay here long.

The door swung shut above me, with a heavy *boom,* plunging me into darkness. I heard a lock snap. It made my breathing louder, *safe for a moment,* but each exhalation ground glass into my lungs. I tried to stand but a wave of dizziness knocked me back to the ground.

I took a quick measure. *The back seems bruised but the head injury will be the worry. I hit hard, so my brain would have smashed into my skull, front and back. Potential sub-*

*dural hematoma. Potential expanding damage. Potential
blood leakage. THINK ABOUT IT LATER!*

He's getting away.

I groped two steps toward the ladder, bent like an old
man, stopped, and threw up. I groped for the flashlight.
It had broken in the fall. In the dark I brought out fresh
ammo. I thanked the Lord, the U.S. Marines, and a long-
ago tight-assed drill sergeant named Dave Gaffney for
making me load guns blindfolded at Parris Island, during
training.

My breathing sounded like ripping fabric. As I touched
the ladder, I heard, up top, slightly muffled by the door,
the unmistakable revving of a four-cylinder snowmobile.
That would be Jens, I guessed.

I envisioned him heading for the ocean, disappearing
into the flood of people escaping from town, over the ice.

In the dark, struggling up each rung felt like dragging
a boulder up Mt. Everest. My breathing sounded like an
emphysema patient's. I tasted sweet, cloying blood. Inside
my back writhed a jumble of snakes. Was the total darkness natural? Or had I suffered some vision loss, too?

The revving sound up top grew smooth and dissipated.
I envisioned a snowmobile heading off. My head hit the
door. I'd reached the surface. Hooking my left arm
around the top rung, I reached with the right and pushed,
but the trapdoor would not move enough to let in even
a sliver of light.

I banged on the door. Each impact sent waves of pain
through my arm, into my chest. I tried yelling for help.

My voice sounded frail to me, like some other, damaged man's voice. The blood in my mouth inexplicably tasted of apples, and a wave of dizziness threatened to topple me back into the dark, but the arm around the rung kept me in place.

Gotta get him.

I reversed the Beretta and used it as a hammer. I banged on the hatch. My voice sounded like a whisper to me. Maybe it was not even coming out at all.

Then I heard a scraping noise, inches away, and an odd clicking, as if an animal, a woodpecker, tapped against the thick wooden door. A beak. Paws with nails. I heard a snort.

"Is someone there?"

The response was only muffled, jagged breathing, heavy, sounding like an animal's.

"Waggy? Winfred? Winger?"

No, not the dog, because now I heard the lock scraping. I heard the metal padlock being moved. Was the dog nosing the thing? Or was a person lifting it?

"Who's up there? Michelle? Is that you?"

The scraping stopped. I called out and got no answer. I couldn't believe that no one had heard all the shooting. Or maybe a neighbor *had* heard it, but was too scared to come over, or had decided to not involve himself, or was using the anarchy out there to mount up on a snowmobile with a good GPS system and drive off, exiting the town.

Trapped.

No, not trapped. *Someone was unlocking the door.*

The scratching sounds stopped. But the door didn't

open. Heart pounding, I reached up and pushed and this time the door moved. I pushed harder and it swung up and fell over, open, made a thunking noise as weak light flooded in. I saw through a blurred film—my vision—the mass of bruised Arctic sky.

Was he still here? Had *he* opened the door? Were the revving snowmobile sounds a trick, as in, *Poke your head up so I can fire?*

I called out, "Jens!"

No answer.

"Who's there?"

Silence.

I couldn't just wait. I stuck the Beretta out and started firing, moving the gun in a circle. I quickly jutted my head up and glanced out, expecting to see Jens, maybe aiming at the door from a few feet off, but I saw Michelle Aitik. She lay still, two feet off, one hand tucked beneath her crumpled body, one stretched toward the door. She was a rag doll. Face in the snow. But the black hair spread over her back was matted with blood.

Christ, Christ, I killed the person helping me.

I made myself keep going. As I struggled out and up top I saw with no relief that I'd been wrong; she was dead, all right, but from this angle, it was clear that the wounds in her back were entry wounds. Clean and smaller, not wider. I'd not shot her. He had.

She'd probably been in the house, heard me firing, maybe heard the snowmobile start up, came out and saw Jens and he'd whirled, fired, and then he'd run for it. Then Michelle, mortally wounded, crawled a couple of feet, smearing the snow, reaching to release me, reaching for the lock on that heavy trapdoor.

My rage bloomed and for a moment drove off pain and dizziness. He'd slept with this woman. Then he'd shot her as casually as a farmer kills an animal. He'd killed four people on the tundra. He'd murdered Karen and Michelle. He'd destroyed the lives of innocent people. He'd used that storage cellar down there as a repository for a bioweapon, a murder weapon. He'd spread the disease from that vial.

I'll kill you. Whoever you are, I will kill you.

I needed a doctor, but there was no time for that. I limped into the garage. Michelle's snowmobile was gone. It had left a fifteen-inch-wide track heading north, up to the road, toward the sea, where Jens Erik, or whoever he really was, had driven off.

The wind was picking up, from the north, and that trail would be gone in minutes. I knew that there had been no time for General Homza to get enough soldiers out on the ice to stop the exodus from town. Not yet.

Go after him.

There was just my Ford for that and a Subaru Impreza in the garage, but both vehicles, even with studded tires, would not be able to follow a snowmobile through smaller openings in the sea ice.

If anyone in those adjacent homes was watching, they would have seen an apelike figure, me, run, hunched over, into the street, a knuckle-dragger with a Beretta, moving sideways, house to house, garage to garage. My ribs were on fire, the headache was worsening. In a subdural hematoma, one side of the brain hits the back skull, bounces off, then the other side hits the front. You're okay at first, but things worsen if internal bleeding continues.

Don't think about that.

Snowmobiles were often kept in yards. Sometimes, owners left keys in ignitions, not so much out of a belief in honesty, but it was tough to steal a snowmobile in a place where everyone knew one another, and many people would recognize the vehicle in town.

Why are you riding around on Gustav's Honda?

In the third yard I passed, I spotted a red-and-white Polaris with a cracked windshield. The key was in the ignition! As I straddled the seat I saw a surprised face, a child clutching a doll, appear at the living room window. The face disappeared. It was replaced by an angry man as I turned the throttle. The snowmobile coughed clouds of blue smoke. I shot from the yard, glimpsing the front door opening and a man in jeans and a flannel shirt running out, shaking a fist.

I bumped up onto the street and felt the track catch and I turned left. Jens's trail led straight to the sea. My back was on fire. The wind blew cross-wise, into my mouth, making it harder to breathe. The brakes were spongy. The pitted wind guard would make visibility difficult. Each bump was torture. I screamed to stay angry, screamed a war cry, screamed as fuel.

I took a shortcut between two homes and down Stevenson Street and Nachik Street and across Egasak onto the ice-sheathed beach. I spotted a moving dot a half mile ahead, zipping west. His track was shallow and the wind made it less visible with each minute. *What if the person ahead isn't him? What if I mixed up his trail with another escapee?*

It better be him. I turned the throttle higher with my right thumb. I sped up.

Which was dangerous.

I left the beach and reached sea ice, but this was no flat plain, no Bonneville salt flats of ice, no smooth skating-rink-type surface where you could drive as fast as the engine allowed. This was an obstacle course; hard, ridged, pitted geography that could hide a hill or make it look like a depression. It could offer a slit of open water as looking solid, a mirage. It could topple a rider as easily as a giant flicked a fly. One second you're speeding along. The next you slam into an outcrop, miss a dip, plunge through an opening, skid sideways and topple. The borough emergency squad regularly attended to people— newcomers usually—who'd suffered accidents on ice.

I sped up again.

So, apparently, did the figure ahead.

I maintained distance but my windshield grew smeary. The horizon merged ice and white air. Featherlike flakes began swirling. I lacked goggles. I needed a thermal snowmobile suit. My fingers were already cramping. I needed mitten liners against hypothermia. And special boots, not the walking kind that I wore. A helmet would be nice, too.

Maybe goggles are in the saddlebags but there's no time to look. At least not until I get past any troops out here.

Wind abraded my face. At thirty miles an hour, the

temperature dropped at least fifteen degrees. Night was falling. That would make it worse. My ribs seemed to be cracking, fractures inside growing longer. I was losing vision, as it contracted at the edges, but I willed it to expand. My headache spread out, deepened. *Thudthudthudthud!*

Pay attention.

I bounced out of an ice rubble field, reached a rise, and leaned forward on the snowmobile for traction. I remembered lessons that Alan McDougal had drilled into me at the beginning of the summer, when he gave Eddie and me a course in basics. I sat back for better weight distribution on the way down the hill.

Ahead of me the terrain went perpendicular. I shot across a hill face, leaning up, away from the drop, into the slope. Jens was a good rider. But I kept pace, riding with one knee on my running board, the other leg out, as I tried to ignore the pain.

Was I gaining on him?

That's when I saw two other snowmobiles closing on me, ahead, a pincer closing from right and left, both machines spewing ice trails, trying to cut me off.

They were Rangers. Rangers trying to expand the blockade. Rangers on confiscated snowmobiles, drawing the cordon closed to cut off seaside escape. They had to be soldiers because civilians would have avoided other snowmobiles. These guys thought I was trying to escape.

Jens Erik had gotten through before the circle closed.

I might not make it.

I sped up, a mistake. The Polaris spun out. I'd been pushing too hard. I bounced off a stubbly rise and was suddenly spinning in a circle. I hit more ice, tilting, almost falling, sliding sideways on an incline as the track fought for grip. The other snowmobiles closed on me.

I saw one man unsling a rifle off his back as he moved.

I gunned the engine and only at the last second realized that the ice had opened here, torn, and looming twenty yards ahead lay a long, black slit of open water!

I slammed on the brakes. The sudden locking almost launched me off the seat. The track caught and spun left and I slid in a fast glide toward open water.

Jens Erik Holte, in the distance, beyond the two snowmobiles, drew farther away.

Ahead of me, the ice began bursting up in puffs, warning shots. The soldiers did not see the open water yet. They were shooting to try to stop me. They thought I could stop if I wanted. But I could not.

Shit, shit!

I stopped before reaching the water.

"Hands up, you!"

I did not see Jens Erik Holte anymore.

He'd gotten away.

THE FIRST MAN, THE SHOOTER, TRAINED HIS CARBINE ON ME AS the second dismounted. From the way One looked at Two, Two was the boss. They held me at bay. I was a prisoner who'd been stopped from escaping. They were in no mood for back talk.

I tried to reason with them. "I'm Colonel Joe Rush. I'm a Marine. I'm working with General Homza. Remember me, from the school? Were you at the school? I'm after a fugitive. I have ID. You need to let me pass."

The plea had no effect. Their attitude was tense and angry, as someone had shot two Rangers. They had no instructions regarding me. They would have been ordered to ignore any pleas from escapees.

Besides, the only people who know about my deal with Homza are the general himself, and Eddie.

But now I recognized one of the soldiers. It was the captain I'd expelled from my hut on the first day of quarantine. Great. Not exactly a friend. But at least he knew I was a Marine.

"You know me," I told him.

He said, flat and hard, "Yes, I do, sir."

"Then let me go. He's getting away!"

The captain turned and peered west. There was nothing there. Jens was gone. The captain turned back. I pointed down at the ice, the fifteen-inch-wide track that Jens had left, but even as I regarded it, it filled with wind-blown grains of snow or ice. It could be anyone's track.

"He's on that snowmobile. He's the one who started the outbreak. You have to let me pass," I said.

But he wasn't buying it, and I detected a measure of satisfaction in this. "We'll wait. I'll call. Meanwhile, you're not going anywhere, sir." He added, "They kicked you off the base, didn't they, sir?"

"I need to talk to General Homza!"

Five minutes passed.

It was cold, standing here, and the pain seemed to rise up in my head and replace thought. The bruising in my head and shoulders ratcheted into a wave, then more waves.

Nine minutes. I was sweating, always a bad thing in the Arctic. The sweat was freezing beneath my inadequately insulated jacket. I was not dressed properly for extended time out on the ice.

"Let me go after him," I asked, through the pain. "Come with me if you don't believe me."

"No can do."

"All of us. Together." My ribs felt as if they were about to burst from my chest, tear out of my parka.

Closer up, the Ranger with the carbine looked young, maybe twenty-one. He regarded me with slightly more sympathy, or at least less aggression. Only a moron would not see how hurt I was. I looked down and saw drops of blood in the snow. Mine. The Ranger became two Rangers, and then the two Rangers merged back into one.

"Sit down, sir," he said. "You don't look so good."

I tried to think. Where had Jens been going? Somewhere specific? Or anywhere as long as he escaped from town? I gazed off in the direction I'd last glimpsed him, a dot, diminishing, but also turning back to land. He'd passed the line of soldiers and had been looping back, as if to reenter the continent behind the line of soldiers on land. Moving southwest, into tundra. What did he hope to accomplish by heading off there?

What lies in that direction? A village? No. There's no village in that direction.

The captain had gotten through to someone on his radio, and was telling him I'd been stopped while trying to escape. I glanced at the GPS on my handlebars. The sky was clearing as night came on. The stars coming out. I looked into the void and saw Polaris, brightest star in Ursa Minor, the Little Bear. And Vega, brightest star in Lyra, the Harp, a sapphire sphere, second brightest light in the Northern Hemisphere constellations, after the North Star.

If that's the North Star and that's Vega . . . Karen was always gazing at stars . . . if Jens was steering a path between them, he'd be heading southwest toward . . .

Toward where?

I told myself to think. But it was hard to do anything but hurt. I looked up again and saw I had three fixed points with which to work, Barrow, and the two stars. Marines learn night navigation in basic training. We go out without compasses and are challenged to find our way. In my head, I considered the 360-degree horizon as a compass, and assigned numbers to angles. I tried to crudely triangulate direction, using the town and stars as fixed points. I extended an imaginary line into the tundra from where Jens had turned south. I envisioned the North Slope map I'd been staring at over the last few months, the tundra areas, the spots Eddie and I had visited during our mission.

I stopped. The pain in my chest grew sharper. I heard my own whispered speculations coming out, more hope, more question than answer, "Lake number nine?"

"What was that, sir?"

"Nothing." I put my head in my hands. Maybe the pain had caused me to err.

I tried to think. I had to be wrong. Because what the hell would he *do* at nine? There was nothing *at* nine. At best there would be a little research cabin, as at lake number four. It would be winter. There would be no people. The lake would be iced over. Why break quarantine, why risk capture to go to that isolated spot? It made no sense.

Oh, yes it does. You just don't understand why. Because you don't know what this whole thing is really about.

Then I thought, *Maybe it's just a coincidence that he's heading toward that lake. Maybe, the second he reached land, he changed direction. He's evading, that's all.*

The captain, I realized, was now actually talking to Homza's adjutant. Number Two kept back from me, eight feet off, carbine aimed loosely. The captain told the adjutant that I'd been injured while "trying to run the blockade."

"That's not what happened!" I protested.

He waved for me to shut up. "He tried to elude."

I slumped forward in the saddle. Even the Rangers could hear breath rattling in my lungs now. I felt ice on my chin and wiped it with a sleeve. But the pain had a benefit. I looked into my guard's face. He'd relaxed.

I heard Eddie's voice in my head, warning, *One, don't do it.* I saw Karen lying in a pool of blood. Any notion of protecting myself was repugnant at that moment. I let the pain take me. It was easy. I slumped forward. It was what my body wanted. I felt the seat slide up my butt and my knees fail. I would have one chance here, just one.

I heard an old drill sergeant's voice in my head. *Adopt a submissive posture, if you're about to try to take away a weapon, Marine.*

I needed the carbine closer. I got off the snowmobile and dropped to my knees. I tried to struggle to my feet. I prayed, *Come closer, just a few steps.* And he did. But three steps wasn't close enough. I started coughing. He said, his glance sliding left for a fraction of a second, toward his boss, "Colonel, why don't you get . . ."

I launched up, hard, screamed in fury and deflected the swinging barrel with my left palm, my head averted in case he fired, which he did. I locked my arms around the carbine and brought my knee up and yanked the M4 back as I made contact. I had the M4 in my hands.

My whole body was on fire.

The captain's gaze had been averted and only the shot got him spinning around. He was too late. Now I had the carbine. I shouted, razors in my lungs, "Down, down, get down, on your knees now!"

The soldiers knelt, expecting me to fire. The captain's look now pure hatred; the other guy's embarrassed, scared as shit. *I don't want to die.*

"Look, I'm not going to hurt you, unless you move. I have to go," I spotted the captain's phone in the snow, probably still on, probably with Homza's adjutant on the other end, listening. Damn.

"Colonel, come with us," the captain reasoned smoothly, friendly now that our situation was reversed. "You're hurt, sir."

He started to get up.

"If you do that, I will fire. Pick up that phone. Give it. Slowly."

I took their weapons and ammo. I took the key off my snowmobile. I motioned the captain away from his Polaris and stole the key. They could not chase me now.

A quick scan of the captain's saddlebag showed a welcome sight; a bunched up thermal snowmobile suit, an extra he'd probably been ordered to give to some Ranger riding without proper protection. I saw thermal gloves.

They'd be sending people after me. Rangers were probably coming right now. I had to get out of here. I'd change clothing later.

I mounted up, armed now at least with two M4s and extra ammunition pouches, each containing three magazines, each of those holding thirty .223-caliber bullets. The M4 can fire selectively, in three-round bursts, or it can be used on fully automatic.

But could I catch Jens Erik Holte even if he was really heading toward lake number nine?

Gotta try.

I told the captain, "Get to General Homza. Tell him, please tell him that I said that Jens Erik Holte is the guy we're looking for!"

No answer.

"Captain?"

"Fuck you," the captain said.

I hit the throttle and almost toppled off as the snowmobile lurched forward. In the left-side mirror two sorry-looking soldiers stood and brushed themselves off, staring at a disappearing Marine colonel they regarded as a full-fledged enemy now.

Pursuers would be coming. I prayed that no one would reach me until I found Jens. I did not know if the *Wilmington* had drones up looking for the sniper. The pain spiked again with the bumping and the lurching. It was everywhere. It was in my skull, chest, hands, and feet. It kept me alert. I let it fuel me. I was running on pain and hate.

The early night sky was beautiful. Vega glowing. Polaris the jewel. But I would much rather have had clouds, no vision, no chance of the drone, no chance of a chopper.

I followed the shallow indentations in the snow, left by Jens's snowmobile, but they were dissipating.

You need to get rid of the sat phone. You need to rip off the GPS. You can't be carrying anything enabling them to track you.

But I could not do that for a little while longer, because I had to call Eddie before jettisoning the equipment. And I had to get farther away before I could stop and make a call.

The wind rose and the tracks disappeared, and I traveled after an invisible opponent.

I navigated by intuition.

Navigated, truth be told, by guess.

TWENTY-ONE

I looped out to sea and, at approximately the place I saw him turn, swung back toward land. The snow here was marked by a mass of crisscrossing tracks left by escapees. They all looked the same.

I hit land again and turned south by southwest and gunned the engine. After ten minutes I judged myself far enough from the soldiers to take a few minutes to change into warmer clothing and take better inventory of what I'd stolen, what I could use.

The thermal suit gave warmth instantly, as did the insulated gloves. The helmet cut down on peripheral visibility, but would lessen the abrasive scouring of wind.

I also found a headlamp, which I affixed to the helmet, and some peanut butter–flavored PowerBars and a thermos that, when opened, gave off steam and smelled of coffee. I drank some for the caffeine jolt. But added awareness ratcheted up the pain.

Also in the saddlebags was a small, plastic snap-up pouch containing a folded terrain map of the region; helpful, but not much since, to me, the geography here looked basically similar, its differences so subtle that an outsider would miss them. At night especially, there were no mountains or forest, trees or boulders. I could match the map to the GPS for a while, but that was risky. As long as I kept GPS functioning, a sat could find where I was.

And there were lots of lakes.

Too many. They call Chile the nation of lakes, and Minnesota the land of lakes, but both pale beside the North Slope, which seems more lake than land half the time.

I strapped one M4 over my back, tied the other by bungee cord onto a saddlebag. I mounted up and the pain flared. The vista looked flat but, I knew from ATV experience, would not turn out to be flat at all. It would trick any rider with dips and falls and sudden ice mounds.

Get going. I took a final glance at the stars. I checked the GPS and decided on the approximate route that would take me to the cabin that the Harmon party had never visited. I needed to call Eddie . . . but if I couldn't let him know where I was, without mentioning specific coordinates, the call would be useless, or worse.

In short, I needed a landmark that we both knew, and no other listener would know. Great.

The lakes I rolled over were similarly long and thin. It would be easy to mistake one for another. The map, clipped to my handlebars, helped a little, and perhaps every once in a while some particular feature might stand out, give an extra hint of where I was.

I headed south by southwest, into the void. I gambled that tracking me by satellite would take time. That the Rangers might not know I had a phone the general had provided, might not know whose stolen GPS unit I carried. And unlike TV shows, where satellites fly around ubiquitous in space, available for surveillance twenty-four hours a day, in real life they're not always overhead. The entirety of Earth's surface is not under permanent surveillance. Unless on a preset route, unless a sat is there at the exact time you need it, you have to *send it* if you want a snapshot from space.

If the Rangers needed a shot now, it could take hours to get equipment in position. My gamble was that there was no satellite above me at the moment.

At top speed a snowmobile can cover one hundred miles in an hour. But to go even fifty on this slick, deceptive surface would be suicide. I kept the speedometer at thirty-five, risked thirty-six, thirty-nine. Several times the Polaris threatened to tip over and crush me.

I mushed over soft spots and skittered across a frozen lake that I'd not known was there until I was on top. The hard ride ended abruptly as the surface grew spongier and I knew I was on tundra again. Mist spread in the sky. The stars were getting dimmer. Uh-oh.

Then, five minutes later I had a break. Coming up fast

was the wrecked remains of a trio of small, lumpy, abandoned sod houses, built a century ago by Eskimos, long unoccupied, probably dens for foxes now.

I've been here with Eddie.

Basically the homes were dugouts with sod roofs. If you didn't know what they'd been, you would mistake them for mounds. The entrances were low so you needed to crouch or crawl to enter. Whale jawbone "frames" supported the narrow entranceways. Crawling in, you risked a fox bite, and smelled the cloying wet-wool/fur and urine residue of centuries of wild visitors.

The sod houses give me a fix for navigation, triangulation, a call.

I eased up on the throttle. The snowmobile glided to a halt. I checked the location of the houses against the map . . . *Got 'em* . . . and looked up again at the stars I could still see. *Three fixed points!* Breathing hurt. So did my head. *Here we go!*

I pulled out the sat phone and punched in Eddie's number, fully aware that someone else might hear everything we said.

I heard ringing.

They might have him at the base, having arrested him. They might be grilling him now. They might have his phone. The ringing went on, four . . . five . . .

"Hey, man," Eddie said. "Where the hell are you?"

Translation, if that was his opener: They're grilling him. They told him to learn where I am.

I said that I needed to speak to Homza, and Eddie responded, "So do I, man." I told him that Jens had fled town and I pursued him. I said that Jens had spread the rabies. I spoke through Eddie to whoever monitored me.

"Uno, tell me where you are? Are you hurt? Those Rangers said you were hurt. We'll send a doctor for you."

Here we go.

"Remember the place we found those dead foxes?"

A pause. He was thinking, adjusting. There was only one place where this had happened, back in June. He said, remembering, slowly, "The foxes. Yeah."

"Well, let's say, with fifty miles to go, I'm heading approximately ten degrees south by southwest from the tip of the fat monkey's tail."

Thank you, Karen, for teaching me about the made-up constellations because I shared it with Eddie. He'd better remember that "the tip of the fat monkey's tail" is the North Star.

Eddie was silent. Then he said, "What?"

"Ten degrees south, and thirty degrees from Flipper's left eye, roughly."

Sound grew muffled. Someone's hand was over his phone. Someone would be demanding of Eddie what I was talking about. Meanwhile, I approximated angles, triangulating, using the horizon's circle as a compass, assigning values and degrees. It was up to Eddie to get to the general now. I could not waste any more time here.

I thought, *Why didn't Homza tell his adjutant about our arrangement? Why did he keep it to himself?*

"You hallucinating or what?" said Eddie. *He knows!*

I clicked off, pulled the battery from the phone,

stomped on the phone, and left it. With a groan of pain I mounted up. I wished I could jettison the GPS, too, but I was still too far from the lake, and destroying the GPS now was too risky. If the stars disappeared, once the sod homes were gone, without GPS there would be no way to triangulate. So I had to hope that the Rangers who had confiscated my particular GPS from a private citizen did not know which one it was.

The pain seemed worse when I started off again. Each buck of the snowmobile a fist striking the inside of my head. You know what they say: A physician who has himself as a patient is a fool. But I was the doctor and I was the patient. I reviewed symptoms. The shots that had hit my body armor had caused massive bruising, at a minimum. The parka had cushioned my fall a little, and my shoulders had done the rest. The problem was the head injury, how bad it was, and how much worse it would get.

I was running on adrenaline, grief, and rampant fury.

And running out of all three.

RABIES FIGURED IN AS ONE OF MANKIND'S EARLIEST ATTEMPTS at creating bioweapons. The disease entered military records in the fourth century B.C., when soldiers in India were advised to dip war arrows in the blood of rabid muskrats. "Anyone pierced by such a weapon will then bite ten friends, and they will bite and infect ten more," the manual Arthashastra said.

By 1500, the great Leonardo da Vinci sketched out a

"rabies bomb," and, in 1650, Polish General Kazimierz Siemienowic tried one, having his engineers mix "slobber from mad dogs" in clay artillery shells.

It didn't work. No enemy caught rabies.

But that didn't stop the experiments. During World War One both sides worked overtime on designing poison gasses and disease bombs, including devices to inflict rabies. By the Cold War, both U.S. and Soviet scientists worked on creating a contagious, fast-acting strain. The reasoning was that even if rabies remained inefficient against humans, due to spread problems, it could be used against cattle, to damage an enemy's food supply.

And now I had a vial in my pocket, and inside it I was pretty sure I carried a new lab strain of rabies, which had been spread intentionally, first to a four-person research team on the tundra, and then to innocent people in town.

But why?

How far off was lake number nine? Fifty miles? Sixty? That seemed like months or years away.

My face was going numb. Snow blew inside the windshield. I felt sand-like granules between my teeth. My skin burned beneath the balaclava. My lungs ached with each breath and I wondered if we could add frostbite to the mix. The Polaris threw up geysers of snow, where wind had it piled, and in other spots, rubbed raw by wind, I bumped over dead, matted brown grass.

Going uphill, the front of the snowmobile rose, and I leaned ahead, adding weight. Going downhill, I downshifted, sat back.

I heard an erratic clicking and realized it was the engine. Something was wrong in there. But I kept going.

I checked the odometer. I'd traveled only thirty-one miles.

I started to see things that weren't there. I saw a gigantic wolf running beside the snowmobile. Ten minutes later I saw the same wolf, sitting, watching me pass.

I saw a mass of office buildings ahead, tall ones, white, at least ten or eleven stories high, except they turned out to be more small mounds when I reached them.

Seventeen miles.

Eight miles to lake number nine.

Six. The clacking noise worsened.

The stars were gone. A fine mist thickened the sky, hung twelve feet above the tundra.

I passed over fresh bear tracks, huge ones. Monster animal. Maybe not a polar bear. Maybe one of those big hybrids, half grizzly, half polar, that have been showing up as the species mix.

I was losing vision.

A good soldier knows when he has to stop for a break, like it or not. I stopped.

ONE MILE TO GO, MORE OR LESS. I ATE THE POWERBAR, AND drank still-warm coffee, sitting in the snow. Then I destroyed the GPS, shot it, actually, while the wind was keening. I was the Spanish explorer Cortés burning his warships when he reached Mexico so his troops had to move forward. No retreat allowed, soldiers. No way back now, except by luck.

I turned the key and the engine roared, coughed, and sputtered. The snowmobile jerked ahead ten feet and died. The gas gauge read half full. I checked the tank.

Out of fuel.

Had there been spare fuel stored in the saddle bags? Nope.

Well, it's probably a good idea not to get closer with the snowmobile anyway. If he's there, he'd hear it. This way, I'll surprise him.

Which made me laugh. Some surprise.

I hooked the M4 over my shoulder, and shoved extra ammo clips into my parka pockets. I made sure the carbine was ready to fire. The M4 was a good weapon, and normally I could hit a target with one from three hundred yards away.

I advanced like a limping ninety-year-old into the wind, head down, scanning my field of vision, which extended a good solid two hundred feet ahead. The snowmobile disappeared. Then so did direction. But I remembered what an Iñupiat friend had taught me last year on an Arctic mission, and it was that in wind, you can use sastrugi, lines created by wind on snow, for direction.

For the past hours I'd been cutting crosswise through line after line of jagged sastrugi. I continued to cut the lines on foot. Either the cabin would show up soon, or I'd simply wander off into the void.

Suddenly I was knee deep, struggling through drifts that sucked me back. The earth's gravitational field grew stronger. Invisible hands grabbed my boots. I discarded the helmet to improve visibility, but what I saw was darkness. Then abruptly the sky cleared a little.

And then I saw the light in the sky.

It was vague at first, more hint than reality, and that became a yellow glow that morphed into a searchlight. It flew low. It flew fast. It flew in from the direction of the coast, *Uh-oh.*

My first thought was *drone,* but then I saw the running lights and realized it was a small plane or chopper.

Did Eddie come through? Or is it the Coast Guard?

As the craft closed, I saw that the running lights indicated a fuselage shorter than the borough rescue squad's Bell. The light didn't move as it would if it was a chopper searchlight, either. The rescue guys had a King Air prop plane, but no skis on it. Whatever was coming was too big for a drone.

And this plane was not searching. No beams or crisscrossing floodlights. No flying in a grid or circular pattern. The craft made a beeline ahead.

This was *not* a craft sent by Eddie, the general, or Merlin and the North Slope Rescue Squad.

This thing was sent to pick up Jens Erik Holte.

And that was when this destination for him—*rendezvous*—finally made sense. And so did the sniper shots back in Barrow, that had started the mass escape from town.

You waited for the right moment, the perfect build-up of rage, fear, and claustrophobia. Then you calmly triggered the break, used that as cover to get away. You'll load your snowmobile on the plane. You'll be one more person swallowed up by the tundra, never found, a mystery.

Who the hell are you?

The plane made a quick approach and then it lowered smoothly and touched down on the iced surface of the lake. As it closed on shore I recognized the silhouette of a Canadian-built Twin Otter, hardiest craft in the High North. It could carry fifteen to eighteen passengers, cargo, or both.

Nobody I knew on the North Slope flew a Twin Otter. It had the range to have come from western Canada, across the border. It could have come from Fairbanks or Wainright. Hell, if it flew low, it could have even originated in Russia, across the Bering Strait.

As it reached shore, and powered down, I saw, in its floodlights, the figure of Jens Erik Holte standing and waving. Friends! The outline of a snowmobile sat beside him, like a trusted horse. Beyond that, in the beam flashed the small, rickety cabin, barely any shelter at all in winter, a concave structure the size of a multi-seated outhouse, even less inviting than the cabin where the Harmon bodies had been found, and a structure that, if the eco lodge went through, was scheduled to soon be destroyed.

Then *soon* became *now*. Something bright and orange whooshed into life on the side of the cabin. No, not *on* the side, *inside, in a window.* It was fire, I realized, from the sinewy tentacles of light, the sense of heat coming off the thing, just from vision, not even feel.

Not just a rendezvous, Jens. Something more.

Destroying the cabin! That's what you came to do! You waited for the plane to arrive, and set the fire.

I made sure that my M4 was ready to fire. The pain in my head exploded, seemed to expand out and threaten to crack through my skull. I was bleeding in there. I trudged forward on a foot that barely functioned, on a fool's errand, a fool's revenge, and I suffered a fool's punishment, pain so pervasive that it was the only thing keeping me moving.

The cabin would burn for twenty minutes and be obliterated and Jens's mission would be accomplished! I imagined that plane flying away again, disappearing into the void.

And then, months from now, a construction company would land here to wipe away the charred remains and burrow into the permafrost with augurs, massive mechanical screws, and up would spring a fine, new hotel, and probably, in the spring, workers would discover a mummified U.S. Marine colonel under snow, maybe half devoured by wolves. Or maybe no one would find the colonel. He would join the centuries-old parade of explorers, missionaries, and scientists who had, for one reason or another, been swallowed up by the Arctic void.

In the firelight I saw figures jumping down from the open door of the plane, spreading out, military guys, wary figures, one bulky-looking man glided into the light for a moment. He was dressed entirely in black. Black parka. Black furred hat. He carried an automatic weapon with a long banana clip, a bullpup or AK.

Three guys—including Jens—quickly loaded the snowmobile onto the plane via a ramp. No more evidence! The fourth guy stood guard, vigilant as a pro even though, to them, probably, no one else was there.

Well, I had one thing to do before they left. If I couldn't stop them, maybe I could get them to leave something behind that would let Eddie and Merlin and maybe Homza, if he wasn't involved, figure out who they were.

I owed it to Karen and Ted, Cathy, Kelley, and Clay Qaqulik and the others who had been murdered. I didn't much care what happened to me at the moment, but I knew, whatever happened, that I owed something to them.

You're not just going to fly out of here.
Eco lodge my ass!

TWENTY-TWO

A U.S. Army M4 assault rifle weighs 6.36 pounds and extends out fourteen inches. The thirty round 60x magazines stuffed in my pockets were lead weights. The carbine had a telescoping butt stock and the gas-operated magazine fired 5.56mm ammunition. I was an excellent shot with an M4 when I was healthy. I was not particularly healthy just now.

That my snowmobile had run out of gas had probably saved me. Otherwise the pilot of the incoming Twin Otter would have seen the headlight, and the men up there might have mowed me down. Circled a bit. Just like hunting wolves from the air. *Bangbangbang!*

I pushed myself forward. No snow falling, but no moon or starlight out. Just a black land and ahead, a slowly collapsing cabin, a jagged circle of orange in which figures moved like Neanderthals silhouetted in the glow of the first fire.

I was in range, three hundred yards, but for accuracy wanted to be closer. I mentally reviewed the invisible part of the layout, outside the light.

The cabin—or what was rapidly becoming a pile of glowing charcoal—sat at the extreme northern end of the pencil-thin lake. The lake extended south in the usual elliptical shape. It was probably a mile and a half from end to end, probably a third of a mile across at its widest. I had no idea of the depth of the water. The rapidly cooling shape of the Twin Otter was parked where it ended, its three small skis atop the layer of white.

Fire. Now. Do it. Kneel down. Shoot.

No, get closer. They'll move fast when they hear shots, and you'll need every advantage.

I pushed through a windblown snowpile and kept going. Suddenly there were two blurred cabins, and then the two merged back into one. I tripped but stayed up. I was losing strength fast. The digging pains in my chest came steady and deep, with or without movement. Four guys, I thought, five including the pilot.

Or are there more inside the plane?

At sixty yards, the flames died down, relaxing into a peaceful orange glow. Evidence gone. The tundra dipped and I almost toppled into a small depression, deep as a golf course sand trap. It was what I needed, a natural shield. I was out of strength, breath, and time.

Carbine in hands, I lay belly down in the granular cold,

as at the old Quantico rifle range. I could hear them talking from here, not words yet, too far, but a rapid, businesslike snap of orders. From the nasal intonations I realized that they might not be speaking English at all.

The snowmobile had been loaded into the Twin Otter. It was gone. Anyone arriving here would assume that the cabin had been hit by lightning and burned, or that a passing traveler had started the fire; drunk maybe, a firebug, or hunter cooking when suddenly something exploded . . . a mystery not worth thinking about. One more collapsed wreck outside the border of human thought.

The guard stood casually in the cold, yet I sensed a tense awareness in him. Two of the guys out there came together and one lit a cigarette.

The balaclava in my crosshairs. If these guys wore armor, I needed a head shot.

I fired.

I didn't wait to see if I hit him because I had to move fast. I swung the barrel and the second head came into view and *crackcrackcrack* and this time I saw the guy go down. They were both down. I rolled left, screamed from the pain. I was on a roller coaster. My head was spinning. The muzzle bursts would have revealed my location, and the sound of gunfire, too. I was aware of figures scattering, moving left and right, throwing themselves to the ground.

Two down. Two or three left.

Whatever was happening inside my head was climaxing. The booming and dizziness came in a roar. I stayed in the depression, peered out and saw orange glow, a charcoal heap, a couple of body-sized lumps in snow, but nothing moving except smoke. They'd found shelter, too.

Someone out there shouted a name. "Andre? ANDRE!"

Then, the same voice, louder, deep: *"Ty v poryadke?"*

Another, coarser voice: *"Zdyes bolit . . ."*

"Kakoy Movoz!" The words ended in a gasping, choking sound, which cut off abruptly.

Russian?

NOW THE DEEP VOICE WAS THERE AGAIN, FROM THE DARK, FROM the left side. But I couldn't see anyone. "Jens?"

"Ya v poryadke!"

That was Jens's voice, but there was no pain in it. The living guys were taking stock.

"Niki?"

No answer.

"Niki?"

So. Niki dead, hopefully. Two dead. At least two more mobile, including Jens, and maybe one more in the plane. Yes, because the lights in the plane went off suddenly. There were at least three of them.

Shooting suddenly erupted out there, coming at me from two locations. It tore up the snow to my left and right. I wriggled back. They knew where I was.

I fired and heard a scream. I needed to move location, but my head was spinning. If they were smart they'd be using hand signals, or whispers, and would come at me from flanking directions.

I told myself to roll right, and crawl out of the depression. But my muscles refused to move. A fine time to run out of gas! It was like one of those nightmares where you are lying on the street and a bus is coming, or maybe you are running away from something, and it is about to hit you. Safety is a foot away. You need to move a little. You try to take a step, but your muscles refuse to operate.

My right leg just lay there, twitching. I couldn't feel it anymore. My hands were tingling, not hurting, but just not there at all.

I rolled onto my back, pushed with the other leg, and backed farther down into the depression. My one chance was that they would assume I'd moved because moving is what they would do. Anyway, I had no choice. My blood was probably filling my brain cavity. The snowmobile ride had worsened my condition. Offensive action was out.

With the pain coming harder, I had to concentrate to move even fingers. Move! I was disembodied, detached from any connection to earth, sight, sky. Vision is a tunnel and mine was contracting. I watched my breath rise and wondered if it dissipated by the time it reached the top of the depression, or whether someone crawling toward me from three feet away would see swirls of condensation that, like cigarette smoke, would pinpoint where I lay.

I listened but only heard my own heartbeat. My fitful breathing sounded like a jet engine to me. I did not hear anyone crawling up there, whispering, flashing signals.

I could only hope that when someone came over the top, they would be directly in front of me, not behind or to the side.

Suddenly the snow turned green, not mildly green, not a hint, but an electric hue that burst onto the snow like lines on a sonar screen. A luminous presence that extended into the depression and danced on my snowsuit and created green spots on the M4 and illuminated a small burrow in the snow six inches to my left. Vole hole. Some animal's hiding place. Emerald lights. Oz of the Arctic.

I thought I was hallucinating but realized it was the aurora borealis, back again, stage lights highlighting the cripple. The clouds had parted. I saw, high above, the pulsating, greatest show on Earth, the glowing star called Polaris, by which I'd tried to summon Eddie, and the northern constellations, Vega . . . and I thought, *Close your eyes, lie here.* But that was a surrender voice. Light meant opportunity. And anyway, at that moment, I heard the vaguest hint of a scraping sound to my right.

The whole tundra was probably bathed in green out there. They'd feel exposed. They'd move faster.

The lights danced and flickered and formed geometric patterns on my parka. The sky and stars were drenched by an undulating curtain of magnetic light.

Silence.

Maybe I'd been wrong about the sound.

No, between heartbeats, it was back. The smallest brushing. Then a pause. Then the sound.

And then, directly before me, two fingers of a three-fingered shooting mitten appeared at the lip of the depression. They dug into the snow. The black top of a balaclava followed, and then a forehead smeared with black.

I shot him in the face.

My cheek lay in the snow with the lights dancing inches away. The lights smelled like Avgas. They smelled like a fired M4. They smelled like the dead man lying at the top of the depression had voided himself.

"You don't look so good, Joe," said Jens Erik Holte's voice from behind me, and slightly left. "You're not shot, though. So, what?"

Something, a rifle I assumed, poked my back. A boot appeared. My M4 lifted away. Jens, kneeling beside me, probed for hidden weapons. It was an expert search and it involved, at one point, using his foot to turn me over, which caused someone to scream. I realized the screamer was me.

"Huh! A vest! I should have known. You're not hit, so what's the problem? You got four of us, Joe. Four!"

He squatted a few feet off, like a tribesman in the jungle. He didn't look angry, though, and he certainly was not hurt. A dark brown fur-flapped hat had replaced his snowmobile helmet. He still wore a thermal snowmobile suit. He was armed with what looked like an AK-47 variation, from the banana clip and length.

There was no rush. He sat down heavily, sighed, and nodded at the dead man, without breaking eye contact. "That was the pilot, Joe. How do I get out now?"

I said nothing. I tried to, but I couldn't.

"You're pretty busted up. I don't know how to fly a plane—just choppers. Do you?"

I tasted something coppery and metallic. Joe Rush, still life in the Arctic.

Jens sighed, disgusted. "I didn't think so, not that

you're in shape to move. Also, my snowmobile's in the plane now, with a busted chain. Yours? The lights showed it, out there. Got gas?"

I managed to shake my head.

"I guess I could siphon fuel from the plane. Avgas ought to work in a snowmobile, don't you think? No? Yes? No? No opinion? What good are you. Help me out here, man."

The northern lights danced across his strong Nordic features. Handsome guy. Adolf Hitler's ideal. He said, "I would have been out of the country in no time, but now, if Homza's got satellites up, shit. Canada is at least two hundred miles from here, and if they're tracking, even if *they* can't reach you in time, they call the Mounties, and *they're* waiting when you arrive."

I managed to force out, "You're Russian?"

"Nah. *They* are. Not me. I hate Russians."

I heard myself whisper, "Who are you?"

"International citizen of the world." He grinned. "One for all and all for one."

My mind was pain. I tried to get words out and he watched, curious about what I would say, now that he was master here. He coaxed me. "You can do it. Try it slow. I need a few minutes rest before I get out of here anyway. Long day, Joe."

"The . . . rabies isn't . . . con . . . contagious?"

"Nah."

"You . . . spread . . . it."

He nodded. "One person at a time, except for the first ones. Damnit, Joe. I put it in Ted's ice cream, the goddamn ice cream. He *never* shares his ice cream. Except Kelley decided to play a joke on him on his birthday, share it with all of them: Ha-ha, Dad, we ate half your precious supply! They all ate it. He was supposed to get sick alone and that would end the project. Stupid teenage joke."

I tried to think. Through the green dancing light, black spots appeared. I forced out, "Why . . . give it . . . why . . ."

"Why give it to others? In town? Come on, man! Think! Once four people had it, we needed to keep you away from *here*, from connecting the deaths to their work. So we created an emergency. We gave you what you looked for. A 'new' disease. We shifted attention. It should have worked."

He stood up. He seemed amused. "I thought you were going to ask me about *her*, but you didn't, Joe. You asked about something else. Marine to the end."

"What is . . . here?"

He made a noise like a game show buzzer. "Gotta go!"

"I'll . . . find . . . you."

"Yeah, yeah." He sighed, getting up. "You'll hunt me down. I can see you're in good shape. Anyway, just so you know? I liked all you people. You are one fucking bird dog once you get an idea in your head. Everyone else, fooled. Gotta go, Joe. Gotta reach Canada."

I tried to claw my way through the snow to him. I managed to move my left hand a whole inch.

I whispered, "Eco lodge?"

"Hey, Joe, remember that time early on in the season, that homemade pizza at the Harmons? That was a good night. Kelley rolling dough. Ted chopping onions. Lillienthal and his nympho sister coming in with that Texas brewery beer? Summer friends."

"Who . . . ?"

"You still haven't asked about *her*. Some fiancée you were, Colonel. Workaholic to the end. Well, you get no sympathy from me. I could shoot you, but hell. Freeze."

He leaned down. I was as helpless as an infant. He stripped off my hat and mittens, and instantly I felt the temperature plunge. He unzipped my thermal suit. He took my M4. He said, "Well! Gotta burn those bodies and get gas!"

He stomped off into the snow, green lights playing on his back. I heard him crunch away, right about the time that the aurora borealis failed and night came back. Show over.

When I was conscious again I heard grunting from some distance off, probably him dragging a corpse toward the fire. I heard a smashing noise, and imagined Jens busting up a dead man's teeth with his rifle stock. Can't have authorities checking teeth on bodies burned in the fire. He'd probably blow up the Twin Otter, too, try to obliterate the record, once he gassed up one of the snowmobiles.

And the evidence here, a burned-down cabin, a blown-up plane. Hell, put it down, Detective, as a cocaine or illegal alcohol delivery gone bad . . . one more mystery of the High North to be written up in the adventure magazines.

. . .

KAREN VLESKA PAUSED AT THE TOP OF THE DEPRESSION, HER long silver hair flying in wind, her mittens wrapping ski poles, her eyes hidden by goggles, her hip jutting out, feminine, petite, perpetually sexy. There was a long red scarf wrapped around her neck, and I understood it hid a knife scar. She'd heard Jens Erik Holte's accusation. *I thought you were going to ask about her, but you didn't, Joe.*

I told her, "I'm glad you're all right."

She said, "I'm not."

I said, "Where are you going?"

She said, "Oh, I'm already there."

"Karen. I love you."

"Funny way to show it, Joe." She skied away.

BACK IN WASHINGTON, BEFORE EDDIE AND I HAD FLOWN TO Alaska this summer, the admiral had insisted that we watch a warning film, an old black-and-white copy of an original made at a German World War Two prison camp, Treblinka. It was one of the films that Admiral Galli came up with from a seemingly inexhaustible supply of archived, classified files, which he regularly used to underline points. We'd pissed and moaned because it was a nice, warm spring day, and Eddie wanted to shop for souvenirs for his wife and daughters, and I wanted to sleep at the hotel.

Instead, we were ushered into the admiral's screening room, space for six, where we slumped into cushioned chairs and, coffee before us, watched a grainy film. We sat up a little. Then we sat up a lot. Eddie grew so sick at what we were seeing that at one point he gagged.

Shot one: three smiling white-coated doctors standing by a bathtub filled with water. Shot two: the biggest, fattest, least-healthy looking doctor waves his hand, and two German soldiers dump lots of ice cubes into the tubs.

The three prisoners look like toothpicks when they lurch in, terrified, eyes swinging between the smiling doctors and the ice-filled tubs. And then, clearly forced, they remove their rags. The man folds his neatly. Maybe once he was a lawyer, or businessman, the kind of guy who draped his clothing neatly over the top of a chair each night, before climbing beneath laundered sheets with his perfumed wife. The woman refused at first to get into the tub. The soldiers pushed her in. The kid was screaming, but the film had no sound reel with it. We only heard the whirring projector and the muted hum of Washington on a warm spring day outside, where cherry blossoms bloomed.

"You two Marines *will not* let yourself get frostbite or hypothermia this summer," Admiral Galli said. "I hate this film and the people who made it. But it's the best graphic warning I know. Watch!"

Watch? Horrified, we couldn't stop. The Nazi doctors slid big red thermometers in the water, and smaller ones in victims' mouths. Someone, an Allied technician likely, had added numbers on the bottom of the screen. The thermometers in the film showed temperature in Centigrade. The added numbers were Fahrenheit, easier for us to understand.

"Body temp, ninety-eight point six," whispered Eddie. The immersion had begun.

The victims began shivering.

The shivering grew worse.

The child shivered more than the adults.

"Keep watching," Galli said.

He'd given us reading material, and I'd skimmed it, but now, facts slammed home. I knew for the Jews in the tubs, as their skin temperature dropped, the nerves on the surface pulled back, pushed blood farther into the body. It was natural triage, the body sacrificing its skin in exchange for keeping organs—heart, lungs, kidneys—warm.

The fingers in those tubs were probably numb by now.

At body temp 97F, the father seemed to pause, and I knew that inside, he'd gone into a pre-shiver, the body's expectation of near convulsions to come.

Fat Nazi doctor said something to skinny one, pointing to his own ears, then Dad's ears, keenly observing, fascinated, probably saying something like, *"Und now ze ears vill begin to hurt him!"*

At 88F, the doctors were looking at blood in a test tube. "Thicker blood," Fatso probably remarked. "At zis temperature, ze blood thickens into natural oil."

By 87F, I knew from the reading, even oxygen was being sent from the outer surface of the bodies into the interior. The three victims were convulsing with shivers. Any air or warmth would be fleeing to the core.

The father clapped his hands over his ears. He was probably trying to block out his jackhammering heartbeat.

The woman moaning, pleading. *Let my son out, at least!*

Tears streamed down the kid's face, as he lifted both

shaking arms to his parents. They could not help him. Fat, happy doctor took notes. Skinny doctor spoke to the boy, with a kind expression, as if reassuring him, as if any minute he'd give the kid a lollipop. Doctor with the limp just watched, left elbow cupped in right palm, right hand stroking chin. Hmm. Very interesting.

The soldiers remained expressionless, on the side.

At eighty-five degrees, freezing victims start to think they're *hot*, not cold, as I now felt, lying in the snow. I had to get my parka off. I was burning up. But my fingers refused to grip the zipper head.

Someone was looking down at me. I gazed up. At an eighty-five-degree body temperature, I knew, people dying of cold actively hallucinate.

The stranger said, in Jens's voice, "I found your snow-mobile, Joe. I gassed it up. Thanks for the loan."

He added, "Feeling chilly, guy? Wish me luck. Off to Canada!"

The stranger—or hallucination, more likely—was gone.

TWENTY-THREE

Major Edward Nakamura, USMC, sat on the right-hand front seat of a U.S. Army Black Hawk helicopter as it raced south by southwest out of Barrow. It flew low. The aurora borealis had ended and a thick cloud cover had returned. The lights of the copter shone in an arc below, sweeping across a white blanket of unrolling, undulating tundra. Major Nakamura tried to batten down the rage and fear and consider what he needed to do.

I hope that Joe is at that cabin.

But the whole attempt to get there had the heavy feeling of too late. Five heavily armed Rangers rode behind. Add Nakamura, that made six. He settled back and felt the fury as a knotting in his neck and jaw, and a line of tension that made his back into a steel rod. His teeth hurt. His eyes throbbed. He could not stop flashing back to the way that General Homza's adjutant, Major Garreau, had refused to listen when Eddie had burst into head-quarters, trying to reach the general.

"Your friend just attacked two Rangers," Garreau had said.

"Just let me talk to General Homza for a minute! He'll explain! We made a deal!"

"The general is busy. If you haven't noticed, we've got a mass escape underway."

Homza was out on the ice, Garreau said. Homza was personally watching the last few yards of open space closed up out there. Homza was directing his field commanders. And after that he was talking to Washington, discussing the situation with the secretary of defense himself.

"You'll see him when he's free," Garreau said.

And then, when Homza had finally walked in, exhausted, and spotted Nakamura in the glass room, he'd raised his eyes inquiringly at the adjutant, cocked his head to listen to Eddie's tale, and as it came out Homza had slumped and looked blank for some moments, turned to the adjutant and said, simply, "Give him what he needs."

Eddie thinking, *I need to take back the last hour that you just wasted. That's what I need.*

Why had Homza kept the arrangement with Joe and Eddie secret? Maybe he wanted credit. Maybe he was playing it safe.

Ten miles to go, Eddie Nakamura thought, eyeing the odometer, calculating distance backward since they'd lifted off from Barrow Airport, less than a half hour ago.

If Joe isn't there, if I figured this wrong, if I misread what he was telling me, I have no idea where he is.

The pilot said, pointing, "Should be ahead!"

There would be no lights to announce the place. They flew by instrument. The spotlights swept over snow and for a moment some animal was there, scurrying away, wolverine, looked like, nature's mass of warm-blooded fury, a fierce creature but one that knew when to run, not fight, knew when to play it smart against bad odds.

Eddie flashed to Homza's face again, a quick flick to that countenance which, up until Eddie told the story, passed along Joe's claims, had always seemed so sure. Eddie had seen the animation go out of it as the weight of realization hit. Homza probably knowing that he'd blown it. Knowing, if Joe was right, if Jens Erik was who they wanted, that many of the general's steps until now had been blunders; the arrest of Valley Girl, the marginalization of Joe, the failure to realize a basic fact of the Arctic, that ice freezes, and then to not have enough troops to handle things when it did . . .

Game over, General, for you.

The pilot said, "That cabin has to be here. Where is it? We're here, but everything looks like everything else. Wait! There." He pointed.

And there it was, in the floodlights, a burned-out wreck of what had been some dilapidated shack. A wooden hut. An escape for researchers. Lake number nine's shelter, now a smashed-up mass of barely smoking charcoal, hissing as the last embers were smothered up by blowing snow.

"I don't see anyone," the voice in Eddie's earphone said.

"Circle."

"I don't see tracks."

"You wouldn't, in this wind. Circle, I said."

The copter tilted and veered and they began a search pattern. Eddie's heart beat loud and hard in his throat. Eddie heard the chatter of talk between the pilot and Barrow, and more talk coming in from Rangers out at sea, on ice, manning the new oceanside barrier. No one else could escape from Barrow anymore.

Big deal. At least eighty people did.

Now he was startled to spot the wreckage of a small plane, also burned, by the lakeside. He frowned, considered ordering the chopper to touch down, so they could continue looking for Joe on foot. If a plane was here, this was definitely where Joe had been heading.

The pilot said, "I don't think anyone's here."

"Then who burned this place?"

"I don't know. Whoever did it is gone."

"Keep circling," Eddie ordered. "I see smoke down there. This is fresh. Shut up and look for my friend."

THEY SAW THE BODY TWO MINUTES LATER. IT WAS A MOUND half buried in blowing snow, an hourglass-shaped lump of white that ended in something dark, like fabric, the half-removed snowsuit. Eddie was the first one out of the chopper. He kept his sidearm out. He knelt by Joe's side.

"Uno?"

No movement. No breathing. No rise and fall of chest. No warmth.

"Oh, man. Uno!"

Eddie thumped on the chest to get the heart moving. He thumped hard. He couldn't figure out why the thermal suit was unzipped. And the hands. No gloves. *Hypothermia victims get confused and take off their clothes.* Eddie unzipped the jumpsuit further, tore off his balaclava, lowered his ear to the bone-white chest, above Joe's heart. Eddie listening. Eddie sitting up and spitting out an order that the Rangers stop making noise, crunching around in the snow.

He's dead.

No, wait.

Do I hear something? Or do I just want to hear it?

Faintly, faintly, he heard it.

"Get him back! Get him in the chopper! Now, now now!!!"

THE HALF-HOUR TRIP SEEMED LIKE IT TOOK A MONTH. RANJAY was waiting at the hospital, where they landed. Ranjay telling Eddie to stand back, let him get close. Ranjay saying, as they wheeled Joe in, that friends do not operate on friends. That friends make mistakes when they do. That doctors should never work on good friends.

"*You're* a friend. I'm going in, too," Eddie said.

"You're not working on him."

Eddie bulled up to the little Indian. Eddie's face in Ranjay's. Eddie wanting to punch the guy, except he saw, in those brown eyes, strength and determination. Eddie slumping. Eddie unable to speak. Ranjay turning and, with the emergency staff, rushing Joe into the operating room.

Ranjay calling back to Eddie, "Come! Major! Come in and see!" Then, as if addressing a child, "But don't touch."

THEY INSERTED A LONG CATHETER INTO JOE'S ABDOMINAL CAV-ity. They wheeled in saline solution, just salt water, but warm, and began the flush. It was like flushing a car radiator. The warm solution was supposed to raise his body temp, but not too fast.

Eddie remembered a story. It was that a capsized boatload of Italian seamen had been rescued from the Atlantic, not from the ocean like the frigid one here, not iced over, but from waters that were only fifty degrees.

The rescuers had carefully warmed the seventeen grateful victims in blankets and poured them coffee. The Italians had recovered nicely, quickly, in no way in as bad a shape as Joe. They stood up, unaided. They walked together to the ship's mess. They were smiling and chatting. Within minutes, out of the blue, all seventeen collapsed and died. Heart attacks.

Can't warm up too fast.

My best friend, Eddie thought, going back in memory. Uno and Eddie at college, in Massachusetts, in ROTC. Roommates. Eddie and Joe at Parris Island, competing to see who was the better Marine. Eddie winning the push-up competition, Uno winning on the obstacle course. Eddie in hand-to-hand combat. Uno, earning his monicker, *Number One,* during war games in the hills, capturing the general of the "Blue" team.

You were always better at strategy than me, Joe.

Eddie watched the monitors. They held steady. Joe's limbs looked less waxy. The pulse rose a tiny bit, and so did Eddie's hope. Ranjay ordered more saline solution brought in. Joe's blood pressure was almost nonexistent. Eddie remembered all the piss-drenched clothes they'd cut away, all the sweat, bodily fluids lost in his body's attempt to warm itself. Eddie saw cold blisters on Joe's limp hands.

Ranjay to Eddie, as they finished. "Now we wait, Major. He was badly injured even before the exposure. He needs a CAT scan. He's got back injury. He's got bumps on the front and back of his head. Major, even if he survives, we may need to do amputations."

"I understand, Ranjay. Christ."

"Let's get some coffee."

"Ranjay, you're a good guy. You're an honorary Marine."

The little man beamed. But then he looked sad. His head wove side to side in the Indian mannerism. *We must wait and see and hope for fate to be kind.*

"Tea for me, please," Ranjay told the cafeteria girl.

TWENTY-FOUR

The wedding started well but then things went sour. The ceremony was held in the small, white-steepled Methodist church in Smith Falls, the Massachusetts town in which I'd grown up. It was October, peak of New England leaf season, and the oaks, maples, and birches had lost their summer green and taken on crisp, bright hues: pumpkin orange, dazzling yellow, maroons in shades ranging from dried blood to the deep rich of an emperor's cloak.

Karen pulled up in a dogsled outside, through a shower of leaves, the huskies puffing as she stepped off the runner, dressed in a clinging white gown that showed her lithe body. I hate big gowns, the hoop kind, that make brides look like they stepped out of an Alabama antebellum ball. My parents smiled at us from the first pew. Behind them sat kids, still ten and eleven years old, with whom I'd attended school, and beside them an old drill sergeant from

Parris Island, odd because he'd died of cancer. The admiral sat beside General Homza. It was a happy scene, with sunlight brightening the stained-glass windows. But then I saw that the scenes depicted on those windows were not from the Bible. Afghanistan didn't show up in the Bible. Neither did a tarp-covered troop truck exploding. In the center window, each piece of colored glass in the mosaic showed a different aspect of the explosion: a shard of metal, a severed limb, roiling smoke.

And the faces on that window—eyes turned toward heaven, fractured into Picasso-like angles—belonged to eight dead Marines, who I'd blown up. Their eyes were the color of sapphires and their helmets reflected the gold of the sun. I'd never met them. I'd seen photos. Depicted in glass, their eyes followed the reverend, as he took a step toward Karen and I.

"Do you promise to lie, honor, and obey?" he said, smiling pleasantly.

"It's not a lie if you do it for your country," I answered.

Karen looked angry at that. Wrong answer. The faces in the pews, when I turned, were sad. Eddie sat in back, trying to tell me something. I heard the sled dogs outside, baying. The air in the chapel grew cold, and my fingers hurt, and I felt the brush of snow on my abraded face.

Karen was walking off without me, out the church.

"I can't pronounce you," said the reverend, and I realized that his voice had deepened and acquired a foreign accent. He still wore vestments but now he'd morphed into Jens Erik Holte. Jens holding a Bible. No, not a Bible, but an advertisement for an Arctic eco lodge.

Jens said, "Lots to see!"

I opened my eyes and saw white ceiling. I heard a roar I recognized vaguely as fighter jets taking off. Through gauzy curtains a low, bright sun flooded in. My fingers really did hurt. They lay beneath clean covers. I turned my head on the pillow and saw what had to be another hallucination, because it was Admiral Galli, in a light gray suit and striped red-and-blue tie, sitting in a visiting chair a few feet away.

The room smelled of tulips. Tubes ran into my arms. I held my hands in front of my face and saw stained wrappings. The pain was fiercest inside the bandages wrapping my right hand.

"He's awake," Galli said.

"I'm not, sir," I said, in the dream. "I'm not awake if you're here."

He stood. He nodded. I smelled the faint aroma of cigars that often came off the admiral. He said, softly, "Homza's out. I'm back. The administration wants a face that reporters like. The quarantine ended. You're awake, all right. You're in Anchorage. Joe, do you remember telling us about Holte? The rabies? The ice cellar?"

"Now I know I'm up, sir. You didn't ask how I feel."

He smiled. His hand on my shoulder was light, reassuring. "You feel like shit, what's to ask? And it'll last awhile. CDC's confirmed it, Joe, rabies not contagious. We found the vial in your parka, where you said it would be. But we still need to figure out where it came from. Colonel, you did a hell of a job."

I closed my eyes. I heard hospital machinery beeping

behind me, heartbeat low, blood pressure could be better. I heard a cart squeak out in the hall. The door was open, and a man was weeping copiously somewhere beyond my range of vision. I smelled Lysol and boiled chicken, boiled string beans and packaged orange juice. The ubiquitous hospital meal. Chicken. The least-fortunate creature on the planet, designed for one purpose, slaughter.

"Yeah, I did one hell of a job," I said.

"I'm sorry about Karen."

I closed my eyes.

"Joe, you're going to have to testify on the Hill."

I opened them.

"In secret. We've got half of Congress accusing us of a cover-up, hiding some weapons program, thanks to someone named Tilda Swann. We've got the other half wanting to double appropriations against terrorists. The quarantine's over but what the hell happened?"

I tried to think. My whole body was a mass of pain. I said, "What story are you putting out?"

"That the rabies morphed naturally. That it was a rogue strain that just died out. CDC's going along. Truth is, authorities in Yellowstone did find a strain that's jumped fox to fox, without bites. So it's *possible* that the disease could evolve. But our batch came from a lab."

"Jens will know the answer. Did you get him?"

I was tired. Fading. The weeping in the hall subsided, and the beeping of the machinery grew low. Someone else came into the room, but they looked hazy and indistinct in sunlight. I closed my eyes. I was exhausted. I was too tired to wonder who was there.

"He's out again," said Galli's voice.

The other voice said, "Did you tell him about his toes?"

"When he's better. One thing at a time. Merlin, are those damn reporters still downstairs?"

NEXT TIME I OPENED MY EYES THE ADMIRAL WAS GONE BUT Merlin was there with Eddie. I was more alert and recognized the unmistakable roar of fighters, F22 Raptors taking off outside, possibly headed north to intercept Russian Bear Bombers. The bombers have started buzzing Alaskan air space recently. They'd stopped after the Cold War. They started again when oil extraction came up as an issue in the Arctic. The bombers never enter U.S. territory. They fly along the border, doing "exercises," often at times when U.S./Russian relations sour elsewhere on Earth. Recently they've buzzed U.S. airspace more and more. I figured I was at Elmendorf Air Force Base.

Merlin looked shy, an expression I'd not seen on him before. He seemed bigger in the small room, dressed in freshly laundered jeans and an ironed, button-up, lavender-and-white-striped shirt, bowhead buckle design, spotted seal vest, bolo tie in walrus ivory. Eddie wore a light blue dress shirt, tie in solid blue, matching dark blue jacket and charcoal trousers, sharply creased.

"What happened to you?" I said, taking in the outfit.

"The admiral paraded me before the governor," Eddie said. "The governor wants details. So does the world. Lotta nervousness out there, Joe, as in: Will this thing come back?"

"Tell *me* details."

"Bottom line, we don't know! Ranjay saved you. Brought you back. It was touch and go for a while, but we airlifted you out when you stabilized. You've been here for a week."

Merlin hung back, shyly, out of character for him. He was a quiet man, but he was not shy. Eddie tilted his head at Merlin, brows up, as if to say, *Tell him.* Merlin pulled a chair close. "Eddie told me about your deal with Homza. You're a hell of an actor, Joe. You convinced me not to trust you. What can I say?"

"I need to tell you that I called Homza when the breakout happened. To ask him to stop people from leaving Barrow. I tried to stop it."

Merlin chewed that over. "I'm fine with that. You did what you had to do. You were trying to stop the spread. If it *had* been contagious, if those people had reached other villages, only God knows what would have happened. We alerted them, too. A couple of snowmobiles reached Wainright, but they were held up. Later choppers brought them back. No charges filed. Enough is enough."

"Thanks for understanding."

"I owe you, Joe. Lifetime offer."

"In that case, one of you tell me about this," I said, raising my bandaged, throbbing left foot.

My whole body hurt and the hammering was worst at the extremities; right hand, left foot. I was familiar with the sort of constant pounding that came from serious bruising. But this sharp burning was one I'd never felt before.

Eddie let out a deep breath. He said, "Who needs all ten toes, right? Like the appendix. Eight toes work fine. Hell, couple of tips gone. Big deal."

I glanced down at my feet, lumps under the light-weight white hospital blanket.

"Two toes on the left foot, Joe. Little therapy, few weeks of new moves, you'll be dancing again."

"I can't dance now."

"See what I mean? This will improve things."

Truth was, I couldn't believe that they'd saved me at all. I remembered my brief conscious time in the snow-bank as a cold dark, a dark that surpasses anything living, a sensation that—if you have a choice, if you can trade a toe or two to keep it away, seems worth it. I would not have thought previously that the loss of a couple of toes could seem small, but compared to the enormity of what had happened, and what I'd lost, they were beside the point. They were not the point at all.

"Eddie, tell me about Jens."

He nodded and swiveled back in the hospital chair and came back with an attaché case, opened it and extracted eight-by-ten magnified aerial photos. The first showed the Alaska pipeline, the lifeline flowing north-to-south from Prudhoe Bay, atop the North Slope, to Valdez, in the south. Not so long ago, 20 percent of America's oil flowed through that pipe. These days it ran one-third full. Land-based oil was drying up. That's why Dave Lillienthal at Longhorn wanted to drill offshore, where they'd esti-mated lay several billion barrels of crude.

But I understood that Eddie's showing me this photo just now had nothing to do with fuel. He was showing me a border, which Jens would have had to cross if he wanted to reach Canada.

"You stopped him at the pipeline?"

"We spotted him there."

He'd avoided a direct answer. I saw a shot of a snowmobile heading out of the left side of the frame, churning snow, toward the pipeline. Next the snowmobile was zigzagging, trying to evade whoever was above. It was like watching a silent film frame by frame. The snowmobile stopped. A figure crouched beside it. Yellow bursts, shots, erupted from the muzzle of the rifle. This last photo had been taken at a steep angle. Now the chopper pilot was trying to evade.

Eddie said, "Homza had the pipeline manned as soon as he got your message. There were already troops there, beefed up because of the quarantine. I'd told Homza that Jens might be headed in that direction."

"Why did you think that?"

"You. It was clear that you hadn't dragged those bodies into the fire. Someone else did, so there was another survivor. We knew you were after Jens. We knew whose snowmobile you'd stolen, and it wasn't there. So I figured Jens was running, he'd taken yours."

I nodded. The logic was right on.

Eddie continued, "The police had been alerted to watch for incoming at the seven villages. He didn't show up. Airports closed. No roads to block. Everyone cooperating for a change because no one wanted a contagious disease spreading. So where was he? He had to be heading east."

I saw it as he described it, and picked up the thread. "You checked and found that the Twin Otter hadn't originated from anywhere in Alaska. You figured the plane had come in low, over a border. What did he tell you when you got him? *Tell me what you learned when you caught Jens.*"

Eddie blew out air and sat back and the posture and expression gave me an answer. The next photo showed a black-clad figure lying in the snow, left arm thrown back, rifle nearby, dark blood by the head. He looked like a dead man half trying to make a snow angel. I felt a hard, angry knot form inside. They'd not talked to Jens at all.

"They shot him?"

"He shot himself."

"Then who was he, Eddie?"

Merlin sighed. Eddie stood up in agitation. "We don't know. No ID on any database from fingerprints or DNA. Nothing from national security. Dental records, zilch. Documents, immigration, forget it. That coast up there is the most porous entry point in the country. There's no customs agent on the entire North Slope. The FBI checked back. So did Amanda Ng and Hess. He didn't come from where he said, even in America. So far, he's a total blank."

A hollow frustration filled my belly. "What about the bodies pulled from the fire? Prints? Clothing? Anything?"

"Burnt up. Teeth smashed. Fillings generic. What I

want to know is why, if he'd escaped, he wasted time go-ing to that cabin? He could have reached Canada if he headed there from the get-go. What was at the cabin?"

"Whatever *was* there isn't there anymore."

A sudden stabbing in my leg made me shift position, and the move shoved photos off the bed so they separated and drifted onto the floor. There they lay, clues without answers, dead men, charred sites.

"We have nothing then," I said, bitter.

"No, One. *You* found the vial, which we took from your pocket. *You* enabled them to end the quarantine. *You* found rabies. All Jens had to do when he wanted to infect someone was stroll over to the supermarket and put a few drops in a food. If it wasn't for you, it would have worked. The phony outbreak would have ended. We all would have gone home."

A pretty red-haired nurse appeared. She told Eddie and Merlin that they had to leave. She said I needed rest. She said they could come back in a few hours.

"We'll be nearby," Eddie said.

Merlin said, "Eddie sleeps in the hall, Colonel. He won't leave here."

When they were gone, the nurse fussed over me and gave me more orange juice and said I needed fluids and said that I must be important because of all the reporters downstairs and all the VIPs who kept calling and asking how I was, telling the doctors to treat me like royalty. She said that yesterday night, when she stopped at a bar after work, a reporter from a Los Angeles–based rag sheet, *Creeps and Celebs*, had offered to buy her dinner and slip her a thousand dollars to take a couple of photos of me in bed.

She said, "I turn on the TV and every channel says something different happened. What did happen, sir?"

I'm going to find out.

"LET'S GO OVER IT ONE MORE TIME," SAID AMANDA NG AS HESS took notes. "I know you're tired. I really appreciate this. Did Jens . . . the man who said he was Jens . . . did Jens ever mention anything about the Mideast, or a connection with a foreign terrorist group?"

"I told you. No."

"Domestic, then. There are several groups in rural Alaska that concern us."

"He didn't mention any connections."

"You said that the men who got out of the plane were speaking Russian."

"No, I said I thought it was Russian. Jens said it was Russian. I don't speak Russian. It could have been something else."

"Did Jens ever say anything to lead you to believe that whoever did this intended to do it again, elsewhere?"

"No."

"Did he make even any casual mention of another U.S. location, even in passing?"

"No."

"Did you ever get the impression that this infection in Barrow was a kind of test run?"

"Test run?"

"You know, try it out in one place, do it in another."

"What's the point of a test run? If you have an infectious agent and you use it, the whole world knows it instantly. Test run? It wasn't a test run. He told me what it was."

"You believe him?" Hess said. Apparently Hess had doubts.

"My turn to ask a question. You said last time that you've put out Jens's photo on TV. Anyone recognize him?"

"We're getting a lot of calls, but no. *It's my father who disappeared! It's Uncle Ed, the pervert! It's the slob who lived next door and used to play loud Irish music!*"

"What about the eco lodge connection?" I said.

Hess sighed. Ng took it more seriously. "There isn't any that we can see. Why? Did Jens mention the eco lodge?"

"No, but he was there! I'm tired. I need to sleep."

"YOU'RE LOOKING BETTER." BRUCE FRIDAY BEAMED. "WE ALL came to see you. Happy birthday!"

They'd flown down on the morning 737 from Barrow, and they were in the room when I was wheeled back from physical therapy. They'd brought a lemon cake. Deirdre McDougal lit candles. I blew them out, watched smoke drift before their faces. Calvin DeRochers lugged in a suitcase. He was headed back to Arkansas when the visit was over, to begin the next year of planning for a return.

"Calvin expects to hit it big next year," he said.

Mikael Grandy brought a gift-wrapped book, *The Es-*

kimo and the Oil Man, about Barrow. He looked incomplete when he wasn't holding a camera. He stayed back, didn't talk much. I'd heard that HBO had accelerated the release of his film. It would be coming out in ten days, while Barrow still filled headlines across the world.

Mikael was booked on an evening flight to New York, with a stop in Minneapolis.

"Sure you don't want some New York bagels?" he said.

"I'm sure."

The McDougals brought a care package from the North Slope Wildlife Department; reindeer sausage, caribou stew, and an assortment of homemade fruit pies that we convinced the nurse to store in a staff break-room refrigerator down the hall. They all had business in Anchorage. The trip was not just to see me. McDougal would attend one more Arctic symposium to be held this week at the Cook Hotel. Bruce would speak on "The Great Polar Bear as the Arctic Warms."

"All this attention in Washington might benefit our effort to protect these magnificent creatures," he said.

Merlin was in town for a meeting of the Alaska Eskimo Whaling Commission, and a final vote on whether to support Longhorn's offshore drilling proposal. Dave and Deborah were back in Anchorage for the year. Leon Kavik had come to scout the University of Alaska campus. The mayor was visiting his sister, who worked in the office of the lieutenant governor.

"Brought you some Tito," said Dave Lillienthal, leaving a gift-wrapped package by the window, with a red ribbon on top. He winked. "I told the nurses it's books."

Tilda Swann pushed to the front of the group.

She looked good in leg-hugging jeans, sharply toed dark leather boots, and a turtleneck beneath a fawn-colored jacket. She wore a silk scarf, moss-green, which highlighted her red hair. Brashness still marked her, but her voice was toned down, at least at first.

She said, "I came to say how sorry I am for your loss, Colonel." But her voice was stiff, her eyes, locked on mine, seemed more wary than sympathetic. Of all the people there, she and Leon were the only two who were not friends.

"Do you mind if I ask you a question, Tilda?"

She seemed surprised. The others watched. She said, "That's what I'm in Anchorage for today, to answer questions. After you, I'll be talking with the guy from the *New York Times*."

Somehow, when she said it, it sounded like a threat, or at least a challenge. I said, "You've got a job with the new eco lodge, I heard."

Her eyes narrowed. "I do."

"To give lectures."

"That's right. I like Barrow. I like the people. I like the remoteness. And that lodge will show people there's an alternative way to make money without giving *them*," she said disdainfully, nodding at Dave Lillienthal, "carte blanche to wreck one more pristine place on Earth."

"Did you meet the owners of the lodge?" I asked.

Her gaze hardened. Sympathy only went so far. "Uh-huh."

"Did they tell you if it's just a lodge, or whether they'll be doing anything else out there?"

Her mouth snapped shut. She shook her head. She was one of those people whose anger appears instantly in the form of blushes, which in her case started at the freckles and burst outward and across the skin, mass by mass.

"I don't believe this," she snapped. "Even now? That lodge is a win-win, and you're trying to link it to what you guys did? Disgusting! Why don't you admit there was a government testing program that went wrong! All this bullshit! Phony hand-wringing. A cover-up was what it was!"

She stormed out. I watched her on CNN that evening, fulminating, her angry face superimposed over a background shot of a herd of caribou, *Live from Alaska*. Her fury seemed magnified, and her British accent gave weight and heft to the accusations spewing from her lovely mouth.

"The North Slope is an American Serengeti," she said. "One of the last unspoiled spots on Earth. We intend to keep it that way."

Eddie sat beside me. "Fiery in bed, I bet," he said with amusement.

"If she'd shut up."

"Hey, you're back," exclaimed Eddie.

I wasn't back. It was wishful thinking. She'd given me an idea, though. I picked up the phone, called Valley Girl.

"It's three A.M. in Washington?" she moaned, even her complaints phrased as questions. "I'm sleeping?"

"Perfect time to go to work," I said.

TWENTY-FIVE

It took a while. But I found him.

Crises bloom and get replaced in Washington. What seems crucial one day is history the next. Who planned the shooting of John F. Kennedy? Did Franklin Roosevelt have advance warning that Japan would attack Pearl Harbor? Did George W. Bush lie to America when he sent troops into Iraq, saying that country hid weapons of mass destruction? Was the quarantine of Barrow a military cover-up, or not?

After the hearings, the talking-head speculations and accusations, after my secret testimony in closed hearings before Congressional subcommittees on terrorism and biowarfare, the admiral let me retire early.

Joe Rush, ex-colonel, at the rural post office, collecting a pension check.

They say you can't go home again, but, as is often the

case, they are misinformed. You can always go home again. Or rather, what is home is inside you, what you carry from childhood. It gets buried during the rest of your time on Earth, but it never completely goes away.

Smith Falls didn't look much different than I'd left it. The hamlet still ran for three hundred yards along a Berkshire river. The church remained the anchor of town. The mechanics and home repair guys still gathered for crisp bacon, fried eggs, and strong opinions at the general store at 6 A.M., where the *Berkshire Eagle* carried the news, not the *Washington Post.* Most of them didn't know who I was. Then word got around, from a clerk at the store.

There was satellite TV in town now, and the kids going past on the school bus were hooked to iPhones, or sending text messages. I stayed away from it, and long-distance calls for the most part. At least personal ones.

I found a small house on a dirt road, a thirty-year-old A-frame built originally for a New York lawyer, and after three decades of life the shabby construction needed upkeep, which gave me something to do. There was a big bedroom downstairs and a small one in the loft up top for an office. The house had propane heat and a woodstove for backup. I was pretty good with the chainsaw. The pile of ash logs grew higher as more trees outside fell sick. Up here, it's the vegetation suffering from fatal disease.

I could not see the nearest neighbor, or rather, it seemed to be a clubfooted, ill-tempered moose that, at 5 A.M. some mornings, limped past, and continued out of view, munching leaves, as if punching a clock.

Most mornings I woke at 4:30 and, in darkness, did

the painful exercises I'd learned in physical therapy. Walking was an education. The nature of balance had changed. But soon I was doing a mile a day, then three, and then I ramped it up, walked faster, started running, started running hills, running trails. The toe loss was a stare gatherer at the town beach.

Not that I cared.

The front stairs needed a new buttress. A century-old pine tree out back leaned dangerously toward the house and had to come down. I stripped off weathered, ant-eaten siding, plugged a gap by the chimney where rainwater was getting past flashing, stripped off the old and put in the new. That's not hard if you're dealing with something inanimate, like a house.

Word got around town that Joe Rush was back, and some of my old classmates dropped in: fatter, older, redder, but awkwardly, if temporarily, welcome.

We reminisced. Would I stay? Did I remember our fifth-grade teacher Mrs. Wilberforce, and the way she wore glasses around her neck on a red string? Did I remember the time that we climbed into the condemned Brady Textile Mill grounds, got sick-drunk on scotch, almost got caught by the Lee cops? Did I remember diving competitions on summer nights at the old granite quarry in Becket?

A world without the admiral, Eddie, and terrorists. A world in which microbes gave you a flu, at worst. They didn't threaten to wipe out a town.

Late at night, I searched.

I sat in the second-floor study, computer glow on my

face, and followed the progress of the Barrow eco lodge, on Tilda's Swann's "Save the North Slope" blog. I took phone calls from Valley Girl, who was working for me off the clock. I think the admiral knew she was doing this, and let it go. He's that way.

Eddie called once a week, checking in, giving me space. Galli called once a month. He was waiting for me to get bored, or anxious, or just to miss Washington. He was hoping I would come back. Forget it.

It was a bad Christmas, very cold for Massachusetts, not so cold for the North Slope. I heard from Calvin, who had tracked me down, and wanted to know how I was doing. He must have told the others. Next I heard from Bruce, the McDougals, Merlin, and Deb Lillienthal. Their e-mails were casual and caring, filling me in on their lives, sometimes shyly mentioning Karen, wondering if I'd be in Barrow next summer season, doing more research.

Oh, just checking in, Joe.

On New Year's Day I phoned Dr. Liz Willoughby, head of the department of sciences at Prezant College, New Jersey, at home. She seemed subdued and said that the FBI had stopped coming around, asking about the Harmons. She said their project had been taken over by an ex-grad student, now an assistant professor. She missed the Harmons, and had not gotten over their loss.

I let her think that I was still actively involved in the investigation, and asked if the ex-grad student would be going out to the lakes again this coming summer and following up, as Ted Harmon would have done?

"Not on lake nine. Dr. Untermeyer will be doing the other lakes. But nine is off limits now."

"Why is that?"

"There was trouble getting permission from the new owners, that hotel going up, up there."

I leaned forward. "The eco lodge?"

"Hotel. Eco lodge. Whatever. They were *rude*, Craig told me. They said no research of any kind will be permitted on the property. They turned down Dr. Untermeyer, even after he offered to stay at the lodge and pay full rate." She paused protectively. "Dr. Untermeyer's grant wouldn't allow that. But he has family money. He would have supplemented the grant with that."

I listened, sipping coffee, watching a deer wandering around the side of my screened-in porch. It looked how I felt. Lost.

She said, "Craig told them he'd be quiet. All he wanted was to row a boat out and use a net to take samples. No machines. No loud noises. He even offered to give lectures to guests for free, about the Arctic."

"But they didn't want lectures, did they?"

"No."

"They were adamant, sounds like."

"I'll say!"

"Maybe they told him—when he persisted—not to bother asking again, next year. That they would never change their minds."

"How did you know?" Dr. Liz Willoughby asked sadly. "Dr. Harmon's comparative study work required a ten-year spread. That will all be worthless now, at that lake."

It was the word *worthless* that did it. I hung up and looked out at a Berkshire blizzard. Snow drove sideways into the house. The fireplace was lit downstairs. It was toasty in here. January in Massachusetts.

In my mind, I saw lake number nine, a cabin reduced to cinders, charred bodies in sizzling snow. I'd looked for secret explanations. I'd sought overcomplicated ones. *Worthless*, Liz Willoughby had said. I heard her in my head again. *Worthless.*

You went back to burn evidence, Jens. What would that evidence have been? Equipment? It would be dumb to leave equipment? Files? In a busted-up cabin? No way! Clothes? F drive? Photos?

What would constitute logical evidence in this case?

I sat up straight.

My heart started racing. I probably should have called the admiral at that point. But I didn't do it. I wanted to do this last step by myself.

WHEN IT COMES TO GOVERNMENT SCIENCE GRANTS, MOST CAN be found in public records. I accessed the websites of the three principal agencies funding U.S. Arctic research: NOAA, NASA, National Science Foundation. I knew which agencies they were because almost all the researchers last summer had been funded by one of them, at least.

I cross-referenced grants with the name Dr. Bruce Friday, way back when, *before* he retired, to see what he'd claimed to study. I read his applications and grant descriptions. I started with the latest one and went back to when he was still a professor, years before he got involved in the polar bear stuff.

Bruce Friday had used Jens Erik Holte as a pilot.

There it was.

I sat back. I felt my blood coursing. My head hurt where I'd hit it in that ice cellar, but maybe this was ghost pain. The moon was up when I made a few calls to Alaska. Dawn was breaking, snow was blowing, and the club-footed moose was straggling past when I called the airlines and booked a flight.

SAS JETS TO OSLO LEAVE NEWARK AIRPORT AROUND 9 P.M., daily, early enough to catch local, connecting flights out of Norway's capital. From Oslo you must hurry to catch the early connection to their Arctic capital. But Oslo has a small airport. Immigration is efficient and posted signs show you the right way to go. I made my second flight with moments to spare, just as the doors were closing.

Two hours later I was wide awake when the Airbus pilot announced our landing. I looked down. Tromso lies along what looked like a deep fjord, or harbor. It is situated at the same latitude as Barrow, but thanks to the warm air from the Gulf Stream, that's where similarities end.

The city of seventy-five thousand looked like a mix of quaint old and sleek new, all emanating *clean*; deep blue water, steeply rising snow-covered bluffs on two sides, a neat downtown, a sprawling college campus, and modest, steeply roofed homes rising in tiers from the commercial area by the water, to the residential one in the heights. It was Currier and Ives in the Arctic. It radiated comfort.

On any given day, in January, the temperature differential between Barrow and Tromso can be as much as one hundred degrees. A check of Google told me that Barrow was suffering fifty below zero temperatures that day. Even the hardy Iñupiats would stay indoors. Venture out and the thickest parka would feel like paper. Sled dogs would huddle in their little homes. Karen, my beautiful Karen, would have bundled up in waffle clothing, explained one more time how the waffle pattern had come from research on Arctic fox skin, gone for a short hike, joked about windchill.

But in Tromso, same day, it was a balmy thirty degrees, bright and sunny, and featherlike snowflakes fell, as if out of some 1950s Paramount Christmas classic: *Santa's Home*. The airport was bright, clean and modern. A new Mercedes taxi took me into town and the chatty driver explained in perfect English that the fare for the ten-minute drive was sixty dollars, since, he said proudly, Norway's currency was the strongest on Earth, after Switzerland's. "From our northern oil and gas," he bragged.

It had been hard to book a hotel in early January, since that week Tromso hosted its annual State of the Arctic Conference. I'd read on the plane, in the online *New York Times*, that the meeting attracted heavyweights from around the world, experts in northern geopolitics, oil company reps, military types, scientists, biomed people, explorers, and Eskimos. There would be shippers speculating on profits from new shortcut trade routes. There would be generals at cocktail parties at the university, talking about defense. There would be adventurers seeking publicity, trying to raise money for expeditions.

Valley Girl had confirmed, after accessing Bruce Friday's credit card records, that he was here, too.

The cab dropped me at a boutique-like hotel where I sipped lobby coffee and waited for a room to be cleaned. Departure hour was 3 P.M. I eavesdropped on a trio of French, Italian, and Colorado-based journalists, in the lobby, speaking English, deciding which presentation at the conference they planned to cover this late afternoon.

Diamond discoveries, or extinction threats?

I asked directions to the university. The lovely blond concierge said I could walk, but that would take forty-five minutes. Could she call a cab for me? Sure. The journalists, overhearing, asked to split the fare.

I said I'd rather not. I had not come to make friends.

The streets were freshly plowed, and piles of snow flanked cobblestone thoroughfares. Schoolchildren wearing cartoon logo backpacks walked by, holding hands. The campus lay on a hill, and there, an hour later, I spotted Bruce Friday in a packed auditorium, as house lights went out, as a screen lowered. Arctic University is the northernmost institute of higher learning in the world.

On screen I saw: "Tromso! Hot Spot for Cold Biotech." The speaker was a Norwegian government speaker bragging about Tromso's "biotechnology cluster."

"Our university is a nexus of research in the High North. We have several successful biotech companies headquartered here. Our government offers aid: Innovation Norway and The Research Council of Norway to spur discoveries. And there is no dearth of private investors! Quite the contrary! Norinnova and KapNord Invest support aggressive research here. We are confident that many helpful discoveries from the Arctic will assist future medical and molecular diagnostics. To say it simply"—she grinned—"much profit for all!"

Bruce Friday sat alone, nodding, midway down the center row. He was recognizable from the mop of chestnut hair, back sloped from bad posture and, glimpsed from the side, the out-of-style wire-rimmed glasses.

The audience was a mixed bag of academics and business people, some in suits, others dressed casually. The speaker was trim and fortyish, in a dark blue pantsuit and white shirt. "The infrastructure for commercial science is great," she said. "Documentation labs, bio-center lab, marine processing facility, all right on this very campus."

How could I have missed this?

Bruce took notes. The audience was riveted. I saw lots of Chinese reps, sitting in tight groups, which is how you knew they were from China, instead of somewhere else. I saw the journalists from my hotel standing in back. Bruce occasionally said something to a woman beside him. The screen presented a roll call of local bio-companies: ArcticZymes, which sought enzyme products from cold-adapted life-forms; Ayanda, pharmaceuticals; Calanus, which harvested zooplankton and might already have come up with a product that worked against type-2 diabetes; Chitinor, which manufactured high-quality bio-polymers from cold-water shrimp, for use in cosmetic procedures; OliVita, which supplied dietary supplements, including seal oils.

It was funny, I thought. Back at home the admiral was a frustrated voice in Washington trying to impress listeners that the Arctic needed attention. Here everyone took it for granted. They planned for it. They seemed ten years ahead of anything I'd heard in Washington, D.C.

After a while there was a coffee break.

I fixed on Bruce.

I stayed out of sight, as he made his way in the crowd to a large hall outside where piles of oily-looking, heavily sugared jelly donuts and strong coffee had been laid out.

I did not want Bruce to see me yet, not when there were people around. I followed at a distance as he wandered idly down a hall filled with exhibits; models of Arctic rescue craft, Arctic clothing, Arctic drill technology, and cold-resistant equipment, its manufacturers claimed.

At five, day over, he joined the stream of conference attendees streaming out into the dark, heading toward parked buses. The buses were there to take participants back to hotels. I feared that I would lose him. I could not follow him onto a bus or he'd see me.

But he walked.

You always did like your exercise, Bruce. You always were a surprise, looking frail, being so hardy.

He strolled along narrow streets, peering into souvenir shops, considering quaint restaurants, skirting the brightly lit harbor as coastal ferries went in or out. There were cross-country ski trails in the hills, I'd read. Hiking.

Trams taking stargazers up a mountain. Tromso was allegedly one of the best places on Earth to see the magnificent aurora borealis.

Tourists from the world over came here to marvel at the lights.

Karen would have loved this, I thought, feeling an ache in my chest, feeling the past.

His hotel was small, well lit, set a block from the harbor, on a snowy square surrounded by restaurants, a gym, and it had an old church in the center. The hotel featured four stars in the window. Bruce was living well, no longer an impoverished scientist needing handouts, or a polar bear activist seeking grants.

I walked to the church. It was locked. I stood on the front steps. I waited.

An hour went by and he came out.

He dressed the same. He always did. Apparently he was paying more for hotels these days, but style wise, Bruce remained Bruce. He never looked back. He meandered past souvenir shops featuring Arctic sweaters, Sami clothing, reindeer-horn handle knives, Laplander carvings. The night was clear. The mountains were visible across the harbor, and the lights marking the tramline sparkled.

Bruce Friday entered a glass-fronted restaurant that looked expensive, judging from the décor seen through the plate-glass window. I watched him pause by the maitre d' station. I saw the man shrug, shake his head, and direct Bruce to a window-side table, for four.

Five minutes later a G-class white Mercedes SUV

pulled up to the restaurant. A suited driver got out and opened the rear door. The shorter man who emerged was middle-aged, wealthily dressed but plain looking. Pudgy, in a dark blue overcoat. Hatless. Expensive gloves. The man walked with a side-to-side gait that gave the impression of an out-of-shape body beneath the sleek outerwear.

The driver pulled the car to the side, kept the motor on, and waited. I memorized the license plate. And through the restaurant window, I memorized the stranger's face.

The man sat talking animatedly with Bruce for forty-five minutes. They drank. They ate. They shook hands and the man left. Bruce lingered over an after-dinner drink. I never knew he liked after-dinner drinks. I was learning all kinds of things about Bruce now that I wished I'd known before.

Bruce got up and shrugged into his coat, went back outside, scanned the sky, and again started walking.

He was restless, curious, or excited. Or maybe it was too early to go to sleep. He headed away from his hotel, and up the steeply rising side streets that took us both away from the port. He trudged across a small, dark city park and I followed him up a zigzaggy series of narrow streets lined by private homes. Nothing big and grand. Everything modest, low, set into the land.

Where are you going?

Sometimes events break in the way in which you want them. Sometimes, after long stretches of difficulty, fate gives a gift. Bruce had his hat shoved low and gloved hands in his pockets. He periodically stopped and peered up at the sky. He seemed to be looking for something. Then I realized what it was. He was searching for the aurora borealis. Bruce the tourist had finished business and, job over for the day, wanted to see the fantastic northern lights.

Oh, you want the best spot for lights? Well, sir, you must get away from the town lights for a better view!

The streets rose steeply. He never turned around. There were a few people walking also; either down toward the commercial strip and the cafés, nightclubs, restaurants . . . or back to their lodging. Most walkers looked young. Couples held hands. No one acknowledged me. In Tromso, I guess, people were accustomed to seeing outsiders. There was a ski-town ambiance. Lots of new people every day.

Bruce Friday reached an area of thick woods, a park I supposed. He hesitated, then walked into the woods. When I reached that spot I saw that he'd followed a narrow footpath, covered with snow.

I followed. The snow was deep, but crusty on top, so my boots sank in only slightly. My ankles did not get wet.

He's walking through the woods. Ah, he's walking out of the trees and onto that meadow or frozen lake. No houses here. This is probably the place that the guidebooks identify as a good spot to see the northern lights.

And suddenly, the aurora borealis appeared.

It showed at first like movie floodlights shining up from the northwest quadrant. Or perhaps those were automobile headlights pointed up, as if a car climbed a steep hill. No, that wasn't it because the floodlights turned to magenta lava and then the whole sky seemed iridescent. I saw what looked like lines on an oscilloscope, pulsing, as if heaven was sending silent messages to Earth. If only someone would look. Or listen.

"Hello, Bruce."

He spun. I was six feet from him, but he knew my voice. He froze, a mix of surprise and horror on his face. Bruce in the same old Barrow parka. The same blue scarf and dark stocking hat. But the eyes were not the same, not when it came to expression. They were animal eyes. They were a deer's eyes, in a headlight.

He started to run.

We were alone and the snow was deep and I was pretty healthy now, missing toes but the therapy and training had worked fine. I caught up with him in less than sixty seconds. He went down hard, tried to fight, tried to scream but I hit him in the solar plexus. *"Ooooof!"* He was strong, but not trained in combat. I probably had enough adrenaline surging through me to power six Marines. I poked his throat where the soft flesh hits the collarbone, not hard, not a kill blow, just a *fuck you*. He couldn't breathe. He started gagging. His hands went, involuntarily, to his throat.

Control yourself, I thought. I had one of those Laplander knives out, pressed to his throat.

"Bruce. Bruce? Answers, Bruce. You hear me? *Answers.* I'm taking you in, if you give me answers. If you don't give answers, I'll kill you right now."

"What are you . . . doing here?"

"No, no. Did you hear what I said? I ask, not you."

"Let me up."

I hit him twice in the face. I heard bones break. Busted nose, minimum. My hand hurt. I felt the fight go out of him. A terrorized look nested in his eyes.

Bruce said, like a ten-year-old kid, snot running freely, "It isn't fair."

Of everything he could have said, this shocked me and I sat back. His breath rose in puffs. He was crying. I smelled the fish he'd eaten for dinner: oregano, curry, the sweet lingering aroma of after-dinner port. I pushed the tip of the knife into him, just enough to draw blood. He moaned. His blood caught the iridescent light.

"All right, all right, stop," he said.

I started it off. "You were a professor. You came to Barrow for research, years ago. After a while you found something at lake number nine. What did you find?"

The crying grew worse. The tears reflected, in small flashes, emerald and violet light. He blurted out, "I lost my wife over this. I lost my kids. My family. I deserve something. All those years. It isn't fair!"

I drew back the knife.

"Cancer," he gasped. "Pancreatic cancer."

"A *cure*?"

"Yes. A cure, Joe."

"An organism? In the lake?"

A nod.

I said, seeing it, "But you couldn't tell anyone while you were a professor, not if you wanted to get the benefits. Your contract gave commercial rights to the school. But if you waited until *after* you retired, made the discovery then, you'd get profit."

"Is that so wrong? It was my discovery. Mine!"

He was blubbering. He was hoping that someone else would show up to see the lights. It was possible. Someone might show up, especially if this spot had been recommended. But at that moment I didn't care if someone showed up. If someone showed, I'd kill Bruce. That was a fact.

In fitful, half-choked sentences he finished the story that Liz Willoughby had started. His life was *not fair* because the school should have let him keep profits. *Not fair* because of the Supreme Court ruling denying discoverers profits from finding a natural gene. He'd waited for years, and when the prize was within reach, the court changed the game. *Not fair* because he had to seek help from a company overseas, a man with a shady reputation; *not fair* because after all the years and secrecy, the Harmons had planned to gather samples at the lake, and possibly make the same discovery Bruce had made.

"You killed them, Bruce."

"Jens did that. I tried to make them stop. I made them have accidents. But Ted kept going. He just would not stop! So Jens was sent. He showed up. It's not my fault."

"And Karen?"

"Jens. Jens is crazy. Jens was a killer. I was nowhere near there. I promise."

"Why did Jens burn down the cabin at the lake?"

"We . . . he and I . . . we went there over the summer.

For samples. Our fingerprints. They were there. You were going to go there, taking a forensics team. You would have found them. My prints. And then, you know . . ."

It made sense. I *would* have had that cabin swept. It would have been normal procedure. I said, "And the eco lodge? What about that? The only reason it's there, is so nobody else can use the lake, right? The whole deal is to bar the lake to research. The deal is phony."

"The . . . lodge will be . . . real. But, yes, he bought it to block off the lake."

"Tilda Swann?"

"Not involved. Joe! You can't synthesize the drug. Not yet. We're trying. *The only place in the world it comes from is that lake.* That lake has to be protected."

Protected?

I felt the energy draining away from me. He babbled that the extract from the lake, in clinical trials on humans, had killed pancreatic cancer in 90 percent of cases. He said it would reduce the death rate by a huge amount. He said it was a miracle, and would save lives, thousands, more, *hundreds of thousands* of lives.

To my question, *Where did the rabies come from?* he answered that it had been designed in Siberian laboratories, during the Cold War. To my question, *Who controlled it now?* he told me the name of the man he'd just met.

"He's not a good man, Joe. I had no choice but to deal with him, don't you see? But after I made the deal with him I wrote a letter," Bruce added slyly. "I wrote down who he was, what we did. I hid copies. He *has* to give me my share. Forty-nine percent! Joe, I . . . can share that money with you."

"The man you just had dinner with."

I envisioned the pudgy guy in the restaurant window, across from Bruce.

"Yes."

"Which hotel is he at?"

Bruce shook his head. Suddenly he was my big helper, not a whimpering victim under a knife. "He flew home, Joe. He was never staying here. He has a private jet. He left after dinner and he's gone by now.

"Joe? Can I get up? I'm cold. I'll cooperate. I'll say what you want, unless you . . . want . . . to . . . share. It won't make up for Karen, I know, I'm sorry. I am. But *we can share, Joe.*"

"Okay, Bruce, we'll share. Get up."

I strangled him.

I PRESSED DOWN AND LEANED FORWARD AND LET MY RAGE TAKE me. I felt my fingers crunch into his neck. He was kicking. He tried to flail. I felt his breath on my face as it spurted out. I felt his life force departing. He sprayed saliva on my chin.

The last wisps, the final vaporized breath of Dr. Bruce Friday drifted, drifted, rose, and was gone.

After a moment I rose, looked around, and the rest of the world came back to me. I was dizzy with spent adrenaline. I bent down and rifled his clothes, took his wallet, his watch, and opened his fly.

On my lurching way down to town, I threw them all into a sewer opening. As for my tracks, once I was on the well-plowed streets again, they were gone. It was like getting away from bloodhounds by walking into a river. The police would find the body, and see size ten and a half footprints. But there would be no trail of those prints into town.

Back at the hotel, the blond concierge was still on duty. She smiled dazzlingly when I walked in. She asked me if I'd enjoyed my dinner. She informed me that the bus to the conference would depart the hotel at eight the next morning, and before that a delicious smorgasbord breakfast—cheeses, cold cuts, oatmeal, eggs, and fruit—would be offered from 7 A.M. on, in a dining room down the hall.

If the other man—the one Bruce had dealt with—was gone, I had no choice, so I called the admiral. He was home and picked up on the second ring. "Joe?"

I laid it out for him. If the police were going to show up, someone needed to hear, now. Galli listened and sometimes made humming noises, thinking. He said, "You have Bruce Friday? The FBI will want a crack at him."

"Death-bed confession, sir. He's gone."

A pause. He understood what I was saying. "You're in Norway now?"

"I am."

"If what you've told me is true, if we can connect the lodge and the deaths and him, believe me, something will happen. The president won't accept it otherwise. I swear to you. I've never lied to you. Come home, Joe. First chance."

I slept soundly, waking only once after hearing footsteps in the hallway. *Police*, I thought. But no knock sounded at the door.

I caught the first flight out in the morning. At Oslo, at immigration, the man opening my passport was curious as to why, after arriving yesterday, I was leaving so quickly.

"Finished my business early," I told him.

He wagged a finger at me. All work is no good. "Next time, plan to stay and have some winter fun," he said.

TWENTY-SIX

They came for him just as dessert was delivered.

Dmitri Turov—nicknamed "the angry man" in the company he owned—sat with his wife, in his favorite restaurant, Khachapuri, on the southern outskirts of Moscow. It was her birthday. She was twenty-eight. She did not like Georgian food, but he did, and he wanted it tonight.

Not a fancy place, but a great one. They sat at his favorite table under the blackboard menu. They started with mouthwatering mujuji, *cold jellied pork, and plates of chopped, minced vegetables, and a terrific walnut dipping sauce for tasty breads . . .* satsivi.

"This food," his wife said, "is too spicy."

"Fine. More for me," he said, mouth full, eating fast.

After that, the karcho *soup—beef, rice, and plum puree—and* chalchokhabili—*a hot soup with stewed chicken. And, of course, no Georgian dinner would be complete without* plov, *rice cooked in broth, smothered by delicious fish.*

He was in a good mood, in superb spirits, actually, because he'd learned that very day that his lawyer in the United States had managed to obtain the letter written by Bruce Friday, stored in an Anchorage bank safe-deposit box. Bruce Friday was dead, in Norway, killed by a Norwegian robber. A few payouts, a little blackmail, a quiet trip into a bank vault, and the incriminating letter was now burned to ashes, floating through some Alaskan sewer drain.

With the letter gone, there was nothing to connect Dmitri Turov with the disaster in Barrow that had panicked the world, humiliated a U.S. president, caused massive expenditures, and left many dead, and the American Congress howling about secret U.S. military programs.

A big mystery that made the Yanks look stupid!

Ha!

He was watching a waiter approach carrying a large copper tray on which sat plates of baklava, and small cups of sweet coffee, when he noticed the front door of the restaurant open and immediately understood that the three men wearing dark suits—men who were not smiling, men whose eyes swept the tables, men whose walk was economic, military— were there because someone was in big trouble among the noisy patrons packing the restaurant.

Hmm, *he thought, like a happy gossip.* Who?

The men walked toward his table.

The angry man's heartbeat sped up.

The lead man walked right up to the table and said, "You are Dmitri Turov, president of Dalsvix Group?"

It had to be a mistake. The leader produced a card identifying himself as Colonel Nicholas Azamat of the Federal Security Service, modern successor of the KGB, Russia's equivalent to the American FBI's National Security Branch, except in Russia, it reported directly to the president. Dmitri looked around for his bodyguards and saw that the table behind him was empty. His wife was gaping. She was not used to him being bossed around.

Dmitri told Colonel Azamat that there must be a mistake, but Azamat insisted that they all leave together. There wasn't really an option to refuse.

Dmitri accompanied the men outside, and entered the back of their armored Mercedes G550. No one spoke. No one answered when Dmitri asked the cause of this visit.

He expected a ride into Moscow proper—where he'd confidently clear up whatever the problem was—but they left the city and rode beyond Moscow's outer-ring road, and onto a newly constructed highway, northwest. Apartment buildings fell away. They passed woods on one side, farms on the other.

Colonel Azamat said, quietly, "Some people are very angry with you. They don't mind what you did. They mind that you got caught. Now you have embarrassed them."

Dmitri thought, It can't be Alaska. No one knows!

Colonel Azamat said, "Now we must do some things to keep the Americans from releasing the story which would hurt us."

Dmitri grabbed for the door handle, tried to struggle.

But it was one thing to beat up a twenty-eight-year-old woman, and another to try to overcome four agents of the FSS. He hinted about offering money. He threatened their careers. He let them know that his cousin Natasha was close to the president.

At length they left the highway, and continued on a narrow, excellently maintained road through thick birch woods, and pulled through a spiked gate and into a walled compound with a sign identifying the four-story nineteenth-century structure ahead as a private clinic.

The escorts got him out of the car as easily as if they were moving a television. They force marched him across a white gravel driveway and up to the thick wooden doors and into what had probably been a duke's country home once, then some prominent communist party member's weekend dacha, and now, from the smell and white uniforms and hushed attitude of hurrying nurses, was some kind of clinic, all right.

The angry man began to shout for help.

Ten minutes later he was in a small, very well-lit, well-appointed operating room, clothes cut away, boxer under-wear torn off, hairy ankles strapped in, like a monkey's, his wrists restrained by manacles as well.

It was insane. They weren't even asking questions. The suited men arrayed themselves in the corners of the room, and everyone just waited. Just fucking waited.

The angry man begged for a chance to explain. He begged to be interrogated. He begged for a lawyer. For a general he knew. For one of the president's aides, a friend.

But the man who walked toward him in doctors' scrubs

was a stranger, tall, broad shouldered, and he moved with a slight limp, as if something was wrong with his left foot. As the doctor bent over him Dmitri tried to explain. Whatever was going on was an error. A fixable error.

The doctor just shook his head as if he had no idea what Dmitri was saying. Then, surprise, the words that he spoke came out in English.

Colonel Azamat materialized beside the doctor, and translated, in an efficient, unemotional voice.

"My name is Colonel Joseph Rush, of the United States Marines."

What? The FSS had kidnapped him out of a restaurant and delivered him to an American? It was insane! It was an insult.

Colonel Azamat continued, "Despite the tension between our two nations, I am here thanks to the gracious cooperation of your president. My country is very grateful for this favor. But we are very angry at you."

Dmitri Turov struggled, but the straps held him tight.

"You killed my fiancée. You almost started a war. You carried out an attack on our soil. In order to make this all go away, your people and mine made a deal. Included in this is that your company will not be making any medicines. Your company is being closed."

Dmitri Turov was apoplectic.

The Marine watched as a Russian doctor produced a small syringe. At the sight, the angry man's blood went cold.

Colonel Rush said, "I bet you can guess what this is."

"You must not give that to me!"

Colonel Azamat translated as Colonel Rush said,

"You'll have a nice room. In the syringe is the rabies that your scientists modified in 1974, that your company took charge of later, and stored."

The angry man had been prepared for pain. For hitting. For a steel rod. If he could hold out for a while he'd be rescued and things would be okay, for him, but not for Colonel Azamat, he'd told himself. But this was different. There was no way to stop the shiny long needle that was inserted into his arm, while he looked on, bulge-eyed.

He watched in horror as the plunger went down.

He watched the amber-colored liquid inside disappear.

There was a mild stinging in his arm, accompanied by some small heat. Then the needle was withdrawn.

The Marine said, "My president said I could ask him for anything. In the end, your people said okay, as long as they made the arrest and administered the shot. I am only permitted to watch. Favor for favor. To avoid worse."

Joseph Rush removed his medical gown and let it drop to the floor, and then, one by one, everyone filed out, to leave Dmitri on the table, shouting that they could not do this to him. Not him!

He awoke in a different room, an observation room, with padded walls and furniture, no window, high ceiling, a vent spewing forth lukewarm air that smelled of diesel fuel and cinnamon.

His shackles were off. There was a single cot. The steel door had a slot, through which, three times a day, healthy meals were delivered. He pounded on the walls. He begged someone for the antidote. He offered money. Whatever they wanted. A job. A car. A girl. A boy.

And every time he looked at the glass, the Marine was there, iron straight, emotionless. He never seemed to need sleep. He never moved in the big chair.

It took two days, then water began to taste funny.

Then the light started to hurt.

At the end, his screams were loud and hideous, and he barked like a dog and foamed at the mouth. No one heard him, because of soundproofed walls. On the far side of the thick glass sat the lone Marine, not eating, not drinking, just watching. Once, only once, Dmitri saw a tear roll down the man's face. Other than that, the expression never changed.

After it was over, the Marine went home.

Keep reading for an excerpt from
the next Joe Rush novel by James Abel

COLD SILENCE

Available July 2016 in hardcover from Berkley Books

I'll never get out of here alive, thought Tahir Khan.

He stepped back from the peephole in his twenty-fourth-floor Boca Raton penthouse apartment, as the quiet knocking on the door continued. Bright sun flooded in through floor-to-ceiling sliding glass doors facing the blue Atlantic, dazzling and still, far below. In early January, seventy-degree air washed in through an open patio door, and he heard the ocean out there, vaguely, insistent as a hiss.

Khan backed from the door and looked around wildly, as if somehow, magically, an escape hatch would appear in the walls. But all was as it had been when he rented his hideaway. The place was costly but ugly and generic; hospital white walls and matching floor tiling, curving Naugahyde couch wrapped toward a giant TV. Bright lime green cushions sat on wrought-iron furniture. The same generic pastel beach paintings hung in a thousand rental condos from Key West up the eastern U.S. coast to New Jersey: still-life conch shells, wind ruffling dune grass, six-year-olds in bathing suits wielding plastic pails.

Khan was tall and stick-thin and he wore a black short-sleeved tropical shirt with a once festive and now sweat-soaked yellow orchid pattern that showed underdeveloped muscles, soft hands, big eyes. He thought, *Call 911 for help? If I do that, I'll be arrested.*

"Hey!" the friendly voice called through the door. "I know you're in there. Open up. I just want to talk."

Khan peered through the peephole again and saw, magnified, like two spread fingers, air tickets, and then the tickets moved away and the smiling face was back, features exaggerated by the lens, ratcheting up his terror.

I'm trapped. I'm finished. He'll kill me.

He'd taken a bus there, because cheapo bus lines accepted non-traceable cash, changed his name on the lease to Phillip Zahoor, and paid a pile of hundred-dollar bills up front for three months, plus a hefty damage deposit. He'd barely left the apartment for the last two weeks.

But they always found you. They tracked you down. They used computers and satellites, databases and old-fashioned footwork. It had been stupid to try to leave. He should have shut up and gone along and battened away his doubts.

"How did you get past the guard?" he called out.

Knock-knock-knock. The thin door looked like it was caving in with each impact, however slight.

Fucking Florida construction. Fucking south Florida

quality work. South Florida, where planned obsolescence meant concrete spalled months after being poured, roofs leaked in storms, doors were as sturdy as in Hollywood sets. Appearance was everything. Quality was a joke. The voice sounded close, male, soft and intelligent.

"Guard? I didn't see a guard."

"I'll call security if you don't leave, Orrin."

No answer. Then, as if the man felt hurt, "Aw, what do you want to say that for? And why'd you leave anyway? After four years? Things are finally about to pop, Tahir!"

Tahir Khan was a twenty-six-year-old ex-biology grad student from Pakistan, still legally in the U.S., although he'd withdrawn from the State University of New York in Albany. Family abroad. Cold sweat flowed from his bald head, shaved two days ago, and ran down his face, where he was trying unsuccessfully to grow a beard. It coursed past his glasses and down his ropey neck and sprouted inside his armpits. His throat was closing. He couldn't breathe. His head pounded. He'd heard the expression "knees going weak" but had never experienced it until now, and he wobbled backward from the door as if, at any second, it would crash in. First thing on getting here, he'd called a locksmith to come and install a deadbolt, and the hearty American voice on the phone had promised, "You betcha! We'll come today!" But no one had shown up. "Our guy got a flu. Sorry, sir." So Khan tried a second place. "We can come next Friday. Is Friday okay?"

Friday was tomorrow.

Now the voice came again through the door and it was patient and soft but inside the patience was something dark. The voice was Midwestern, reasonable on the surface. It was confident and quiet. "If I wanted to hurt you, I could have done it last night at the fish restaurant. Or this morning when you walked on the beach, Tahir."

Tahir felt hope stirring. "You were in the restaurant?"

"You ordered mahi mahi. Me, I prefer lobster. With butter. And lots of dark beer."

Tahir risked the peephole magnifier again, saw Orrin's plain and forgettable face. There was absolutely nothing memorable about the man. He seemed composed of a collection of bland features. Height, half an inch short. Face, almost round but not; nose, one of those computer-generated combos of common features of humans, two holes for breathing in a functional pasted-on knob. He was a genetic mix of average. You could see him straight on and forget him if a breeze distracted you. His skin was tanned. His tropical shirt, worn loose, featured a racing cigarette boat pattern. The baseball cap said Marlins, as it did on ten thousand people walking around here. The left hand held up the Delta tickets again. Orrin's smile looked genuine. It always did. But Tahir had seen the kind of damage the man could do. The doughy body was illusion.

"See? One for you. One for me. What are you going to say if you call the police, anyway? You know what they will do to you? Open the goddamn door and let's go."

Tahir considered it. His two-bedroom penthouse sat above a concrete patio on the beach side, three blocks from the inland waterway in the west. At this height, any tourists walking on the beach would be beyond earshot if he screamed, and his next-door neighbor, a snowbird psychiatrist from Manhattan, was away for the weekend at his daughter's wedding on Long Island.

Tahir was thinking, *I should have gone back to Pakistan*.

He'd been in Florida for nine days, and during that time the only human being he'd had contact with for more than five minutes was the real estate agent. *I need to rent something today*, he said. He'd paid cash at Best Buy for a TV, which he'd sat staring at, waiting with dread for the BIG NEWS to break, the thing he'd been working on. Cash in the supermarket, where he'd stocked up on food for weeks. Cash to the cabbie who'd taken him here.

No motel for him. No lodging where he had to sign a registry book, even with a false name, because handwriting could be tracked. He'd been drilled on techniques. The people looking for him would check hotels and motels. They'd bribe desk clerks. Watch security tapes. Send phony tourists to sidle up to other guests and start conversations. They'd sit in cars in front of hotels.

So after he rented this place, other than a daily walk on the beach to keep from going crazy, he'd stayed inside and watched TV. Sometimes waiting for the BIG THING, sometimes just mindless fluff: *Judge Judy. Wife Swap*. Anything to keep him half sane as he tried to figure out what to do next. Tahir Khan had become one more anonymous figure trudging the Florida tide line, watching porpoises offshore at sunrise, and other fins, bigger ones, less benign life looking for something smaller to eat. Tahir among the handful of sleepless retirees, young lovers who had been up all night making impossible promises, sunburned tourists getting one last longing look before boarding the plane back to gray Newark or Pittsburgh. And among them, one fugitive, running from the biggest mistake of his life.

The plan had been to sit here for a few weeks, get distance and decide when to try to get out of the country and sit out the disaster that was about to begin.

But now the doorknob turned and Orrin Sykes somehow just stepped into the apartment. How could he have a key? The private security guard downstairs was "here twenty-four hours a day," the rental agent had promised. Khan had pushed it, demanded of the woman, "What happens if someone gets past security," and the beefy guy behind the desk had laughed, nodded at video monitors showing elevator interiors, and said, poking his chest with pride, "Ex ATF," as if that guaranteed that no intruder, no stranger, not even a ninety-year-old cripple would pass his station without proper ID.

But Sykes was a ghost, and now the man stood just ten feet away, same distance as the phone. For an instant Tahir flashed back to a film he'd seen in freshman biology class, too many years ago. It had been called *Animal Camouflage*. It had featured creatures; a certain frog, a moray eel, a crab, all of which looked beautiful, and rarely moved, and then with sudden shocking aggression would lunge. A tongue would flick out. A mouth would open. Whatever life form had been innocently feeding nearby a moment before would be gone, and the killer would be sitting there again.

"Come on, Tahir. Pack a bag. Let's go home."

"Really?"

"What do you think, I'd hurt you? You're valuable."

He started to feel relief. The sweat flow dissipated into a trickle. Was it possible? He began to babble, as he moved backward, toward the bedroom, toward his ratty suitcase in the back closet, all the time watching for Orrin to lunge.

"I didn't tell anyone. Who would believe it, right?"

Sykes nodded. "You had doubts."

"I admit I thought about calling a reporter. Or the FBI. I did. I considered it. But I didn't do anything. I just wanted to get away. For a little while. To think."

"Think."

"Everyone needs time to think."

"I know I do," Sykes agreed, nodding.

The bedroom was down a short hallway from the living room, and gave Sykes a view of all the other rooms in the condo. Kitchen, empty. Bathroom, empty. Guest bedroom, empty. Master bedroom.

"No one really here," Sykes said.

"I told you that."

"I was just checking," Sykes said.

Tahir opened the mirrored, sliding closet door with shaking hands. He reached up for his suitcase. He actually felt Orrin move before, it seemed, the reflection did in the three mirror panes. Tahir did not have time to turn. In the mirrors three meaty arms circled three skinny throats and three Tahirs were lifted bodily off the carpet. There was an awful cracking sound and he watched his head spin around. Orrin's face remained expressionless.

In a freshman biology class at SUNY, Tahir had heard

a professor say once that after a human being is killed, the brain keeps functioning for a few more moments. Now his brain processed that he was being carried back into the living room, and that he was hanging over the patio railing. *Wow, I am dead,* he thought, falling, the concrete flecked with shiny mica, its squares forming a chessboard, the empty squares coming up fast.

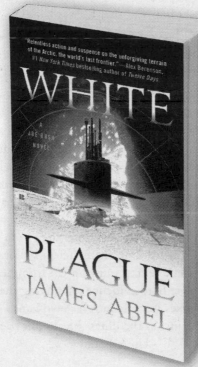

COMING SOON FROM

James Abel

Cold Silence

A Joe Rush Novel

While trying to alleviate the suffering of thousands in drought-stricken, war-torn Africa, ex-Marine doctor and bioterror expert Joe Rush receives a plea for help from a member of his old military unit, who is currently working as a geologist in a chaotic region of Somalia.

Joe arrives on the scene to find an entire group of people showing horrific symptoms of an ancient sickness that was once thought to be sent as punishment from heaven. But before Joe can get hard evidence identifying the illness, a local warlord takes matters into his own hands—and the proof is gone, just as the illness breaks out back in the United States.

This outbreak is not a curse from God. It's a well-coordinated, meticulously planned attack with a specific goal that could overturn global stability and kill millions. And the only one who can stop the downfall of civilization is Joe Rush...